JOSEPHINE COX

with GILLY MIDDLETON

A TIME TO REMEMBER

HarperCollins*Publishers*

HarperCollins*Publishers*
1 London Bridge Street,
London SE1 9GF

www.harpercollins.co.uk

HarperCollins*Publishers*
1st Floor, Watermarque Building, Ringsend Road
Dublin 4, Ireland

First published by HarperCollins*Publishers* 2022
1

A catalogue record for this book
is available from the British Library

ISBN: 978-0-00-812822-7 (HB)
ISBN: 978-0-00-812852-4 (TPB)

Set in ITC New Baskerville Std 13/17pt
by Palimpsest Book Production Limited, Falkirk, Stirlingshire

Printed and Bound in the UK using 100% Renewable Electricity
at CPI Group (UK) Ltd

MIX
Paper from
responsible sources
FSC
www.fsc.org
FSC C007454

A TIME TO REMEMBER

Josephine Cox was born in Blackburn, one of ten children. At the age of sixteen, Josephine met and married her beloved husband Ken, and had two sons. When the boys started school, she decided to go to college and eventually gained a place at Cambridge University. She was unable to take this up as it would have meant living away from home, but she went into teaching – and started to write her first full-length novel. Josephine won the 'Superwoman of Great Britain' Award, for which her family had secretly entered her, at the same time as her novel was accepted for publication. Sadly Josephine passed away on July 17th 2020. Her strong, gritty stories were always taken from the tapestry of life.

Josephine said of her books, 'I could never imagine a single day without writing. It's been that way since as far back as I can remember.'

Gilly Middleton has been involved with fiction all her working life. She lives in Sussex, where she likes to go to the theatre and to watch cricket. She has been a huge fan of Josephine Cox for many years and feels very privileged to have worked with her.

Also by Josephine Cox

CHAPTER ONE

IT WAS NEARLY mid-afternoon by the time Eliza Bancroft had finished helping to tidy up the Short Cut, the barber's shop where she worked. The floor was swept clean of all hair clippings, the chairs were wiped down and neatly aligned, the mirrors were polished, the combs and clippers cleaned ready for the next morning, and the towels dropped off at the laundry just round the corner. It was half-day closing on Wednesdays, but she seldom managed to get the whole afternoon off. Still, the work was enjoyable and interesting, the clients were mostly friendly, and Eliza's colleagues – Harry Mulligan, the owner of the business, a kind man of about thirty-five, and a good boss as well, and Theo Gilmore, more than ten years older than Harry, with dark good looks, gentlemanly manners and a natty taste in shoes – were, in her opinion, the perfect people with whom to share the tiny premises. You had to get on with folk when the entire workplace

3

comprised one room into which were crammed two washbasins and two barber's chairs, and a couple of spare seats for the waiting customers.

'Right, I reckon we're done, Harry.'

'Nice work. Thanks, Liza. Off you go then, and p'raps I'll see you later if I drop in at the Waterloo.'

'I'll look out for you. There's a few other folk singing, too – I think Seamus's band are booked – but Theo and I will be doing some numbers mid-evening.'

'Aye, I expect he's gone home to polish his shoes,' laughed Harry.

'Ha, I reckon he'll be having a last-minute practice. We've got some new songs tonight – new to us, that is. He's written some linking passages and he wants them to be perfect.'

'I look forward to hearing them. Cheerio for now, love.' Harry unlocked the door, on which the sign had been turned to display 'Closed' for over an hour, and let her out into the street.

It was a beautiful spring day and Eliza decided to walk home from the barber's, tucked away in a side street close to the cathedral in the centre of Blackburn, taking the long but scenic route home via Corporation Park to the little terraced house she shared with her mother, Maureen. On the way she stopped at a street stall to buy Maureen a bunch of daffodils, a cheering little present of her favourite flower.

She hoped to be able to persuade her mum to go to the pub that evening to hear her and Theo perform their short programme of popular songs from musicals, but Maureen had been looking tired and wan lately and would likely say she'd prefer an early night again. A lively evening spent in good company might well lift her mother's spirits, but Eliza wouldn't nag her to go if she didn't feel up to it. Maureen had been weary and, truth be told, looking a bit miserable for a few months now, though she hadn't complained of any ailment to Eliza, who hoped her beloved mum wasn't hiding anything serious from her.

Eliza was beginning to have her suspicions as to what might be the matter. Maureen had mentioned her ill-mannered boss a few times – his temper, his lack of consideration, and the hectoring tone in which he always spoke to her – and Eliza had heard his name occasionally from her customers, too. The gossip had not been complimentary, although she never joined in or let on that she knew of the man, of course. Discretion was the ultimate watchword at the Short Cut, and Eliza knew that she'd be letting Harry down badly if she broke this golden rule.

Then again, the low mood could just be Maureen's age – but what age was that? She was only in her forties and had years ahead of her yet. Heavens, she might even remarry! Eliza's father had been dead for well over a decade now, and Maureen had brought up her two daughters by herself, working hard at various unskilled jobs while her girls were at school, and some-times in the evenings, too – cleaning offices and the like. Through all those years Maureen had remained strong and resolutely cheerful, devoting herself to her children, doing her best to give them a happy and settled childhood.

Now, when she might have got used to the heartbreak of her husband's illness and death, her sorrow blunted, though never healed, by the passing of the years; when her life should have been easier with her daughters grown up – Sylvia married, and Eliza working at the barber's and helping with the household bills – and with a clerical job at the brewery that had promised interesting work and a chance to use the skills she'd worked hard to attain at a course of evening classes, Maureen seemed sapped of spirit and energy. It was almost as if she had used herself up and had lost the strength to cope with any setbacks at work. Her enthusiasm and pride in getting the job had carried her along for several months, but gradually, over the past year, her shoulders had become increasingly slumped, as though bearing a heavy burden, and her step had lost its spring. She was beginning to look defeated, her brown hair was starting to fade and her face was showing a few lines.

Eliza wound her way slowly along the park's broad pathways, clutching her flowers and humming one of tonight's more soulful tunes. She noticed the first bright green leaves appearing on the trees, admired the neat flowerbeds with the park's own daffodils nodding. A robin hopped across the path and fluttered into one of the shrubs as she passed. It was such a cheerful time of year: all this new life and, with it, raised hopes after the long, dark months of an exceptionally cold winter. *If only Mum could rally as these gardens are doing,* Eliza thought; *if only she could find the strength to blossom again . . .*

Eliza paused in her walk to consider. Her mother clearly wasn't going to just snap out of it – whatever was wrong. It was up to her daughter to get to the root of the problem and do what she could to help. Maureen had devoted her life to her girls and now it was time to do something for her in return.

'I hope, Mrs Bancroft, that you won't be *too much* longer with that letter I need to sign,' huffed Herbert Nicholson. 'I have to get away by four o'clock today. I believe I made that perfectly clear to you this morning. I do wish you would at least take *some* notice of what I tell you.'

'I shall bring it in directly, Mr Nicholson,' Maureen replied. *And if you hadn't changed your mind – twice – after I'd typed them all, I would have finished the lot ages ago, you'd have left already, and I'd be able to get on without you breathing down my neck.*

Maureen's strategy to keep calm while working for her short-tempered, ill-mannered and dithering boss had been simply to decide the choice was his: she could either type the same letter three times until he finally made up his mind exactly what he wanted to say, or she could type three different letters instead. Office hours did not allow her to retype all the letters several times and still catch the post and do all her other duties every day. She reminded herself of this often, but in practice it wasn't easy to keep up the pretence of cool indifference, especially with his carping and sniping, unfairly implying she was not only slow, but could do nothing right.

How frustrating it was to have her efficiency constantly undermined by the stupid man's indecision, which meant even the most straightforward tasks took up most of the day and she often had to stay late to finish off, tidy up and do the filing – all with never a word of appreciation or acknowledgement that it was he who was at fault. More annoyingly, everything Mr Nicholson asked her to do was always described as 'urgent', no matter how trivial, as if he had to chivvy Maureen into applying herself, when in fact she was a very conscientious worker. Even the letter he'd dictated to the council this morning – without asking Maureen whether she would mind if he were to give her a private letter to type for him, nothing to do with Felbridge Brewery – had been 'urgent', although it was only about the streetlight outside his house shining into his bedroom window. There had been several of this kind of letter recently, also with not the slightest gratitude expressed for the favour Maureen was doing for him.

Maureen released the paper from her typewriter and took the top copy through to the inner office for Mr Nicholson to sign.

'About time, too,' he snapped, writing his name with a flourish of his fountain pen and underlining it for added importance – as if he was the sovereign, Maureen thought. 'Right, I'm going to go now, at last. Mrs Nicholson and I are attending a classical concert this evening – a string quartet, I believe – and we're meeting up with some very important people beforehand. Make sure this letter goes in today's post and that your desk is cleared before you leave. I don't want to see papers heaped untidily about the place when I come in tomorrow.' His own vast desk – tooled leather and mahogany veneer – was completely empty, as it was every evening before he departed.

'Yes, Mr Nicholson,' Maureen said, wondering if there was ever an end to his criticism. When had her desk ever been left in a mess? 'Have a nice time,' she added pointedly, his cue to show some good manners and wish her a pleasant evening, and she took the signed letter as he tucked his fountain pen into his inside jacket pocket.

He walked out without saying goodbye and then Maureen heard him smarmily wishing Stella, Mr Felbridge's secretary, a pleasant evening as he passed the open door to her office, further down the corridor. Stella had the ear of Mr Felbridge, and everyone knew it was wise to keep in with her.

I do hope he's got time to go home first and change that shirt, thought Maureen, quickly typing the envelope, *otherwise he'll be greeting these 'very important people' with a nasty little ink stain on his front.* She felt slightly guilty for not drawing his attention to it, but she quickly shrugged off the feeling: he'd only have got into a paddy and started shouting if she'd said anything, and anyway, it served him right for being so rude. Perhaps Mrs Nicholson would find him a clean shirt to wear – urgently.

'So Herbert's gone already?' It was Stella, bringing a cup of hot tea for Maureen, a digestive biscuit balanced on the saucer. 'Thought you could do with this, Maureen, what with the day you've had. The man's a nightmare! We could hear him bellowing self-importantly down his telephone in our set, and a couple of times I had to close Mr Felbridge's door.'

'Very *important* business,' said Maureen, with a tired smile. 'Thanks, Stella. I haven't had time for a cuppa, what with retyping the same letters all day while he makes his bloomin' mind up what he wants to say, and every single thing being so "urgent".'

'I don't know how you put up with it,' said Stella, perching on the corner of Maureen's desk.

'Nor do I, sometimes. I used not to mind, but just lately . . . the endless little criticisms, the continuous bad temper – it's like I'm enduring a punishment rather than simply being at work. I'm really starting to feel fed up. You know, kind of like: is this all my life is worth – typing letters for some ill-mannered fella whose every word to me is deliberately chosen to make me feel small and useless?'

'Oh dear, you *are* feeling low! Shame Herbert doesn't appreciate your efforts, but then I don't think he ever appreciated his previous secretaries, either. Everyone else here gets on so well with all the others. I've never heard Mr Felbridge being less than charming to anyone, whatever their role. Do you want me to mention Herbert's behaviour to him?'

'Best not. Herbert will only give me a harder time for telling tales, I shouldn't wonder. But I don't know why he thinks rudeness is acceptable, or why he's so full of his own importance.'

'I think,' said Stella, lowering her voice, although they were alone, 'it's because he hasn't much – importance, I mean. Or at least what authority he has is still a novelty to him, and he doesn't wear it lightly.'

'Mm, he is a bit of a bully. And a snob.'

'Quite.'

'But still, though I recognise it, it's hard to take. I'm beginning to feel I'm as useless as he's continually implying I am.'

'Anyone would, if their confidence was constantly being eroded. Try to ignore him. He's just ignorant. Anyway, where's he gone to so early?'

'Hopefully home to change his ink-stained shirt, but then it's "a classical concert, a string quartet, I believe".'

'So he doesn't even know what he's lucky enough to be going to hear? Philistine,' said Stella, who liked classical music and on whom a string quartet would not be wasted.

'I think the point of the evening isn't the music, it's the "very important people" he's going with.'

Stella rolled her eyes. 'Well, give me your letters to post – I'm just taking Mr Felbridge's – and you drink your tea and enjoy a bit of peace while you get on without "Mrs Bancroft! Mrs Bancroft!" every three minutes.' She did an astonishingly accurate impression of Mr Nicholson.

'Ah, Stella, you're an angel. Thank you.'

As she set about filing her carbon copies and distributing memos into the pigeonholes for the internal post, Maureen wondered whether she ought to think about searching for a new job, working for someone who was pleasant and appreciative. How wonderful it would be to look forward to coming to work, as she had once done; to face the week ahead on a Monday as a happy prospect rather than as five days of servitude to be endured. Of course, if she left she'd miss Stella, and there were others with whom she was on friendly terms, but, by heck, she'd be glad to see the back of Mr Nicholson. Still, the job came with reasonable pay and she certainly needed that. Perhaps she was just being silly to mind her boss's unfortunate manner. There were plenty of jobs where she'd have to put up with worse – she knew that from experience. At least it was mostly warm and always clean in the offices of Felbridge Brewery. No, she was just feeling tired, and disappointed with the job, having started it the previous year with such high hopes. *Put up and shut up and be glad of what you've got,* she told herself. *After all, you're luckier than many.* With her clerical experience limited to this one position, she knew she'd be fortunate to walk straight into another office job.

It was still daylight when Maureen let herself into her neat little house. Not too late home this evening, but, goodness, she was tired.

'Mum, hello,' called Eliza from the kitchen. 'I'm making corned beef hash with those leftovers. It won't take long. Do you want an egg on top?'

Maureen came into the kitchen and sank onto a chair pulled up to the kitchen table, on which Eliza had placed a vase containing the flowers she'd bought. 'Yes, please, Liza. Ooh, daffodils, my favourites. So pretty.'

'For you, Mum. But you look whacked. Here, let me pour you a cup of tea. Are you all right?'

'I'm fine, love, just a bit tired, though it is only Wednesday. But these daffs will cheer me, thank you.'

'Only two more days to the weekend for you,' Eliza grinned.

'Aye, thank goodness.' Maureen felt her shoulders slump.

'What's Herbert done now?' Everyone referred to Mr Nicholson as 'Herbert' behind his back; even Eliza, who had never met the man.

'Oh, it's nowt.'

'Well, it clearly isn't.'

Maureen sighed heavily. 'I don't want to make a fuss . . .'

'Tell me, Mum. I'm beginning to get really worried about you. You look all in these days and it's time I knew why.'

Maureen felt the discretion she'd always tried to practise melting rapidly away and she let rip with her frustration. 'Liza, I honestly don't know how much longer I can stand the man. I've always known he's demanding, can't even be bothered to be polite unless it's to people he's trying to impress. He's so rude, it's as if he's deliberately trying to undermine me. Nothing I do is good enough or appreciated, although I really don't think I'm bad at the job. And his temper is terrible. He explodes over nowt. I didn't mind at first – it's just a job, after all, and not a difficult one, plus I'm using the skills I learned at my evening class . . .'

'I know, and I was that proud when you went for the job and got it, just like that. But I'm very sorry it's not what you were hoping it would be.'

'Maybe I was expecting too much. It isn't all about me, is it, love? It's about the brewery business. I'm just a minor cog in the wheel.'

'Yes . . .' Eliza frowned, 'but, Mum, you shouldn't have to put up with owt that makes you unhappy. I'm afraid Herbert Nicholson isn't a very nice man. Whatever he says to make you doubt your ability, it's not that you can't do the work, it's that you can't deal with him. And that's not your fault, it's his. He's unlikely

14

to change, so maybe you should look for a job else-where. How about I get the local paper tomorrow and we can go through the vacancies together?'

'Oh, but I do like it at the brewery—'

'No, Mum, you like the *idea* of the job at the brewery, and you like Stella and those nice people in accounts. Herbert snapped you up for the post of his secretary as soon as you'd gained your shorthand and typing speeds. You were so pleased – Sylvia and I were, too – but it soon became clear the man's a jumped-up idiot without a jot of common courtesy. You've given that job a lot longer than I would be able to, but everyone has a limit and he's really wearing you down now. He's just a silly little man – we all agree. But you're looking like the weight of the world is on your shoulders and . . . well, I am worried. There's nowt else up, is there? You're not ill or owt?' Eliza turned from the stove, spatula in hand, and looked directly at her mother.

'No, sweetheart, I'm fine. Just a little disappointed that I don't like working for Herbert after all. It's just the constant chipping away at my confidence, the little things that are nowt in themselves, but add up to a great black cloud over the whole job.'

Eliza left off her cooking and came over to give her mother a hug.

'Honestly, Mum, if you can't bear it any longer, I'm sure we can manage for a bit on my wage from the Short Cut. I'm learning to cut hair really well now, not just wash and sweep up, and when Harry thinks

I'm good enough to do the job unsupervised, I'll be paid more. Plus Theo and I get a bit for the singing and playing, of course, although that really is *only* pocket money.'

'You're a good girl, Liza, but you won't have to keep us both, I promise.'

'Mum, you've just got stuck down a dead end, that's all. You need to find a way out, and when you do, you'll be off at fifty miles an hour, grinning from ear to ear and with the wind in your hair.'

'I'm not sure that's ever been me, love.'

'Too busy putting everyone else first, being the best mum in the world to your girls, but Sylvia and me have found our feet now, and maybe it's just time you did, too. It's not too late to strike out with summat new, Mum, summat for yourself. I just want you to be happy.'

'Ah, love . . .'

'Anyway, why don't you come to the Waterloo this evening? Theo and I are doing a couple of songs from *Easter Parade*. I know how you loved that film and, though I'm no Judy Garland, Theo's done some nice piano arrangements. It'll be fun.'

'Oh, I don't know . . .'

'Always easier to say "no", Mum; always better to say "yes". C'mon, let me get a couple of eggs in the pan, we'll eat up this hash, you put on a frock, and so will I' – she looked down at her trousers and rather shapeless Fair Isle pullover – 'and we won't even be late home. Please?'

'All right, all right, give me a chance.'

'Great. And tomorrow we'll start looking for summat better for you. Summat worthy of you. You're too good for Herbert Nicholson, just remember that. Don't worry, Mum, it'll be OK.'

'Yes, love, of course it will.'

The music was performed in an upstairs room at the Waterloo pub, and the audience paid a few pennies to go up to listen. There were some chairs and tables where neighbours liked to meet up and exchange news, although most people just stood around with their drinks. The crowd, mainly friends and family of the performers, were very appreciative: favourites and encores were requested.

Maureen watched her younger daughter putting on a very lively performance, standing next to Theo, whose long fingers flew over the keyboard of the Waterloo's upright piano, pushing the ancient instrument to the limit of its capabilities.

Maureen marvelled at how her tomboyish girl was transformed in the low lighting of the room. Eliza's dark eyes sparkled, and she looked so pretty in a bright print frock, her short, straight hair combed out to look elfin and delicate. Harry had cut her hair short as his Christmas present to her, and Maureen had been shocked when Eliza first came home looking like a beautiful boy. Now she'd got used to it, acknowledged the style suited her and thought it very attractive.

Certainly Eliza's voice was appealing, singing popular tunes from films and shows, and all eyes were on her as she performed a solo to Theo's accompaniment.

Then they sang a duet. Theo had a remarkable voice and a huge range, so that he could sing Paul Robeson numbers or croon as lightly as Fred Astaire. Maureen thought he was probably in his mid-forties – his hair greying slightly at the temples, although his handsome face remained unlined – but he was curiously young in his outlook: a reader of comics and children's books, a lover of silly jokes and the ludicrous plots and catchy tunes of film musicals. Like Eliza, he was dressed to be seen this evening, but then there was always a snazziness to his clothes, and especially his shoes. This evening they were blue and white – unlike anything Maureen had ever seen a man wear before – and matched his boldly striped shirt.

Maureen had been a little shy of Theo when she had first met him at one of the Waterloo's musical evenings, but she'd grown very fond of him in the months since then. It put her mind at rest to see what warm and good-hearted people Eliza worked with in the masculine world of a barber's shop. When Eliza had decided to make hairdressing her career, she'd said from the outset that she wanted to work on men's hair rather than 'mess about with smelly setting lotion and, worse, perms'. She wanted to learn to cut with the precision a short, neat style required, where real skill was needed and mistakes could not be disguised.

She'd been fortunate to find a mentor in Harry Mulligan, a man with an open mind, who saw her talent and enthusiasm. Many barbers might have thought a young woman would be an oddity in their business, creating an awkward atmosphere in an establishment that was traditionally men only, but Harry was not one of them.

Looking across the room now, Maureen saw one of Harry's vast number of cousins: Anna-Marie, a pretty, dark-eyed girl, who was a friend of Eliza's. Anna-Marie smiled and waved when she saw Maureen was looking her way, raising her glass in a mimed tribute to Eliza and Theo. Maureen started to gather her things to sidle over to say hello, but immediately she was waylaid.

'Hello, Mum. I didn't think I'd see you here.'

It was Sylvia, Maureen's other daughter, and with her was Desmond Gower, her husband. Desmond was clutching an almost empty pint glass, and Sylvia had not much left of a port and lemon.

'Hello, love. No, I wasn't bothered about coming, but Liza persuaded me and I'm glad she did. She's very good tonight, isn't she?'

'Not bad,' said Sylvia. 'She's a way to go before she's Judy Garland, though.'

'Most folk have a way to go before they're Judy Garland, Sylvie,' said Maureen. 'Don't be mean.'

'I was just saying . . .' Sylvia looked a bit put out.

'Anyway, how are you, love?' asked Maureen. 'I haven't seen you for a week or two.'

'Busy, Mum. We're rushed off our feet at the shop. Can't think why.'

'Maybe it's women making new frocks for spring,' suggested Desmond, as if this might be an original idea.

'And what would you know about haberdashery?' asked Sylvia, although it all sounded perfectly obvious to Maureen. She decided to keep quiet if Sylvia was being snappy. Already Maureen could feel the atmosphere of romance and glamour created by the beautiful Irving Berlin songs dissipating with Sylvia's sour mood.

'Nowt at all,' Desmond responded calmly. 'Maureen, can I get you another drink? Lemonade, is it?'

'Thanks, Des, but I think it's time I was going, if Liza's finished for the evening.'

'It's early yet, Mum,' said Sylvia. 'Why don't you stay and chat for a bit?'

Maureen could see the rest of the evening being given over to whatever was currently occupying Sylvia's mind and, although she liked to know what was happening with Sylvia and Desmond, she hadn't the strength to listen to the likely catalogue of complaints about the draper's shop in general and the haberdashery counter – where Sylvia worked – in particular, or about Sylvia's colleagues, about Desmond, about their neighbours . . . She knew from experience that Sylvia would not be very interested in what was going on in the lives of her mother and sister, and although that was, at least in part, how it should be – a mother was there to support her children, in Maureen's opinion – it would be polite of Sylvia at least to express an interest.

'Mum, there you are. Did you enjoy our set?' It was Eliza with Theo in tow, a glass of Scotch in his hand.

'Loved it, sweetheart, and so did everyone else. Theo, that was smashing, especially that linking part between the songs.'

'Thank you, Maureen, and thanks for coming in to see us. It's good to know we've got our best people in the audience – Sylvia and Desmond, too, I see . . .' He kissed Sylvia in the direction of one cheek and shook hands with Desmond.

'New dress, Liza?' asked Sylvia, eyeing it.

'Old, but new to me: made over. I saw it in a pawn-broker's, of all places, and it was pretty big, but Mum helped me cut it down to size.'

'You'd never know it wasn't originally made to measure,' said Theo, beaming at Eliza.

'Well, you would if you knew owt about sewing,' said Sylvia. 'Next time, Liza, ask me, and I'll show you how to put a zip in properly at the side.'

'Thanks, Sylvie,' said Eliza drily. 'OK, Mum, are you ready to go home or would you like to stay for a bit? There's a table over there big enough for all of us.'

'I think it's time we went, love, if you don't mind? Work tomorrow, and I am a bit weary.'

'I'll take you home, if you like,' said Theo. 'Then Eliza can stay and chat with her sister.'

Eliza, who was standing slightly behind Sylvia, was shaking her head and mouthing 'No!'

Maureen saw, but Sylvia said, 'Good idea, Theo. Bye, Mum,' and started to move towards the empty table.

'No, we'll go together, Mum. Theo, you stay and finish your drink. Mum and I saw Harry earlier and you might find him downstairs by now. Anna-Marie's probably with him, and one or two other Mulligans. Mum's ready for her bed, I reckon, and I haven't quite the staying power of you and Harry for an evening out . . . yet.'

Theo promised to collect Eliza's pay for the evening and give it to her the next day, helped them on with their coats, made sure they'd got their bags and their keys to hand, led them downstairs and opened the outer door for them, asking if they were sure they would be quite safe walking home.

'Don't be daft, Theo,' laughed Eliza, 'it's only the next street.'

'Well, you go carefully. Good night, both, and thank you again for coming to hear us, Maureen.'

'It was a pleasure, Theo.'

And it had been. But as they walked down the lamplit street arm in arm, and the lights and noise of the Waterloo faded away behind them, Maureen felt her spirits lowering again.

'It's OK, Mum,' said Eliza, guessing what she was thinking. 'Like I said, no need to put up with owt that makes you unhappy. We'll look for summat better for you tomorrow. It'll be all right, you'll see.'

'Course it will be, Liza love.' Maureen tried to smile.

Would it, though, she thought. Was there a suitable job out there for a middle-aged widow with only a little secretarial experience? Or was she stuck for the fore-seeable future with Herbert Nicholson, his bullying, his dithering and his rudeness? How much longer could she stand it, or would she have to leave – even be sacked by the horrible man, as nothing seemed to suit him? If that happened, until she found another job, or even worked two or three different ones, as she had when the girls were younger, they'd be scraping along with barely the rent covered on what little Eliza earned at the Short Cut.

CHAPTER TWO

THE FOLLOWING DAY, Maureen returned from the
brewery, once more feeling browbeaten and
disappointed after another frustrating day: typing the
same letters over and over until Mr Nicholson finally
made up his mind what he wanted to say, fielding his
constant impatient and barbed remarks, pouring
frequent cups of tea for him while not having the
time to drink a single cup herself, and even being
sent out to order flowers for him to give to his wife.
('Oh, just get something brightly coloured – whatever
those things are you see this time of year. Surely even
you can manage that. But can you do it urgently
because it's her birthday tomorrow?') It had been
difficult for Maureen to concentrate on her work
while, in his office just the other side of the wall from
her desk, Herbert Nicholson shouted into his telephone, boasting about the very important people he'd
met the previous evening.

Eliza had got home not long before her mother, having also stayed late to cut a client's hair at a discount, which she did as part of her training, and was just putting a cheese and onion pie in the oven to heat when Maureen shuffled dejectedly in and sank down onto a kitchen chair. Fortunately, Eliza already had a pot of strong tea brewing under the cosy on the kitchen table.

'Ah, Mum, how was it today? No, don't answer; I can see how it was. Well, I've got a copy of the *Telegraph* and later we can see if there's a job that would suit you better, if you like?'

'Thanks, love.' Maureen looked at where the *Northern Evening Telegraph* lay on the kitchen table. She felt too tired to want to bother with it now, though. Maybe a cup of tea would help her gather her strength to peruse the job vacancies.

Eliza had one poured and in front of her even as she thought this.

'And there was some post for you, Mum; came just as I was leaving this morning.'

She handed Maureen a long, thick brown envelope. Unusually, the address was typed parallel to the short side rather than the more conventional way round. Maureen felt her heart start to race: she remembered from when her husband, Jack, had died that this had been a characteristic of solicitors' letters. But what could a solicitor be writing to her about now?

'Are you going to open that, Mum?' prompted Eliza. 'Looks official . . .'

26

'I'm not in the mood for bad news. Still, better see what it is.'

Eliza handed her mother a knife from the cutlery drawer and she used it to slice along the envelope's flap.

She drew out a letter folded in half lengthways, with a smaller piece of paper clipped to it. She pulled it off and turned it over. It was a cheque for just over twelve thousand pounds, made out to 'Mrs Maureen Bancroft'.

'What . . .?' Words failed her.

'What is it, Mum? You've gone completely white.' Eliza glanced at the sum on the cheque, her eyes widened and she sat down. Then she reached over and took the letter from her mother's hand. Maureen seemed to be in a state of shock. 'Good grief, can it be possible? Who's Cecily Stevens? Is she a relation?'

'No, love,' said Maureen, slowly, 'no relation at all. She is . . . she was a lady I used to work for, quite a long time ago now. She wasn't all that old then, but I went to clean her house, do some shopping for her, sometimes cook her lunch, help out generally. She was arthritic and also not brought up to manage very well for herself – a sweet lady but not practical – so I went in every day.'

'I don't remember you talking about her.'

'This was when you and Sylvia were quite young and still at school. You were both full of your own activities, so it's possible you weren't really aware of the people I worked for. Miss Stevens was just one of my employers. I had a few at the time. Anyway, she and I got on

27

especially well, and I reckon she liked to have company and someone to talk to as much as she needed the help. She liked a chat . . .' Maureen looked away, thinking about kind Miss Stevens, with her house full of pretty objects – watercolour paintings and delicate porcelain – the little cat she had doted on, her fondness for violet-scented chocolates . . .

'She's left you a fortune . . .' breathed Eliza, quickly reading the letter. She was smiling but also puzzled. 'Oh, Mum, this is marvellous. So much money . . . but such a strange thing to do after all these years. Did she have no one else in her life?'

Maureen looked taken aback. She put the cheque carefully to one side on the table, sat back in her chair and took a sip of her tea. 'Yes, it's astonishing. I'm sorry the poor lady's dead . . . Her brother went to live with her and she didn't need me any more after that, though we kept in touch for a while – Christmas cards and the like. He was older than Miss Stevens, and I think her only close relation.' She glanced at the cheque again. 'You don't think it's a mistake, do you, love?'

'How could it be? The letter looks official, with the name of the firm of solicitors printed all smart at the top, and it's definitely addressed to you, Mum.'

'I can hardly take it in . . . But what am I supposed to do with this cheque? I usually only deal with cash.'

'You'll have to take it to a bank and open an account, Mum.'

'But what if I go to the bank and they wonder what an ordinary sort of woman like me is doing with all this money? It could turn unpleasant if they don't believe what I say.'

Eliza laughed. 'Don't be daft. I'll go with you, if you want, and we'll take the letter to prove how you came by the money. The cheque is *for* you, made out to you. Now stop worrying – this is really good news, not summat else to make you anxious on top of working for Herbert.' Her smile broadened as the thought struck her: 'And, Mum, you don't have to work for Herbert any more, either. You can be shot of him.' Eliza put the letter on the table beside the cheque and took Maureen's hands in hers. 'Oh, Mum, it's wonderful. You can do anything you want to now. Not only do you not have to work for Herbert, you don't have to work *ever again* if you don't want to. The bank will pay you interest on the money so, provided you don't spend it all at once, you can have a nice income from it to live off.'

'Spend it all at once! Now who's talking daft? And I've always gone to work – what would I do with myself all day if I didn't go to work?'

Eliza could see that far from being delighted by her good fortune, her mother was fretting. Maybe the day had been especially trying, running about after Herbert, and she would feel calmer after something to eat and a good night's sleep.

'Look, Mum, I understand why this will take some

getting used to, and you'll want to have a proper think how to go on from here, but I'm sure Miss Stevens left you the money in her will because she wanted to make you happy, not worried. Telephone the solicitor tomorrow – ask Stella if you can phone from her office – and then you can set your mind at rest.'

Maureen nodded. She picked up the cheque again and reread it, her hand trembling.

'Put that in a safe place with the letter and p'raps you'll see it in a different light tomorrow,' suggested Eliza.

'I feel like the rug has been pulled from under my feet and I'm sent topsy-turvy, not sure where I'll land.'

Eliza got to her feet and gave her mother a hug. 'You'll always have me and Sylvia to help you, Mum, and we won't let you lose your way. I'm sure there'll be some clever fella at the bank only too willing to advise you, too, if you're depositing all that money with them.'

'Yes, love, thank you,' Maureen muttered. She smiled, but to Eliza it looked like an effort.

'And the other good thing is that there's a pie in the oven and it must be nearly ready. You set the table, Mum, I'll dish the pie and we'll raise a toast to Miss Stevens with a fresh pot of tea.'

Maureen looked relieved the subject was back on familiar ground. 'Yes, love, pie and a nice cup of tea.'

* * *

Next morning, Maureen set off for work with the solicitor's letter, the telephone number printed at the top, tucked safely into her handbag, although she felt compelled to check a couple of times that it hadn't mysteriously disappeared during the bus journey.

She had a word with Stella straight away about using her office telephone. Stella's only concern was to be assured that there was nothing wrong with Maureen, no illness she was keeping quiet about, and she said she'd let Maureen know when she could make her phone call in private.

'I don't know what's the matter with you today, Mrs Bancroft,' said Mr Nicholson, towards the middle of the morning. 'You seem to be working more slowly than ever, if that were possible. It's not the weekend yet, you know. Do at least *try* to apply yourself to what you're paid to do, otherwise I might be docking your wages for today.'

'Yes, Mr Nicholson. I'm sorry to hold you up.' She knew she had been distracted, her mind not entirely on the job, but, even so, she had done all the letters and memos he'd asked of her. She took the blotter from his desk, the signed correspondence inside. Sure enough, as usual, most of them were rewritten with deletions and additions in heavy black ink, his handwriting untidy, and instructions to Maureen were scrawled in capital letters in the margins, as if they were being shouted at her. None of these could be salvaged in any way and they would all have to be completely retyped.

'I want those in the lunchtime post. They're urgent,' he barked at her. 'You'll need to stop wasting time and get a move on.'

They're not that urgent, you stupid man. What difference does it make, providing they're posted today, before the weekend?

For a moment Maureen thought she might have said this out loud, so vivid was the thought.

Soon after Maureen had sat down again at her typewriter, Stella put her head round the door to the outer office and silently beckoned Maureen to come to her own, just down the corridor.

'I'll go and take round the internals while you make your call, Maureen. Mr Felbridge is busy in the boardroom and I'll be a few minutes.' Stella showed Maureen to her desk, gathered up her memos and closed the door gently behind her.

Five minutes later, Maureen had made her call to Lambert and Goldsworthy, Solicitors and learned that the legacy was very far from being a mistake. The solicitors had acted as executors and Miss Stevens had bequeathed the savings in her bank accounts to Maureen Bancroft and the money from the sale of her effects to a distant cousin.

'Miss Stevens's brother predeceased her,' Mr Lambert explained, 'augmenting Miss Stevens's already considerable estate with his inheritance from their parents. I am glad to be the bearer of the good news of your legacy, Mrs Bancroft, although we all mourn the death of Miss Stevens. Please be assured Lambert and

Goldsworthy will be pleased to be of service, should you wish to draw up your own will or, indeed, need any other legal service or advice.'

'Thank you, Mr Lambert,' said Maureen. 'You're very kind.'

'May I suggest, Mrs Bancroft, that you pay the cheque into your bank account at the earliest opportunity?'

'Yes, Mr Lambert. I, er, agree that would be best.' Better not to tell him that she didn't have a bank account.

'My good wishes to you, Mrs Bancroft,' said Mr Lambert, 'and I hope you gain much happiness from your legacy.'

'Thank you, Mr Lambert. Goodbye,' Maureen said shyly, and replaced the receiver. This important legal person was so polite and attentive, as if he thought she was someone who mattered. Now, she should go to a bank and open an account as soon as possible.

There was a soft tap at the door and Stella put her head round.

'You all right, Maureen?' she asked, seeing her colleague had finished her phone call. 'Not bad news, I hope. You look a bit . . . gone.'

Maureen straightened her back, took a deep breath and pasted on a smile. 'Thank you, Stella, no, not bad news at all. And I'm grateful for the use of your office and telephone – thank you.'

'So long as you're OK . . .?'

'Yes, Stella, I'm just fine.'

Maureen went back to her own office and Mr

Nicholson's letters, her thoughts whirring. Now she knew for certain that the cheque was genuine, and she had had time to think about the astonishingly large amount of money, its presence in her pantry was beginning to worry her, and the important business of opening an account would be all done and dusted if she just got on with it today, before the bank closed for the weekend.

Right, just finish this little lot and then I'll go. I'll say I'm not well and need to go home . . . No, that would be a lie. I'll just say I have to go, then do so. Oh, but he'll want an explanation . . . I'll say I've been called away urgently – ha! – and I'm going . . .

'Mrs Bancroft, where have you been? I've been calling for you for the last ten minutes. I have a very urgent letter I want you to take down and I'd appreciate it if you'd hurry up with those others, too, and stop wasting my time. Oh, and would you bring me a cup of tea straight away?'

'Of course, Mr Nicholson. Tea first, and then the urgent letter, or is the letter so *urgent* it can't wait?'

Herbert Nicholson looked for a second as if he thought he'd misheard. Then: 'Tea, Mrs Bancroft, then the letter. Chop chop.'

It was these last two words that finally pushed Maureen beyond the limit of her patience. Her heart was pounding and she felt the colour rising in her face, but she was blowed if she'd let him speak to her like that one more time.

'Mr Nicholson,' she said, forcing herself to meet his eye, trying to control the tremble in her voice, 'I'll thank you not to address me as if I were a pit pony. I'm not your servant, I'm your secretary, this is paid work, not some kind of punishment I must endure, and plain good manners are not too much to expect of anyone.'

'Mrs Bancroft—'

'Let me finish, please, Mr Nicholson. I had high hopes of this job when I started, but before long I began to see how things were – see how *you* are: someone who tramples on those he regards as his inferiors, who chooses to be rude to folk he thinks won't answer back, and kowtows to those he regards as his betters. Someone who seems not to have learned even the most basic rules of civilised behaviour.'

Herbert Nicholson opened his mouth in astonishment but no sound came out, which gave Maureen the chance to unburden herself further. She had nothing to lose.

'I think, Mr Nicholson, that decent folk, far from being impressed, will think that makes you a bully and a snob.'

'Mrs Bancroft—' Mr Nicholson's face was puce, as if he was about to explode with anger, but Maureen was grasping this opportunity to air her grievances and she wasn't going to stop now.

'And as for "urgent", it's just another way of browbeating me, implying I sit here wasting time doing nowt unless you keep cracking the whip with your "urgent" all the time. It's insulting. It turns out, Mr Nicholson, that you are a bad boss and you're impossible to work for.'

'How dare—'

'So I'm off now. I'm going and I'll not be back. I'll leave these urgent letters here for you.'

She gathered herself, controlling her shaking hands, and gently placed the open blotter back on his desk, the inky amendments and boldly worded instructions to herself displayed prominently. Then she turned on her heel and left Herbert Nicholson's office for the last time. She gathered her bag from under her desk, her coat from the peg by the door, and walked out without looking back.

She would not go without saying goodbye to Stella and the friendly people in accounts, and she hurried round to explain briefly that she was leaving – she'd had enough – and promised to be in touch. More than anything she wished to avoid meeting Herbert Nicholson in the corridor on her way out.

By the time Maureen had crossed the brewery yard and let herself out into the street, she was feeling much lighter of heart. She'd said what needed saying, what she now knew she'd been longing to say for many months. That job might have been a step up from being a cleaner or a home help, but it had turned out to be a terrible strain on her nerves and now, at last, she was free of it.

* * *

'So, Mum, you're looking a lot happier,' beamed Eliza when she got in that evening to find her mother already in the kitchen with her pinny on, bustling between the stove and the pantry, and humming quietly to herself. 'I take it you telephoned those solicitors.'

'I did, love. Mr Lambert was very nice. He explained all about the legacy and, like you, he thought I ought to pay the cheque into a bank without delay. So I did. I opened an account this afternoon.'

'Good news, Mum. Did you have to take the afternoon off work to go and do that?'

Maureen grinned as she poured boiling water into the teapot. 'I'm never going back, love. Herbert was that rude to me I just couldn't bear it any longer. You were right: what the legacy means right now is that I won't have to put up with that awful man ever again. I don't know what I'll spend the money on, but already it's bought me my freedom from that miserable job and I've been giving thanks to Miss Stevens, God rest her soul, all afternoon.'

'Mum, I'm so pleased. You look years younger already, like you've shed a heavy load. I've been that excited all day, almost bursting with happiness at your news, but I promise I haven't told anyone. How did you get on at the bank?'

'Oh, love, I was nervous to start with, what with everyone looking so important and serious. And the place was huge inside, with all these great lights hanging down on chains. When I presented the letter and the cheque at the counter, they asked me to wait. I thought for one silly moment they might be going to call the police, like I said yesterday, but I reminded myself that they could call Mr Lambert and he'd explain if they had any doubts. Anyway, a very smart young man soon showed me into the manager's office, would you believe? Then it was all "Mrs Bancroft this" and "Mrs Bancroft that"; tea and biscuits, too! About halfway through all the fuss and paperwork, I saw the upper of one of my shoes had split across the crease and it was all I could do not to laugh when those posh bank folk – all starched collars – were making such a lot of me.'

Eliza smiled, too. It was so good to see how quickly her mother was regaining her sense of humour, now she was out from under the cosh of Herbert Nicholson's oppression.

'And why would they not, Mum? You're one of their customers now and they need to keep you happy if they want you to leave your money in their vaults.'

'They were falling over themselves to offer their services, it's true, but I don't expect I'll be bothering them much . . .'

Eliza went over and hugged her mother. 'Dear Mum, you are lovely. I doubt your riches will ever spoil you.'

'I should hope not. Now, we've a nice bit of haddock I got at the market on the way home. Are you going to Theo's this evening?'

'I intend to, unless you'd rather I stayed in with you,

what with your news. I don't want you sitting here alone and getting worked up about it again.'

Maureen thought for a moment or two. 'Would you mind if I came with you? I promise not to interrupt your practising, but it'd be nice to listen to your singing and Theo's lovely playing, and just feel like . . . like I'm on holiday; like I've had a little evening away, a treat.'

'A holiday . . .' mused Eliza. 'Yes . . . course you can come with me, Mum. Theo is always pleased to see you. We'll just practise our pieces and you can sit comfortably on Theo's sofa and drift away on a cloud of Fred Astaire and Ginger Rogers classics. Better close your eyes, though, 'cos Theo looks nothing like Fred Astaire – or Ginger Rogers . . .'

Maureen laughed long and loud, rather more than Eliza thought the joke was worth, but she realised it was a release of all the tension her mother had been feeling recently, and it was a pleasure to hear.

A holiday, though – now that really was a good idea. When had Maureen last had more than a day or two off work? Eliza decided to give some thought to that and then see if she could persuade her mother to have a proper break. If Maureen went right away from here, somewhere quite different, it would give her a breathing space, a chance to come to terms with her new wealth and decide what she wanted to do with her life now she could do almost anything she wanted.

CHAPTER THREE

'FIVE, SIX, SEVEN, eight . . . one, two . . . No, no,
dear, you come in on "one". Let's try it again, shall
we? Both hands up over the keys, remember. Five, six,
seven, eight . . .'

Would this hour of purgatory ever end? Barbara Hayle
took a deep breath to steady herself and counted, but
was unable to prevent Jane Saunders, a stolid little girl of
eight, and possibly the least promising child Barbara had
ever taught to play the piano – which was saying a great
deal indeed – coming in a beat too early and thumping
out 'The Pixies' Dance' as if hammering in nails.

'All right, Jane. Those pixies are a little heavy on
their feet. Try to think of them dancing on their toes,
nice and light, like this.' Barbara demonstrated a few
bars, then asked Jane to copy her. 'When you're practising at home, if you count aloud it will help you keep
time. So, scales and counting, keep it light and pretty,
and that left hand up, and I'll see you next week.
Mummy's waiting in the hall for you.'

'Thank you, Miss Hayle.'

The child slipped off the long piano stool and trotted away to her mother, clutching her music, and Barbara followed to see the pair out through the wide front door with a smile. She closed the door gently behind them and, exhaling with relief, sank onto one of the chairs she provided for waiting parents in the lofty hall, closed her eyes and enjoyed the sound of silence.

Never mind, girl, just keep thinking of the money.

She had three piano pupils on a Saturday morning – two down, one to go – and three elocution lessons to give in the afternoon, but if she was quick there was just time for a fortifying cup of tea before Doreen Perks arrived. Barbara sighed. Oh, no, Doreen Perks! Or rather, Doreen Perks's mother . . .

On the kitchen table, Barbara saw the letter that she'd picked up off the mat first thing and hadn't had time to open. The envelope was addressed in a familiar hand but she couldn't think immediately whose writing it was. While the tea brewed, she slit open the envelope and withdrew a thin lined sheet of paper that looked as if it was from a Woolworths writing pad. She glanced at the end and saw that it was signed 'With best wishes from Maureen'.

Of course . . . Maureen Stubbs – Maureen Bancroft, as she now was – her old best friend from school, or at least Maureen had thought so; Barbara had never been one for very close friendships. It had definitely been a case of opposites attracting: Maureen's gentle quietness; Barbara's need to have an audience and put on a show.

And Maureen had been a very willing audience, only too keen to supply the praise and admiration that Barbara loved. Maureen's softly spoken parents had been quite a contrast to Barbara's own – Barbara's father, tired and intolerant in the evenings, shouting and lashing out after his long days at work, her graceless and harassed mother not quite coping with all her children of various ages – the older ones getting into mischief, some of it serious, the younger ones constantly demanding to be fed or washed or comforted. Barbara loved to go to Maureen's house after school. There, the loudest voice was her own, there was abundant applause and admiration, and the most severe chastisement was no stronger than kindly guidance or, on very rare occasions, mild expressions of disappointment. Everything about Maureen and her parents was modest and low key. Young Barbara was convinced she brought some much-needed glamour and excitement to their small, dull lives, and she loved it that all eyes were on her.

Maureen had been a sweet-natured girl, an only child, rather shy, very like her mother, and from what Barbara knew of her since they'd grown up – their friendship now kept up by the intermittent exchange of letters as they'd made their own lives in different worlds – she hadn't changed much. Maureen's letters were usually full of news about her daughters, on whom she clearly doted, though Barbara wasn't sufficiently interested to remember how old they were or what they did. She had a vague recollection that

Maureen had done a shorthand and typing course or some such a few years previously. Poor woman – was that really the most exciting news in her life? Barbara, in turn, had told Maureen all about her theatrical career, the famous names she had worked with in variety, and the applause she received whenever she was persuaded to emerge from her semi-retirement in her large country house and graciously take on a guest appearance.

Mousy Maureen, Barbara thought, looking at the cheap writing paper with a sneer. It was amazing that, despite their differences, they had kept in touch. Barbara was certain that Maureen looked forward to receiving her letters rather more than she cared to have Maureen's, but it seemed such a small thing, really, to bring a little sparkle into the poor woman's dull life.

Barbara turned the letter over – it was written on both sides, the writing on the reverse showing faintly through the cheap paper – and read it carefully.

> *28 Mafeking Street,*
> *Blackburn,*
> *Lancashire*
> *19 April 1956*

Dear Barbara,
I hope you are well and enjoying life. It's a long while since we last met, although I'm always so pleased to get your letters and hear of your latest news.

A TIME TO REMEMBER

I've been thinking about you and wondering how you're getting on since we last corresponded at Christmas. Then, you mentioned receiving so many invitations to appear in the glamorous world of variety. I do hope you aren't working yourself to the bone. I'm sure you have lots to tell me and I hope to be able to hear it all soon.

I have decided to have a little holiday. My girls are too busy to take time off work just now, and the first person I thought I'd like to spend a few days with otherwise is you. I keep remembering the fun we shared when we were at school together, and what good friends we were.

Do you remember that hotel in Somerton-on-Sea where we worked that summer? I sent for some brochures and I see it's still there. I thought it would be fun to go back, but for a stay, sleep in the lovely soft beds we used to make! It's not the same folk who owned it then, but it still looks nice in the picture. I don't have a car, but we can easily get to the Yorkshire coast by train, with a few changes. I thought perhaps four or five days next month, but I'm flexible and can fit in with what and when would suit you.

I expect you're probably busy starring in some wonderful show and this is the last thing you've got the time for, or perhaps even want to do at all, but I'd love to see you. If you are able to come, and you fancy a little break and a chance to catch up, then tell me when you're free and I'll book the rooms, my treat.

I look forward to hearing from you.

With best wishes from Maureen

Well, there was a surprise.

Barbara put the letter back on the kitchen table and poured herself a cup of tea, thinking about Maureen Bancroft and her holiday. Was the holiday dependent on whether Barbara went too, or was Maureen intending to go anyway, maybe even alone? 'My treat' implied that Maureen would pay for the rooms, but that was a puzzle. She'd never given the impression of having any money to spend before; rather the contrary. Barbara thought hard, trying to remember what Maureen did for a living. She had thought it used to be something quite menial, like cleaning, and more recently she worked in an office somewhere, but the offer to pay suggested there had been some change in her circumstances. Interesting . . . Either that or this was now a very cheap and possibly ghastly hotel! Such a curious invitation out of the blue . . .

The hotel they'd worked in had been clean and attractive, and had felt smart to the young girls without being too daunting. The owners, who had been connected in some way to Maureen's father, had been very kind, giving Barbara and Maureen so much time off that their working summer had been as much their first seaside holiday away from home as it was helping out and waitressing. It had been the late 1920s, a bit of a golden age: the First World War long over, lively new music to dance to, and the new style of shorter frocks to wear, which were fun and comfortable, even if, for Barbara and Maureen, they were second-hand

and altered to fit. Barbara had spent her first wages on having her hair cut fashionably short – she smiled now, remembering; this might have been the start of her lifelong love of trying new hairstyles – although Maureen had felt unable to part with her plaits. The girls had cleaned the rooms and helped with the laundry, waited on the guests at breakfast and for what they'd learned to call 'dinner' – which was, in fact, 'tea' at home – and they'd had great fun at the beach in their time off. Looking back, Barbara could now see that they had been little more than children really, and the afternoons building sandcastles with colourful buckets and spades had been the kind of innocent fun that children far younger also enjoyed . . .

The doorbell jangled loudly and Barbara put down her cup of tea and went to let in Doreen Perks and her mother. Passing through the hall on her dainty heels, she stopped briefly in front of the ornately framed mirror to check her lipstick wasn't smudged and that her curls were still lacquered prettily in place. A pot of highly scented hyacinths stood on the hall table, and Barbara turned it round to show the blooms to their best advantage. Never mind dreaming about holidays at the seaside, there was work to be done – and what work young Doreen and her mother were.

Mrs Perks had booked piano lessons for Doreen to start with, but after a few weeks she had suddenly remembered – or so she told Barbara – that she had once learned to play herself and wished to, as she put it, 'brush the rust off my talent'. So far as Barbara could tell, Mrs Perks had never played before or, if she had, she was badly self-taught, and certainly she was a long way from ever truthfully being able to describe herself as having a talent.

Barbara adopted the dazzling smile she'd learned as a chorus girl – the kind of smile you had to perfect even when your feet were killing you – and swung open the door on its smooth, deep hinges, the brass letterbox – inscribed with the name of the house, The Manor, such a smart draw for those to whom these things mattered – glinting in the spring sunshine.

'Welcome, Mrs Perks and Doreen. It's a pleasure to see you again . . .'

Barbara sank down on her sofa and reached for the blanket she kept handy to save having to light a fire in the drawing room. Goodness, what a day . . .

She knew she had dozed off because when she opened her eyes there was a man standing at the foot of the sofa. She sat up, her hand flying to her mouth in shock.

'Oh! Oh my . . . Oh good heavens, Brendan, it's you! You nearly frightened the life out of me. How dare you let yourself into my house? How did you get in, anyway?'

'Hello, Barbara. You left the door unlocked, didn't you? I just walked in, called out a couple of times, then found you in here, having a nice little doze. Had a hard day, have you, old girl, teaching the tone deaf to

play that big piano and the snobs to speak proper?'
He grinned, showing slightly crooked teeth in his otherwise handsome young face.

'Don't be mean, Brendan. And less of the "old", if
you please. I've had the most awful day. I don't know
who are worse, the piano pupils or the elocution
ones. There was a new client this afternoon, a man
from Blackburn called Herbert Nicholson, desperate
to sound "posher". Absolutely ghastly. Some days I
just hate the lot of them – stupid, talentless, horrible
little people.'

She stood up to face him. He was unable to sit without
crowding her, because the sofa was the only seating in
the entire large and echoing room.

'What time is it? Would you like to stay and I'll cook
you dinner? It's only sausages and mash, I'm afraid. I
didn't know you were coming, but I can make it stretch.'

'No, thanks, I'd rather not risk your cooking. I'll
leave you to enjoy your tea in peace. I reckon you must
need a bit of peace after the row some of those pupils
of yours must make.'

'Actually, you're welcome to stay. It can get a little
quiet in the evenings . . .' She tailed off, knowing she
was in danger of sounding pathetic. She might enjoy
spending an evening with Brendan occasionally . . .
but then again, perhaps not. It was the company she
wanted, not Brendan. He couldn't be relied on to be
pleasant. For a while she'd kept a canary in a cage. It
had been a winsome little thing and its pretty song had

brightened her days. Since it had died, just after Christmas, she felt the silence of her solitary hours more than ever. Maybe she should get another caged bird. Or a dog . . .

'I only came to deliver that rent I owe you,' said Brendan. 'Envelope's on the table in the kitchen.'

'Thank you,' said Barbara crisply, determined not to sound too grateful.

'I'll stay while you check it. Save you counting it as soon as I've gone and then we can *both* agree it's right.'

Barbara raised an eyebrow but said nothing. She led the way into the kitchen where a brown envelope now lay on the table, withdrew some red ten-shilling notes from it and quickly counted them.

'Thank you, Brendan. Yes, it's right.'

'We've got a good arrangement here: me paying you rent for the use of those outbuildings for my storage, far from prying eyes – which would just be empty and wasted, probably full of rats if I didn't use them – and that allows you to continue to live at The Manor. You told me yourself you can't afford to keep it up since Marty popped his clogs, left you without a penny to your name, the bank breathing down your neck and, from what I gather, half Lancashire chasing you to settle their bills. Not quite so free-spending these days, are you, Babs?' He smiled nastily.

'Yes, thank you for reminding me, Brendan. I have to admit I am having to rob Peter to pay Paul, and every month there seems to be less to go round to any of them. The worst of it is that wretched loan Marty and I took out. I've still got that hanging over me – after all this time it feels like I'm paying for nothing – and the people at the bank are absolutely ruthless. I'm quite certain they'd make me homeless if I got in arrears. They have no sympathy at all about what The Manor means to me. I've had to rein in my spending in so many ways that it's becoming really quite hard to maintain any sense of style. There's nothing so dreary as economising.'

Brendan laughed. 'I bet, Babs. Forgotten you're just the same as the rest of us, have you, for all you look and sound like a toff?'

Barbara chose not to answer that. Instead she said, 'As you say, Brendan, we've got a good arrangement. I love The Manor, and the smart-sounding address is very good for business, but it's beginning to wear me down, trying to keep everything going: something always needs repairing or seeing to, or someone needs paying. Some of this rent you've given me will go towards getting the window frames repainted, at least at the front, and the rest straight to the gardener. I have to pay him. I can't afford gossip about unpaid bills in the village.'

Brendan looked suddenly alert. 'First I've heard of a gardener. You're getting very grand in your old age, girl. Who is he?'

'Mr Gathercole, he's called. He's an old man who lives just down the road. He comes here as and when:

cuts the lawn, tidies the garden, trims the hedges. Heavens, you didn't think I did the garden myself, did you?' She trilled with laughter.

'Never thought owt about it. Your garden, your problem. So this Gathercole – he doesn't ever put your mower and rake, or whatever it is he uses, in those buildings I'm renting, does he? You see, you said that space was free for me to use. I wasn't reckoning on sharing.' Anger crossed his face, and for a moment he looked just like a small child who wanted to keep his toys to himself.

'Don't be silly, Brendan. I told you those outbuildings were empty. I wouldn't lie to you.'

'Wouldn't you, Babs?'

Under the intensity of his belligerent stare, Barbara looked away. Annoyingly, just for a moment, he'd looked exactly like his father. 'I don't use any of them at all – except for the garage, where I keep the car, of course.'

At the mention of the car, Brendan rolled his eyes.

'Mr Gathercole has the lawn mower and the gardening tools in the shed at the back.'

'You quite sure?'

'Yes, of course I'm sure.' Barbara frowned. 'What's the matter? I would hardly be renting the space to you and using it myself, would I?'

'Course you wouldn't,' Brendan said drily. 'How's the car running, by the way?'

'I expect it's fine. I haven't been out in it much lately.'

'A lot of car for one person, Babs. I know a fella who'd be interested if you were thinking of selling it. He'd do you a deal and I wouldn't want much of a cut. Maybe a little Austin would suit you better. I can get you one of those, second-hand but reliable. Be cheaper to run, even if it wouldn't be so flashy to be seen in.'

'Second-hand Austin indeed! I'm not parting with the Alvis, Brendan. It was Marty's pride and joy. I promised him I'd look after it. Anyway, I like it. It suits me. It's good for my image and that's useful.' She tossed her curls and straightened her back.

'I know, Babs, but circumstances change. Maybe that big old car has become a bit of a vanity item.' He looked around the huge kitchen, the table isolated in the middle of the blue lino floor like an island in an ocean, a glazed cupboard along one wall containing the meagre remnants of a once-grand dinner service, Barbara's lunchtime crockery unwashed but in a neat little pile on one corner of the vast draining board. 'Bit like this house, eh?'

'I'm selling neither the house nor the car, Brendan, so don't get any ideas.'

'Up to you, Barbara. But you know where I am if you change your mind. Right, well, I think I'll be off. I'm busy this next week – there's a lot happening in the house clearance business – but I'll not disturb you with my coming and going.'

As he turned to go, he seemed to catch sight of Maureen's letter lying on the table. It was right beside where he had left the envelope of money, so Barbara knew immediately this was an act. He'd already seen the letter and read it, of that she had no doubt.

'Heard from a friend, have you, Babs?'

'And what if I have? Can't you mind your own business?'

'Ah, don't be like that, love. I'm glad for you. It's nice to keep up with old friends, especially ones who can afford to take you on holiday. I thought the rich crowd had dropped you after Marty went out in a box.' He laughed. 'Seems like you still know someone interesting. I expect you'll be working on this friendship.'

'Actually, this is completely unexpected, but I admit I'm intrigued. Still the old address, but no hint as to how Maureen can suddenly afford to be so generous.'

'Perhaps I should go round and ask her. Sounds like she's had a bit of luck. If she's rolling in it, she can take me on holiday too.'

'For goodness' sake, Brendan! This has nothing to do with you. It's a private letter, in case you hadn't noticed, although I'm sure you had.'

'Course it is. Thing is, I'm just wondering, if you're planning a little trip, if you'd like me to keep an eye on The Manor for you. Could keep an eye on this Maureen's place in Mafeking Street, too, while she's absent.' He winked, smirking. 'All you have to do is let me know when you and your friend are going to be away.'

'Good heavens, you mean move in here?'

'Don't be soft! What would I do in a big posh house

with nowt in it but a grand piano? It's bloomin' freezing in here, too. No, I meant would you like me to keep an eye on the place, come round and make sure there's no one been trying to break in, pinch your stuff.'

'What stuff?' Barbara laughed, despite being annoyed that Brendan had read her letter and was being devious and awkward. 'Any burglar would have an impossible task to get the piano out and there isn't anything else worth stealing.'

'No, I meant just make sure everything was all right. Like I said, you just tell me when you and Maureen plan to be away. There's a lot of villains around, Barbara, and a woman like you – alone – wants to take care of her assets.'

Barbara gave him a very hard look. 'If I do go away for a few days, I'll let you know. Now, thank you for the rent, Brendan.'

'You see, I could always move Mum in here to keep an eye on things . . .'

'What! Are you mad? Whatever reason you may have to suggest moving Mum in here, it isn't to keep an eye on things. That canary I used to have had a better grasp of what was going on than our mother would.'

Brendan seemed to find this extremely funny and he laughed loudly.

'Anyway,' Barbara went on, 'I'd never get her to leave . . . although she'd hate the noise the pupils make . . . and it's too cold for her. And besides, she'd have the place looking like a pigsty in no time.'

Brendan's laughter subsided and he mopped his eyes showily with a grubby handkerchief.

'I can always get a rise out of you, Barbara . . . I'll see you soon,' he grinned. 'You take care, love, and think about what I said. Mebbe you need a little holiday, and with me you've got a trustworthy fella to keep an eye on the gaff for you.'

'Yes, thank you, Brendan, I'll bear that in mind. But if you even suggest to Mum she could move in here, I'll never speak to you again and you can forget about renting the outbuildings.'

'All right, Babs, it was only a joke. No need to get uptight. Ta-ta for now.'

He went out into the hall, his footsteps beating sharply on the stone flags. The front door opened soundlessly and then Barbara heard it closing firmly behind him.

Gaff, indeed! Really, how on earth did Brendan get to be so rough? Well, Mum, of course. And Dad. As for moving Mum in . . . the day she moves in here is the day I leave for good.

Barbara went to her fridge to get the makings of her dinner. There was just one sausage – she remembered now she'd eaten the other one the previous evening – and in the larder, two small potatoes and a tiny tin of peas. It was a good thing Brendan had declined the invitation to stay to eat. She could just imagine his sneering face and cruel laughter.

*　*　*

The following morning Barbara lay in bed with the eiderdown pulled up high against the early chill and thought about her life as it was now.

To the residents of the village of Buckledale, nestling in the fells north of Blackburn, she was Miss Barbara Hayle, former star of variety and light comedy theatre, a glossy and glamorous presence in the village, who opened the Christmas fête and graciously gave out the prizes, and who lived in the largest and most beautiful house, The Manor. From there, she taught piano and elocution to those lucky enough to be able to afford private lessons, and sprinkled a little stardust on village life generally. So went popular opinion, and Barbara continued to cultivate that with every atom of her being.

The reality was rather different from this view, and it was increasingly a struggle to marry the two.

Barbara sighed, pulled the eiderdown up higher around her ears and tried not to frown. She had enough problems without creases in her brow.

Say, for instance, she managed to save up enough money from the lessons and the rent Brendan paid her for the use of the outbuildings to have someone round to do the maintenance that was needed on the window frames, she'd have to remember to close all the curtains so the workman couldn't see into the empty rooms. In most of the bedrooms there was now not a single stick of furniture remaining, and downstairs it was not much better. The furniture had been sold off over recent years, piece by piece. Somehow, living beyond their means hadn't mattered when Marty had been alive. It was part of their devil-may-care attitude to life; they were above the ordinary considerations of thrift and economy because they had style by the bucketload. Now Marty was dead, though, taken by cancer at the age of forty-nine, and Barbara felt the responsibility of The Manor weighing heavily, with money so extremely tight.

She lived in a beautiful grand house that she loved. She loved its elegance, she loved its important-sounding name and she loved the picturesque setting. She loved being the celebrity of the village, the person everyone greeted in the street and smiled upon, and The Manor was all part of this act – her stage setting. She could no longer imagine herself without it, yet it was also a terrible drain on her small income. But how could she give it up? It was inextricably bound up in her memory with her marriage to Marty – those brief, happy years of shared love and living the high life – and now it was all she had left of those golden times; that and the car. Without those she had nothing; she was no one.

Marty had bought the house for a song five years ago. It was old-fashioned, remote from the bright lights and utterly impractical, but he was bored with the life of a theatrical impresario, and the idea of 'retiring to the country' and becoming 'lord of the manor' had overwhelming appeal. That was what he had told Barbara at the time. He'd asked her to marry him and they'd had a dazzlingly romantic whirlwind wedding at a registry office, and then a honeymoon in Rome. He hadn't mentioned that he was ill until he could no longer keep it hidden from her.

Barbara's star, which had never reached anything approaching dizzying heights, had begun to wane long before that, with pretty, talented, eager young actresses jostling for the parts she wanted. She'd taken a few wrong turns in her career, too, and the roles offered to her had become small and infrequent by the time she'd caught the eye of handsome, charming Marty, who had begged her to come to live with him at The Manor. She'd thought it would be fun to be married to Marty, who was such a good catch, to be his 'lady of the manor'. Now she was bound up in that role, the only leading lady she'd ever been, even as it brought her nearer to bankruptcy with every passing month. The lady of the manor was now a widow who taught lessons by the hour, with a big house and a big car to maintain, a loan to pay off, like a ball and chain weighing her down, and a stack of unpaid bills on her desk.

The arrangement with Brendan over the outbuild-ings had been a necessity in the end. She didn't really want him hanging around the place, lowering the tone, bringing a whiff of the city terraces to this reinvention of herself, but she needed the rent he paid, and he might as well put the empty buildings to good use rather than her renting the space to a stranger, who might gossip about her. She just hoped Brendan would keep his head down and pass unnoticed in the village.

On the whole, he did prefer to keep his business activities quiet, she'd learned.

And Brendan had known Marty, of course, and liked him, so far as Brendan liked anyone, despite the age gap of well over twenty years. It was nice to hear someone else say Marty's beloved name. It kept him out in the world, somehow, for all he had been dead for two years now. Darling Marty, how she missed him . . .

Barbara blinked back threatening tears. She decided it was time to brave the cold bedroom and the even colder bathroom. Ridiculous to lie here in bed, weeping and feeling sorry for herself.

Later, having drunk two cups of tea and called them breakfast, Barbara put on her coat and went out to see if Brendan had already brought any of his house-clearance storage to the outbuildings. He hadn't made it clear whether he'd put the place to use yet and she was curious to see what kinds of things he was currently dealing in. Maybe there would be something she could even use herself, or just whisk away without his noticing and take to a saleroom.

These buildings were screened from the side of the house by a thick bank of laurels. The gravelled drive from the front gate divided into a carriage drive, with a spur curving off to the right and behind the shrubs to garages. It was impossible to see this from the house windows, which was exactly the way it was designed.

The first of the doors were to the garage that housed Barbara's beautiful car. Next were three further sets of double doors, opening onto the spaces now rented out for cash to Brendan.

Oh, he really had been busy! As she approached, she saw that there was a stout new hasp and a padlock attached to the next doors. The other two sets of double doors, when she looked, were locked in the same fashion. Well, Brendan must be doing well if he needed to keep the things he'd acquired so secure. Either that or he was up to no good and liked the remote location. Then again, he probably didn't trust her not to have a look round and help herself. She'd just have to wait for her opportunity. The main thing was that he was paying her in cash for the storage, and paying her on time as well.

Barbara went back to the house, brewed another pot of tea and took her cup and saucer to the music room to play a few old show melodies, her mind turning to yesterday's letter from Maureen Bancroft.

It was tempting to take up the invitation to go on holiday. She'd have to cancel some of her lessons, of course, which would mean a loss of income, but she hadn't had a holiday for ages; not a proper one since Marty became really ill. It would be nice to get away from the awful teaching, even for a few days, and it would be bliss to sleep in a warm bedroom for a few nights. But could she afford to go? There would be *some* expenses, even if Maureen had offered to pay for the room: drinks and dinners, tips, plus petrol for the car. There was no point in paying the train fare and having the fuss of changing and possible delays, and all the soot from the engines, and having to find and tip porters for the luggage, when she could just take the car. Besides, the car made an important impression: it defined who Miss Barbara Hayle was, like a mobile version of The Manor.

And, she had to admit, she was curious as to why Maureen had invited her on holiday now and what could have happened in Maureen's life to make this sudden invitation possible. Undoubtedly there was something there that Barbara needed to know about . . .

Barbara stopped playing and went upstairs to where she kept her cash savings hidden in an envelope under the chest of drawers in her bedroom. She drew out the notes and counted them carefully, then counted them again to be sure. There was enough to cover a short holiday, she thought, especially as Maureen was paying for the hotel . . . and anyway, since when had Miss Barbara Hayle put sensible economy before fun? The answer was: too often lately. The old Barbara – the Barbara that Marty had loved – would have laughed in the face of thriftiness and ordered another round of drinks.

Well, it was long overdue time to bring back the old Barbara, and Maureen had given her the perfect excuse. It was even possible – depending what Barbara discovered about her friend – that a little holiday with Maureen might prove to be a very good investment for the future.

CHAPTER FOUR

'PLEASE DON'T WAIT, Liza. I'm sure she'll be here in a minute and I'd hate you to be late for work.' Maureen's excitement at the prospect of meeting up with her old friend and departing for their holiday was beginning to be overtaken by anxiety.

'It's all right, Mum. If Barbara *is* here in a minute, I shan't be late anyway. Harry knows you're going on holiday this morning and he said he could spare me first thing so I could see you safely away.'

'It's good of him, love. Now, I just want to be sure I've got my cheque book' – Maureen was extremely mindful of the whereabouts of her new cheque book, never having had one until very recently – 'and my purse.' She rootled around in her handbag. 'Try not to forget to water those houseplants, love, and if you could just make sure you've put all the rubbish in the bin for tomorrow . . .'

'Mum, will you please stop fussing? I'm twenty years

old and I was brought up by you, the best and most reliable mother in the whole world – do you honestly think I'll forget how to go on in the short time you're away?'

'No, love, of course not. And don't forget there's a cake in the tin, and I've filled up that there fridge for you.'

'Yes, Mum, I did notice,' Eliza laughed.

The fridge was just about the only thing her mother had bought for the house since she'd inherited Miss Stevens's money last month. Unused to buying much food, or having a fridge, she had stocked it sparingly for the two of them until the previous day. Now it held enough to feed a family for a week, never mind Eliza on her own for a few days. There was even a chicken and a little shop-bought apple pie, and some cream!

'I might ask Anna-Marie and Theo over to share some of those lovely things, if that's all right?'

'Of course. Invite who you like, love.' Maureen looked at her watch again. 'Oh dear, I'm sure we agreed nine o'clock. Do you think I might be mistaken?'

'No, Mum. Mebbe she's just got held up or summat. She'll be here soon, don't worry.' Eliza was doing her best to sound reassuring but she, too, was starting to worry. It would be awful if the first holiday her mother had had in living memory got off to a bad start, and Eliza didn't want to go to work and leave her mother waiting alone if Barbara wasn't going to turn up at all.

'Oh, now, should I take my umbrella, do you think? I don't know if this good weather is forecast to hold . . .'

'Mum, please stop fretting. The more you take, the more there is to remember to bring home.'

'You're right, Liza. Of course you are . . . but mebbe I should take my headscarf, just in case.'

'If you want. Shall I fetch it down while you look out for Barbara?'

Eliza knew little about Barbara Hayle, other than that she was an old school friend of Maureen's. She wondered if Barbara was also unused to going far from home and, although she had offered to drive, was – now the day had arrived – a bit nervous at the thought of the long journey. On the other hand, the lady was, or had been, an actress, apparently, which didn't sound like the kind of profession a timid person would choose.

Eliza saw Maureen's headscarf straight away on her bed. It was a much-washed plain navy-blue woollen square with a modest decorative fray edging. Eliza held it to her face briefly: it smelled of home, of comfort . . . of Mum.

Please, let her have a lovely time and bring her home safely, Eliza prayed. *And, please, never let her change, except that this good fortune brings her the happiness she deserves . . .*

'Oh, my goodness! Ooh, Eliza! Eliza!'

Eliza rushed downstairs to find her mother dancing up and down on the doorstep and fanning her face.

'Good grief,' Eliza muttered.

Just pulled up at the kerb was the longest and shiniest

vehicle either of the women had ever seen. It was cream-coloured and shaped like the kind of car that might be driven by a film star, all spacious and rounded and smooth. Its soft top was down and concertinaed neatly under a cover at the back, and the seats were red leather. Sitting behind the steering wheel was a woman who might have been Maureen's age but who looked like a goddess.

'Blimey . . .' breathed Eliza, then made a big effort to pull herself together. One of them had to; Maureen was now speechless. 'Not quite what we were expecting, eh, Mum? C'mon, let's go and say hello to Barbara.'

She led her mother gently forward while the goddess extracted herself elegantly from the car and stepped round to the pavement to greet her old friend, extending a slim hand with beautifully manicured fingernails, painted bright red, which exactly matched her dress with a swishy skirt.

'Maureen, I'm so sorry to be late. I . . . got held up. But I've been so excited to see you again. It's been far too long . . .' She bent forward – she was taller than average and her heels were high, as was her broad-brimmed hat, held in place with a feathered hatpin – and kissed in the direction of Maureen's cheek, as close as the hat would allow. She smelled of some lovely perfume that probably was not, Eliza thought, made by Yardley.

Could this really be Mum's old school friend, Eliza wondered. She sounded exactly like a BBC announcer.

'Lovely, lovely . . .' Maureen murmured, looking Barbara up and down, and then visibly gathering herself before she became absurd. 'Barbara, you're amazing, a sight to behold, and so is that car. It's so good to see you again, and so kind of you to take us. But I really think that hat will blow off with the car roof down. Would you like to borrow a headscarf, love?'

Barbara put her head back and trilled a pretty laugh, then pulled out the long fancy hatpin and took the hat off to reveal pretty blonde curls. 'Quite right, Maureen. You always were the practical one. But I've got a little scarf in the car for when we're properly on our way. And you must be . . . Eliza, am I right?'

'Hello, Miss Hayle.'

'Oh, Barbara, dear, please.'

'Barbara.'

They shook hands.

A crowd was gathering up and down the road, people drawn to their doorsteps, peeping through their front windows, some even venturing out into the street to get a better look at the scene.

'I'd ask you in for a cup of tea, Barbara,' said Maureen, 'but I don't know if you'd want to leave the car.'

'Goodness, are there criminals?' said Barbara, her eyes twinkling mischievously.

'No, but there are little boys with sticky fingers. And I'd hate one of them to climb in and try a bit of pretend driving.'

'Well, let's be on our way then,' said Barbara. 'We

can always stop for tea if we see somewhere nice. It's a beautiful day so let's make an occasion of the journey.'

It's all a bit of an occasion already, thought Eliza, and they haven't even left the street.

Eliza brought Maureen's case out from the hallway and handed her the headscarf she'd fetched from upstairs. 'I think you'll be needing this, Mum,' she said. 'I'll just pop the case in the car, if you show me where, Barbara?'

The little case was stowed, Maureen was seated in the passenger seat, and Barbara tied a silk scarf over her blonde curls and donned a pair of sunglasses. Maureen kept glancing at her as if she couldn't believe she was seated in this car next to this woman.

'Bye, Mum. Have a lovely time. Bye, Barbara . . .'

Even the gathering crowds of neighbours were waving as Barbara drove away, Maureen turning in her seat to wave to Eliza until the junction at the road end took her out of sight.

'Eliza, Eliza!' It was Louisa next door, beckoning her over. 'Who was *that*? I'm not sure we've had the pleasure of seeing that person round here before.'

'She was a bit of a surprise, wasn't she?' Eliza smiled. 'She's an old friend of Mum's, that's all I know,' she added discreetly.

'Looks like your mother's gone up in the world, moving in such fine circles. She'll have her work cut out keeping up with that one, unless I'm mistaken.'

'I reckon Mum's feet will stay firmly on the ground, Louisa. I don't think we need worry that she won't want to know us,' Eliza laughed, and started to move away to lock up and get off to work.

'So where is it they've gone, love?'

'Just to the seaside for a change of air, nowhere special; be back very soon,' said Eliza. She gave a cheery wave of farewell and decided she'd better go inside to escape the attention. She closed the front door firmly behind her.

Oh dear, it would have been far better if Maureen had gone to the station and caught a train. Then the neighbours would have been none the wiser. It was impossible to do anything in Mafeking Street without everyone knowing about it. Now they would all be wondering why Maureen Bancroft had gone off for a holiday with someone who looked a bit like an older version of Grace Kelly.

So far as Eliza knew, up until now only she and Sylvia had been in on the secret of Miss Stevens's legacy. Of course, Sylvia had had to be told but, in the privacy of Sylvia's front room one Sunday afternoon, Eliza had impressed on her older sister – in no uncertain terms – the importance of zipping her lip.

'It's Mum's secret to tell, not yours, Sylvie.'

'Can't I just tell Des? A husband and wife don't have any secrets. You'd know that if you were married, Liza.'

Eliza had taken a deep breath and refused to rise to the bait. 'The more folk you tell, the more likely the secret is to get out. It's not a bad thing *not* to boast about having money, is it? Why would you want to tell anyone Mum's business? It's for Mum to tell who she wants to, and when she's good and ready.'

'But it's good news to spread, isn't it?'

'It's not *your* good news, though, Sylvie. Mum's told you and me because we're her daughters and she knows we're happy about her good fortune, but she trusts us to keep quiet. I'm not telling anyone, not even Anna-Marie, or Harry or Theo, so if this gets out we'll all know it's because *you* blabbed. You wouldn't want to betray Mum's trust, would you?'

'Course not. Don't be horrible, Liza. I wouldn't betray anyone.'

'Good! Because if folk did get to know about the legacy, they might think Mum was a soft touch. There might be begging letters on her doormat every day, so instead of Mum enjoying her legacy, she'd be bombarded by heart-breaking tales from unfortunates – not all of them honest, likely as not – asking her to send them money to settle their debts, or because they need an operation, or because their children are ill. Imagine how Mum would worry then. All the joy would vanish and she'd end up fretting about folk she'd never met and sending her legacy to them. So Miss Stevens's money, far from being a good thing, would just bring Mum worry and misery.'

'Oh, Liza, do shut up. You don't half go on some-times.'

Well, now the astounding presence of Miss Barbara Hayle had certainly opened the way for speculation. Best to leave through the gate from the backyard into the ginnel behind the houses and go to work that way, Eliza thought. With luck, by the time she got home this evening, the neighbours would have the concerns of their own day to occupy their minds.

Barbara drove well and quite fast. They headed north and east. Maureen was very conscious as they left Blackburn that heads were turning in the street at the sight of the beautiful car, and its driver. She knew no one was looking at her, which was a relief. Barbara seemed not to mind the interest, but even so, all this attention must surely be very wearing after a bit.

'My, Barbara, but this is lovely,' said Maureen. 'I don't think I've ever seen a smarter car. It turns heads wherever you go, I'll be bound.'

'Oh, I can't say I've noticed,' said Barbara. 'I use it all the time so I kind of forget it can cause a stir. But I'm glad you like it.'

'Was it difficult to get the time off for this holiday? From what you say in your letters, you're terribly in demand for these special guest appearances. It must be nice to be asked, but also not to have to work if you don't want. I'm so grateful to have your company.'

Barbara turned briefly to Maureen, a twinkle in her pretty blue eyes. 'Well, I had to call in a favour or two, but I told the producer that I really *need* this holiday. In the end he understood and they changed the running order of the show. He said he was sorry to lose me but they'd just have to manage.'

'He clearly has a high regard for you, Barbara. Where is it you were appearing, love? Is it nearby?'

'Not terribly.'

Maureen saw that Barbara was concentrating on the road now, so she kept quiet, not wanting to distract her. It wasn't at all attractive on this initial stretch of the journey. The route was urban and the air heavy with smoke from industrial and domestic chimneys.

Soon Barbara said, 'I'm so sorry, Maureen, but I think perhaps we need to put the roof up. What do you say?'

'Mebbe. The air's a bit mucky round here.'

A couple of minutes later, Barbara pulled off the road beside the yard of a factory building where there were men standing around taking a break from their work.

'Tell me what to do and I'll give you a hand,' offered Maureen.

'No need,' beamed Barbara. 'It'll all be taken care of.'

She stepped out of the car, all tall and slender, her red dress a beacon in the grey surroundings, and stood smoothing down its skirt. Then she removed the sunglasses and looked about her, as if surprised to find anyone else was there. By now the men had stopped chatting or were looking up from their newspapers at the sight of this beautiful blonde and her amazing car.

'You all right, love? Need a hand?' one of them asked. He ground out his cigarette underfoot and beckoned some of his workmates over.

'Oh, goodness, yes, please. That would be wonderful. I just need to put the roof up. Do you think you might be able to do it for me?' Barbara looked suddenly helpless and vulnerable. 'It's quite tricky, I'm afraid.'

Of course, the men were only too pleased to show that they wouldn't find it tricky at all and in moments the roof was up and fastened securely.

'So kind . . . so very kind,' Barbara murmured. One of the men even opened the door for her and handed her into her seat. 'Thank you . . . you've been such a help . . .' She flashed her wonderful smile, graciously including all her helpers in the beam of her gratitude, then drove on with an elegant wave of her hand through the window.

'Well, I never,' said Maureen, and then gave herself up to gales of laughter. 'You little tinker!'

'They were very glad to help. It's probably made their day,' said Barbara with a slight shrug, but Maureen saw a twitch of laughter cross her face, too.

As they travelled north-east the big industrial towns were soon left behind, and the countryside became beautiful with majestic hills patterned with dry-stone walls, sheep clinging to the steep fields.

'Are you all right with leaving The Manor empty while you're away, love?' asked Maureen. 'Only I don't like to think you might be anxious about it.'

'It is indeed empty,' said Barbara with a curious twisted smile. 'But my brother Brendan is keeping an eye on it while I'm away.'

'It's good you have someone you can trust. I imagine you've some lovely things in your house and you'll want to keep them safe. I'm not sure I remember Brendan, though I do recall you have quite a few brothers and sisters. I do remember a younger sister, Enid, and an older one, Maggie.'

'Oh, yes, Enid's very much still on the scene,' said Barbara, in a way that implied she would prefer not to see Enid. 'She lives not far from you. I don't see any of the others much, though, except Brendan. He's the baby of the family, much younger than the rest of us. He's around some of the time, especially now Marty's gone.'

'That's good of him. I'm sorry about your husband. You must miss him.'

'Every day,' said Barbara. 'He was such good fun; had real style. It was him that found us The Manor to live in.'

'A wise husband to have set you up in a lovely home. A woman alone has enough to cope with, without worrying about the roof over her head. My Jack always said property was a good investment, but we never got beyond renting, ourselves. Still, me and Eliza manage nicely together.'

'Good . . . good.'

Her mention of Jack brought rushing into Maureen's memory his one encounter with Barbara. It was not long before he and Maureen were married and, as a treat for Maureen's birthday, he had bought tickets for a variety show at the Grand Theatre in Blackburn, in which Barbara was appearing in the chorus. Maureen had written to Barbara at her theatrical digs – Barbara left home as soon as she started working, and never went back – to let her know she would be there and saying she hoped they could meet up afterwards. But when Maureen and Jack went to stand at the stage door, as Barbara had directed, she emerged with a whole gaggle of other chorus girls and introduced Maureen as 'my little friend from school' – 'as if you were a pet dog, not her best friend,' Jack said afterwards. 'Can't stop, darling,' Barbara cooed in a very affected way. 'The girls and I have a date with some very strong drinks and some even stronger men.' The chorus had all giggled and tottered away, Barbara with them. 'Thank goodness she didn't invite us to join them,' said Jack, clearly unimpressed.

How strange that this incident should have flown into Maureen's mind. She had completely forgotten it until now. It was such a long time ago, and both she and Barbara had been very young at the time. She'd forget about it again. The holiday wouldn't be like that.

'Shall we stop for a cup of tea, Barbara?' asked Maureen as they approached a market town. 'Would that be all right?'

'Of course. Good idea.'

'I should have thought to pack us a flask and some cake.'

Barbara looked askance. 'Oh, I'm sure your cake is delicious, Maureen, but it's not very practical, picnicking in an Alvis.'

'No, I suppose not. It's just not what I'm used to . . .' She tailed off. She had been about to say that she wasn't used to going to teashops, but she'd already made up her mind to try to avoid this kind of conversation. She really must get used, instead, to having the means to do exactly as she wished and to think a bit bigger than her old life, restricted always by having to economise. It was the habit of a lifetime to be thrifty, though, and so difficult to break that habit in just a few weeks. Maybe with Barbara showing her how, she'd learn a more stylish way of behaving.

Barbara found a space to park in the market square and the two women got out of the car and straightened their backs. Already Maureen noticed a few people turning to look their way. It made her feel self-conscious, but Barbara didn't seem to notice.

Maureen tried out the attitude of mind she'd resolved to practise from now. 'Let's walk along a bit and see where looks really nice, shall we?'

Barbara agreed and they strolled up one side of the main street and then down the other. There was only one teashop.

'It doesn't look much,' said Barbara.

Maureen had been about to suggest they go in, but she didn't want Barbara to be disappointed, especially as she was doing all this driving, and the place didn't look particularly special.

'We could try the White Hart,' said Barbara, indicating an old coaching inn across the road from the central market square.

'The pub? For tea?'

'It's an inn, Maureen, a place that caters for travellers, as we are.'

Maureen was doubtful but Barbara was already leading the way across.

Maureen's face must have betrayed her hesitancy because Barbara stopped at the door and smiled. 'It's all right. If we don't like the look of it, we can simply turn round and leave,' she said kindly. 'Just say if it doesn't suit you.'

Inside, the inn was full of deliberately old-fashioned character, with horse brasses and pictures of coaching scenes displayed on the walls. A man in a suit appeared instantly and showed the women to a table in the many-paned bow window. As he settled them comfortably and took their order for tea and scones, he kept glancing through the window, his eyes roving across the road to where the car was parked. Maureen guessed he had seen their stylish arrival.

The tea was delicious, the scones light, and the service, at the hands of a young woman whose glance was also drawn across the street to the car, was quick and friendly. Maureen noticed that Barbara, who looked younger than her, although they were in fact the same age, was always served first. She didn't mind this as she understood that Barbara's stylish glossiness made her seem important, in charge.

'Please tell me about this role you've turned down for a holiday with me,' said Maureen. 'I hope you won't be disappointed, but I'm right glad you chose to come with me.'

'Oh, it was nothing, really, Maureen. Just a bit of playing the piano, and a speaking part, too.'

'When did you learn to play the piano, Barbara? I don't remember you doing that when we were younger, or that your parents had a piano.'

'Ah, I'm no concert pianist, but I can play well enough for the roles I take,' said Barbara, looking modest. 'I learned to play not long after I first left home, and I can say with all honesty I put my heart and soul into it.'

'So professional and committed, going all out for what you wanted. I admire that.'

'Well, it certainly led to things I could never have foreseen,' said Barbara quietly, and then gave a big smile. 'Now, well, it's quite a big part of what I do, so it's a useful skill to have learned.'

When it came time to pay, the bill was presented to Barbara, but while Barbara was distracted, searching in her handbag – probably looking for her purse, Maureen thought – Maureen reached across to take it and insisted on settling it. She left a generous tip for the young waitress. Then the man who had greeted them, and who Maureen thought must be the manager, practically bowed them out through the front door. Barbara bestowed one of her wide bright smiles upon him in thanks.

'Thank you, Maureen. That was delicious, and made a nice little break,' she said as they walked back to the car.

'You were right to choose the inn,' said Maureen. 'I would never have thought of that . . . never have dared to . . .' She broke off. She was doing it again: betraying her lack of confidence and how unused she was to doing what she suspected Barbara must consider even quite ordinary things, like going out to share a pot of tea somewhere nice.

Barbara looked at her in a speculative way but didn't reply. Instead she said, 'Are you ready to go on?'

'Yes, please,' said Maureen quietly.

She still felt excited about the holiday, but she was beginning to realise that her life and Barbara's had taken very different paths since that memorable summer thirty years ago, when they'd been best friends and enjoyed such a special few weeks working and playing together at the seaside hotel. For a moment she wondered if she had made a mistake with this whole enterprise and should have stopped at home, and then she berated herself. Barbara had already proved herself an asset. She did have a very charming way of getting exactly what she wanted – Maureen had fleeting memories of a couple of occasions when what Barbara wanted had prevailed over what anyone else had wanted, including her best friend – and, surely, what she wanted from this little trip down memory lane was exactly the same as Maureen did: two old friends spending an enjoyable holiday together. Why else would she have agreed to come with her?

* * *

The Yorkshire Wolds rolled out prettily before them in the late afternoon sunshine, the road lined in white from the May blossom and cow parsley, as the Alvis sped along towards Somerton-on-Sea.

'When I was little, whenever we went to the seaside, I would crane my neck to catch my very first glimpse of the sea,' said Maureen. 'I'd be nearly exploding with excitement. Mum pretended we were in competition – who's going to see it first? – but of course she always let me shout out before she did. It was usually Blackpool then, but I do remember coming here with you that time and looking out from the train.'

Barbara smiled and nodded. 'I think every child lucky enough to go to the seaside plays that game,' she said. 'Is your mother still alive?'

Maureen sighed. 'No, neither she nor Dad is.'

Barbara slowed down a little. 'I'm sorry. I remember them; they were kind. I used to like to go to your house. So much less . . . less chaotic than ours, with the others, all the noise and the mess.'

Maureen could still recall something of those lovely afternoons after school. They would do their homework together at her house, and then play card games, or Barbara would show off a dance she'd learned from her older sister, or teach Maureen songs she'd heard on the wireless. Maureen had no brothers or sisters, and her parents had a lot more time and patience for their daughter than Barbara's had for her. Maureen once overheard her mum saying to her dad that Barbara

was 'a bit of a little madam, and such a show-off', but
she always made her welcome and sent her home with
a piece of cake 'for later'. There had been another
occasion when Maureen's mother had said to her, 'You
don't have to do everything Barbara tells you, you know,
love. You can do what *you* want to sometimes, instead.'
But mostly Maureen had happily followed Barbara's
lead. Besides, Barbara preferred her own ideas for the
games they played and could be scathing about
Maureen's. 'Boring' and 'babyish' were words she liked
to use to describe them.

'Do you see much of your family, Barbara? Are *your*
parents still alive?'

'My father isn't.'

'And your mum?'

'Still the same, as far as I know. I don't have a lot to
do with her.'

There was a finality to Barbara's tone that prevented
Maureen from pursuing the subject. She didn't want
to upset her friend if there had been a serious falling-
out, and she did remember that Barbara had never
had much to say in her parents' favour.

She was about to change the subject from families,
in case she was treading on sensitive ground, when
Barbara said, 'I liked the look of your daughter Eliza
this morning.'

*Was it only this morning? It feels like days since we left
Mafeking Street. More gadding around today already than
I've had in many years put together.*

'Such pretty hair; great sense of style, I could see straight away,' Barbara added.

Maureen was pleased to field a compliment about Eliza. 'Yes, she's a credit to me. She sings, too. Oh, nothing like the kind of performances you do, Barbara, not proper theatre, just in a pub, with her friend Theo playing the piano, but I think she's good.'

'Is Theo her boyfriend?' Barbara asked, interested.

'Not really, although they're good friends. I can see how fond he is of her. But he's more than twice her age, a widower. They work together in a barber's shop and do the performing in the evening in our local pub, the Waterloo. They sing popular songs from films and musicals. It's just a bit of fun, that's all.'

'So Theo's more your age, Maureen?' The question was full of implication; teasing.

'Don't be daft.'

Barbara laughed and they sped on towards the sea and their holiday.

It was Barbara who spotted the sea first and called out, 'Oh, the sea! Look, Maureen, the sea!'

They smiled at each other, remembering all at once what it was like to be young and have the prospect of days of fun ahead of them. At that moment Maureen saw a fleeting carefree expression cross Barbara's beautiful face, as if she'd lifted her guard.

It's going to be all right. We'll have a wonderful few days and come away the best of friends again, thought Maureen.

She and Eliza had discussed whether she would tell

Barbara about the legacy, and had concluded that this was a situation Maureen would have to play by ear; that she'd know if and when it was the right thing to do.

'I don't want to get into a position where I feel that I'm deceiving her,' Maureen had said. 'That would be horrible, as if I was a dishonest person. After all, I'm sure she won't be hiding anything from me . . .'

CHAPTER FIVE

'DID MUM GET off all right on her holiday this morning, Liza?' Sylvia asked.

'In the end. Barbara Hayle turned up late and poor Mum was getting in a flap, but they went off happily enough then.'

Sylvia pulled up a wooden chair from the table next to hers and indicated Eliza was to sit down beside her. It was Wednesday evening, and they were in the upstairs room of the Waterloo. Eliza had just arrived and was looking round the busy room for Theo, who appeared not to be there yet. Desmond and Sylvia were already halfway through their first drinks.

'Go and get Liza summat to drink, Des,' Sylvia ordered, tugging at her husband's sleeve to get his attention.

'No, don't disturb him,' Eliza said. 'I'll get my own in a minute, when Theo gets here.'

'It's no trouble,' declared Sylvia, speaking for Desmond. 'When Theo gets here, he'll whisk you off, all charm and devotion, and I shan't see owt of you for the rest of the evening. Never mind him, I reckon you've got summat to tell me . . . Do us a favour, love, and get Liza's drink,' she told her husband again.

Desmond was talking to a friend from work, but he broke off and immediately got up to oblige. 'What's it to be, Liza, love?' And when she hesitated: 'No, I insist.'

'Oh, thank you, Des. I'll have a small shandy, please.'

Desmond nodded to Sylvia's glass on the table. 'I'll bring you another of those, shall I, Sylvie?'

'Please, Des . . . So, Liza, what is this Barbara Hayle like?'

Eliza's eyes sparkled with mirth. 'Guess.'

'What? Don't be daft – how should I know? Tell me.'

'Well—'

'Hello, Liza . . . Sylvia.' It was Anna-Marie Mulligan, Harry's cousin. 'You two look like you have news to share. Shall I go away?'

'No, course not,' said Eliza, just as Sylvia opened her mouth to say that that was a good idea. 'I was just about to tell Sylvia about Mum going on her holiday this morning with her friend Barbara.'

'Oh, yes, I heard all about that,' said Anna-Marie, who lived in the next road along from Mafeking Street.

'So it's all round the neighbourhood,' said Eliza. 'I might have guessed it would be.'

'What is?' asked Sylvia, but Anna-Marie was off on her own tack.

'All the fellas round our way can speak of nowt but

the car, although I don't reckon any of them actually saw it for themselves.'

'Well, it was a sight to behold,' said Eliza.

'What about it?' asked Sylvia, but Anna-Marie was sticking to her narrative.

'Louisa-next-door-to-you told Ma Gould, who told Mrs Davis at the shop, who told Mum, that the lady had a huge hat like Margaret Lockwood wears in that film, and a fur coat and a diamond necklace. But I don't believe it about the diamonds.'

'*What!*' gasped Sylvia.

'You needn't believe it about the fur coat, either, Anna-Marie, although the hat was quite big, and the car was amazing.'

'Mum's gone on holiday in a huge car with a film star in a fur coat?' said Sylvia, eyes wide.

'No, do listen, Sylvie. The car and the hat were big but there wasn't a fur coat. Or diamonds. I don't know who made that up, but there were definitely no diamonds or furs.'

'Oh, thank heaven for that,' said Sylvia. 'I don't want Mum getting any ideas now—'

'Don't be daft,' said Eliza, aiming a gentle kick at her sister's foot under the table. She feared Sylvia was half a sentence away from saying something she should keep quiet about.

'So what is this film star like?' asked Anna-Marie.

'I don't know that she's a film star. I gather she is, or was, an actress in the theatre.'

'Oh . . . like Sybil Thorndike?' asked Anna-Marie, disappointed.

'I don't think so. Variety. She looks nothing like Sybil Thorndike. More like Grace Kelly, but Mum's age. She's very pretty, though, and her clothes were nice.'

'Tell me,' begged Sylvia.

'Well, the big hat, and a red dress with a wide skirt, which was just the same red as the seats in the car.'

'Her frock *matched the car*?' Sylvia looked as if she couldn't believe her ears.

Desmond brought over the drinks for Sylvia and Eliza. 'Oh, hello, Anna-Marie. Can I get you owt to drink, love?'

'No, thanks, Desmond. I've just seen Harry and our Patrick with Michael McBride in tow so I'll go over and say hello.' She gave a meaningful smile to Eliza. 'See you later, Liza. Bye, Sylvia . . . Desmond.'

'Bye, love,' said Desmond.

Sylvia looked cross. 'Heck, she's annoying,' she said when Anna-Marie was barely out of earshot. 'Like some silly schoolkid, mooning over Michael McBride.'

'She's my friend,' said Eliza, 'and so is Michael. Now I've just seen Theo, so if you'll excuse me . . . Thanks for the drink, Des. I'll catch you both later, mebbe after our turn.' She got up and moved away, leaving Sylvia frowning, her lips pursed.

'Now what's the matter?' asked Desmond. 'I only went to get some drinks and when I get back you've got a look on your face like someone's done you a bad turn.'

'No I haven't,' snapped Sylvia. 'It's just that Mum's gone on holiday with this actress Barbara Hayle, who used to be her friend years ago, and it sounds to me like she's trouble.'

'What d'you mean? What did Liza say?'

'Nowt much. It was all Anna-Marie Mulligan repeating some stupid gossip about what this woman looks like. She's obviously completely out of Mum's league, and I gather Mum's gone away with her in a big car.'

Desmond looked confused. 'And how is that trouble, love? No reason to think this lady didn't come by the car in an honest way, especially if she has a glamorous career. I reckon it's part of her image, like. If she's an actress she'll be used to being . . . I don't know . . . larger than life. Better not to begrudge Maureen a bit of summat special. Heaven knows, your mum has had little enough special in her life – apart from her daughters, of course.'

'I just don't want Mum's head to be turned by flashy things. Apparently, this Barbara was wearing a great showy hat and a red dress, and the car is huge and has even got red seats!'

'By heck,' said Desmond, trying to picture the scene. 'I wish I'd seen it – the car, obviously, love.'

'Mm, so do I,' said Sylvia, dourly.

Eliza and Theo finished their song and took their bows to enthusiastic applause from their audience.

'Well done, Liza,' beamed Theo. 'Quite the little Fred Astaire.'

Eliza laughed and reached up to put an arm around Theo's broad shoulder. 'Quite the big Fred Astaire,' she grinned.

'Ready to go home?'

'I think so. I've already seen Anna-Marie, and now she's sitting with Michael McBride I'll never get her attention again anyway. Sylvia's in a bad mood about Mum's holiday so I'd rather avoid her.'

'Come on then, we'll collect our coats and our pay – and I don't think that'll weigh us down on the walk home – and I'll see you safely back. It's lonely letting yourself into an empty house.'

'Thanks, Theo.'

It was only a short walk and the street was properly lit, but Eliza was glad of Theo's offer. When they'd got their coats on and had been paid, they set off, the lights and noise of the Waterloo fading behind them as they turned the corner.

'Mum's been so generous,' said Eliza. 'She's got in some lovely food for me to eat while she's away, but I think she's overdone it a bit. Would you like to come over one evening and share it? Only if you want to, but I'd be pleased if you did. I'll ask Anna-Marie as well. Seems mean not to share when there's so much of it.'

'Yes, please, I'd love to,' grinned Theo. He patted his stomach. 'As you can see, I'm vastly underfed and I appreciate you taking pity on me. But tell me, Liza, are you a good cook?'

Eliza laughed. He wasn't in the least overweight and cut quite a fine figure now she came to consider it. 'I'm all right; I can do simple things.'

'Right . . .' said Theo thoughtfully.

'Oh, don't let my lack of cooking skills put you off. It usually turns out fine.'

'*Usually fine.* I see . . .' said Theo, nodding his head, his expression serious.

'What?'

'I tell you what: you provide the food, the venue, and the pleasure of your company and that of Anna-Marie and anyone else you see fit to invite, and I'll do the cooking. Is that fair?'

'Can *you* cook, Theo? I didn't know that.'

'I wouldn't have offered if I couldn't. I can do a lot of things – you'd be amazed. Not tight-rope walking, you may not be surprised to learn, and I've never fancied being a steeplejack, but, yes, I can cook.'

'Then it's a deal,' said Eliza, as they arrived at her front door. 'Come and cook on Saturday, and amaze me.'

It was very quiet in Mafeking Street, no one about and all the curtains closed. Few lights showed behind them: people tended to leave for work early in the morning, many at the cotton mills, and long working days didn't make for late nights. The Wednesday evenings at the Waterloo were low key compared to Fridays, which were altogether a louder, wilder affair, and not the kind of audience to appreciate the modest glamour of Theo and Eliza's repertoire.

Eliza put her key in the lock, opened the door, and turned to say good night to Theo. But even as she opened her mouth to speak, she heard the slamming of a door very close by – inside the house. She saw Theo had heard it, too, and in a moment she was over the threshold and had the hall light on.

'Let me,' said Theo urgently, almost physically picking her up to move her aside and let him squeeze past.

Eliza was hot on his heels as he rushed into the kitchen and switched on the light. The window in the back door had been smashed and it was immediately obvious that someone had put an arm through the hole and turned the key, which was kept in the lock. Vicious-looking shards of glass and a few drops of blood were strewn across the floor.

'Careful of that,' said Theo as he stepped over the mess as best he could, opened the door and hurried out into the backyard. Again, Eliza was close behind and they were just in time to see the black-clad figure of an agile man disappearing over the high wall into the ginnel that ran parallel to the street.

'Quick, where is the key to this gate?' asked Theo, helpless to follow the same route out.

'In the drawer in the kitchen table. You get it. I'll go round to the ginnel and see if I can see him there.'

'No, Eliza!'

'We'll miss him if I don't,' she said, running back inside, through the house, out of the front door and down the road to the narrow passage between two of the houses that led to the back alley. It was dark here and she could see little. It was too late to wish she'd stopped to grab the torch from the drawer where the key was kept. She stood looking up and down, straining her eyes to see if anything moved, trying to breathe as quietly as she could, though her heart was beating audibly. After a few moments, Theo emerged through the gate of Maureen's backyard, further down. He had found the torch and he swept the beam slowly up and down the alley and then over Eliza, standing helplessly in the dark, looking very young and anxious with her coat over her second-hand frock.

'He's gone,' she said, and walked down to meet Theo, who lighted her way towards him with the torch. 'I didn't get a proper look, did you?'

'No, just a man in dark clothes and a pull-on hat, fit enough to scale the wall, that's all.'

They went back through the gate and Theo locked it.

'I think I left the front door open,' said Eliza, and Theo went quickly inside to see, while she followed slowly. She locked the kitchen door behind her, although the broken window hardly made it secure.

Theo came back to the kitchen with Ted, Louisa's husband, from next door.

'Heard you running up the street, love, and then I saw the door open, so I came to see if you are all right.'

'Oh, Ted, I think we've been burgled. The back door pane is broken but I don't know how long the man had been in the house. We disturbed him but he escaped over the back.'

'He might have just got here when you came home,' said Ted. 'With any luck he won't have taken owt.'

'I'll go and call the police,' said Theo.

'There's a police box at the end of the next street, or you could telephone from the Waterloo,' Ted said.

'Right. While I do that, you'll stay with Eliza, won't you?'

'Course.'

Theo went out, and Ted advised Eliza not to clear away the broken glass in case it contained any clues for the police about the intruder.

'I'll board up that window for you when the police have been, love,' he said.

Theo quickly returned with a constable he'd encountered, entirely by chance, in the street, and questions were asked, the answers noted down, the door and shattered glass examined, and a torchlight search of the backyard and the alleyway behind accomplished as well as it could be.

The constable said he'd be back in the morning to examine 'the crime scene' in daylight, and that Eliza was to look carefully around the house and list everything she thought had been stolen.

Ted was hammering a piece of wood over the broken window and Louisa had come round with a tray of mugs of cocoa by the time the police constable had finished his questioning and left.

'I think you should go home now, Theo. You've been a real help, but it's getting very late,' said Eliza.

'Yes, but I don't like to leave you here by yourself. You're bound to wake in the night, imagining you can hear that man breaking in again.'

Louisa tutted. 'You'll scare the life out of her, suggesting that,' she scolded. 'I reckon he'll not come back after you disturbed him. He wasn't keen to be seen. Still, I'll stay over with you, Eliza, love. I'll sleep on the sofa and keep the coal shovel handy, just in case.'

'Good idea,' said Ted, smiling approvingly at his statuesque wife. 'It'd be a brave fella that took on my Louisa, especially when she was armed.'

Theo gave Eliza a little hug, patting her back. 'I'll tell Harry what's happened, of course, and you'd better stay here tomorrow until the police have been and searched out the back in daylight. That will give you time to have a good look round to see if anything's missing, too.'

'Thank you, Theo. And thank you for everything you've done.'

'Dear Eliza . . . you know I'd do anything . . . all I can to help.' He patted her back gently again and then left, and she heard the front door closing quietly behind him.

'Sorry about last night,' said Eliza, arriving at the Short Cut halfway through the following morning.

'Why, love, what've you been up to?' smirked Tommy Parker, an old boy who liked to sport very short hair and bushy side whiskers. He was sitting in Harry's chair with wet hair and one towel across his front, another round his shoulders. Harry was concentrating on trimming round his right ear.

'It's no joke, Tommy,' said Theo, expertly clipping around the nape of Fergus McBride's neck. Fergus was Michael's grandfather, another regular at the Short Cut. 'Eliza's mother's house was burgled last night.'

'No! Outrageous! Did you catch the blackguard?'

'He got away,' said Eliza, 'but the police have been and Ted-next-door's got his cousin to come round and re-glaze the back door, and I've learned my lesson about keeping the key in the lock.'

Tommy huffed. 'Time was, before the war, when folk could leave their doors unlocked and never find any intruder in the house. Things have changed, and not for the better.'

'Is your mother all right?' asked Fergus, his voice deep because his chin was right down on his chest.

'Thanks for asking, Mr McBride. Luckily Mum wasn't there at the time.'

'Was owt taken?' asked Tommy. 'You'll have checked everywhere?'

'I have and I can't see that owt's gone. I think mebbe the burglar was disturbed before he'd got far. The police don't reckon he'll be back, having just missed being seen once.'

'Not back to yours, mebbe, Eliza, but he'll be trying his luck elsewhere, you mark my words,' said Tommy sagely. 'There's a lot of it about – burglary. If I had my way, those filthy fellas would be strung up and—'

'Anyway, it could have been a lot worse,' said Harry. He was well practised in heading off contentious conversations, and Tommy Parker was well-known for his trenchant views on crime and punishment. 'Now then, Eliza, I reckon you could brew us all a pot of tea and then have a quick sweep round, and then I'll let you shave off Tommy's sideburns.'

'No one touches these here sideburns but you, Harry Mulligan, and no one at all shaves them off,' said Tommy fiercely.

Then everyone started on their extreme side-whiskers stories, the atmosphere lightened and the subject of the burglary was dropped.

By the time the morning was over, and Eliza had cut a neat short back and sides, as well as tidied up around Harry and Theo, she was feeling a lot happier. She was quite certain that everyone was right, and she needn't fear to encounter that particular burglar ever again. The really good thing was that with all the glass swept up, the door re-glazed and nothing missing, so far as she knew, there was very little to distress her mother when she returned. Of course, Eliza would have to tell her, but she'd be able to make light of it and emphasise what a help Theo, Ted and Louisa had been.

The question was, though, why had anyone thought to burgle the house at all, a modest little terrace, just like all its neighbours? The thief appeared to have run away with nothing, but what had he hoped to find? The attempted burglary couldn't possibly be linked to Maureen's inheritance from Miss Stevens, could it? No, that was impossible. No one but Maureen and her girls knew anything about it.

CHAPTER SIX

'Let's have a little stroll along the seafront,' suggested Maureen. 'I need to walk off that huge breakfast, delicious as it was, and I'm keen to see if the place has changed at all.'

'Me, too,' agreed Barbara, although Maureen noticed she had eaten little. She hoped Barbara wasn't ill – she really had a very small appetite – but she looked quite well. Perhaps preserving that beautifully wand-like figure had become second nature.

Barbara was wearing a neat pair of slacks this morning, with a warm-looking jumper and smart lace-up shoes, which reminded Maureen of the kind of shoes Theo liked to wear. Barbara had brought very little luggage with her, from what Maureen had seen, but everything she had was expensive-looking and matched everything else. The collar of Barbara's soft wool coat was turned up just so – like those models on the front covers of magazines, Maureen thought – and bold lipstick and sunglasses adorned her face, as yesterday. Maureen wished she had these kinds of clothes, this kind of look. The breeze could be gusty off the North Sea and, as they set off on their walk, she found she was continually making a grab for her skirt to hold it down as the wind snatched at it. It was too cold for sandals, and her shoes looked all wrong at the seaside: as if she was wearing town shoes and not on a holiday by the sea at all. Even her summer dress looked inappropriate, somehow, and that was brand new. She didn't usually care about these things, or even notice them, so what had got into her today? Could it be the glossy presence of Barbara that was making her dissatisfied with her clothes? Certainly Barbara did look lovely, Maureen acknowledged, and she noticed the eyes of other people, both in the hotel and here on the promenade, assessing her in an admiring way, too.

The promenade was quiet this early in the day: there were just a few old people about, who probably lived in Somerton-on-Sea, and no families on the beach as yet. A couple of people walking dogs wished the women a cheery good morning, and two men in overalls were sweeping up the sand that had blown in from the beach. The kiosks that sold ice cream and beach toys were closed, and the row of prettily painted beach huts, which Maureen and Barbara remembered and were delighted to see hadn't changed at all, showed no sign of life yet this morning.

'You look just right, Barbara. I wonder if I ought to get summat similar to wear.'

'Oh, but don't you have . . .? I mean, thank you, it's nice of you to say, Maureen. Of course, we can go and look at the shops, if you'd like to?' Barbara smiled her lovely smile. 'A bit of shopping might be fun.'

'Yes . . . yes, I think I'd enjoy it with you to help me choose.'

They walked along, Maureen talking about how pleasant the hotel was and what had brought back memories, and Barbara agreeing, and offering, 'Do you remember . . .?' a few times, so that Maureen felt very relaxed and happy to have her old friend's company. She'd felt the same at dinner the previous evening, when they'd reminisced about their time here, working at the hotel in the 1920s, noting what had changed, and teasing out shared recollections.

'Such a relief to get away from my parents,' Barbara had remembered.

'Oh, I rather missed mine, for all that we had fun,' said Maureen.

'Did you? I don't remember that . . .'

Maureen had shrugged that off. It no longer mattered, and if Barbara had forgotten her friend's terrible homesickness when they'd first arrived, so much the better.

'I wonder you haven't been back here before now,' ventured Barbara now, leading Maureen to a bench that overlooked the beach. They sat down and Barbara moved close. 'Do you have many holidays? I expect you've been away quite a bit with your charming daughter Eliza. Or maybe with your other daughter and . . . and her husband?'

'Oh, no. I've never been able to afford a holiday away at all until now,' said Maureen, the truth out before she knew what she was saying. It wasn't in her nature to be secretive, or to lie by implication or omission, and she found it so difficult not to have the kind of conversation she had told herself to avoid, especially with Barbara, who was so friendly and open.

'Gosh, Maureen, that's very sad. I'm sorry to hear it and I realise I'm lucky indeed that you asked me to come with you on this holiday. Please excuse me for asking then, but I can't help wondering, after what you've just told me, do I detect a change in circumstances? I hope you haven't suffered a sadness, although I know your Jack has been gone many years now. Tell me,' she lowered her voice confidingly and leaned in to Maureen; she smelled of the headiest scent of roses, like a summer flowerbed in Corporation Park, only better, 'did you win the football pools?' She trilled her pretty laugh, which Maureen found strangely infectious.

'No, not the pools, Barbara.'

'Ah, but I suspect my guess could be, as they say in the quizzes "getting warm". Mm, let me think . . . Now, Maureen, are you a betting woman? Did you perhaps win some money on an outsider at Aintree?' She laughed again. 'Oh, please tell me you put your life savings on a horse and it romped home ahead of the field, bringing you a fortune with it.'

'Honestly, Barbara, do I look like a betting woman?'
Maureen smiled. 'I'm not at all the kind to go to the
races.'

'I did think that was a long shot, but you are something of an enigma, Maureen, and I'm very intrigued.'
Barbara beamed at Maureen to convey this was a
compliment, then paused, thinking in a rather arch,
theatrical way. 'No, it's no use, I'm completely stumped.
You'll have to tell me.'

Somehow this had turned into a game and Maureen
was feeling almost compelled to join in with her vivacious
friend. However, it wasn't yet too late to draw back.

'Well, I did decide I wasn't going to say owt to anyone.
Not until I thought the time was right. I don't want
folk thinking I'm getting above myself, or having *expectations* of me.'

'Good heavens, Maureen, of course I entirely respect
your decision. You must do as you think best. But I
should be very sorry if you thought you couldn't trust
your old friend, especially when there are just the two
of us here together. You see, I'm just starting to be a
little anxious, what with the hotel being so comfortable,
and the food there so delicious, that you haven't at all
. . . *miscalculated*, because you are by nature so very
generous.' Barbara adjusted the collar of her soft blue
coat against the wind and gazed out at the grey sea
through her big sunglasses. 'I expect you think I'm
being very silly to worry about you,' she said.

'Worry? Oh, Barbara, I'm so sorry, I never meant to

worry you. Quite the opposite: I meant what I said. This little holiday really is my treat to you, for old times' sake. You see . . . it's true, I've had a bit of luck.' Maureen paused to gather her thoughts, trying not to be insensitive. 'Well, it wasn't luck at all really, because the lady died, and I did like her, and I certainly didn't look to gain anything . . .'

'You mean you were left some money,' said Barbara, stating a fact rather than asking.

'Oh!' Maureen had avoided referring to Miss Stevens's legacy since she had opened the bank account and then told Sylvia about it. The fact of it hung in the air between herself and Eliza every day but was seldom mentioned aloud. Eliza, like Maureen herself, wasn't in the habit of spending, and would never persuade her mother to buy anything she didn't want. Apart from the fridge, which they both agreed was a good idea, and the few new summer clothes (which Maureen decided she didn't like very much now she was here and wearing one of the dresses in the face of a stiff North Sea breeze), she had hardly even thought about how to spend the money. It was out of sight at the bank, and there it would mostly remain, until she decided what she really wanted to do with it. And now, suddenly and unexpectedly, her friend had brought the fact of its existence out quite plainly and openly into the light. It was almost shocking.

'Yes . . . yes, you've guessed right, Barbara. A lady I used to work for left me some money and, truth be told, I'm not used to it.'

'I'd never have guessed,' said Barbara, deadpan. 'Honestly, Maureen, it's nothing to be ashamed of. I take it, as you told me you left your job at the brewery because you didn't like your boss, that you have enough to live on, at least for now, without having to work?'

Well, goodness me, thought Maureen, *this must be how rich people talk: just treating their wealth as a matter of fact, openly acknowledged instead of something to be hushed up in case it offends folk or incites them to envy. Miss Stevens just bought what she liked and never made a fuss about it, but nor did she hide the truth that she was very well off. She had a houseful of pretty things, but it was simply a nice way for her to live, not a form of showing off. I can see I've got a lot to learn. Mebbe I should be more like Barbara. It was lucky I thought of inviting her. Now I'm being shown what it is to live with a bit of style.*

'You're right, Barbara. I am a most fortunate woman and I won't ever *have* to go to work again. But, you see, that's left me at rather a loss. I'm not used to having the time and the means to do what I want, and I *don't know* what to do with myself, or even what I want to buy. I thought this little break, away from my home and everything I've known for years, would help me to see things differently. Thank goodness I invited you to join me.'

Barbara squeezed Maureen's arm. 'That's very kind of you, Maureen. But I, too, am at a loss . . . to know how I can help. I'm not much of one for giving advice, or following it, I'm afraid.' She gave her charming little laugh. 'But I'm so glad you've confided in me. I was afraid I'd misread the situation and it is, after all, always better to come right out and be honest about things, don't you agree?'

'Yes, you're quite right, Barbara. I didn't mean to mislead you at all.'

At that moment a little dog on a long lead came over to say hello. Barbara patted its soft head.

'What a pretty dog you have,' she said to the owner, who was an elderly man in a sports jacket and flat cap. 'So friendly, too.'

The man smiled. 'Kind of you to say. She's my only companion now my wife has passed away. She means the world to me.'

'I can see why you love her so much,' said Barbara. 'What is her name?'

'Mitsy,' said the man.

'Hello, Mitsy. Aren't you a pretty girl, then? I just love this breed of dog – so cute and very intelligent.' Barbara made a fuss of the dog, who reached up and put her little paws on Barbara's knee, presenting herself to be admired. 'Well, we'll look out for darling Mitsy another morning, won't we, Maureen? And you, too, of course, Mr . . .?'

'Elphick.'

'Mr Elphick. So lovely to meet you and Mitsy.'

By now the old man's face was full of admiration for Barbara, Maureen saw. He hovered, as if finding it difficult to tear himself away, and then, with obvious reluctance, eventually touched his cap to Barbara, then to Maureen, and continued on his way.

'Adorable,' said Barbara, presumably of the dog.

'I think you've made a friend there, Barbara. I don't know how you do it,' said Maureen. 'You really have a knack of pleasing folk.'

'It's just acting, Maureen; giving people what you know they want. But I have been thinking about getting a dog myself.'

'Really? Wouldn't that be difficult when you're away starring in a show? Who would look after it?'

'I'd take it with me, of course. A little companion in my dressing room. Everyone would make such a fuss of it; it would be the most spoiled and adored creature.'

'Let's walk down to the end and back and see where we can get a cup of tea, and you can tell me all about the theatre,' said Maureen. 'I know nowt about plays or theatrical life but I'm longing to hear about the amazing folk you get to meet, if you wouldn't mind?'

'Not at all,' said Barbara. 'And then, maybe this afternoon we can have that shopping trip you fancied, if you like?'

The shops on the main street in Somerton-on-Sea were on a broad avenue leading from the promenade to the centre of the town: pretty, shady with trees and very smart. Neither Maureen nor Barbara remembered anything of the shops, but now Maureen noticed that two of the three women's clothes shops were rather expensive-looking, with elegant window displays.

'Which do you think we should try first, Barbara?' asked Maureen.

A tiny look of impatience flittered across Barbara's face. 'Whichever you like, Maureen.'

'Only you look so lovely that I think the one that appeals to you will be best.'

Barbara smiled then. 'All right, let's go in here, Crosby's. Nice accessories in the window.'

Maureen had never had cause to use the word 'accessories' before. Maybe that's what she was missing. The shop looked very plush and, to Maureen, a little forbidding.

She wasn't in the least surprised that the assistant approached Barbara first. Why would anyone notice her when Barbara shone so brightly?

They looked along a rail of dresses – Barbara holding them up against herself and turning to the mirror with an elegant little twirl, which Maureen wanted to copy but felt too shy to attempt in case she looked silly – then at some beautiful light cardigans, much softer than the one Maureen had bought the previous week in Blackburn, and even at some fine wool trousers, very like the ones Barbara was wearing. Maureen was persuaded to try on a pair, then another, with matching jumpers and cardigans. Soon, with Barbara's encouragement, it was like a dressing-up game and Maureen forgot her caution, forgot even to look at the price tags, so exciting was the afternoon, so completely unlike any other afternoon she'd ever enjoyed, with herself as the centre of attention and nothing too much trouble. The changing room was festooned with garments on hangers, and pretty jumpers and cardigans were piled on the counter, ready for her to try.

'Help me decide, Barbara,' she pleaded as the time passed and she began to feel overwhelmed by the choice. By now the assistant was bringing items out from the stockroom, and the manageress had come over to supervise and offer an opinion, while Barbara went to browse the silk scarves and fine leather handbags on another counter, bringing a few back with her for Maureen to see.

Eventually, looking flushed at receiving many compliments, and also because the bill, totted up and handwritten in triplicate, had made her feel a little breathless, Maureen left Crosby's clutching several smart carrier bags with cord handles and tied with glossy bows at the top. She was now the owner of a whole new summer wardrobe, and she had never been so thrilled to have new clothes in her whole life.

'Goodness, Barbara, that was quite an adventure,' she said.

'Fun,' beamed Barbara, who'd had the manageress and the assistant under her own direction long before Maureen had made up her mind.

'Thing is,' said Maureen cheerfully, remembering Eliza's made-over frock from the pawnbroker's and Sylvia's home-made clothes put together with a discount from the draper and haberdasher's where she worked, 'I can always give them to Eliza and Sylvia if I have no use for them once I get home. I'm sure the girls will love them, and they're pretty much the same size as me.'

'But why wouldn't you have a use for them?' asked Barbara. 'You have to wear clothes if you want to be decent and warm, so why shouldn't they be these ones?' She took some of the carriers from Maureen and they strolled on slowly back towards the hotel.

'Well . . . in case they get spoiled, when I'm doing the housework and that,' said Maureen hesitantly. Something in Barbara's expression told her this was not the right answer, but it was the only one she could give.

'Do you remember when we were young, about the age we were when we came here?' Barbara asked. 'Well, of course, we didn't have many nice clothes, except perhaps one thing for best. Saving a favourite dress "for best" was what we did, how we'd been brought up.'

'Yes, of course . . .'

'And what a mistake that was! I had this lovely summer frock, flowered muslin with a layered skirt. I think it had belonged to my older sister, Maggie, who'd been given it by a boyfriend, and then she'd parted with him and given the dress to me. Anyway, I loved that frock but, it being my favourite, it always seemed too special to wear, even though it was just a pretty summer dress – it was to be saved "for best" – so I hardly ever wore it. One day I had a party to go to and I was looking forward to wearing it. But when I took it out of the cupboard, it smelled stale and it had a couple of moth holes and, worse, it looked a bit old-fashioned as well as too short. So I never really got to enjoy it because "best" occasions don't happen often enough. It was all a waste.'

'That's a real shame,' said Maureen.

'It was. So as soon as I was able, I decided that I should try to make every day a "best" day. After all, what use are clothes except to be worn? Why not look as good as you can, make getting dressed each day a treat, enjoy wearing beautiful things instead of letting them languish unseen, to be eaten by moth grubs?'

'Goodness . . . I hadn't thought of that,' said Maureen. 'But, you see, Barbara, if I'm all dressed up, my friends and neighbours might think I'm getting above myself.'

'They won't think that if you're not, Maureen. It doesn't mean wearing the wrong clothes, like going to the shops in an evening gown. It just means looking nice, like you've bothered; like you value yourself.'

'Yes . . . yes, I see what you mean.'

'So enjoy your beautiful new things yourself. Don't give them away.'

'I s'pose if Sylvia and Eliza want new clothes, I can just buy them for them,' said Maureen, as if it had only just occurred to her. 'Oh, I'm sorry, Barbara, I know this sounds mad, but I just can't get used to having the money to do as I like. It's all . . . it's too big a change of circumstance, too much to take in.'

'So you've tried not to think about it at all?'

'Yes . . .'

'But isn't that a bit like what I said about the clothes? Are you saving the inheritance "for best" and not enjoying it?'

Maureen thought about this. She feared Barbara was correct about this, too, and that she was being silly. Perhaps Sylvia and Eliza secretly thought she was very mean because she hadn't gone out and bought them lots of new clothes, or whatever else they might want: a car . . . even a new house. There had been the fridge, of course. Maureen blushed to think that the fridge, and the cheap holiday clothes she'd come away with – along with the holiday itself, of course – had been her sole purchases. She was a bad mother with a mean spirit. She was a stupid and pathetic person with no imagination, no vision, no dreams . . .

'Barbara, I fear you're right,' she said in a small voice. 'I think I've been a fool. Thank goodness I asked you to come here with me and show me summat beyond my own silly narrow ideas. Over the years I've got so used to trying to make ends meet, it's hard now to look up and see there's already a . . . a rosier outlook.'

Barbara swung the carrier bags nonchalantly, beaming her bright smile at Maureen. Then she said, 'Maureen, if I have helped you, even a little, it has been my pleasure. That's what friends are for, isn't it? We've had such fun this afternoon, haven't we? It's really very simple to broaden your horizons, you know. You've done it already, and if you practise it you'll soon get

112

used to living a different way. You can spend your money on yourself and your family and friends – whatever pleases you and perhaps helps others, too. You just decide what you want – *really want* – and then you go and do it.'

'Is it really that easy?' Maureen asked.

'Well, sometimes you have to wait for the opportunity to arise,' said Barbara, 'but then, when it does, you only have to recognise it, and there you are!'

They continued their walk towards the hotel.

'I reckon when we get back I should put on some of these new things, all soft and warm, and go and sit on the beach and have a little think . . . a little dream in my new clothes about my new self; face up to my changed circumstances and consider the choices and opportunities I have.'

'What a lovely idea,' approved Barbara. 'And I hope you won't mind if I join you. I'd love to hear what you'd like to do, Maureen, where you'd like to go in life now you've the chance. It's all so exciting. I'm never short of ideas about what the good things in life are, and I love to share my thoughts. It's just so nice to have someone to share them with.'

'Yes, of course. All these years we've been in touch and now, just when I need someone who knows what's what to guide me, we've met up again. I feel so lucky, Barbara, love.'

'So do I, Maureen. And I think we're both going to have an absolutely splendid holiday.'

CHAPTER SEVEN

IT WAS SATURDAY evening and all the lights were on downstairs at number 28 Mafeking Street. Theo, wearing a huge blue-and-white-striped butcher's apron, which entirely by chance matched his blue-and-white shoes, was busy preparing vegetables. Eliza had opened the back door a few inches to let out some of the heat from the kitchen, which was beginning to make her face flushed.

'Oh my, Theo, that smells delicious,' she said, unable to resist peeping in the oven at the roasting chicken, and the potatoes sizzling in dripping.

'Uh-uh, Liza, no peeking. Best to keep the heat in,' said Theo, chopping carrots into neat batons. He'd already made something called a syllabub for pudding, which he promised, with a comical wink, contained 'secret ingredients', which he'd brought with him in a bag and kept hidden from Eliza's sight, 'so as not to dispel the magic', and the creamy-looking pudding, like a captive cloud, was sitting in Maureen's pretty glass trifle bowl in the new fridge. 'How about you open that wine I brought, and we'll have a crafty sip before the others arrive?'

Eliza's hand flew to her mouth. 'Oh, no, Theo, I can't.'

'That's OK. No need to fret. I'll show you how.'

'No, I mean I *can't.*' She started to laugh. 'We don't have a corkscrew!'

They were both laughing now.

'I'm sorry, Theo, I never thought,' said Eliza, recovering. 'We're not really drinkers here – not that I'm implying you're a drinker! Oh, you know what I mean . . .'

'Jake at the Waterloo will lend us one. I'll just go now and ask.'

Eliza looked worried. 'But you can't leave me with all this! What about the chicken and the potatoes, and when do I put these little carrots on? And where does the orange fit in with all this?'

'Calm down. I'll only be gone five minutes.'

'Well, go now then, please, before summat needs summat doing to it. And don't forget to take your pinny off.' She flapped him out into the hall and he departed, doing a bashful impression of Oliver Hardy on the doorstep.

Theo had barely left when Anna-Marie and Michael McBride arrived.

'We met Theo in the street,' Anna-Marie said, 'so we know it all. He says I've to keep you calm.'

'I am calm,' said Eliza, fanning herself exaggeratedly, 'but I won't be if he's not back soon.'

'Here, I brought these,' said Michael, handing over two large bottles of beer. 'Something smells wonderful, like Christmas dinner. Are we celebrating?'

'No, just sharing. Mum's gone off on her holidays—'

'I told you about the film star and the car, Michael,' Anna-Marie reminded him.

'—and she thought I might starve without her, so she left me all this lovely food. I need my friends to help me eat it.'

'It's good of you to invite us, Eliza,' said Michael.

Theo reappeared with the corkscrew then, so the wine was opened and the crown cap of one of the beers removed, drinks poured. Theo disappeared happily to continue cooking the feast, drink in hand, leaving the others to lounge about in the sitting room.

'Have you heard from your mum at all, Liza?' asked Anna-Marie.

'Not a word, but I wasn't really expecting to. There's hardly been time to send a postcard. She'll be back tomorrow.'

'Are you going to tell her about the burglary?'

'*Attempted* burglary. Of course. It wouldn't be right to keep it from her – it's her house – but I think any danger of the burglar coming back is past. He didn't take owt, so far as I know, and everyone's been so helpful. So it's really a tale of how kind Theo and our neighbours are, more than anything else. I'll try to tell her about it in such a way that she won't be worried.'

Anna-Marie and Michael nodded their approval, and drinks were sipped as news and gossip were exchanged. After a few minutes, Eliza excused herself and went out to the kitchen, taking the bottle of wine with her, to see if Theo was all right, slaving away on his own.

Theo was cheerfully humming one of the tunes he'd played the previous Wednesday, while stirring some flour into the roasting tin to make the gravy. He didn't see Eliza standing in the doorway, and she paused to admire his assured cooking skills and also to notice for the first time how his slightly greying hair suited him and how, wearing an apron and looking a little over-heated, he had no vanity about himself, only a love of good clothes. That was really so attractive . . .

She cleared her throat. 'Er, Theo, I just wondered if you're ready for a top-up.'

He glanced round at her and for a second the unguarded affection in his face disconcerted her. Then he grinned and the moment was gone.

'Ah, the wine fairy, right on cue. Yes, please, and if you could just add a glug to this pan, too, I'm sure that will be the magic touch it needs.'

Eliza did as he asked. 'Smells delicious.'

'The wine fairy's magic,' Theo said modestly.

Soon the company was gathered round the dining table, which Eliza and Theo had moved to a central position in the front room, and which was neatly set for four. Theo brought in the chicken on the biggest plate he'd been able to find, to applause from everyone else for his efforts.

Grinning, Theo said, 'I say, I say, I say, which side of a chicken has the most feathers?'

'The outside!' the other three chorused, giggling and raising their glasses to him.

Everyone was tucking in to the splendid feast, complimenting Theo on his efforts and passing round drinks and the gravy boat, when there was knock at the door.

Eliza, with a roll of her eyes, went to see who it was, not expecting anyone halfway through a Saturday evening.

'Sylvia! Des! Come in.'

'By heck, Liza, love, summat smells good,' said Desmond, stepping into the hall behind Sylvia.

'Liza, what's all this?' asked Sylvia, hearing the murmur of voices from the front room. 'We came round to ask if you'd like us to fetch you a fish supper. I thought you'd be here by yourself, not living it up with Mum away.'

'It's just Theo, Anna-Marie and Michael, come to share some food Mum left for me.' Eliza couldn't help herself adding: 'It's all right, Mum said I could have them round.'

'And here's me thinking you'd be sitting here all alone.' Sylvia sounded almost disappointed that this wasn't the case.

'It was kind of you to think of me, both of you,' said Eliza, wondering whether she'd taken from Sylvia the chance to show herself to be a thoughtful older sister. 'There's masses of food. Why don't you come and join us?'

'Mum left you so much food? And it smells like Christmas dinner! Why didn't you ask us over in the first place?' asked Sylvia. Suddenly she looked cross. 'I reckon you're only asking us now because you've been found out.'

Eliza took a deep breath. She wanted to get back to her friends and her dinner, and she also very much didn't want the evening spoiled by the dampening presence of Sylvia in a bad temper. Sylvia's mood could turn in seconds on any chance remark. *Oh, no, why did I have to open my big mouth and ask them? I should have said we'd nearly finished eating or summat. Too late now.* 'There's nowt to be "found out" about, Sylvie. I've got friends round. Mum agreed. If you'd like to join us, you can.'

'Well, I would,' said Desmond, grinning and edging past Sylvia to the front room doorway. 'Hello, everyone. Here's a nice surprise. Sylvie and me thought we were taking pity on Liza, all on her lonesome, and it turns out we're the ones to be pitied. Eh, but that chicken looks good. Did Liza cook it?'

'Theo did,' said Anna-Marie.

'Man's a genius,' added Michael.

'Sit yourself down, why don't you, Desmond?' said Theo, who'd heard the conversation in the hall. 'Anna-Marie, love, do you want to just grab those two chairs and I'll fetch some more plates?'

'Ta very much,' said Desmond. 'Come on, our Sylvie. Don't stand there gassing while the food grows cold.'

Sylvia came in, passing Theo in the doorway as he went to the kitchen. 'Someone's making himself very much at home,' she murmured. She surveyed the scene, taking in the food, the bottles half empty, and the happy faces of the friends around the table.

'Right, well, if you're sure I'm not putting you out, Liza . . .'

'Sit down and Theo will carve you some chicken. Help yourselves to vegetables.'

'Isn't that Mum's special Christmas plate, Liza?' asked Sylvia.

'Mebbe . . . I don't know,' said Eliza evasively. 'Please would you pass those carrots, Michael . . .?'

The Gowers were served and everyone got on with their dinner, though the atmosphere was now less relaxed.

'And *you* cooked this chicken?' asked Desmond of Theo, eating with enthusiasm, helping himself to more of the delicious crispy roast potatoes.

'Men can cook, you know,' snapped Sylvia, before Theo had a chance to accept the praise graciously. 'At least some of them can. Not you, obviously,' she added. 'Good thing Theo's got a talent for cooking, eh, Liza? You could learn a lot.'

Eliza caught Anna-Marie's eye and decided not to reply to the barb. 'Glad you're enjoying it,' she said quietly instead.

Drinks were passed round and Theo went to open another bottle of wine.

'So kind of you to bring all this,' said Eliza when he came back.

'We'd have brought some drinks ourselves if we'd known you were having a feast,' said Desmond. 'In fact, why don't I nip over to the Waterloo, get a few more beers?'

'Really, there's no need, Des, but thank you,' Eliza said. She didn't want her guests waiting in front of cooling food while Desmond went to the pub. On the other hand, if he *were* to leave the table, she wished that he'd take Sylvia with him and not come back. The evening had got off to such a promising start, and now Sylvia had introduced an abrasive tone, like a blast of cold air. Why couldn't she just be nice?

When the main course had been devoured, Eliza refilled everyone's glass before taking the first of the plates through to the kitchen. Theo followed with the scant remains of the chicken on the platter.

'Sorry . . .' hissed Eliza. 'I could hardly tell them to go away.'

Theo smiled. 'It's OK. Don't let her upset you.'

'Mebbe even Sylvia will be so in awe of the pudding, she'll find herself wanting to enjoy the lovely evening, instead of trying to be disagreeable.'

'Well, it does contain the secret ingredients, so maybe they'll work their magic, mellow her mood,' said Theo, waggling his eyebrows in a comical fashion.

When the table was cleared and the plates piled into the sink, Theo brought in the syllabub and Eliza followed with a stack of little glass dishes she'd found at the back of a kitchen cupboard.

Sylvia broke off some story she was telling about a colleague she disliked at the shop to say, 'Liza, I hope you asked Mum if you could use those. They belonged to Grandma Bancroft and Dad inherited them from her.'

'Mum said I could use anything I wanted,' said Eliza, which wasn't true as she and Maureen hadn't had that conversation; there had been no need. She felt cross even answering Sylvia now, in front of her friends.

'Well, I suppose Mum can have as many dishes as she wants now,' said Sylvia.

Eliza looked hard at her but didn't say anything. With luck, no one was taking any notice. She suddenly felt nervous, as if a ticking time bomb might be about to go off, and that bomb was Sylvia, her indiscretion and jealousy fuelled by a few drinks. Maybe the syllabub wasn't a good choice of pudding in the circumstances, but Theo couldn't have foreseen Sylvia descending on the party, and anyway, he'd made it especially for Eliza and it looked delicious. And it was too late to worry now.

The syllabub was served up into the elegant little dishes and everyone took up a teaspoon and tasted it.

'Oh, my goodness!' gasped Anna-Marie, her eyes huge and round. 'Theo, this is just the best thing I've ever tasted. This is . . . well, it's like—'

'—the food of the gods,' Michael finished for her grandly. 'It's like the Ancient Greek gods would eat on Mount Olympus.'

Everyone but Sylvia was smiling and agreeing, and Anna-Marie dug Michael playfully in the ribs. 'Will you just listen to the man, waxing poetical.'

'*Is* it Greek?' asked Desmond, and everyone roared with laughter, except Sylvia, who seemed to be threatening a sulk, as she had from the moment she realised there was a party going on to which she hadn't been invited at the outset, and Desmond, who joined in the laughter after a few seconds, but clearly didn't know what he'd said that was funny.

'Theo, this is amazing,' said Eliza. 'What's in it?'

'It's just cream and a few things to flavour it.'

'Nice things . . .'

'Very nice,' agreed Anna-Marie. 'I think I'm going to have to have a lie-down – and then have seconds!'

Everyone laughed loudly, even Sylvia, and Theo looked pleased.

Eliza said, 'I think we should raise our glasses—'

'. . . while we still can . . .' interjected Michael.

'. . . while we still can . . . to Theo and his wonderful cooking. This is the best dinner ever!'

'To Theo!' the others chorused, and Theo went a bit pink and beamed his thanks.

He looked around the assembled company and then his gaze rested on Eliza. 'Thank you,' he mouthed silently and the look in his kind brown eyes was exclusively for her. She felt, for a moment, strangely shy, then gathered herself and gave him her widest smile.

Soon the syllabub was completely finished, and the company was feeling possibly a little too well indulged. Theo produced a real coffee pot from the bag of secret ingredients he'd brought, and made some strong coffee on the stove top, and Eliza brewed a pot of tea for those who preferred it.

'Well,' said Sylvia, occupying Maureen's favourite armchair in the sitting room where everyone had gone to rest their stomachs and avoid looking at the dirty crockery left on the table, 'this has all been rather a surprise. But perhaps this is the shape of things to come, Liza.'

'Oh, I think it's a one-off, Sylvie. Mum doesn't go away on holiday often, if ever before now, and she only left me the lovely food as a treat because I wasn't going with her and she wanted to make sure I ate properly.'

'There's properly and there's pushing the boat out! It was nowt short of Christmas dinner! But then Mum's always spoiled you. I wasn't going with her, either, but she didn't leave me a chicken and a fancy pudding,' said Sylvia.

'I expect she thought you and Desmond would be managing very nicely for yourselves, you having each other; and anyway, the pudding was made by Theo.'

'And very good it was, too,' said Michael cheerfully, determined to keep the evening on track, raising his coffee cup in salute to Theo.

'Mum could have given me some lovely things to eat while she's away,' persisted Sylvia tipsily. 'After all, she can afford to eat like this every day now. I think she's been really mean not buying owt for me. I'm her daughter, too, *and* I'm the eldest. At least you've got the fridge. She could have bought *me* one.'

The others looked puzzled and also uncomfortable. Even through a haze of wine, beer and syllabub, Anna-Marie and Michael clearly realised this conversation, whatever it was about, had no place in the evening. Desmond was looking utterly at sea, as if his wife had started speaking a foreign language, and Theo, who was almost sober, caught Eliza's eye and read her panic.

'Right, Desmond, I can see it's getting late and Sylvia looks ready for her bed,' he said.

'But the washing up . . .' began Desmond.

'It's fine,' said Theo firmly. He lowered his voice. 'Better go, I think. It would be a shame if Eliza got upset after all her efforts.' He looked at Desmond in a meaningful way and Desmond eventually twigged.

'Er, right, yes. Come on, Sylvie. Time to go now. You're looking tired, love. A nice long lie-in tomorrow, mebbe.'

'And we have Mass in the morning, early, don't we, Michael?' said Anna-Marie, who had long ago given up attending Mass.

'We certainly do,' agreed Michael, not missing a beat. 'Are you and Sylvia coming, Desmond? I think you're walking our way, are you not?'

126

Eliza smiled her thanks. 'It's been a lovely evening. Thank you all for coming.'

'I still think Mum could have bought me a fridge full of nice food,' whined Sylvia, edging into the hallway behind the others. 'It's little enough to expect when she's got all those thousands in the bank.'

Eliza's heart was pounding furiously now. Should she let Sylvia and Desmond leave with Anna-Marie and Michael, or keep them here until Sylvia could be persuaded to shut up? Goodness only knew what Sylvia might say on the walk home.

'Maybe you and Anna-Marie should go ahead after all, Michael, and we'll perhaps find Sylvia another cup of tea before she sets off,' suggested Theo.

Anna-Marie and Michael exchanged puzzled looks. 'Er, yes, OK, then . . . Thank you for such a lovely dinner. We've had a grand time. I'll see you soon, Liza,' said Anna-Marie.

'Yes, I'll explain everything then,' said Eliza quietly, though how she would explain she had no idea. She had promised her mother she would keep quiet about the legacy, and now look!

She waved off her friends with smiles and thank-yous all round. It seemed a forlorn hope that in the morning they would have forgotten what had been said. Still, there'd be time to worry about that then.

'Are we going or are we staying, then?' asked Desmond.

'We'll just let Anna-Marie and Michael set off. You wouldn't want to crowd them,' said Theo diplomatically.

'Anna-Marie is such a silly girl. She's been making sheep's eyes at that lad all evening,' muttered Sylvia.

Eliza bit her lip, although she was fast running out of patience.

Sylvia wandered into the kitchen and made straight for the new fridge. She opened it and peered inside.

'I wish I had one of these,' she repeated to anyone listening. 'P'raps I'll just ask Mum to buy me one. What else did you manage to wheedle out of Mum, Liza? Champagne, mebbe? A nice piece of fillet steak?'

'Oh, do shut up,' said Eliza. 'I told you, Mum was just being nice because she'd left me alone and wanted to be sure I ate properly.'

'Sylvie, what are you on about?' asked Desmond. 'Talking about your mum buying fancy stuff for you – why would she do that?'

'Well, she's bought all this for our Liza, so why shouldn't she do so for me?'

'But we don't live here, Sylvie,' said Desmond. 'We do for ourselves. I don't expect your mum to give us owt.'

'You would if you knew how much she's worth,' said Sylvia, and Eliza gasped in horror at her boldness.

'Be quiet, Sylvia. It's nowt to do with anyone but Mum.'

By now Theo had edged out to the doorway, torn between good-mannered discretion and not abandoning Eliza to Sylvia's unpleasantness, while Desmond stood with his mouth slightly agape, looking from his wife to his sister-in-law and back again, utterly uncomprehending.

128

'What do you mean?' he asked.

'Well, it's time you knew, for all Mum and Liza are trying to keep it hushed up, like it's a dirty secret and not a cause for celebration. Mum's been left a fortune in someone's will. She'll never be short of money again. She can buy whatever she wants for the rest of her days.'

'What she *wants* to do, Sylvia,' said Eliza, 'let me remind you, is keep quiet about it – at least for the time being. She's only had the money for a couple of months. She hasn't got used to it yet, and she hasn't decided what to do with it. And that's why it was agreed – between us all – that we wouldn't say owt to anyone about it until Mum is ready. It's her money and it's her decision.'

'*I* never agreed!' snapped Sylvia. 'It was you who told me to be quiet. Well, I'm not shutting up just because you tell me to. I reckon you just wanted to take control, let Mum spend her money on you and leave me out of it.'

'Oh, for goodness' sake, what on earth makes you think Mum and I would be against you, would be planning to leave you out, even if I was *rude enough* to think Mum's legacy had owt to do with me? Mum will decide for herself, in her own time, what she wants to do.'

'Well, I haven't seen owt of the money yet, have I? I reckon you're starting as you mean to go on. I'm not the one with a new fridge stuffed with delicious food like we only usually get to see at Christmas, am I? I'm not the one having fancy dinners with my friends, holidays by the seaside.'

Eliza could feel her anger rising like molten lava in a volcano. 'How dare you criticise Mum for having a holiday? Shame on you! After all she's done for us in her life, never having owt nice to look forward to and always putting us first, and now she's gone away for five days – *five days*, Sylvia, not even a week – and you can't even be pleased for her. You disgust me with your envy and spitefulness. Poor Mum! If she could hear you now, she'd be sad to think she'd raised you, behaving like this.'

'You speak to me like that?' shrieked Sylvia. She stepped forward to box Eliza's ears but Desmond caught her arms and restrained her.

'Sylvia, stop it. You're sounding like a madwoman.'

'Mad? I'll show you how mad I am, Des.' She struggled to free her arms but Theo appeared then to help Desmond.

'Come on now, Sylvia. It's the drink talking. Potent old brew, wine and beer and syllabub. Sit down now and be calm,' Theo said, gently but firmly leading her to a kitchen chair. 'Eliza, best just go and sit it out awhile,' he said quietly over his shoulder. 'Now then, Sylvia, how about another cup of tea and then a walk home in the cool night air . . .?'

'It's OK, Liza, they've gone,' said Theo, quietly closing the front door on Desmond steering Sylvia in the direction of their home.

Eliza's cross little face peered out of the sitting room. 'I heard. Thank you. I'm so sorry the lovely evening was spoiled by my mean, stupid sister. I can't bear her when she's like that: all envious and hateful. I really wish I'd told her and Des to go away when they first showed up.'

'Don't worry, Liza. It wasn't your fault. Blame it on the syllabub!'

Eliza gave a crooked smile. 'That's what she'll say when I next see her: "The syllabub made me do it." Nothing's ever her fault.'

'Ah, forget about her. She's gone and is now the responsibility of poor old Desmond.'

'Yes, poor sod. It's bad enough having Sylvia as a sister; imagine being married to her.'

'I said, forget about her.'

For a moment Theo sounded quite firm, and Eliza was reminded that he was many years older than her, and many years wiser, too. She was conscious she'd sounded childish and silly.

'It's getting late and you need to get home,' she said in a little voice.

'What, and leave you the washing up? That wouldn't be very chivalrous.'

'But you did all the cooking. And anyway, I don't think I'm going to be doing the dishes tonight. There's heaps of them, and Mum won't be back until at least the afternoon. I know I'll regret it in the morning, but I'm going to leave them.'

'Actually, Liza, I entirely agree with your slovenly inclination. Best thing to do would be to go to bed, have a nice rest, and tackle it in the morning when everything will look so much brighter.'

'Except the washing-up pile itself, which I reckon might have grown.' She cast a despairing look around the kitchen, every surface covered with used crockery, pans and cooking utensils.

'I agree, but I'll be here to help you with it, so you've nothing to worry about. I'll leave the bag of secret ingredients here and collect it then. Eight thirty sound OK to you?'

'*What!*'

'Ha, I thought that would get you going. No, my dear Eliza, let's say ten o'clock, but promise not to start without me.'

'Promise. I think that's one promise I can keep.'

'Don't start fretting again. We've had a good evening. Good night, Liza.'

Eliza saw him to the door. 'Thank you for everything, Theo. Sorry about Sylvia, but the rest of the evening was lovely.'

'I enjoyed it, too.' For a moment he raised his arm and Eliza thought, with a sudden and surprising thrill, that he was going to caress her face. But then he quickly lowered his arm and said, 'Sleep tight. See you in the morning.'

'Ten o'clock, not a minute before,' Eliza reminded him. 'Good night, Theo.'

She waved him off, watching him until he was out of sight, then quietly closed the front door, wishing he could stay longer, thinking about earlier when their eyes had met.

Dear Theo, what a kind man. So good-looking and so talented. Where had he learned to cook like that? The chicken had been delicious, and nothing too much trouble to make perfect. It had been a lovely evening – almost.

Don't think about Sylvia.

As she went up to bed, Eliza decided she'd rather not have to think about Sylvia ever again, but then she berated herself for being horrible. Oh dear, perhaps that meant they were more alike than she really wanted to admit . . .

The difficult problem to face, though, was what to tell Mum now that the news of her inherited fortune was out. She'd return from her only holidays for years, full of the joys of a lovely little break with her old friend Barbara, only to find her daughters had fallen out and her secret legacy was a secret no longer. She would be so disappointed, so anxious. The burglary attempt paled in significance next to this. What a disaster!

CHAPTER EIGHT

'**B**ARBARA, LOVE, WE'VE had such fun. I'm so glad you agreed to go with me on this little holiday.'

'Yes, haven't we? An escape from real life.' Barbara sighed as she drove westwards, her car filled with luggage on this return journey, what with their original cases plus Maureen's new wardrobe of clothes and the presents she'd chosen for her daughters.

Maureen was taken aback at her friend's response. 'But, Barbara, love, your whole life is an escape from real life! All those plays and shows you've been telling me about . . . the big names . . . the fancy costumes you get to wear . . .'

'Only an escape for the audience. It's just work for me, a job that I need to do, increasingly now I'm entirely relying on myself for support, as I have had to since Marty died. But you know all about self-reliance, of course, Maureen. And . . . I haven't told you this before as I didn't want to spoil our lovely time, but I fear there may be bad news about my next part. There were rumours before we came away about the backers pulling out and . . . I wouldn't be entirely surprised if, when I get home, I learn the show isn't going ahead after all.' She sighed again and bit her lip. 'I was very much looking forward to it – was banking on it, in fact.'

'Oh dear! That's a shame. But you'll be offered another part soon, won't you, Babs? A star like you will be snapped up when folk hear you're free.'

'Mm, maybe . . .' A look of anxiety crossed Barbara's beautiful face. 'It doesn't always happen like that, I'm afraid. At least not nowadays.'

'Oh, Barbara, I'm sorry, but try not to worry. It may all work out for the best,' said Maureen, surprised to see a tear at the corner of her friend's eye.

Barbara wiped it away discreetly and sniffed, visibly pulling herself together. 'Yes, I expect it will.' She didn't sound very hopeful. In fact, she sounded glum.

It was then that Maureen suspected Barbara had been worrying all this time and had been terribly brave and selfless, putting aside her fears so as not to spoil the holiday. Now, with the Alvis eating up the miles towards home, she was having to face reality.

'Shall we stop for lunch in York?' suggested Maureen kindly. 'My treat, of course, to thank you for going with me, making this little holiday such a wonderful time.'

'That's very kind of you, Maureen. If you're sure . . .?'

They found a nice place to eat, despite the limited choice of venues on a Sunday, and Maureen said she'd buy them both a traditional roast lunch. She chatted all the while about how much she was looking forward to seeing Eliza and Sylvia, and telling them about the holiday, but Barbara was quiet and evidently preoccupied.

As they were drinking their coffee, Maureen, glancing round to make sure there was no hovering waiter or other diners within earshot, said, 'What is it, Babs, love? You can tell me. I can see you've summat on your mind and it's dragging you down. Are you really fretting about the show not going ahead?'

Barbara nodded, unhappiness now written all over her face. She put down her cup and looked at Maureen, hardly able to disguise her anguish. 'Oh, Maureen, it's such a worry. I'm so grateful to you that you've enabled me to put all thought of it aside for these last few days and think instead of all the good times of the past, but I fear I'm going to find it a little difficult to . . . well, to manage without this role. I really need it, you see.' She lowered her voice and Maureen leaned in to be sure to catch what her friend was saying. 'It isn't so easy when an actress gets to a certain age, I'm starting to discover. The starring roles . . . well, they seem to want young girls for so many of them that the kind of parts for me are *not quite* as available as they once were.'

'But you look so lovely, Barbara, I can't think they'd find anyone prettier, and you've gallons of experience and – what's the phrase? – star quality. I'm sure the audiences flock when they see your name on the bill. From what you've told me, you've been doing ever so well.'

'Oh, Maureen, you're very sweet, but I'm afraid in the world of the theatre, these days I'm *just beginning* to be stuck between two kinds of role: too old to play the beautiful young lead and too glamorous to play the older women. Neither Juliet nor the Nurse, if you see what I mean?'

'But what about Juliet's mother?' asked Maureen, in all innocence, taking Barbara literally. 'I don't know much about that play, or any other, really, but I seem to remember that's one of the parts.'

'*Juliet's mother* . . .' said Barbara, in a way that let Maureen know this was not a helpful answer. 'I don't think I'm the motherly type, Maureen, do you?'

'No, I suppose not,' said Maureen quietly.

She thought about Barbara going home to her house – a house called The Manor, which implied grandeur and probably a lot of expense on upkeep – and finding a letter on the doormat informing her that the show in which she was to star was cancelled and she had no work. Barbara lived alone now Marty, her husband, was dead. The house would be empty and silent; there would be no shoulder for Barbara to cry on, no reassuring hug, no one to share a pot of tea with while deciding on a plan to overcome the setback. There would be no lively, cheerful daughter like Eliza to welcome her mum home and chat about the happy few days away. Poor Barbara.

And she had said she was going to find it 'difficult to manage' without this show going ahead. Maureen knew all about the difficulty of managing; in the past she'd always just rolled up her sleeves and got on with whatever employment she could find. But it would be different for Barbara. Maureen had a sudden image of Barbara taking a job as a home help or a cleaner, turning up at the house with her stylish blonde curls tied up under a turban, pulling on her Marigolds and dunking her mop in a bucket of ammonia, and the lady who owned the house saying, 'Good heavens, aren't you Barbara Hayle, the celebrated variety star?' It would be too humiliating for Barbara, a far greater let-down than it would ever be for anyone who was a nobody to start with . . .

Maureen came out of her daydream to find the waiter asking if she required anything else, or just the bill.

While she paid for the lunches and insisted that she, rather than Barbara, left a tip, Maureen's mind was working in sympathy with Barbara's plight. She thought about how kind Barbara had been over the past few days, how patient and encouraging in the face of her own shyness in fancy shops, and her inexperience in restaurants and tearooms, how Barbara had helped choose the new outfits that made her feel graceful and attractive, possibly for the first time ever. How Barbara had suggested new food for her to try for dinner at the hotel every evening, which always turned out to be delicious. How Barbara had driven them both up and down the Yorkshire coast, and inland, too, in her amazing car, to visit beautiful gardens, picture galleries and stately homes open to the public, and picturesque seaside towns with wonderfully clean fresh air and quaint cottages – places Maureen would never have got to see by herself. Really, now she thought about it, it was Barbara who had made the holiday, given it far broader horizons than it would otherwise have had. If she hadn't gone with Barbara, Maureen knew she would have just kept within her own very limited experiences, eaten what she had always known, worn the same old clothes – or the regrettable new ones she'd chosen for herself in Blackburn – and not seen a fraction of the places they had managed to visit.

More importantly, Maureen had felt frightened of her new wealth, frozen by inexperience and indecision, and – Barbara had been right – instead of enjoying it she had been keeping it 'for best'. Well, no more! What was the use of having money if she wasn't going to enjoy it, do something with it, make it count? It wasn't as if there was not enough. Now, as she and her best friend strolled back to the car, and a couple of onlookers – admiring the Alvis as people did wherever it went – stood aside to let them pass, she reminded herself of the resolution she'd made on the beach after that shopping expedition on the first day in Somerton: to live a new life, the life of a woman of means. Not a timid, careful, thrifty woman, who was afraid to dream because those dreams were never likely to be realised, but a woman with imagination and the ability and confidence to make her dreams real.

'Don't fret, Barbara,' she said as she climbed into the passenger seat and settled back to enjoy the last leg of the journey to her little house in Blackburn. 'I shan't let you sink or swim alone. You let me know if that show gets cancelled, and I'll be round to make sure you're all right. I know we grew up together and times were tough in them days, but you've moved on since then – got used to a different kind of life through your own talent and hard work. I admire and respect that, lass. After all, in a way it's what I've been doing for myself and my girls, but we've simply been moving in different circles.'

'Dear Maureen, how good you are,' said Barbara, her eyes glistening with unshed tears. 'I am truly touched by your kind heart, but I would never want to be a burden on you.'

'Burden! What nonsense you talk. We're friends, have been for years. We might have lost sight of each other, but we've never lost touch. Now we're back together.' She laughed. 'Somerton-on-Sea has united us again. Now, I'm intending to have a telephone installed – I expect my neighbours would like that as they can come and use it – so if you give me your number, I can call you up. It'll be quicker than writing.'

Barbara told her and Maureen wrote it carefully on the back of her much-depleted cheque book.

'Don't worry, Babs,' said Maureen, tucking it safely back into her bag, 'I'll see you right.'

* * *

It was late in the afternoon when Barbara drove in at the gate of The Manor and parked in front of the house. A few pigeons cooed their welcome home, the wind gently rustled the trees in her garden, and there was the distant grind of a tractor engine in the fields beyond. Apart from that, silence. No Maureen wittering on. Oh, that woman could fuss for England!

It was good to be home, to be back at The Manor. Her love for the house and the status it gave her never faded, however much of a financial burden it was proving to be. Its upkeep was on top of the loan she and Marty had taken out to cover some unforeseen expenses, and several that they had foreseen all too well and should have avoided; it was secured against the house, and so she could never fall behind on payments. The holiday with Maureen had given her a lot to think about, though. Had she really been away only since Wednesday? In some ways it seemed like weeks.

Had it been a mistake to assume her 'successful actress' persona at the start? Possibly – she was having to work on the story of the cancelled show now – but that role was in her veins, her default position, and the alternative was not pretty. The failed auditions, the insincere expressions of sympathy or, even worse, the curt dismissals as too old, too young, not right, no talent – she could not face all that again.

Has-been . . . washed-up chorus girl . . . second rate . . .
'Stop it! Shut up!'

Had she said that aloud? No, no, be quiet! It was treachery even to think that; to remember her own mother's cruel words. She was Barbara Hayle, celebrated actress in variety and light comedy theatre, a beauty, a talent, the woman on whom Marty had bestowed his love. As the lady of the manor in Buckledale, she had found a role in life that suited her, she'd practised it, she'd *lived* it, and she'd be damned if she'd give it up now.

Barbara straightened her back and took her bags out of the car. She found her key and opened the big, shiny front door. There was no post on the mat, which was a surprise. For one mad moment she almost expected to see the letter telling her the show had been cancelled, she'd made such a habit of mixing invention with reality. Perhaps Brendan had been in and moved any mail that had arrived. In the end she had given him a key so he could keep an eye on The Manor for her while she was away.

She closed the door, and the house became totally silent. Not even a clock ticked.

She saw that the flowers in the vase in the hall were dead, the water stagnant. Well, it wasn't the kind of thing she'd expect Brendan to notice or do anything about. Her footsteps beat loudly on the stone flags as she went to the kitchen, ran the tap for a minute or two, and then filled the kettle and set it to boil; took the tiny teapot for one person off the shelf . . .

Later, as she unpacked her suitcase, Barbara's mind

143

turned again to Maureen. Who'd have thought Maureen Bancroft would have inherited a fortune? She'd obviously never had two pennies to rub together before now, and she was completely out of her depth. Barbara smiled as she thought of Maureen in the dress shop. The poor woman hadn't a clue, and it was only because she'd had Barbara there to help that she'd been willing to buy some smart new clothes. Barbara recalled how she'd let Maureen think the shopping trip was all her own idea. Then she'd made dull and dreary Maureen feel good about herself, given her the boost she'd never had before, so that now she was so grateful she thought they were best friends again. She had been very easy to manipulate. Barbara had made over Mousy Maureen in her own image, now she came to think of it, though Maureen hadn't the advantage of her face or figure, of course . . .

Barbara rummaged in her case and pulled out a silk scarf printed with pink roses. It was a little something that she felt Crosby's, the dress shop in Somerton-on-Sea, had *owed* her for bringing them so much custom from Maureen. She had been quite justified in slipping this neat little *commission* into her coat pocket when the assistant and the manageress's attention had been otherwise occupied. She delved again into the bottom of her case and extracted a small leather clutch bag, which would look very well with her winter coat. This had been a little trickier to procure, but the key to success had been, and always would be, distraction.

She'd learned that in a brief and regrettable career as a magician's assistant. Handbags or white rabbits – the principle was the same.

'Naughty girl, Barbara,' she mock-chided herself, grinning. Just because she didn't have any money, it didn't mean she shouldn't have nice things; that she should lower her standards. Barbara Hayle, variety star, only ever wore stylish clothes and had quality accessories. Nothing else would do.

After she'd unpacked and hung up her few clothes, which swung freely on their hangers in the spaciousness of her vast wardrobe, and put her hat carefully back in its box, the crown stuffed with tissue paper, Barbara went back outside to take the car round to the garage.

Having locked the Alvis safely away, she checked, out of interest, to see if Brendan had secured all the outbuilding doors with those padlocks he'd attached. The first two were firmly fastened but the third, surprisingly, was just hooked through the hasp. You had to look closely to see that the lock had not quite clicked into place: obviously a mistake.

Barbara made a mental note of the exact position of the lock so she'd be able to put it back just so. Then she slipped the padlock out and swung back the door.

It was early evening now and the low sun cast shadows into the interior. Nonetheless, she could see there was quite a lot of furniture lined up along the back wall. She went in to look closer.

Some of the furniture was clearly rubbish: shabby

junk, cheap originally and now horrid with age or misuse. She opened a desk drawer and found it stuffed with old Christmas cards. Sad. Fortunately, there was none of the nasty old stained furniture one might expect to have to collect in the house-clearance business: no appalling old mattresses or sagging, greasy armchairs and sofas. At least it looked as if Brendan had had the sense to dispose of these straight away.

Barbara saw now that all this furniture – most worthless, although there were some better pieces – featured drawers or cupboards. There were desks, sideboards, wardrobes, dressers and linen presses. Well, he would be careful to go through that little lot just in case anyone had left anything valuable. House clearance was very much a game of chance, Brendan had once explained to her. 'If folk are daft enough to let me take away their dead relatives' furniture without bothering to search through it first, then that's their lookout.' There wasn't a huge amount of money to be made from clearing houses, and some were apparently a lot of work – filthy, with junk piled up everywhere and disgusting, vermin-riddled horrors waiting to be uncovered – but Brendan got to sell on anything he could salvage via his junk shop in Blackburn, and his dream was to discover a long-forgotten hoard of cash or jewellery or a gold watch put away in a 'safe place' and overlooked.

Barbara tried the central top drawer in a desk and found it locked. Interesting . . . She opened the right-hand drawer, hoping to find the key, but there were only a few letters, nothing valuable-looking, and no key. Then she tried the drawer at the other side, which contained nothing but a large dead spider. She shut it hastily. She didn't think she had the stomach for house clearance. You had to deal with an awful lot of dross in the hope of finding some elusive treasure. She gathered herself to look in one of the drawers below, hoping not to discover any more spiders . . .

'Looking for summat, are you?' said a voice right behind her.

Barbara leaped in surprise and turned to see Brendan standing close, grinning mockingly.

'Good heavens, Brendan, don't do that. I nearly had a heart attack.'

'So I saw,' he smirked. 'Well, what are you doing here?'

'I own this property, in case you've forgotten.'

'And I rent it from you, in case you've forgotten. Don't come the high-and-mighty with me, Babs. You were having a little nose around, weren't you?'

'You'd left the door unlocked. I was just seeing if everything was all right.'

'Were you indeed? And how would you know what was all right and what wasn't, eh?'

Barbara ignored the question and stood her ground. 'Well, considering this place is full of junk, you seem to be awfully uptight about me having a look.'

'Well, that's up to me, isn't it? My stuff, my business. Not *your* business.'

'All right, all right, I'm really not interested in your shabby junk, anyway. I was just going.'

'Just going to what?'

'Just *leaving*.'

'Off you go then.' He stood back and swept out his arm in a gesture showing her the door.

What on earth had got into him? He was clearly feeling shifty about something. 'Oh, let's not fall out,' said Barbara. 'I saw the padlock wasn't closed and I was just curious. Is that so difficult to understand? Why should you mind if I take a peek at your junk? After all, you've obviously been in my house, and I expect you've had a good nose round these last few days.'

Brendan did not stoop to deny it, and Barbara was pleased she had taken her entire envelope of cash with her on holiday. With Brendan it was always better not to lead him into temptation.

'Anyway, I'm home now, if you want to give me back the spare key . . .?' she said, stepping back out into the evening sunshine and watching Brendan close and lock the door.

'Haven't got it with me, have I? I'll bring it next time.'

'You do that. You haven't even asked me if I had a good holiday.'

'Sorry, Barbara. Did you have a good holiday?' he asked sarkily.

'As a matter of fact, I did. Very nice woman, Maureen Bancroft. Kind, motherly, sympathetic—'

'All the things you're not.'

'Don't be mean. Generous, too. She paid for the holiday and all I had to do was drive her around.'

'So she's got money, after all?'

Barbara narrowed her eyes. '"After all" what, Brendan?'

'Well, she lives in Mafeking Street, Blackburn. Doesn't quite add up, to me. Worth something, is she?'

'Not that it's any of your business, but yes, she's newly come into an inheritance. She's far too refined to say how much, but I gather it's a pretty substantial amount.'

'Lucky woman.'

'Keep away, Brendan. She's my friend, not yours.'

Barbara walked with him down the drive to the road, where he'd left his van parked beside the gate.

'I hope you won't be leaving that there regularly. Park round the side when you're here,' said Barbara. 'It looks like I've got the pest controllers in.'

'Funny.'

'What have you done to your hand, Brendan?'

He glanced at his left hand, which was wound about with a grubby bandage, as if he'd forgotten about it. 'Oh, just cut it on some glass when I was round at a house. You never know what you'll come across in my business.'

'Perhaps you should wear gloves. Would you like me to put a clean bandage on it?'

'Nah, it's OK. Did it a few days ago and it's nearly better, thanks.'

'I'd ask you to stay to dinner but—'

'You're too embarrassed about my van parked here.'

'Silly boy. No, I was going to say, I haven't got anything to eat.'

'Ah, well, never mind. Another time,' said Brendan, climbing into the van. He closed the door and started the engine. Then he wound down the window. 'I thought I'd go and get some chips. I know a place that's open. Care to come, if you've nowt in? You can tell me all about your holiday, all about Maureen Bancroft.'

Barbara thought for a moment or two. Sharing her thoughts about Maureen Bancroft with Brendan was a bad idea, at least for now. She'd be far wiser to keep them to herself.

'No, thanks, Brendan. I'm not a big eater of fried food. Go carefully and I'll see you soon. Don't forget to bring the key back.'

He drove away with a wave.

Little bastard, thought Barbara. For all Brendan was family, she didn't trust him an inch.

She strolled back up to the house and let herself in, not too bothered that there was nothing to eat, as the roast lunch in York had been substantial. So, early to bed, a quick trip to the village shop first thing, and then it was back to the piano and elocution lessons. Only, now, if she played a careful hand, if she was prepared to go slowly and not rush in, there was a hope that a change in fortune was on the horizon.

Maureen, although she hadn't said how much she was worth in so many words, had hinted that it was a substantial amount. She wanted to live her dreams, she confided rather touchingly to Barbara on the drive home from York, but she talked only of having a garden, which Barbara, with a garden so vast she had to have Mr Gathercole to tend it for her, didn't think was much of a dream. Still, Maureen had only a backyard with a coal shed in it, so maybe a flowerbed or two was something to aspire to in her eyes.

Maureen was in every way an ordinary person, a little person with a little life. The fortune she'd inherited was an ill fit with that. In fact, it was totally wasted on her. Far better that Barbara, with her style and taste, should have it. It was surely fate that, just when her own financial situation was becoming too difficult, Maureen and her legacy had turned up. All that remained was to plan the strategy for the handover of the money.

'Don't worry, Babs, I'll see you right,' Maureen had said. It was looking promising so far.

CHAPTER NINE

'DID YOUR MUM get back all right yesterday?' asked Harry as he prepared for his first customer of the morning. 'Arrived home in style, as she left, in that posh car with that friend of hers?'

'Yes, she's home fine, thank you, Harry,' said Eliza, putting the kettle on to make the first of many pots of tea of the day. 'And yes, the car made just the same spectacle,' she smiled, winking at Theo. 'And everyone turned out in the street to look, like before. I'm surprised you have to ask, word gets round so quickly.'

'How was the holiday?'

'Good, thank you. Mum's come back full of the joys; had a great time, went all over the place. I'm so glad she was persuaded to go away. It's done her a lot of good.'

'Aye, your mum's not one for giving herself many special treats,' nodded Harry, 'but we all need to get away from time to time.'

'Did you tell her about the burglary?' asked Theo. 'She wasn't too upset?'

'She calmed down once I explained that nowt had been taken and only the back door damaged. She was just glad you'd been there to help, and that Ted and Louisa next door were so good, too. She's decided to have a telephone installed, which would have been useful last Wednesday, although we hope we won't have another emergency any time soon.'

The doorbell rang loudly, announcing a scruffy-looking man and his four-year-old grandson.

'If I let you cut mine, will you do the little lad's for free, Harry?' the man asked.

'No. If you're looking to take advantage, you can sling your hook, Billy,' said Harry. 'The lad needs to learn you don't get owt for nowt in this world. If he's old enough for a proper haircut, he's old enough to know it costs money.'

Billy Cuthbert sighed. 'Thought you'd say that, but it was worth a try.'

'Tell you what,' said Harry, as if the idea had suddenly dawned on him, 'I'll cut yours at the going rate and Eliza can do the lad's for half the price. How about that?'

'It's a deal,' said Billy cheerfully.

Theo turned away to hide his smile. Eliza, as the junior, always cut for half the price of Harry and Theo.

'C'mon then – what's your name, young man?' asked Eliza.

'Albert . . .'

'Albert Cuthbert?'

'Yeah, I know,' said the boy mournfully. 'Me mum wasn't thinking, I reckon.'

'Well, sit down here and I'll wash your hair and then you can read that *Beano* while I give you a trim – what do you say . . .?'

The day passed in busyness, although Eliza found her mind wandering to Maureen's homecoming the previous afternoon.

The car had arrived outside in the grey street as showily as it had the first time, and Barbara stepped out as if in a spotlight, wearing exactly the same clothes and looking fabulous. It was as if the scene of the previous Wednesday was being played in reverse, only with a lot more luggage to unload. The bond between Maureen and Barbara had evidently strengthened, though, with hugs goodbye and even promises to telephone, which surprised Eliza.

Then there had been the inevitable brewing of a pot of tea while Maureen chatted about her holiday and Eliza wondered how to tell her mother that Sylvia had announced the news of the legacy to four people on Saturday evening and that there had been an attempted burglary.

'So,' said Maureen, sitting down in her favoured chair in the sitting room with a cup of tea, 'I'll unpack in a minute, show you my new clothes, and I've got presents for you and Sylvia, too.'

'Mum, you shouldn't have,' said Eliza without thinking. She was so used to Maureen never having the money for special treats that she'd spoken out of habit, momentarily forgetting the legacy.

'Ha, love, that's the way I was thinking, too, before my holiday, but I'm trying to put those days behind me, to move on and live like a woman whose life isn't all about scrimping and saving and doing without. I can afford to think differently now, and I certainly never meant to be mean either.'

'I never thought you were mean, Mum – not for a moment – but I've been hoping you'd feel better able to cope with the money after your holiday away; have some new ideas about what you'd like to do now, mebbe.'

'I'm working on those, but in the meantime I'm definitely getting a telephone installed. Ted and Louisa, and anyone else we know, can come and use it, too.'

'I wondered when I heard you saying to Barbara that you'd telephone her. I expect a lot of our neighbours will be asking to use it, as you'll have the only telephone in the street,' said Eliza. 'But the thing is, Mum . . . well, I'm afraid the news about the legacy is out.' She held her breath. She'd been dreading breaking this news.

Maureen put her cup down slowly. Then she said, 'Well, I don't reckon it matters now, love. Summat Barbara said made me think the money would be wasted by keeping it hidden and not enjoyed. "Keeping it for best", she called it, like a favourite frock that gets wasted 'cos you never wear it, and I could see I was very lacking in imagination to think I could just go on as I always have, hide the money away from others and myself, and not take opportunities to spend it openly, as I've every right to do. Miss Stevens wouldn't want me to live like I've always done and not enjoy her legacy, just for fear of offending folk or because I was too stupid to think out a new way to live.'

'So you told Barbara?' asked Eliza.

'Of course I did. She was beginning to worry about me, bless her. She thought that I'd miscalculated and offered her a holiday I mebbe couldn't afford to pay for, and she didn't want me to be embarrassed. She was very sweet about it, and she has such an open way of discussing things that it would have been wrong to try to hide the good news, try to cover it up. It would have been lying to her, really.'

'Good . . . well, that makes me feel better.'

'Was it you that said summat?' her mother asked Eliza.

'No, it was Sylvie, of course.' Eliza told her mother about the dinner party she'd had and how Sylvia, under the influence of wine, beer and syllabub, and jealousy about the fridge, had blurted out about the legacy.

'Well, no harm done,' said Maureen, getting up to pour herself another cup of tea.

'I'm glad you think that,' said Eliza, a bit crossly because Sylvia *had* betrayed their mother's secret, and now seemed to have got away with it, too, which wasn't right.

'Oh, love, it sounds as if you've had a falling-out, but it turns out not to matter what Sylvia said, so just forget about it and be nice to each other.'

Eliza took a deep breath to calm herself and then told her mother about the attempted burglary.

'Right, I'm all finished here,' said Eliza at the end of the day.

'Well done, Liza. Nice work on Albert Cuthbert this morning.'

The three of them grinned at each other.

'Poor lad,' murmured Theo. 'I'm finished too, if you're going my way . . .?' he asked Eliza with the raise of an eyebrow.

'Yes, I'm off straight home. Come by ours and say hello to Mum. I know she's keen to thank you for looking after me on the evening of the burglary.'

'No need for that, but I'll be pleased to see her looking well and relaxed after her holiday.'

They left Harry to lock up and set off in the direction of the park, taking the scenic route on this fine May evening.

'So?' asked Theo. 'I've been dying to ask you all day.'

'When I told Mum the news was out, she didn't mind at all. She's told her friend Barbara and she's come back from her holidays with a whole new attitude to the legacy.'

'Well, that's good, isn't it?'

'Mm, mebbe. I was that worried about telling her,

and I'm still cross with Sylvia, who only blabbed out of drunken spite.'

'But how would it have been better if your mum had been upset?' asked Theo. 'It's all turned out for the best really.'

'I s'pose,' said Eliza. 'Yes, you're right, of course. It's just typical of Sylvia, that's all.'

'In which case it can't be helped,' said Theo.

They walked on a little way into Corporation Park, Theo enjoying the flowerbeds, stopping to smell a rose, really looking at the colours, admiring the trees in full leaf. Eliza, however, was preoccupied.

Theo led her to a bench by the path and they sat down. He leaned back, closed his eyes and breathed deeply. After a few minutes he opened his eyes again and sat up.

'All right, Eliza, I can tell you're fretting about something else. Your mum knows about the burglary and she isn't too worried, and she knows the news about her inheritance is now circulating the streets of Blackburn – and it'll be the talk of the Short Cut before the week is out, I bet, so you'd better practise your strategy for fielding the questions – and she doesn't mind about that either. What else is it that you're worrying about?'

Eliza breathed out slowly and tried to get her thoughts in order.

'I feel a bit mean,' she began tentatively. 'It's just a feeling I have . . .'

'About . . .?'

'Mum's friend Barbara. You see, Mum had such a lovely holiday with her. I can see she's got some colour in her face and she looks nothing like as worn and tired as she did before she went. She went shopping with Barbara and she's come back with a whole lot of nice clothes – I mean *really* nice, all quality things and colours that match, like nowt she's ever worn before – and she's talking about not saving owt for best but making every day a day when it's worth the effort to look nice.'

'But surely that's good? We all like to have beautiful things. I'm fond of a good shirt and some decent shoes myself.' Theo raised his feet, regarding his shiny brogues fondly.

'I know, but it's such a big change in Mum. She's never talked like this before.'

'That's hardly surprising, Liza. She's never had a legacy before. When, yesterday morning, you explained to me what Sylvia had been talking about, I thought it a bit, well, hard to understand that your mum had had the money for all those weeks already and it had seemed to make hardly any difference to her. Maybe this Barbara has done her a favour, showing her a freer way to live, not hindered by having to scrimp and save after a lifetime of doing so. Maureen had got into the habit of living as she had to, and habits can be hard to break sometimes.'

'Yes, and I don't want to spoil owt for Mum. I told

her at the beginning that she can do as she likes and I mean it. But there's something about Barbara Hayle . . . it sounds really strange, I know, but it's as if she's *playing* at being an actress.'

Theo turned on the bench to look more directly at Eliza. 'How do you mean?'

'Well, when she first drew up in the big car that everyone's been talking about ever since, she was wearing a really huge hat, quite impractical for a long drive with the car hood down, and she just knew all eyes were on her, I could tell: she was playing the role of the star of the show. I'd no idea until then that Mum's friend was actually a star. And the car was a part of that, too. It was like a stage prop, a part of her act. She couldn't just have an ordinary sort of car, could she?'

'I suppose not, but then in a way we'd be disappointed if she did, wouldn't we? You see, you can't have it both ways, Liza; you can't expect her to be a larger-than-life glamorous actress but go around looking and behaving like everyone else.'

'True. But I've never heard of Barbara Hayle, except as an old friend of Mum's, have you, Theo?'

'No, I can't say I have, but perhaps she was a big name in the theatre here when I was working abroad, or in the army.'

'I didn't know you had lived abroad,' Eliza said, turning in surprise to look at Theo.

'That's where I learned to cook – in France before the war. Anyway, you were talking about Barbara Hayle . . .'

'If she's a star, why does she have to put on quite such a show? Doesn't she ever give herself a day off? It's a kind of double mask: a star actress playing a star actress. I don't know . . . mebbe I'm being daft and it's summat I know nowt about. I just don't want Mum, who isn't an actress and doesn't have to put on a show, to fall too much under Barbara's influence. Mum's not Barbara. The clothes are lovely, but I gather from what Mum says that Barbara was in charge of the shopping expedition and even decided where they were to go. I reckon it was Barbara decided what she was to buy, too. They're Barbara-type clothes, if I'm not mistaken.'

'Maybe Maureen just needed her advice. I'm guessing she hasn't had a lot of experience in smart shops, and if this Barbara knows what's what, why wouldn't she ask her?'

'Oh, I expect you're right. I just worry that Mum wasn't so much doing what she wanted but more what Barbara was somehow directing her to do.'

'Why would Barbara do that, do you think, Liza?'

'I don't know. Mum hasn't had anyone quite like Barbara in her life before, and mebbe she's a little bit starstruck, and Barbara, for some reason I don't under-stand, is . . . is taking advantage of this, or at least lapping it up.'

'But didn't you tell me they were childhood friends?'

'Mm, they were, but Miss Barbara Hayle's come an awful long way since then. The voice – that accent was never found around here – and the look, the attitude. I'm not sure why she'd want to take up so much with her childhood friend. They've little in common any more, from what I can see.'

Theo got to his feet and held out his arm for Eliza to walk on with him. 'But they found enough in each other to enjoy their holiday together, didn't they? We all evolve, Eliza, we're all changed by our experiences and collect our own baggage as we go through life,' he said gravely. 'At least I hope we do. Allow your mother to be changed by her good fortune. She's a sensible woman and she won't let it spoil her. And if she ever looks like getting carried away, she has her daughters and her many friends to set her right.'

'You're right, Theo. Thank you. I don't want to be mean about Mum, or Barbara. It's just that this is all such a big thing for Mum; it's too important it should all work out well, do you see? It's her big chance after she's had so few. I expect I'm just being soft, and I need to broaden my own narrow horizons, too.'

'Just see what happens, Liza, that's my advice. Wait and see.'

When Eliza let herself and Theo in at 28 Mafeking Street, they found Maureen looking far from relaxed and happy. Rather, she was tearful and anxious, wringing her hands and pacing the sitting room.

'Mum? What's the matter?' asked Eliza, alarmed. 'Not bad news?'

'Oh, Liza, I'm that glad to see you. Hello, Theo, love. Come on in and I'll make us a pot of tea. I don't know if I'm being daft or if it was burgled, but I can't find my engagement ring.'

Whatever Eliza had been expecting to hear, it wasn't that.

'Now, sit down, Mum, and tell me when you first noticed it gone. Then we'll have a look for it.'

'But I've looked everywhere,' lamented Maureen. 'I realised after Barbara and I were on our way to Somerton that I'd forgotten to put it on before I left. I don't always wear it, as you know, and I leave it on the dressing table in that little tray. Anyway, I never thought owt about it until this morning, after you'd gone to work. Then I suddenly remembered and rushed up to look, thinking what you'd said about the burglary, and I couldn't find it anywhere.'

'Oh, no! Oh, poor Mum. You're absolutely sure you didn't take it with you, in your handbag or summat?'

'Of course I am. I've *told* you, I always leave it in the tray and I'm certain I hadn't put it on.'

'I'll go up and look, just in case. Theo, sorry to ask, but would you just put the kettle on, please, while I have a search round upstairs . . .?'

Eliza rushed upstairs and hunted around her mother's bedroom, then took a quick look in all the obvious places, but she hadn't noticed the ring in the last few days and it was with a sinking feeling that she acknowledged that it might well have been stolen by the intruder.

Just when she thought the burglary was all a nasty little something-and-nothing incident that they could all put behind them, it had reared its ugly head again.

She went down again slowly. 'No, Mum, I can't see it either. I'd have noticed it on your dressing table when I went in to open and close the curtains each day, I'm sure. I never gave it a thought, and if I had I would just have assumed you'd been wearing it when you left. Oh dear, I think we're going to have to tell the police that we think it's been taken and give them a description. I don't know what else there is to do.'

Maureen nodded. 'You weren't to know I'd forgotten to put it on, love. It shouldn't have mattered. We've never been burgled before.'

Theo came back with cups of tea on a tray.

'Thanks, love,' said Maureen. 'Well, I suppose after nearly a week since that fella broke in, it will wait until tomorrow. I'll go to the police station and report it in the morning.'

'Try not to get upset, Maureen,' said Theo. 'We'll have another look in a minute.'

'Thank you, Theo, and thank you for all the help you were to Eliza when you both nearly saw the burglar. But I've been searching for my ring all day.' Maureen was looking tearful again. 'My Jack gave me it when I promised to marry him and now I've lost it. Oh, I can't bear to think it's been stolen from me, after all these years.'

'Would you like me to go to the police now?' suggested Theo.

'No, I'll go tomorrow,' Maureen said again. 'I'll write out a description of it, the setting and cut of the stones and anything I can remember of the hallmarks. You never know, it might turn up.' She didn't sound hopeful.

They all three had another look round, but they knew in their hearts that if the ring was still in the house it would have been found by now.

Eventually Theo went home and Maureen allowed herself a little weep over the ring before pulling herself together.

'Sorry, our Liza, this is hopeless. There's nowt to do but what I've already said.'

'You're right, Mum. And just because you've reported it stolen to the police, it doesn't mean it won't turn up. We'll still keep a lookout.'

'Thank you, love. Now, life must go on . . . I did manage to get in a bit of shopping from Mrs Davis between my searches. She kept looking at me in a queer way, like I'd got two heads or summat, and in the end I just had to say: "Mrs Davis, I can guess what you've heard and it's probably an exaggeration, but I shall be able to spend a little more with you this week. How about a couple of pieces of that nice ham and some very lean back bacon?" And of course she stopped staring then and got to it, so it's ham salad tonight, love, which I hope will suit.'

'It will, Mum. Thank you.'

Later that evening, as they sat knitting, reading and listening to the wireless, as they always had, Maureen cleared her throat a couple of times as if she were about to speak and then thought better of it.

'Mum?'

'It's nowt, love.'

'I wonder, could you be thinking the same as me?'

'Go on, Liza.'

'Well, it's odd how we've never been burgled in all these years until you inherited Miss Stevens's money. Yet you, me and Sylvia were the only ones who knew, and Mr Lambert, the solicitor, of course. And I don't think he'd have owt to gain and everything to lose by gossiping. Who'd have thought, seeing where we live, there'd be owt worth pinching? Yet the timing of the burglary suggests to me that mebbe someone knew about your good fortune, and thought your little house might hold summat it was worth breaking in for, even with the risk of being caught.'

'Oh, Liza, you're right. That's exactly what I'm thinking. And I just don't understand it at all.'

Their eyes met, their faces filled with anxiety. Who could possibly have known about Maureen's legacy *and* where she lived?

CHAPTER TEN

BARBARA'S WEEKDAY MORNINGS and early afternoons were largely given over to teaching adults to play the piano or practise elocution, children usually being at school then. This morning one of her piano pupils was an elderly man called Esmond Raygate-Galsworthy, which ridiculously unlikely name Barbara suspected he'd invented for himself. Not that she had any reason to sneer at invented names. Barbara Wilmot had believed you could call yourself whatever you wanted, and when she had gone for her first audition at the age of sixteen, she'd decided to reinvent herself with the name Barbara Hayle, and so she had remained.

Mr Raygate-Galsworthy claimed to have been born in a dressing room at the old Liverpool Empire Theatre, and he name-dropped continually about his theatrical connections. He came to The Manor not for tuition, but to enjoy playing Barbara's grand piano, and she in turn relished being paid for an hour of duetting with someone who could play well, even if he did wheeze like a bellows all the while, and gush heavy-handed compliments, which she mostly pretended she hadn't heard. She suspected that his mother had been the only woman ever in his life, but she didn't want to risk him wheezing any closer than the other end of the piano stool.

She had just seen him out with the very welcome receipt of an envelope containing payment for her time – the other good thing about Mr Raygate-Galsworthy being that he paid immediately and in cash – when she heard her telephone ringing in her little study where she did her paperwork.

There was time to answer it before the next client was due to arrive, but should she risk it? Of course, it could be someone wanting to book lessons, and the more pupils she had, the more money she made, which was an increasingly desperate necessity. On the other hand, it could equally be someone asking why they hadn't yet received payment for the maintenance on the car, the tuning of the piano, the fine stationery order, the painting of the front (but not the back) window frames of The Manor, sweeping the chimneys, the logs for the fire, even the sheet music that Barbara ordered for her pupils. These were just the outstanding bills she'd run up since returning from her recent holiday, in addition to the regular expense of her maintaining her blonde hair and replenishing her cosmetics. There was also an agreement with a wine merchant to pay in instalments for some rather special cases, which, absurdly, dated from when Marty was alive and the wine merchant had been 'a chum', and which was still continuing, despite the fact that Marty had been dead for two years and the wine had long ago been drunk. Barbara could not afford to drink wine at all these days. And, of overriding importance, and at the head of the lengthening queue to be paid, there was the loan from the bank, which had paid off numerous previous creditors who were now being replaced by these others. It really was too bad that these people couldn't just leave her alone, Barbara thought peevishly. She was beginning to run out of excuses to put them off.

Barbara even owed money to Mr Gathercole now, who had mowed the lawn and deadheaded the roses twice without being paid anything. Barbara knew this was risky, and she was breaking her own rule: she could not afford gossip to circulate in the village. If people knew the celebrated variety star was beginning to run up a debt with an elderly man who helped her out with her garden, then maybe she wouldn't command quite the respect she was used to.

The villagers of Buckledale had taken Barbara and Marty entirely at face value: they owned The Manor and drove a big car, therefore they were wealthy. And how else had they accumulated their fortune but by being the very best at what they did, as Marty and Barbara had hinted at often, in far-off theatres in thriving cities, where quite possibly no one from round here had ever been? If their fame had been achieved in London or Birmingham or Edinburgh, Buckledale felt privileged that the renowned theatricals had chosen to retreat to the peace of this pretty village to shelter from the relentless glare and fatigue of the bright lights. Barbara did not want anyone delving any deeper than what they had been told. And, as Barbara and Marty both knew, people, on the whole, really did believe exactly what they were told.

The telephone was still ringing. Better answer it. Whoever it was would only call again if she didn't, which was a nuisance during the lessons.

Barbara went into the little room, leaving the door open.

'Hello?'

She'd taken to answering without giving her name. Once or twice she'd pretended to be her own cleaning woman: 'Naw, Miss 'Ayle's away . . . summat in Town. I don't reckon she'll be back till the end of the month . . .'

'Barbara, is that you? It's Maureen. I was beginning to think you must be away.'

'Oh, Maureen. Oh, thank God it's only you.' The relief was real and intense for a moment.

'Heck, love, what's up? Is summat the matter?'

Barbara sank down onto the chair in front of her desk, whose surface was untidy with outstanding bills, her cheque book and scribbled calculations on the backs of envelopes, where she'd been trying to work out who to pay next and who would be paying her next and, most importantly, *when*. She put the envelope with Esmond Raygate-Galsworthy's money in it on top of her open diary.

'Oh, Maureen, I don't want to burden you with my problems, it's just that . . .' Barbara allowed her voice to break, just enough to imply she was being terribly brave.

'Babs? What is it? You're starting to worry me.'

'It's that show I think I told you about, Maureen – that starring guest role. Did I mention that it was all a bit in the balance, that it might not go ahead?'

'You did, and I've been thinking about you and hoping it'd all worked out after all. And now I've got my telephone put in and you're the very first person I'm calling. It's that exciting, just being able to call you from my own hallway and not have to go out and queue, and then feed in coins and press different buttons.'

'Good . . . good. I'm glad for you, Maureen. That's excellent news, but I'm afraid things are not nearly as rosy with me. The show is cancelled! Oh, Maureen, I don't know how I'm going to manage.'

'I'm right sorry to hear that. So disappointing for you, love. But chin up. You seem to have been doing just fine so far, from what you've told me. I'm sure it's only a temporary setback and you'll land a new role in no time.'

'If only it were so easy. You see, the show was cancelled while we were away on our little holiday – oh, didn't

173

we have a nice time together? I keep thinking about those lovely few days, and it worked so well that I'd got the car so I was able to take us all over the place – and my agent just can't seem to find anyone right now with a role for someone like me, as I think I mentioned to you: a *little* too old to play the heroine and much too young for the character parts or the crones.'

'That's a shame – too old, I mean. I know you had high hopes of this show.'

'Was *banking* on it, Maureen, *banking* on it. You see,' Barbara lowered her voice, became confidential, 'it costs quite a bit to keep everything going in a house this size, even the basic upkeep. I can't just close down the place and go and live in a hovel somewhere until my luck changes. I know I'm probably being a bit silly but I am very worried.'

'I can hear that, Barbara. A hovel indeed! I reckon you're getting things a little out of proportion. C'mon, love, pull yourself together and get thinking straight. Now, I did say, when you first talked about how worried you were, that I wouldn't let you sink or swim alone, didn't I?'

'Yes, I do remember you were kind enough to say that, now you mention it, Maureen.'

'Because I understand, I really do. It's hard for a woman alone. When my Jack died, I had no choice but to go out and do whatever it took to keep my girls in decent clothes and give them enough to eat. For a little while I was working at three different jobs, what with the home helping and the office cleaning and a little job I had in a hardware shop four afternoons a week . . . But then I'm not a clever person like you, with a talent for owt special. You don't want to be wasting that talent doing summat that's not your kind of thing.'

'Quite right . . .' Barbara said faintly.

'So, why don't I lend you a little bit to tide you over until your . . . your agent finds you a new part?'

'Oh, Maureen, I don't—'

'Now, I don't want to hear any protests, Barbara. It's nice to be in a position to help out a friend.'

'Maureen, you really are so kind,' said Barbara, sounding tearful while feeling relieved that she didn't have to remind Maureen of her earlier offer to help out.

'Don't cry, Babs. You *made* that little holiday, with your company and your kindness, and, as I say, it's nice for me to be able to do summat for you in return.'

'Thank you, Maureen. That is so generous. But what if I couldn't pay you back straight away? It would make me feel awful to be beholden, and you might need the money yourself.' *Better make sure she won't be breathing down my neck, nagging me for a swift repayment. The last thing I need is Maureen whingeing at me, in addition to all these others.*

'Oh, don't worry about that,' said Maureen, and Barbara could tell from her voice that she was smiling. 'I shan't lend you more than I can afford to, and then you can take your time and pay me whenever you are able. That way I shan't feel out of pocket and you won't be worried.'

Better and better. 'Dear Maureen . . .'

'Now, why don't we meet up and I'll write you a cheque? Shall I come to you or do you ever come into Blackburn? You are welcome here or we could go out to lunch – my treat, of course.'

'Yes . . . let's meet in Blackburn one day next week. I'll need to check my diary . . .'

'Of course, Barbara. Call me when you've done that. And try not to worry.'

'Thank you, thank you,' said Barbara, thinking that Maureen's proposal of lending 'a little bit to tide you over' was perhaps not the kind of sum that she really needed. She'd have to put some serious thought into this, decide what would be the most she could decently ask for now, and then soften Maureen up for further sums later, when she'd got used to the idea that Barbara lived on a rather grander scale than she did herself. It wouldn't do to reveal too quickly how bad things had become. Maureen might think she was profligate and foolish . . .

Barbara noted down Maureen's telephone number and then they said goodbye. Barbara realised immediately then that she'd forgotten to feign an interest in Maureen and her daughters, and how Maureen was getting on with her plans for reshaping her life. Ah well, Maureen was probably quite happy in her little house in Blackburn where she could let her neighbours in the street come round to use her new telephone.

The doorbell rang. As she went to answer it to Mrs Latham, who was slightly deaf and who liked to play everything very loudly and slowly, Barbara stopped momentarily to check her appearance in the hall mirror: perfectly styled curls, red lipstick, pale blue cashmere jumper tucked neatly into her narrow, tailored skirt. She passed the hall table, bending to smell the roses from the garden, which she had arranged elegantly in a cut-glass vase.

Then Miss Barbara Hayle fixed her professional smile in place and opened the front door to The Manor, her heart lighter at the thought of Maureen Bancroft's cheque.

At the end of the day Barbara made herself her dinner – a single soft-boiled egg and a piece of toast with a pot of weak tea – and when she'd eaten it at the vast kitchen table, she went outside to enjoy the long summer evening. It was June now, and the roses, which were a feature of her large garden, were glorious. She wondered vaguely whether she could open the garden to the public and charge people to come in to admire the beautiful blooms, but there would be all kinds of problems with having visitors, and Brendan was always nervous if he thought anyone could be catching sight of his store of junk. Since that evening when she'd returned from Somerton, Barbara had not found the outbuilding doors unlocked again, although she was always curious to see if she could get in.

Thinking of Brendan, she went across to the outbuildings now. She thought she'd heard a van that might be his earlier, but in the quiet countryside sound travelled far, which could be misleading. Sometimes she was aware of his comings and goings, but he didn't often come up to the house to say hello. He could be guarded and unsociable as well as awkward and sarcastic.

Of course, she inspected the doors on the buildings, and of course they were padlocked. But as she turned away, the low evening sun glinted on something on the gravel and she went over, searching, leaning her head this way and that to try to catch that sparkle again.

There!

She fixed her eyes on the position of the stones and knelt down to look. Caught in the gravel was something metal and shiny. Barbara carefully moved the dusty pieces aside and picked out a ring: what looked like tiny diamonds set in a circle to resemble an open flower. What on earth was it doing here? As far as Barbara was aware, no woman had any business along this drive, so it must belong to Brendan – perhaps it slipped out of a drawer in a load he'd been paid to remove from a house. Of course, this was exactly the kind of thing he hoped to find among the dross; the very reason that he did the job.

She wrapped the ring in her handkerchief and put it in the pocket of her jacket. It occurred to her then that if there was one piece of jewellery lying on the drive, there might be something else of worth that had fallen out of some piece of furniture as Brendan had unloaded it. She carefully searched the gravel, moving slowly, her eyes scanning the stones methodically. The sun was sinking all the time: less likely to catch the glint of a gem now. Well, she'd come and have another look tomorrow.

Back inside the house, Barbara went to the kitchen, unwrapped the ring on the table and examined it. Yes, those clear stones were almost certainly diamonds, although they were very small – just chips, really – and the gold band was thin and well worn, tiny scratches dulling its shine. Barbara imagined it was the kind of cheap ring that had once meant a lot to the woman to whom it had been given, but now she was dead it had been forgotten about by her relatives and put away in the back of a drawer. Still, it was a pretty little piece. She slipped it on her right hand and held it up to catch the overhead light. It fitted and would make a sweet little dress ring, a trifling embellishment that was nicer than a bare hand on the right occasion. It wasn't worth her taking it anywhere to sell.

As this thought passed through her mind, Barbara acknowledged she had never intended to return the ring to Brendan. Maybe there was other jewellery yet to be discovered in his latest load of second-hand furniture, but this ring had been lying on *her* drive and *she* was taking possession of it. Finders, keepers.

Just then a thud followed by a horrible squawking sound came from the drawing room, sudden, violent and eerie in the silence of the big house. Barbara leapt to her feet, her heart pounding, breathless with shock. What on earth could it be? It didn't sound human!

She grabbed the heaviest implement she could see at a glance, a hammer for tenderising meat, and tiptoed out into the hall and to the drawing-room door. She could hear a scrabbling, flapping sound and a raucous cry, very loud, repetitive and unsettling. She silently pushed open the door and peered nervously in, ready to flee if she had to.

A bird was lying in the hearth in a small scattering of soot, flapping one wing uselessly. The wretched creature must have fallen down the chimney. Was that possible? Thank goodness the chimney sweep had been recently, otherwise the mess might have been terrible.

Barbara approached slowly, then put the meat hammer down on the sofa. She didn't want to frighten the bird, which seemed to have broken its wing, in case it escaped from the hearth and spread soot over the carpet. She regarded the bird from a safe distance, wishing it would just shut up, and wondering what on earth she could do. It was probably a starling – they roosted in the trees along the edge of a nearby field – and it had a sharp-looking beak. Barbara paced up and down, observing it but trying to wish it away. Ugh, it was disgusting with its witchy purple-black feathers with a strange greenish sheen, like old black clothes. She couldn't just leave it here in the hope that it would vanish back up the chimney. That certainly wasn't going to happen. She'd have to do something.

Right . . . just deal with it and in three minutes it will all be over.

Barbara took an old newspaper from the log basket and unfolded it. Then she spread the whole paper over the injured bird, wrapped the sheets underneath and round to make a parcel, and raced through to the kitchen with it, the bird still emitting the occasional distress cry. It weighed surprisingly little and she'd wrapped it so tightly there was no chance of its escape. She had to put the bird parcel down to open the back door, but then she quickly took it up again and, holding it at arm's length, carried it outside at a sort of stooping run round to the back of the house, across the lawn and down to the rose beds beyond, as far as she dared. She didn't want to hold the horrid thing for any longer than necessary, what with the beak and the soot, and probably fleas or lice.

Quickly she laid it on the garden next to where Mr Gathercole had left a spade sticking out of the flower-bed like a grave-marker. Then she withdrew the spade from the soil, took a deep breath and hit the bird parcel as hard as she could with it. She gave it another blow to be sure, then stood back and gathered herself, breathing hard, her eyes on the newspaper, crumpled, the dreadful parcel flattened and silent.

But what to do now? Her hands flew to her hot face as she paced round. She couldn't open it, face what she had done and dig the murdered bird a grave.

Horrible bird. Horrid ugly thing. Serves it right for coming into my house.

In the end she decided on the coward's way out. Mr Gathercole would deal with the remains when he next came here. She grabbed an edge of the newspaper and dragged it upwards. Eventually the mangled body of the starling tipped out onto the earth, where she left it with just a fleeting glance of revulsion. Holding the newspaper away from herself between one finger and a thumb, Barbara quickly turned away and went round to the back door again, lifting the lid on the dustbin and depositing the grisly paper shroud inside.

Then she went back into the kitchen and scrubbed her hands. It was only then that she saw she was still wearing the ring, and she remembered she had already decided to keep it when the bird fell into the drawing room, almost as if the two events were connected. Now it was over, that whole incident seemed bizarre, almost like some receding bad dream.

Dusk was descending; she could see the sunset through the window, a narrowing red-gold line on the horizon. Barbara went to lock the doors before she went to bed. From the kitchen she could see three dark birds sitting on the wall. Perhaps they were starlings waiting for their friend, who would never join them again. She shivered, thinking of that sharp beak, that terrible insistent cry . . .

CHAPTER ELEVEN

T HE BELL ON the Short Cut door jangled merrily to admit a tall, youngish man with astonishingly bad hair. Eliza thought it was a shame he'd allowed it to get so untidy, as beneath the clumpy cut that he may have done himself several weeks ago, he had quite a striking face.

'Morning, sir,' said Harry. 'Theo and I are fully occupied at the moment. You're welcome to wait until we've finished,' he indicated the seats beside the door, 'or, if you'd prefer not to wait, Eliza, our junior, can cut your hair.'

Eliza now had a chair for her own clients, even though she was still learning, and she undertook her work under Harry and Theo's discreet direction. Despite floor space in the Short Cut being even tighter with the three barber's chairs, they were working well around each other.

The man eyed up Eliza, who was eyeing up his

appalling hair, and then glanced at his watch, which she saw was expensive-looking with a lot of pinkish gold, quite a surprise when the man himself was so scruffy.

'*Can* she cut hair?' he asked Harry.

'I wouldn't have offered her skills if she couldn't,' Harry replied matter-of-factly. 'Eliza, what do you think?'

'I reckon I could make you look very smart, sir,' Eliza said.

'Only I haven't got all morning while she faffs about.'

'We don't do faffing here,' said Eliza, not liking being treated by the man as if she were invisible. 'Would you like me to cut your hair, or would you prefer to wait for Harry or Theo?'

'Or maybe you'd like to go elsewhere?' suggested Theo mildly, not even looking up from his own work.

The scruffy man looked taken aback, perhaps that the slightly unlikely trio in this tiny barber's presented such a strongly bonded team.

'I'll risk it here,' he said, 'but if she messes up, I'll not be paying. Is that clear?'

'If you think you're getting away with a free cut just by complaining at the end you can think again,' said Harry. 'I'll be the judge of whether the cut is good enough. And I don't like my staff insulted, so if you'd like to address yourself to Eliza personally, you'll find she doesn't need an interpreter. Is *that* clear?'

The man didn't answer, but turned to Eliza then.

'Well, *Eliza*, I reckon I'll let you show me what you can do. God knows, I've tried every other barber hereabouts, and it's clear they're a bunch of idiots. I need this mess cut and it would be hard for you to make it look worse. I just didn't expect to find a pretty young girl working in a barber's, no insult intended.'

'Please sit down here, Mr . . .?'

'Wilmot.'

'. . . Wilmot, and you can tell me how you'd like it to look . . .'

The ill-mannered man made an effort to be chatty while Eliza was cutting his hair, but Eliza was soon wishing he'd just shut up and stop his awkward conversation. It turned out that he had a second-hand furniture shop a couple of streets away.

'If you've summat you want to be rid of, I'll be happy to take a look, see if I reckon it's worth owt,' he said. 'The Remove, my place is called, just the other side of Church Street.'

'Oh, yes . . .' said Eliza, concentrating, not really wanting to talk to this man who'd already shown himself capable of rudeness, and slightly nervous that – although she knew Harry would stand up for her, and indeed was quite prepared to fight her own battle – there might yet be an argument about paying at the end, which no one would want.

'And I've lots of stock. I'm sure I can do you a deal if you came by and summat took your fancy.' He winked at her.

'Thank you, but I don't need any furniture,' said Eliza. 'Now please can you lower your head a bit more . . .?'

'I'd have thought a pretty girl like you would be putting things aside for her bottom drawer,' said Wilmot.

'I've no need of that.'

'Got a boyfriend, then, Eliza?'

'I think that's a private matter, Mr Wilmot.'

'Is that a yes or a no, love?'

Theo beat both Eliza and Harry to responding.

'Miss Bancroft has many admirers, Mr Wilmot, and a few of them are in this room.' He stopped what he was doing and gave Wilmot a long look, as did his client, Mr Richards, who had known Eliza since she was a child. Wilmot looked away, only to meet, reflected in the mirror, the cold eyes of Harry and his client, another old fella with protective feelings towards the young woman he'd known for years. There was a moment of complete silence in which no one moved.

'Miss Bancroft . . . right . . .' Wilmot said quietly. 'I'll remember that.'

After that he sat back thoughtfully, as if reflecting on his behaviour, and the others chatted in their friendly way around him, Harry and Theo making a very deliberate point of including Eliza in their exchanges so that the bad-mannered man could either join in agreeably or be ignored.

Mr Richards got up to pay and leave, turning at the door with a friendly wave. 'See you at the Waterloo as usual next Wednesday, Theo and Eliza.'

'We'll look out for you, Mr Richards,' said Eliza, raising her scissors in farewell.

In the end Eliza made an excellent job of Wilmot's hair, cutting off plenty and restoring what remained to a neat style.

He paid without any fuss after all, tipped Eliza a decent but not generous amount, and left whistling and looking very pleased with himself.

It wasn't until they'd seen out the last of the customers at five o'clock that the barbers were able to revisit the subject of Mr Wilmot.

'I'm glad he paid up and left without any complaint,' said Eliza.

'Vile creep,' said Theo, with such venom that Eliza was taken aback. 'It's a wonder he's not scraping his knuckles on the ground.'

'Ah, c'mon, Theo,' said Harry. 'He was just a wide boy trying it on – with Eliza, who made it clear she was *deeply* unimpressed, and with me about the payment. We've all seen it before and I don't doubt we'll see it again.'

'Doesn't mean we have to put up with it, though, Harry,' Theo said crossly. 'That one comes in here again and I bag giving him a slow, very close shave with a cut-throat razor. Let's see how cocky he is then.'

'Oh, I think he got the message, Theo,' said Eliza. 'I expect he'll find somewhere else to have his hair cut another time. After all, there's no reason why he should come back here.'

'Well, let's hope he doesn't,' said Harry. 'We don't need his business.'

* * *

Maureen had to admit she'd been totally mistaken. She remembered telling Eliza that, as she'd worked all her adult life, she couldn't imagine what she'd do if she didn't go to work. Now she found so many things to do in a day, she couldn't believe she had ever thought time spent not working would be time wasted.

Take today, for instance. She'd been to several estate agents of the smarter kind and expressed an interest in their finding her a house with a garden. She didn't need anywhere *very* big, she told them, but she had other requirements, especially about the size and potential of the garden – she'd made a list and typed it out on the portable typewriter she'd bought herself – and she was a cash buyer.

The estate agents had all taken a lot of trouble to supply Maureen with details they hoped would interest her, and she'd taken away some of their literature to consider. Maureen was finding it easier these days to deal with the kind of people that she might once have found intimidating. That was a hidden bonus of Miss Stevens's legacy: she could afford to present herself as a woman of means and was quite prepared to walk away – in her own polite way, of course – if the goods or service did not meet her hopes and expectations. With her new-found confidence, she realised that these were just people doing their jobs, and there was no need to feel shy or as if she was a trouble to them.

At lunchtime Maureen met up with her old friend and colleague from Felbridge Brewery, Stella Martin, and they chatted together very happily over some delicious food in a café Maureen had found in Lord Street. Stella hinted, with a naughty twinkle in her eye, that the news of Maureen walking out on her job as Herbert Nicholson's secretary had spread around the brewery in no time – 'I wonder how that happened' – and Mr Felbridge himself had recommended Maureen's replacement: Miss Ramsbottom, a terrifying older woman who had formerly been a games mistress in a girls' school and did not allow Herbert to put a foot out of line.

'Actually, she's completely charming when you get to know her,' said Stella, 'and it's all a bit of a joke, but not one that Herbert's in on because he hasn't taken the trouble to show any interest in her as a person. No one likes him, and since everyone learned what a bully he is – if they ever had any doubts – he's pretty much ostracised by the rest of the workforce. Now he knows what it's like not to enjoy going to work. Personally, I think he'd be wise to find a job elsewhere. I might even suggest that to Mr Felbridge if I hear Herbert's been making any complaints.'

'Stella, you are brilliant,' Maureen said, chuckling. 'I honestly think you just about run that brewery all by yourself. Now, let me pay for these lunches. You were always so kind when I was feeling down, and it's a pleasure to see you and hear your news and how things are at work.'

'Well, that's very generous of you, Maureen. But are you sure?'

'Of course, Stella.'

Maureen had explained her new situation in life as 'having a little bit of luck', and she was happy to treat her friends without making a big show of it or making them feel uncomfortable.

As they got ready to leave, Stella asked Maureen whether she would like to go to a classical concert with her.

'I'll go with you if you want someone to go with, Stella, but I have to say it's not really my thing. I'm fonder of the Light Programme than the Third.'

'No, well, we all have our own tastes. I did wonder whether I might ask Mr Felbridge, who I know likes orchestral music, if he'd like to go. What do you think? Would it seem . . . inappropriate?'

'Mm, I know what you mean, love. You'll have to play it by ear. It might be that he would love to go to a concert but he hasn't got anyone to go with, Mrs Felbridge being dead these last ten years, I understand. Mebbe *he'd* like to ask *you* and he thinks *that* would be inappropriate.'

'I hadn't thought of that possibility. Oh dear, it's all so complicated.'

'Or you could pretend you have a spare ticket because you've been let down at the last minute and you can just mention this in a casual fashion – check his diary first and make sure it's a day you know he's free – and then if he wants to go with you, he might offer to take up the ticket. If he doesn't want to go, he won't; he'll just say, "That's bad luck," or summat.'

'Heavens, Maureen, you are clever. I hadn't thought of that. It would be worth getting a second ticket just in case. I'll make sure it's a popular programme so there's a good chance I can return it if Mr Felbridge doesn't want to go with me.'

'Let me know how you go on, Stella, love.'

They parted with promises to meet again soon.

Then Maureen took her estate agents' details with her to Corporation Park, where she sat on a bench in the Italian Garden and enjoyed the summer weather while reading through them. What luxury it was to have the time to sit in this beautiful garden. Perhaps one day she'd have a garden of her own – perhaps quite soon. A couple of the house details looked worth pursuing. She'd ask Eliza and Sylvia what they thought . . .

It was especially important to consult Eliza about the new house because there was, Maureen thought, a strong possibility that Eliza would be living there, too. Maureen was thinking about a place big enough for the two of them to live together but each to have her own space, so that Eliza could have her friends round and not feel they were encroaching on her mother.

Of course, there was always the chance that Eliza would marry . . . would marry quite soon . . . Would marry Theo?

That made Maureen stop to think. They were very good friends, quite clearly enormously fond of each other, and Theo was such a dear man. He was quite a bit older than Eliza, though.

What are you thinking, Maureen? He's more than twice her age!

It was easy to forget that, because Theo had such a youthful way with him, and certainly Eliza herself didn't seem at all concerned about the difference in their ages. But it was quite a lot of years, which meant that by the time Eliza was in her forties, Theo would be old. Oh dear, Maureen thought, she would not wish on any woman the terrible sadness of widowhood . . . There were so many women soldiering on alone because of the war or because their husbands had succumbed to ill health, as her own Jack had done, and as Barbara's Marty had, that it seemed rash to choose deliberately to take this path, especially when Eliza herself was only twenty.

Thinking of Barbara, Maureen wondered when she'd hear from her. Barbara had said she'd look in her diary and let her know when she could come to Blackburn, although Maureen thought as Barbara was semi-retired and currently unemployed, possibly her diary wasn't packed with engagements. How did Barbara spend her time all day at The Manor? She'd mentioned having a garden, so perhaps she pottered around in it, tidying her flowerbeds and listening to the birds singing, when she wasn't being asked to do guest appearances in variety shows or take the lead in an amusing play. What a wonderful life that sounded.

As Barbara had made such a success of her theatrical career, it was likely that she was only strapped for cash in the short term. Maureen didn't want to insult her by offering her a large loan as if she thought Barbara was in serious financial difficulties – as if she thought she had mishandled her affairs and was feckless with her spending. After all, with her lovely car and elegant clothes, Barbara was obviously doing fine. This was just a minor setback, which Maureen would be very pleased to be able to resolve with a cheque.

Barbara's telephone rang just as she was seeing out her final pupil of the day. It was late afternoon and she was tired and in low spirits.

Should she answer the phone? There were still all those people she really wished to avoid speaking to. As ever, she decided it was no use hiding; they'd only ring back.

'Hello?'

'Barbara?'

'Enid? Is that you?' Barbara's heart sank. She'd almost rather field a call about an unpaid bill than speak to Enid, who didn't telephone often but when she did it was usually to nag her about something to do with their batty, cankerous mother. Enid could be short-tempered and self-righteous, and she seemed unable to understand that Barbara was simply not interested in dealing with their mother. If Enid wanted something done for Annie, then she could jolly well do it herself.

'So long since we spoke you've forgotten what I sound like? I'm ringing about Mum.'

Barbara sighed loudly and impatiently. 'What's the matter with her now?'

'Nowt, I hope, though she's looking older these days.'

'Well, she *is* old. So . . . are you going to tell me or do I have to guess?'

'What? Oh, yes, Mum wants to see you.'

'Well, I'm not especially keen to see her. I don't want to have to go all the way to Blackburn when I don't even know what I'm going for, do I, Enid? I'm a very busy woman.'

There was a moment of silence in which Barbara's younger sister had clearly gathered herself because she came back stronger.

'You're a very selfish woman, Barbara, I know that much. Mum wants to see you and I think you should go. She's an old lady and you haven't visited her for ages. It's not that far for you to go, and I reckon you could just make the effort, after all she's done for you, and behave like a proper daughter to poor Mum. Mebbe you can spare her an hour or two of your precious time? Is that too much to ask?'

'Goodness, Enid, so fierce . . .'

'Well?'

Barbara had decided to cancel her lessons the following Tuesday to go to meet Maureen, so it seemed silly not to combine this with a quick visit to her mother since Enid was so insistent. Then, she hoped, Enid would be satisfied and not bother her for a while.

'All right, then. It just so happens that I am about

to arrange to see someone else in Blackburn on Tuesday next week, so it won't be too much of a bother to see Mum before that. I'll be there at eleven o'clock.'

'I'll tell Mum to expect you, Barbara,' Enid said drily. 'Mebbe she'll *bother* to make you a pot of tea.'

'Will you be there?'

'Don't be daft. I'll be at work. You'll have to deal with Mum yourself.'

'Well, that's a relief anyway. I'd rather avoid facing two harridans.'

'Goodbye, Barbara,' Enid said, annoyingly cool, and put the phone down, leaving Barbara without the last word she so wanted.

Well, I can't avoid going to see Mum for ever, can I? Though I suppose I could . . . It's probably something and nothing. Perhaps she just wants a fresh face to be nasty to. At least that cat Enid won't be there.

Barbara wrote 'Mum, 11 o'clock' in her diary for the following Tuesday, above where she'd pencilled 'Maureen?' Her bad mood had not been improved by the conversation with Enid and she threw her pen down carelessly onto the desk. A splash of ink shot out onto the top sheet of the pile of bills, and she hastily reached for some blotting paper to mop it up. It was very irksome that the tiniest spill of ink could get onto so many things, horrible little spots of black over everything on the desk, and now, she noticed, on the sleeve of her favourite blouse, too. This was all Enid's fault . . .

CHAPTER TWELVE

Today was not an occasion for the car. Barbara took the bus to Whalley, from where she caught the train to Blackburn. From Blackburn station she decided to walk to her mother's house. The weather was fine and she had come suitably dressed – which meant nothing showy or too stylish. Mum could be unkind, even spiteful. She liked to accuse Barbara of getting above herself.

Barbara set off like a woman on a mission to get the morning visit over and done with. Eventually she reached her childhood home in the modest residential street of terraced houses, not far from where Enid lived, where her mother now lived alone. It was an uphill walk to number 52, the front door painted black, but dull and grubby. Barbara had her own key; after a couple of attempts she managed to turn it in the lock and get the door open. Had no one thought of oiling the lock?

'Mum? Mum, it's Barbara.'

'In here.'

Goodness, she'd developed an old person's voice, querulous and weak, so unattractive. Barbara went down the narrow passage, scuff marks on the skirting board and the wallpaper beginning to peel at the top, to the room at the back, dreading to think what she would find.

There was a smoky coal fire in the grate and the room was hot and stuffy. Her mother was sitting in a sagging armchair, which Barbara remembered had once been covered in pink moquette but which was now beige with fade and grubbiness. She was surrounded by dog-eared piles of cheap weekly magazines, old newspapers, used tea mugs, some knitting in a lurid shade of pink – it looked like a baby garment – and with hideous orna-ments of cute children and kittens, ugly vases of thick pottery and moulded glass on the table, the shelves, the windowsill. The window at the back was covered with a yellowed net curtain and, in the dim light it allowed, Barbara saw everything in the room looked dirty and was covered in a thin layer of dust.

She half expected to see her mother was dusty, too, but she was just old and frail-looking, her clothes ill-fitting and creased, smelling of old age and liniment. She looked thinner than when Barbara had last seen her, except for her ankles, which were puffy, the worn slippers on her feet misshapen and broken down under the strain of her swollen feet.

Barbara had thought she would just breeze in, see what her mother wanted, field the inevitable criticism and insults, then breeze out again to go to meet Maureen and forget all about the horrible morning visit. Now she saw it would not be so easy to do that. What was Enid thinking, letting their mother live like this? Annie was Enid's responsibility! On the other hand, Annie Wilmot had never been a neat or tidy person and her home had always been a showcase for her state of mind and everything that was happening in her chaotic life. Maybe she even liked living like that, felt comfortable with it. Any tidying and cleaning she had ever done had almost immediately become a waste of time, Barbara remembered. Enid, with her job, a husband who was apparently a bit of a handful, and three children to cope with, had probably thought not to spend too much of her time here. Barbara certainly didn't want to.

'Hello, Mum. Are you all right? You look a bit peaky, what I can see of you in this dimness.'

'Don't go messing with them nets, Barbara. You know we're overlooked and I don't like folk looking in. I'm all right. Just getting old, that's all. Are you going to make me a cup of tea?'

Barbara smiled ironically. 'May I have one as well?'

Annie grinned in return, showing grubby, uneven teeth with gaps Barbara thought had not been there the last time she'd seen her mother. 'You can if you make it.'

'All right, I'll go and do that. Enid telephoned me and said you wanted to see me.'

'I'd have thought it wasn't necessary for me to ask you to visit, especially after all this time. Most daughters don't need a summons or an invitation to see their mothers.'

'Don't start, Mum. You know what I mean. You're not dying, are you?'

A sly look came over Annie's aged face. 'I might be.'

'Well, if you can hold off death until you've told me what this is all about, I'd be very grateful,' said Barbara.

'I'm sure you would be,' muttered Annie. 'Can you go and make me a cup of tea?'

Barbara noted the request was made as if her mother had forgotten she'd already asked, but she didn't say anything.

She braved the kitchen, where it was, thankfully, a little cooler, and spotted the kettle, its outside splashed with dried-on food deposits. Every surface in the kitchen was covered in crumbs, unwashed dishes, crockery yet to be put away, lists on scraps of paper in a deteriorated version of Annie's handwriting, shaky and laboured . . . The sink was filled with cold, dirty water, like a contaminated pond. There was grease clinging to the top of the stove, and the windows were opaque with smears of fat and dirt.

Barbara tried to avoid any part of herself touching any part of the kitchen furniture. She wished she had some oversleeves to protect her fine cardigan, and when she looked for an apron and found one hanging on the back of the door, stiff with ancient stains, she decided her clothes would remain cleaner if she didn't wear it.

She found two cups and saucers that didn't look completely unwashed, brewed a pot of tea – having first rinsed away a stale brew with a film on top of it – and found the milk in the larder under a beaded doily to keep the flies off it. It didn't smell very fresh but it was all there was.

She took the cups of tea through to the back room. Annie had not moved from her seat. Barbara put the cups and saucers down on top of a pile of magazines and looked around to see if there was anywhere clean to sit down.

'What's the matter?' said Annie. 'Too grand to sit in your own mother's living room now, are you?'

'Mum, what's happened? It's not very clean, is it? It never used to be quite *this* bad.'

'What do you mean? It's not mucky. I do my best. You wait until you're my age, then you'll see it's not so easy to put on airs and graces.'

'Even so—'

'Even so nothing, Barbara. Now, are you going to stand there like Lady Muck, looking down on me and making out you're too dainty in your ways for a cup of tea in your own mother's house, or are you going to sit down and listen to what I've got to say?'

Barbara moved a pile of newspapers off the sofa and onto the floor, then brushed a couple of woodlice, which had been hiding underneath the papers, from the seat. Then she sat down, thinking she'd have to have a bath and put all her clothes to wash when she got home.

'All right, Mum, please tell me what you wanted to see me about.'

'Brendan.'

Barbara took a long breath. On the few occasions she'd seen her mother in her adult life, Brendan was a subject that always came up. That was inevitable, Barbara supposed, though, heaven knew, she'd seen more of Brendan in these last few years than before. Wasn't that enough? Brendan was old enough now to take responsibility for himself, and he really shouldn't be worrying his mother.

'What's he been up to that you ask me to come all this way to discuss it? Couldn't you have gone round to Enid's and used her telephone to call me?'

'No,' said Annie, 'because I reckoned if you made the effort to come here for once in your life, you wouldn't then just ignore what I said. If I telephoned from Enid's it would be all, "Yes, all right, Mum,"' – Annie put on what she thought was an impression of Barbara's cut-glass accent – 'and then you'd just forget that we'd ever spoken and I'd asked you to do summat. Even though I hardly ever ask owt of you. Well, it's about time you started doing summat for me. And you know why, my lady.'

'Yes, all right, Mum.'

Annie smirked.

'So are you going to tell me what's the matter with Brendan, Mum?' asked Barbara.

'I reckon he's turning into a bad 'un.'

'Oh, for goodness' sake, this is hardly news. Brendan's always been a wide boy, one for a bit of the dodgy deal. He's a chancer, hoping for a lucky break with every house he clears. If people are silly enough to pay him what he asks to take away their junk without sorting through it first, then that's their lookout.'

'If he doesn't watch it, I reckon he's going to get in some serious trouble, one way or another.'

Barbara didn't want to hear this. Brendan was his own man – he was well into his twenties now – and he wouldn't be taking the slightest bit of notice of what she or anyone else advised him to do. Better Annie just saved her breath and let Barbara leave and go to meet Maureen.

She sighed. 'Mum, he's a grown-up. He's not a child who's misbehaved in class and needs the back of his legs slapping.'

Annie looked cross. 'Don't you do that sighing and long-suffering thing with me, Barbara. I think you ought to make an effort with him. He doesn't listen to me any longer. He thinks I'm just a poor old woman who's getting a bit soft in the head. He doesn't know what I've heard.'

'What have you heard?' asked Barbara, wishing she could just leave now. She really, really didn't want to have to deal with any trouble Brendan was heading towards. Nor did she want to be here reassuring her mother about some half-misunderstood gossip. How could Annie have heard anything worth hearing anyway?

'This house-clearance business, it's not always folk who *want* their stuff removed, if you get my meaning.'

Ah . . . so not nothing, then.

'Oh, come now, Mum. He's got a shop behind Church Street where he sells on the junk he clears. If it wasn't legitimate, he'd be found out straight away. Anyone could go in and spot their goods if he's taken them without permission or purchasing them, and then they'd call the police and the game would be up in no time.'

Annie, instead of answering, ignored Barbara's attempt at playing down the whole business, and drank down her tea in a long series of gulps, dripping some down the side of her cup and onto her pinafore.

Is she actually doing this on purpose? Oh, gosh, but this room is hot and stuffy. If I don't leave in the next five minutes, I'll start to smell like it does in here!

'Never mind the tea, Mum, tell me who told you all this about Brendan. How can you possibly know anything when you hardly ever leave the house?'

'You know nowt about me, Barbara. How can you when you're never here?'

Barbara saw she was now on the back foot and her chance of leaving at any moment was decreasing.

'Yes, all right, Mum.'

'Come round here, telling me this and that, as if you

know anything at all,' Annie said as if Barbara hadn't spoken, holding out her empty cup, leaving the saucer on top of the magazines, 'and turning your nose up. Thankless hussy! Yes, I saw the way you looked at my room . . . the way you look at me.'

Barbara took the cup, reached for its saucer and went to the kitchen to pour another, breathing hard. Probably it was the heat in the room, but she felt a little light-headed. If she didn't get out of here soon, she'd probably faint, and she dreaded the thought of making contact with her mother's living-room carpet.

She came back in with the tea and put it down in front of Annie.

'Right, Mum, just tell me why you think Brendan's heading for trouble.'

'Well, it's my friend Mary who told me.'

'Mary? Who's Mary?'

'My friend. Her that I see at the shop.'

'Please, Mum, for the love of God will you just tell me what your friend Mary told you about Brendan?'

'There's no need to take that tone, Barbara. She said that she thought Brendan might be getting himself into trouble.'

'And how does she know this?' Barbara ground out.

'Because her granddaughter told her. Her granddaughter said to Mary as she thought our Brendan might be handling some things that weren't legal.'

'Is that it?'

'It's what she said.'

What a lot of nonsense, just a cock-and-bull tale to get me to come here. What on earth could Mum's friend Mary know about Brendan?

'Right . . . well, thank you for telling me, Mum. I shall speak to Brendan, don't you worry. And now I think I need to get out . . . go . . . I've got someone else to see.'

'What? Already? But you've only just got here.'

'There's more tea in the pot if you want it, Mum.' Barbara stood up and brushed down the back of her skirt. She felt clammy with sweat, and the oppressive, stale, sooty smell of the room was making her desperate to leave. She picked up her handbag and looked around to make sure there was absolutely nothing else of hers here. She would not want to come back to collect it, if so.

'Bye, Mum. Thanks for the tea. Don't worry about Brendan; I'll speak to him. You take care now . . .' She waved herself out of the room, practically ran to the front door and burst out into the street, slamming the door behind her.

Oh God, but that had been like a vision of hell: the heat, the mess, the smell, the ghastly vision of creeping decrepitude that her mother had become. The memories evoked that neither of them could ever leave behind . . . Barbara leaned back against the house wall for a moment, her eyes closed, breathing deeply the comparatively fresh air.

'You all right, love?'

206

It was an old lady leaning out of the front door of the house next door. Barbara didn't remember ever seeing her before. Her hair was in curlers under a gauzy headscarf, and she was dressed in a crossover pinafore just like Annie's and a pair of blue carpet slippers with nylon fur trimming.

'Yes . . . thank you. Yes, I'm quite well, thank you,' said Barbara, swallowing down threatening nausea. 'Just a little . . . overheated.'

'Can I get you owt, love? A glass of water?'

Barbara longed to say yes. The woman looked kindly, but she was Annie's next-door neighbour, and Barbara knew she could not withstand any questioning about herself and her mother, never mind any censure.

'No, thank you. No, I'm just going. I'm fine, thank you,' gasped Barbara, and left at the quickest walk she could manage.

She looked at her watch when she had put a couple of road-lengths between herself and her mother. She had almost an hour before she was due to meet Maureen in Lord Street. She'd wander in the direction of the park, perhaps find the conveniences and wash her hands in cool water, then walk among the beautiful gardens and try to think calm thoughts.

'Barbara, it's lovely to see you,' said Maureen, standing up from the café table to lean over and kiss Barbara's cheek. 'Oh, but are you all right, love? You do look a bit peaky.'

Sinking down onto the chair next to Maureen, Barbara remembered this was the very thing she had said to her mother. The word 'peaky' did not conjure a flattering image, and Barbara was used to being told she looked amazing. After even such a short time in her mother's house, however, she didn't feel amazing at all.

Alarmingly, she felt her composure start to slip. The awful experience of the visit this morning had affected her more than she'd realised. She took a couple of deep breaths.

'A glass of water, perhaps?' suggested Maureen, immediately summoning a waitress confidently and asking for a jug of water. When it appeared, she quickly poured a glass for Barbara.

'Here you are, Babs. Sip it slowly . . . take your time.'

Barbara did as she was advised and soon felt better. It was then that she noticed Maureen was looking pretty, with her hair done beautifully, and she was wearing one of the dresses Barbara had helped her choose from Crosby's, in Somerton-on-Sea, but with a pretty little jacket that Barbara didn't recognise from their shopping expedition.

'Mebbe you need summat to eat?' suggested Maureen. 'I never think you eat enough, Barbara. That can make you feel faint.'

'No, it isn't a lack of food,' said Barbara. 'I've just been to see my mother and, quite frankly, she's the limit, she really is.'

'Oh dear. Does she still live in the same house as she did when we were little?'

'That's right, Avery Street, but it's worse than ever now.'

'How's that, love? Haven't your brothers and sisters moved on by this time? I remember it was full of folk and their stuff, but I can't think there's so many living there now.'

'Yes, only the younger ones, Enid and Brendan, are still in Blackburn, and they don't live there, although they are close by. Mum's by herself. No, it's the way she lives, all the mess. She was always untidy, but it's as if she never throws anything away. The air was so stale . . . I don't think a window has been opened for years, and the room was very hot. I think Mum's getting forgetful, too, which doesn't help the social situation. It's really very trying.'

'That's a shame. Forgetfulness is one of the drawbacks of old age for some, of course, and I reckon it can't be helped, but what about the mess? It sounds to me like your poor mother can't manage any longer. She probably doesn't really want to live in a mess, but it's easier than having to bother with it when she's old and frail, do you think? She has to put up with it and perhaps pretend she doesn't mind because it's how it has to be. She probably needs a bit of help, someone to clean and tidy round for her.'

'Well, it isn't for me to have to bother with it,' snapped Barbara, at the end of her tether now Maureen was showing so much sympathy with Annie. 'I can't be coming all this way to see about my mother's mess. Enid lives nearby – it was her that phoned me and told me Mum wanted to see me – and she could help Mum clean and tidy. Enid's got teenage children, too. She could ask them to lend a hand. I wouldn't expect Brendan to do anything to help, of course. He couldn't even put out my vase of spent flowers when I was on holiday.'

Maureen looked very disappointed, far more saddened than even Barbara felt a vase of dead flowers warranted. For a moment Barbara wondered if Maureen was disappointed in her, but it was patently unreasonable to think she could be there to clean her mother's house when she lived miles away in Buckledale.

'Well, that's men, I suppose,' Maureen said. 'They quite often seem not to notice when summat needs squaring up or cleaning. You have to explain it. My Jack was always a help in the end, but I had to do the explaining first.'

'I don't think for one moment Brendan would be round at Mum's with the carpet sweeper out if I *explained* about the mess,' said Barbara, looking genuinely amused.

'Mm . . . Right, Barbara, you're looking loads better, so shall we have a bite to eat? I think that young waitress is ready to take our order . . .'

When they had chosen their food, Maureen excitedly told Barbara about how she was thinking of moving

house and the kind of place she was looking for.
Barbara couldn't imagine that Mousy Maureen would
ever make such a big change, the woman was so suited
to her modest Blackburn terrace, but she hid her
scepticism and made all the right noises. Then the
conversation moved to Maureen's daughters, which
didn't interest Barbara at all, and then somehow
turned back to Annie and her mess. Barbara suspected
that Maureen's years as a cleaner gave her an interest
in other people's dirty houses.

'I've got a bit of an idea,' said Maureen, after they
had declined to order puddings but had asked for a
pot of tea. 'Please, might I have your Enid's telephone
number? Would you mind, love?'

'No, of course not,' said Barbara, thankful that
Maureen would be the one calling Enid to suggest that
she should go round to their mother's with some
scouring powder and a mop. Good luck with that: Enid
took after Annie in temper, though not untidiness. Still,
it was up to Maureen. Barbara was keeping well out of
it. Maureen would encounter Enid's impatience and
rudeness and she'd soon realise why Barbara kept a
distance. And if she braved Annie's house herself, she'd
encounter another ill-tempered and embittered
harridan and she'd quickly dismiss anything Annie told
her as the ramblings of a batty old woman – and not
a very nice one, at that. She had to look Enid's number
up in the back of her pocket diary and Maureen wrote
it down, also noting Enid's married name of Cawley.

The tea came and Barbara wondered when Maureen would get round to the point of the meeting, which was to write her a cheque. She'd thought carefully about how much to ask for, and had calculated a margin that allowed her to pay the instalments due on the loan for a couple of months, plus her immediate bills, including the painter, the piano tuner and Mr Gathercole (the wine merchant could wait), and leave enough for some stockings and a new hat for autumn. A new hat did a lot for an old coat, and the coat was plain enough to allow a completely different look with new accessories . . .

Barbara realised her mind had been wandering.

'Sorry, Maureen, what was it you said?'

'I was saying it's so nice to see you. We've had such an interesting chat that I nearly forgot why we were meeting up. I think my mind is so full of ideas these days that it's hard to hold them all in. Anyway, I've written you a cheque, Barbara, and I don't want you to think you have to hurry to pay it back. Like I said the other day, I'm not lending you owt I can't afford so you just take your time. I know myself how a short-fall one week can seem like the end of the world.'

One week? What is she talking about?

Maureen discreetly passed an envelope across the table to Barbara. It had her name written neatly on the front, but the envelope itself was of inferior size and quality. Obviously, Maureen was using up her Woolworths stationery. Barbara only hoped the cheque wasn't of inferior size, too. Hadn't they been going to discuss a sum between them? Maybe she just thought they had. Now she came to consider, she couldn't quite remember what Maureen had said. Still, she could hardly open negotiations now, nor rip open the envelope at the table and examine the cheque.

There was nothing for it: she had to accept it graciously and just hope it was something like the amount she needed.

They said their goodbyes and Maureen thanked Barbara for meeting her and also for Enid's telephone number, which made Barbara smile. Maureen would soon see the irony of that! Then Maureen went off, presumably to her little house in Mafeking Street, and Barbara walked towards the station and the train to Whalley.

As soon as she was sitting in the second-class carriage, Barbara tore open the envelope Maureen had given her and drew out the cheque.

It was for fifty pounds.

Barbara felt she could cry with disappointment. What on earth had Maureen been thinking? This wouldn't meet all the unpaid bills on top of the loan, never mind leave enough for some nice new autumn clothes.

The answer, Barbara knew only too well, was that Maureen had been thinking exactly what Barbara had told her: that she was a fabulous success who had semi-retired in some splendour, and was short of funds because one guest appearance in a show – of which she was offered many and could afford to pick and choose – had been cancelled. It was absolutely maddening, but of course Mousy Maureen would never make the grand gesture or see the bigger picture unless it was presented to her with a sign and flashing lights. Maureen had got this so very wrong because she was a small-minded, mean and stupid woman, but it was very, very disappointing.

The question was, what to do now? Just how much should she tell Maureen?

CHAPTER THIRTEEN

ALTHOUGH BARBARA HADN'T mentioned whether or not Enid Cawley had a job, Maureen thought she might well be working, which would explain why she hadn't the time to sort out her mother's house. She decided to telephone Enid early the following morning, in the hope of catching her before she went to work.

'Good morning, is that Enid? My name is Maureen Bancroft, but you may remember me as Maureen Stubbs, a friend of Barbara's years ago. I saw Barbara yesterday, she mentioned you and I asked her for your telephone number.'

'Oh, yes . . . yes, I do remember you, Maureen. Heavens, that's going back a bit. You used to come round to ours sometimes, although Barbara mostly preferred to go to your house.'

'Well, it's about your house – where your mum lives – that I'm calling, Enid. I do hope that you won't think

I'm interfering, but Barbara said your mum still lives in the old place – Avery Street – and she . . . well, she could probably do with a hand to keep the house straight.'

There was a pause and Maureen hoped she hadn't caused offence.

'Mm, so Barbara suggested you call me and tell me my mum needs a hand, did she?'

'No, no, not at all! I wouldn't dream of telling you what to do. Oh dear, what must you think of me? No, I gather that you're busy, with a family and mebbe a job . . .?'

'I'm about to set off to go to it.'

'. . . and I don't have to . . . that is, I don't work at the moment and have time to spare, and also I used to be a cleaner, and I thought mebbe, if it was all right with you, and you thought your mum wouldn't mind, I could go and see her and give her a hand getting the place straight.' Maureen realised she was gabbling but she was determined that Enid shouldn't think she was instructing *her* on how to look after her mother.

'And why would you do that?' asked Enid. 'You'll know Barbara never lifts a finger – she's far too grand – and it's a bit rich her expecting folk who aren't even family to help Mum when Barbara herself can't be bothered. I remember she used to boss you around a bit when we were younger. If she's bossed you into this now, you won't want to do it. It'll be quite a big job, and although Mum's mellowed with age, she's still not easy to deal with.'

'It's kind of you to warn me, Enid, but I haven't been

bossed into anything. It was me that suggested it, not Barbara. I just thought it'd be summat I could manage, what with having the time and knowing about cleaning. Just to help out, as I knew your mother years ago.'

'All right,' said Enid cautiously. 'Used to be a cleaner, you say?'

'Private houses and offices, for years. I've seen all sorts. I don't suppose your mother's house will be the worst I've come across.'

'But how much do you charge?'

'Ah, Enid, love, I'm not taking on your mother's house week in, week out. I'll make a few visits, if you agree and if she doesn't mind, and just help her to get straight. Once she's back on track it'll be far easier for her to cope. I won't expect to be paid for that.'

'Out of the goodness of your heart?' asked Enid, as if she couldn't believe this could possibly be true.

'Well, I have the time and I sort of understood from what Barbara was saying that all the responsibility fell on your shoulders and you already had enough to do. There's no catch, Enid. It's a genuine offer of a bit of help, nothing more.'

'Well, put like that, how could I refuse, Maureen? It's right good of you. Let me have a word with Mum and see how she takes the idea.'

Eliza pulled her frock over her head and performed the slightly awkward manoeuvre of poking her right arm through the armhole, then zipping the fitted bodice up at the side on the left. Time and again Maureen had offered to buy her a smart new dress to wear while she and Theo sang at the Waterloo, but Eliza, though tempted, had put a lot of work into making over this second-hand dress and was fond of it. Besides, Theo had said she looked good in it.

When Eliza had applied her makeup and combed her hair, she went downstairs to collect Maureen, who was in the sitting room, looking at the latest batch of details of houses for sale.

'Oh, I don't know, Liza,' she sighed, putting a heap of papers on the table next to her chair, 'the choice is massive and there are more in the post every day. It's almost like a full-time job just going through, ditching the bad 'uns and the ones that aren't where I might want to live. I think it would be easier just to stop here. At least I know I like the neighbours.'

'Why wouldn't you find new neighbours you like equally well? You wouldn't stop being friends with Louisa and Ted and the Mulligans just 'cos you've moved, so then you'd have even more friends.'

Maureen smiled. 'That's a good way of looking at it,' she said.

'And you don't have to move if you'd really prefer to stay here, but you have been talking about wanting a garden for years, and now you have the chance to get one. I wonder, if you didn't move house, whether later, when you're old and mebbe not up to it, you might wish you'd done it when you could.'

'I've been thinking the same. And I've never really been one not to do summat just because it was a bother. I'll put the best of these to one side for you to look through and see what you think.'

'Thanks, Mum. The good thing is that you can take your time until you see exactly what you want. There's no hurry, like a job or a school to fit in with.'

'What about your job, Liza? If I found the perfect house but it was a distance from the Short Cut, would you want to come with me and mebbe work elsewhere?'

'If it is the perfect house for you, Mum, I'd be glad you'd found it. I'd have to have a think, though. I'd be sorry to leave the Short Cut, that's for sure, but nothing lasts for ever, does it? Or I could stop here, take over the rent of this place.'

'I wouldn't want to derail your life, though, love.'

'I'm not worried that you will. I expect we'll always find a way forward, Mum. No reason to think things won't be as good, or better.'

Maureen looked at her daughter. She had the optimism of youth, yet she sounded so level-headed. Sometimes it was hard to remember that Eliza was only twenty.

'How did I ever get to have such a good girl?'

'Because you're the best mother in the world.'

'Go on with you . . .'

They gathered their bags and cardigans and set out into the light evening.

'I spoke to someone on the phone today, love,' said

Maureen as they walked towards the pub. 'Enid Cawley, she's called. She's Barbara Hayle's younger sister.'

'Goodness, I didn't know Barbara had a sister, but then why would I?'

'She has at least one older one as well, I think. I can't quite remember, but there are several brothers and sisters. Anyway, when I saw Barbara for lunch yesterday, she gave me Enid's number and I phoned her. We knew each other slightly a long time ago, of course, although it was Barbara I was friends with. I don't know if I'd even recognise Enid now. It seems their mother, Annie, is getting old and finding it difficult to manage – you know, keep her place looking nice. Barbara isn't interested in helping, or is too busy. Enid sounded a bit fed up about Barbara because she herself has a family and a job and very little time to do what she must, never mind take on her mother's house as well. But she was perfectly friendly with me once she understood why I was calling.'

'Is that what you phoned her about, Mum? Her mother's house?'

'I wondered if I could help Annie, if she's struggling a bit. I wouldn't want to interfere, but it sounds as if she needs someone to tidy her house up, get her back on track, and mebbe get her shopping in.'

'That could be a lot of work, Mum, and she's not your family. I take it she lives in Blackburn.'

'She does, and not too far from here. I can see that for Barbara, out in Buckledale, it wouldn't be easy to pop in, even if she wanted to, but I don't mind going round. After all, if there's one thing I do know, it's how to clean a house.'

'What about her other children? Can they not help?'

'I think they've all moved away, except for Enid and one of the brothers. But, well, men aren't always the best at noticing housework needs doing.'

'Mostly true, I expect, except for Theo. His house is lovely. He really cares about things looking good.'

Maureen looked speculatively at Eliza. 'You're very fond of Theo, aren't you, lass?'

'Everyone likes Theo, Mum.'

'I reckon that's true, although some like him even more than others,' said Maureen with a quizzically raised eyebrow.

Eliza refused to be drawn. Instead she said, 'Anyway, we were talking about Barbara's mother. If this Enid thinks you would be helpful to her mum, and Annie would accept the help, then you could go and see. I don't want you to be up to your neck in someone else's dirt, though.'

'Ah, sweetheart, I spent many years up to my neck in other folk's dirt – not Miss Stevens's, I hasten to say; she realised she needed some help long before things got difficult. But I think it's because I feel so lucky with the money,' she lowered her voice as they were still in the street, 'that it's only right to be giving a little bit of the free time it's bought me to others.'

'Mum, you're an angel, you really are.'

'Not yet, I hope, love.'

'Just don't be putting yourself out. You've done enough of that over the years. We were so thrilled that day you heard about the legacy, that it could buy you your freedom. Don't give up that precious thing, will you?'

'I shall not,' said Maureen. 'I value it too much. But Enid's going to sound out her mother, see if she remembers me and if she'd like me to go round.'

'I can't think that the old lady would mind a bit of help. I just wonder that Barbara, who seems to live very high on the hog, doesn't just put her hand in her pocket and pay for her mum to have a cleaner, though. It's the obvious thing if she's too busy to help her herself.'

'Mm . . .' said Maureen vaguely. She didn't want to lie to Eliza, but she hadn't mentioned the cheque she'd given Barbara and, since the holiday, she was slowly revising her view of her old friend. She was beginning to have some suspicions that, with Barbara, all was not quite what she had once thought; what she'd been led to believe.

The Waterloo was busy, the noise spilling out from the open upstairs windows into the street as Eliza and Maureen approached. The atmosphere inside was lively, though not too raucous.

Sylvia and Desmond were upstairs, Sylvia chatting with Patsy, a friend of hers from the shop, and Anna-Marie was with Michael McBride at the bar, ordering drinks. Eliza and Maureen waved to them and Anna-Marie pointed out her mother, sitting at one side of the room.

'Thought you weren't coming,' said Sylvia, breaking off what she was saying to Patsy.

'Course I was. Just got held up talking about Mum's house move,' said Eliza, and Sylvia rolled her eyes. 'Hello, Patsy. I like your dress.'

'Butterick pattern, love. I'll lend it to you if you promise not to make it up in the same fabric.'

Eliza nodded. 'I know the rule. Thank you.' It was so easy to forget she didn't have to wear home-made any longer if she didn't want to. Her pay was now all her own, to do with as she wished. Maureen refused to allow her to contribute to the running of the house.

Maureen was found a chair beside Agnes Mulligan, and Jake, the landlord, came over and asked her what she'd like. Since the news of the legacy had seeped out, Maureen had the privilege of special treatment at the pub, though Jake kept it respectfully low key. He remembered Jack and had always liked the Bancrofts; good fortune could not have come to a nicer woman than Maureen, in his opinion, and she was always generous with her rounds when she came to the Waterloo on Wednesday evenings.

Maureen ordered a round of drinks for her family and friends and then settled down to talk with Agnes, who had left her twins in the care of Patrick this evening, and was full of hope that he would be taking up an apprenticeship at a garage very shortly. Her husband, Connor, who had 'a tin ear' and couldn't tell one song from another, was downstairs with his friends from work.

Eliza went to stand at the back of the room to breathe the fresh air through the open window. From here she would have a good view of the musicians who were scheduled to play before her and Theo, now preparing to take their turn. But where was Theo? She craned her neck – not here yet.

'Hello, Miss Bancroft,' said a voice right beside her, and she turned to see the customer from the Short Cut the previous week, the one who had been rude.

'Er, Mr . . . Wilmot? What are you doing here?'

'Thought I'd come over this way and listen to the music. I've heard there's some good entertainment on Wednesday evenings.'

'Well, these three are very good,' said Eliza, indicating Seamus Mulligan, another cousin of Harry's, who played the fiddle, and Thomas and Bert Richards, grandsons of the old fella who had also been in the Short Cut the previous week. They sang folk songs and sea shanties, and called themselves All At Sea.

She very obviously turned her full attention to the trio, whose performance was a delightful combination of traditional tunes and words, and mildly saucy improvisation, and deliberately did not look at Wilmot again. But when the music had finished and the enthusiastic applause had died down, he was still standing beside her.

'Would you like another drink, Miss Bancroft?'

'No thanks.'

'I'd like to buy you a drink to say I'm sorry for being so rude the other day.'

'You were a bit rude, now you mention it, but I'd forgotten all about it until you said.'

'Me and my big mouth!' He slapped his hand comically to his forehead. 'Should have kept quiet about the other day and just offered you the drink.'

'That would have been a short conversation as I've said no thanks.' But Eliza couldn't help smiling.

'It would, but then I'd have gone on to say you're looking very pretty in that dress. Are you all smart because we're to have the pleasure of hearing you sing?'

'And what would I have said then?'

'You'd have laughed and told me to stop being an idiot, because you're a modest kind of girl and you've known all the fellas around here since you were born and they're mebbe not so hot on the compliments as they should be so you're not used to being praised.'

'Well, they're certainly not big on flirting, Mr Wilmot, if that's what you mean.'

'I'm glad to hear it. A poor fella like me doesn't want an army of rivals vying to chat up the girl he's taken a fancy to.'

'Goodness, Mr Wilmot, you certainly lay your cards on the table.'

'I feel I should, having been so rude to you when we first met. Oh, and there I go again, reminding you what a fool I am. Please, Miss Bancroft, can we start again and I'll try not to be a fool any longer? My name is Brendan Wilmot – how do you do?' He extended his hand for Eliza to shake, grinning to show his uneven teeth.

'How do you do, Brendan Wilmot?' She shook his hand rather reluctantly. She did not want to be unfriendly and slap him down, but in all honesty she would really rather not be chatting to the man.

'Brendan . . . please.'

He was waiting for the obvious response.

'And you may call me Eliza.'

'And *are* you singing this evening, Eliza?'

'How did you know that?' she asked seriously.

'Just a lucky guess, and maybe the pretty frock was a clue, as I said. Do you take requests at all?'

'You don't even know what type of music Theo and I sing yet. You might not want to make a request.'

'Ah, but I hear you are very good and I do have an ear for a polished performance. I don't think you'll be wasted on me, Eliza.' He looked intently at her.

'So, you knew all along that I would be singing. It wasn't a guess at all.'

'Clever girl. I can see I'll have to keep my wits about me to keep up with you.'

'Why would you need to be keeping up with me, Brendan? After all, we've hardly met: a haircut and then again just now.'

'And a very fine haircut it is, too. I'm grateful for your talent, Eliza.'

'You haven't answered my question.'

'Well, mebbe I'm just thinking you're worth keeping up with.'

Eliza raised an eyebrow at his obvious flirting. He was charming when he made the effort – and he was making a big effort – and he really did have very attractive blue eyes.

Just then Theo appeared at Eliza's other side.

'Ah, Mr Wilmot, it's a surprise to see you here,' he said. 'Eliza, are you ready? We're all ready for you.'

Eliza realised then that the piano had been moved from the side of the room into the front and centre, and she hadn't even noticed.

'Yes, I'll be right there,' she said. 'Bye, Brendan,' she called over her shoulder as she went to take her place to sing.

'What did he want?' asked Theo as he sat down and sifted through his music.

'Nowt really. Just said sorry for being an idiot when he came for his haircut.'

'Well, let's hope he's not an idiot still,' said Theo. 'Right, shall we start with "Me and My Gal" . . .?'

Eliza and Theo's turn went especially well, with Theo improvising between songs and Eliza's voice clear and bright over his accompaniment. They finished as they'd started, with a duet, their voices harmonising sweetly as they looked at each other and re-created, with nods and little hand movements, the dynamics and embellishments they had practised.

The applause was well deserved. It was as she straightened from her final bow that Eliza saw Brendan Wilmot standing by the door to the stairs, looking right at her in a very appreciative way.

'I thought he'd have gone,' Theo said, noticing where she was looking. He started collecting up his music, and picked up his glass of Scotch from the top of the piano, standing aside to let a couple of hefty types move the heavy instrument back to the side of the room.

'Looks like he's just going now,' said Eliza.

'Hmm,' muttered Theo.

Brendan had been charming but also very flirty. He was a bit overpowering, truth be told. Or maybe she just wasn't used to that kind of attention. And how had he come to be here, on an evening when she and Theo were singing? To her knowledge he'd never been to the Waterloo before. He must have been asking around. That made her feel uncomfortable, rather as if she had been followed.

'You OK, Liza?'

'Yes, I'm fine.'

'Wilmot wasn't bothering you earlier, was he? You didn't look like you needed rescuing, but I have to say I didn't take to the man at all when he turned up at the Short Cut.'

'No, not bothering me, Theo. I'm just wondering why he's fetched up here now, that's all.'

'What did he say?' asked Theo, guiding Eliza back towards her family and their friends round a big table.

'He said he wanted to buy me a drink to make up for his rudeness last week.'

'That sounds innocent enough, anyway. As I say, I haven't taken to the man – he *was* rude to you last week – but at least he has the grace to try to make up for it. Of course, you refused; he isn't your type at all.'

Eliza laughed. 'Do I have a type?' she asked. 'And how are you such an expert, Theo?'

'Well, Liza, I have made a close study of types and I think I know them all. And I'd say you were way out of Mr Wilmot's league.'

'So, in your view, definitely not my type.'

'Nor mine. I shall not be letting that blighter buy me a drink though he begs me on bended knee.' He beamed at Eliza.

'What are you two grinning at?' asked Harry, coming over and touching his glass of Irish whiskey to the Scotch that Theo was holding.

'Oh, just disparaging that Wilmot fellow, hanging round like a spare part,' said Theo dismissively.

Just then Sylvia came over and took Eliza by the arm. 'Tell me how the house-hunting is going,' she said. 'Please tell me Mum hasn't found owt she likes?'

Theo and Harry went off to talk with old Mr Richards and his grandsons, and Eliza followed Sylvia to a pair of chairs in the corner, which Desmond had evidently been working hard to keep free for them.

'Well?'

'No, she's not visited any of them yet. She has so

many details through the post every day, it's like the week before Christmas. She was saying earlier it's a full-time job to sort through them all and then there are more the next day.'

'I expect it's because she's only just started looking. There'll be fewer before long.'

'Yes. Anyway, that's how far she's got.'

'Oh, thank goodness.'

'Sylvie? Don't you want Mum to move to a new house, take the chance of a new life for herself now her' – Eliza lowered her voice as Maureen and Sylvia also did in public if ever they referred to the legacy – 'circumstances have changed? She's said countless times over the years that she'd like to have a bit of garden, so why wouldn't she get on and look for summat suitable now? I can just see her with a spade and one of those flat wooden baskets with flowers in them, like you see in pictures.'

'But what about us?'

'Who?'

'You and me.'

'Sylvia! For goodness' sake, don't be such a baby. You've got your own home, and a husband to share it with, and you love your job in haberdashery. You're all settled.'

'Yes . . . but I still need Mum. We both do.'

'Of course, but I don't suppose she'll go off the face of the earth, or even very far from Lancashire – or very far at all. Lots of the details are for places nearby or even in Blackburn. But we've got to let her spread her wings now, when it's her big opportunity.'

'I s'pose . . .'

'Oh, c'mon, Sylvie, she's always put us first. Let's make sure that we repay her by not standing in her way. She's a mum in a million and she deserves our support, whatever she decides to do.'

'Of course,' said Sylvia in a small voice.

'Sylvie? Is summat up?'

'No . . . no, nowt.'

'Good. Please, don't think the worst. It'll all turn out for the best.'

'Why do you think that?'

'Because thinking it makes it more likely to happen. We've got to keep Mum's spirits up and make sure she doesn't get anxious about moving house. It needs to be only a good thing for her and we're here to make sure of that.'

'If you say so, Pollyanna.'

'I don't know what's got into you this evening, Sylvia. Do you want another drink? Will that cheer you up a bit?'

'No, thanks.'

Eliza looked closely at Sylvia. It wasn't like her to turn down a drink. 'Are you OK? You do look a bit pale, now I come to look at you.'

'Yes, I'm fine, thank you, Liza. And of course you're right about Mum. I didn't mean to be snappy. I'm just a bit tired, that's all. Look, I think it's time me and Des were off as we've work tomorrow. I'll pop round later in the week and take a look at some of these

231

house details. I don't want you and Mum to find summat completely impractical, halfway to Kirkby Lonsdale and cut off in blizzards for most of every winter, and you being all optimistic about it.'

'Quite right, Sylvie. Come and keep our feet firmly on the ground,' said Eliza.

'I'm having such an enjoyable evening, love,' said Maureen, 'that I might stay for a bit. Agnes has said that she and Connor will walk round our way and see me home.'

'That's good, Mum,' said Eliza. 'But I think I might go now. I've got work tomorrow and whatever time Harry and Theo leave, they'll still be at the Short Cut before me in the morning.'

'Ask one of them to walk you home, then. He can be back in a few minutes. Or ask Des.'

'OK, Mum. And I won't wait up.'

'Ha, I'll not be that late, Liza.'

Eliza looked round for Harry or Theo but could see neither of them. Maybe they had gone downstairs. Desmond was nowhere to be seen either. He and Sylvia must have gone, as she'd said. Eliza collected her cardigan and bag and went down. The taproom was heaving with customers, and the air was opaque with cigarette smoke. Eliza could feel her throat growing raspy and sore with merely putting her head round the door. She didn't know if Theo and Harry were there and she didn't fancy going to search in the scrum. No, better just to leave and trot off home by herself. It was no further than the next road and she'd be there in five minutes.

The cool evening air was welcome after the fug of the Waterloo. She stood outside, breathing in the sooty air, the best Blackburn could manage, then set off in the direction of Mafeking Street.

Suddenly Brendan Wilmot was beside her.

'Eliza, I've been waiting for you.'

'Oh, Brendan, you made me jump.'

'I didn't mean to frighten you.'

'I'm not frightened, just surprised to see you. I thought you'd gone a while ago.'

'So you were looking for me, were you?' he grinned. 'Are you walking home alone?'

This was a difficult one to answer. She didn't really want to say so to this man she didn't know, who had obviously been asking about her, who had tracked her down to the Waterloo on a Wednesday evening and waited outside to catch her when she left. She wasn't ready to tell him where she lived either, although she didn't quite know why. On the other hand, it wasn't far, the streetlights were lit and there were still people around. Here was Ted from next door, arriving at the pub now.

'Hello, Ted,' said Eliza. 'If you see Theo or Harry, please will you tell them that I'm just setting off back?'

'I will, Eliza. You take care, love.' Ted glanced in Brendan's direction. 'And is this fella escorting you home?'

'No,' said Eliza, just as Brendan said, 'Yes.'

'Yes, I'll see Eliza home safely,' he elaborated.

'Good night, then,' said Ted, and disappeared inside.

'Now, I'd better do as I said and escort you to your door,' said Brendan.

'There's really no need.'

'There's every need. Can't have you making your own way.'

'It's not far . . .'

'No, but even so.'

They set off side by side, Eliza keeping a little space between herself and Brendan.

'So how long have you been doing the singing?' asked Brendan. 'You're very good.'

'Thank you. A couple of years. My mum likes the old musicals, and if we ever went to the cinema, we'd come away singing the songs, what we could remember of them. We still sing along to the wireless. Mum likes the Light Programme.'

'And how do you come to be singing with that old fella – Theo, is it?'

'Old? Theo's not old.'

'Older than you. Older than me, too. We're more of an age than you and he are.'

'When someone's a good friend their age doesn't matter – you don't even think about it,' said Eliza, trying to explain the agelessness that was so much a part of Theo. 'Anyway, I started working at the Short Cut and we got chatting and it turned out that Theo likes the same kind of music. As he plays the piano, too, we began from there.'

'Do they pay you at the Waterloo for singing? They should do.'

'Only a token amount. We don't do it for the money. It's just for fun.'

'Still, you must be glad of what they do pay?'

'What do you mean?'

Brendan shrugged nonchalantly. 'Well, we all have to make our way, don't we?'

'Of course,' said Eliza, thinking the conversation had gone in rather an odd direction and wanting to change the subject. It sounded like he was fishing to see if she needed the money.

'Tell me about your shop,' she said.

'Ah, The Remove. It's part of my house-clearance business. Anything that's suitable goes into the shop to sell on. Con, who works for me, makes over some of it, if it's worth it: a repair, a new coat of varnish or paint, that kind of thing. Come and have a look. You'd be very welcome.'

'I don't need any furniture,' said Eliza. 'It would be a waste of your time if I came to look round.'

'It wouldn't,' said Brendan, turning to look intently at her.

By now they were approaching Eliza's home and Brendan, who was slightly ahead of Eliza, slowed, then came to a stop outside.

'I'd really like to see you again, Eliza. I've had a great evening.'

'I don't think you heard much of the music. If you want a haircut, you know where the Short Cut is.'

'That's not what I meant.'

'Thanks for walking me back, Brendan, and mebbe I'll just see you at the barber's.'

'You're going to keep on working there, then?' he asked.

By now warning klaxons were going off loudly in Eliza's head and she felt for her door key in her pocket. Why had she let this creepy fella walk her home? She should have gone back into the pub and found Harry or Theo when she'd encountered Wilmot outside.

'Look, Mr Wilmot, whatever you think you know about me, you're wasting your time. And now I'm going to say good night.'

She raised her hand with her key in it to put it in the lock, but Brendan took hold of her arm, his big hand encircling her wrist.

'Please, don't go. I'd really like to get to know you better, Eliza. I reckon you're just the kind of girl for me,' he said.

'Let go of me,' Eliza said. 'How dare you touch me?' She struggled to free her arm, trying to push him away with the other one, but he held her tighter. 'Let go, you're hurting me.'

'Just listen—' He leaned in close and his eyes were like flints in the dim light.

'No, you listen. Let go of Eliza now, Wilmot.'

It was Theo, looking and sounding as if he wasn't to

be messed with. Eliza had never been so glad to see her friend.

'Or what?' sneered Brendan. But Theo had distracted him and he loosened his hold on Eliza.

'Or this,' she said, reaching back and delivering the hardest slap to his face that she could.

'Ow, you little b—'

'What's all this noise?'

Now Louisa was at her door, armed with her coal shovel.

'This vile man had his hands on Eliza,' said Theo, 'and if he doesn't make himself scarce at once, I'll make sure he regrets it.'

Brendan was clutching his face. Despite that, he clearly wasn't going to retreat so easily.

'You've got it all wrong, you stupid man. I only want to get to know Eliza.'

'I'll give you stupid,' said Theo, moving in, and – to Eliza's astonishment – in a single second he had Brendan face down on the pavement with his arm bent up behind him and Theo's knee pressing into his back. 'Now, if you don't get the picture, you're even dimmer than I thought you were. Off you go before Louisa brains you with her shovel. We won't be seeing you at the Short Cut again, or at the Waterloo either, will we?'

Brendan lay there, gritting his teeth at the pain in his arm and shoulder.

'*Will* we? I didn't hear you.'

'N-no,' grunted Brendan.

'You see,' added Theo, 'I suspect you'd really hate to have your name brought to the attention of the police. And that's why you won't be bothering Eliza – or me or Harry – again, isn't it?'

This seemed to have the desired effect, because when Theo loosened his grip, Brendan scrambled to his feet and was away down the road at a shambling run without looking back.

'Good grief!' said Louisa, hefting the shovel as if she regretted being denied a part in the brief skirmish. 'Who was that?'

'A rude and ignorant ne'er-do-well, an opportunist,' said Theo.

'A chancer,' added Eliza. 'Trying to question me about my circumstances.'

'You all right, love?'

'Yes, thank you, Louisa. Thank goodness you both appeared just then. What a horrible man. And he was trying hard to be charming earlier.'

'An act he couldn't keep up long,' said Theo. 'Come on, let's get you inside, Liza. I'll see Eliza safely settled, Louisa – Maureen will be back soon, I think – and I don't believe we'll see that rascal around here again. The mention of the police rather put the wind up him, plus we know where to find him if he ever causes any more trouble.'

'Please don't mention anything of this to Mum, Louisa,' pleaded Eliza. 'It was all over in seconds, no harm is done. You know how anxious she was when she found she really had been burgled, and I'd hate her to get all worried again, especially as there's no reason.'

'If you say so, love. But I'll be keeping an eye open for that one. If you're worried about him, you come and tell me.' She held up the shovel in her substantial hands, a fierce look on her face.

'Thank you, Louisa. I will.'

Eliza at last opened the front door and went in, switching on the hall light. Theo followed and closed the door gently behind him.

'How did you know—'

'What did he—'

They spoke together.

'You first, Eliza.'

'Thank you for coming to rescue me. I expect Ted told you I'd set off home with that man.'

'He did, of course. I'll say one thing for this neighbourhood, people really do look out for each other. Why didn't you come and ask me or Harry to walk with you if you wanted to go home?'

'Because I was daft. I thought: it's only a short way and I'll see folk in the street that I know. But I'd just left when Brendan Wilmot sprang out of the shadows and insisted he'd escort me home. He was all right to start with, but then he said some odd things and I began to get suspicious.'

'What did he say?'

'Come and sit down, Theo, and I'll tell you.'

He followed her into the sitting room and they sat side by side on the sofa.

'Well, first of all he knew that I'd be singing at the Waterloo this evening. Nothing too strange about that, except that then he was asking if we got paid for our performance. Why would anyone think to ask that, especially when they don't know the person they're asking? He seemed to be digging to see whether I would admit I don't need the money. And he asked me if I was going to continue to work at the Short Cut. It was as if he knew about Mum's legacy, but *how* would he know? He's nothing to do with us. And the really creepy thing was that when we set out and I said it wasn't far to go home he seemed to agree, almost as if he knew. Then, when we got within sight of here, he was the one to slow down and stop right outside. He knew where I lived already.'

'Mm, I agree it looks that way. Perhaps he followed you home one time.'

'I hate the thought of that.'

'So do I. But I doubt you'll be bothered by him again. Mention of the police seemed to do the trick.'

'How did you know to say that?'

'I didn't. Just a lucky shot that hit the target. He's the type who might well be of interest to them.'

Eliza smiled, despite feeling shaken by the incident. 'So we're back to types again, are we, Theo?'

'Told you, Liza, I know all the types.'

'Well, Brendan Wilmot was certainly trying to turn

on the charm earlier, but when he started to give himself away and I made it clear I wanted nowt to do with him, he got angry.'

'Perhaps he was also angry with himself because he'd allowed you to rumble him.'

'Mebbe . . . And now you can tell me, how did you learn to floor a man like that? I was amazed. You were so quick, he was down before he even knew what was happening.'

'Ah, it's just a move I learned in the army.'

'Well, it was lucky for me you remembered it.'

'Lucky for me I didn't put my back out,' said Theo, deadpan.

'Theo, there's summat else – and please tell me if I'm being daft – but when I asked Louisa just now not to tell Mum about that horrible man because she got so anxious about the burglary, I suddenly had a thought – you don't think Brendan Wilmot had owt to do with that, do you?'

'I wouldn't have thought so . . . I don't know. You mean because he appeared to know where you live, and the burglar knew that Maureen wouldn't be here when he broke in?'

'Mm, put like that it looks a bit far-fetched. Just two things that happened and not connected at all.'

'It's more likely that the burglar and Brendan Wilmot are just a couple of chancers: two among many, unfortunately. I can't explain why Wilmot should have heard about your mother's inheritance and want to check if it's true, but you and your mum know there are a lot of people round here who would do their best for you. Never be afraid to ask for help . . . even if it's only a safe escort to your door.'

'Thank you, Theo. You are such a good friend.'

He looked into Eliza's dark eyes for a moment, seemed about to say something else, but evidently thought better of it. Then he leaned across and gently kissed the top of her head.

'I'll see you tomorrow,' he said, and then left without looking back.

Eliza heard him closing the front door quietly behind him. She leaned back on the sofa and closed her eyes. She really wished he hadn't gone, that he'd kissed her mouth – properly kissed her – so she could kiss him in return. She hardly dared to admit, even to herself, that she might be falling in love with Theo Gilmore.

CHAPTER FOURTEEN

BARBARA PAID MAUREEN'S cheque into her account
at her bank in Clitheroe. She had written Maureen
a short note to thank her on one of her stiff little
notecards with her address embossed across the top,
having decided that she could not bear to speak to
Maureen on the telephone in case her voice betrayed
how utterly inadequate she thought the sum was.

How could Maureen have been so mean with her
best friend? But then, thought Barbara, rather pityingly,
it wasn't entirely unlikely that Maureen, who had never
had any money in her life before that old lady left her
a legacy, should think that fifty pounds was quite a lot
of money. It was probably rather more than Maureen
had earned in a year when she still worked. It was,
regrettably, quite a large percentage of what Barbara
herself earned, giving piano and elocution lessons.

Disappointing, yes, but Maureen's cheque was a
bonus, and at least it allowed Barbara to pay what was

due on the bank loan – such a relief – which in turn allowed her to continue with the expensive roof of The Manor over her head. It also met a few, though not all, of her unpaid bills. She thought the painter could perhaps wait a little longer for his money, but she had to pay Mr Gathercole immediately.

Barbara had drawn some cash out of the bank, and as soon as she got home and had put away the car, she carefully counted out the correct amount. She took one of her thick creamy envelopes from her desk in the little study, wrote Mr Gathercole's name on the front with an elegant flourish, put the coins inside and sealed it. Then she went down the road to his cottage, which was just a few minutes' walk away.

Barbara opened the little wooden gate set in a stone wall abutting the lane and entered Mr Gathercole's pretty front garden. The doorbell was literally a bell beside the door with a rope attached to the clapper. Barbara rang it rather self-consciously; it sounded rudely intrusive in the quiet of the afternoon.

There was quite a long wait and then Mrs Gathercole came to the door. She was a very small woman in her seventies, with straight grey hair and little round glasses. She wore the ubiquitous crossover pinafore, and her legs were encased in beige lisle stockings. Barbara had barely met her before and thought she looked a sweet old lady. It must be an occasion for her to have a visit from the owner of The Manor, her husband's cele-brated employer.

'Good afternoon, Mrs Gathercole,' said Barbara, graciously, looking down from her height.

The day was sunny and Barbara was wearing her broad-brimmed hat to shield her complexion from the sun. The hat not only added to her height, but made rather an impression, as Barbara well knew; one that had had the desired effect with the clerk at the bank earlier, but that Barbara realised now, too late, was not appropriate here.

'Miss Hayle, what a surprise. You've come to pay that money you owe us at last, have you?'

'Indeed I have, Mrs Gathercole.'

'Well, it's about time. It's not nice to keep folk hanging on for what you owe. If you can't afford owt, you have to do without, not expect other folk to provide for you for free.'

'I'm sorry, Mrs Gathercole, I'm afraid I've been extremely busy and I just . . . overlooked that Mr Gathercole had yet to be paid.'

'You mean you forgot? Well, it's odd that you forgot twice, isn't it, Miss Hayle? When you asked my Bill to come round and mow your grass a second time, didn't that remind you that he hadn't been paid for the time before? He told me he even mentioned it to you himself, though he's not the sort to be making a fuss.'

'I—'

'You see, Miss Hayle, most folk round here are just ordinary types who live within their means. No one owes owt that's not paid immediately and so no one goes short. As I say, if you can't afford, you have to do without, then save up for it, not scrounge off others.'

'Scrounge?' Barbara was taken aback to hear so blunt a word from this little old lady at the door of this pretty cottage. Had Mrs Gathercole sworn at her she could not have been more shocked.

'Aye, I think that's the right word, isn't it? Cadge, like?'

'Well, I'm sorry you feel the need to take that tone.'

'I'm sure you are, Miss Hayle, but I'm only saying what I think you ought to hear and then there'll be no repeat.' She looked at Barbara very carefully through her glasses, her eyes hard. 'Now, are you intending to give that to me?'

She held her hand out for the envelope, which Barbara was still holding, having been distracted by the unexpectedly fierce reception.

'Thank you, Miss Hayle. I'll check it's right and let you know if it isn't.'

'It is right, Mrs Gathercole,' Barbara said, feeling as if she was up before the headmistress for some silly, selfish, schoolgirl error.

'Well, I should hope so after all this time. Goodbye then, Miss Hayle.'

Mrs Gathercole turned away and firmly closed the door.

Barbara felt her face flaming with fury. How dare that old woman treat her like that? Who did she think she was? The cheek of her!

There was nothing to do but turn for home, well and truly bettered. Barbara straightened her back and put her nose in the air, deliberately not looking at the cottage in case Mrs Gathercole should be at the window, watching her departure. She slammed the garden gate shut behind her and walked back to The Manor. It was only when she was inside her own house with the big door shut that she allowed herself to drop her guard and give in to the anguish that horrible encounter had caused her.

Well, maybe she'd be pruning her own roses from now, mowing her own lawn. See how Mrs Gathercole liked it when her husband didn't have the prestigious Manor gardening job any longer . . . Hateful old woman!

But she knew this was just nonsense and she would not be doing her own gardening.

Maureen had arranged with Enid Cawley to go round to see Annie on a Saturday morning when Eliza was busy at the Short Cut.

She set out on foot and, crossing King William Street, she saw Stella Martin, looking pretty in a bright summer dress and carrying a basket of shopping.

'Stella, Stella, hello,' called Maureen.

'Maureen. It's good to see you. How are you and how is the house-hunting going?'

'I'm well, love. I'm going to view a couple of houses in Clitheroe next week.'

'That's good. I hope you see one you like.'

'Thank you. I'm trying to be all calm and sensible about it but,' Maureen grinned, 'I have high hopes and I can't help being excited.'

Stella held up crossed fingers and smiled. 'I have a little news of my own,' she said, looking unusually shy for a moment. 'Thank you for your idea about having a spare ticket for a concert and letting Mr Felbridge know about it.'

'And?'

'He accepted without a moment's hesitation. Not only paid me back for it, as you'd expect, but insisted on paying for mine as well, and then took me out to dinner.'

'Oh, Stella, that is good news, love. Dinner as well. He must be keen.'

'I think so. Of course, we're still Mr Felbridge and Miss Martin in the office, but outside of the brewery we're definitely James and Stella now.'

Maureen hugged Stella. 'I'm so glad, love. He's such a kind man, not stuck up or grand with folk, for all he owns the brewery and has such a head for business. Should I be thinking about a new outfit and matching hat?'

'Oh, it's much too early for that, Maureen. I'm not in a hurry. Let's just see what happens.'

'I'll telephone you next week after I've seen the houses, and we'll meet for lunch and exchange our news, if you like?' said Maureen.

They said their goodbyes and Maureen headed off to Avery Street, where she had arranged to meet Enid.

She knocked on the scruffy door of number 52 and it was opened by a tired-looking woman who might have been in her late thirties. Maureen looked for any resemblance to Barbara but, apart from Enid's height, there was none at all.

'Maureen, I recognise you, though it's many years since we last met. Enid Cawley.' Enid held out her hand and Maureen shook it. 'Come in and say hello to Mum. I'm sorry, the place is a bit of a mess but . . . you know.'

Maureen stepped inside the clammy-smelling hall, where the skirting was scuffed and the floor needed sweeping. 'Don't you worry, Enid. I understand, and it's why I'm here,' Maureen reassured her, keeping her voice low. 'I just hope your mum will let me help her get tidy. Once you've persuaded a person to let you help, then it's pretty much a straight road, but the thing is not to muscle in, be bossy and upset her. Let's see how it goes. If she doesn't want me round here then I shan't come again. It wouldn't be right.'

'Well, I wish you luck. I've wasted a lot of time trying to persuade Mum to let me clean round, but the persuading takes so long, and I'm that busy with everything else I have to do. You can't just go in and ride roughshod in your mother's own house, though, can you?'

'Course not, love. And I know you've got your own job to do as well as a family to take care of. No one thinks badly of you.'

'Thank you. The others are all gone from round

here except Brendan, who's hopeless. Barbara's in Buckledale, so a few miles away, of course, but she's even worse than Brendan, and might as well be on the moon for all the time she spends visiting her mother. It's all rather fallen on my plate. I'm that grateful you're offering to try, but Mum can be quite . . .' she lowered her voice to a whisper, '. . . difficult and . . . well, see how you go on.'

They went into the living room at the back. It was very hot and the light was dim through the soiled net curtains, but Maureen could see the place was very untidy and very much in need of a clean. Annie was sitting in a tea-stained armchair, reading a magazine. A selection of used cups and mugs were lined up on the table in front of her.

'Hello, Mrs Wilmot,' Maureen said. 'Do you remember me? I'm Maureen Stubbs, as was. I'm called Maureen Bancroft now. I was friends with Barbara years ago, when we were at school.'

'Oh, aye, I remember you, Maureen Stubbs. Shy little thing, you were. Nice and polite, too, though you used to let our Barbara boss you around something terrible.'

Maureen nodded. 'Probably. I telephoned Enid the other day and she said why didn't I come round to say hello.'

'Well, you're here now. What do you want?'

'Just a visit, see how you're doing. A little chat and a cup of tea, mebbe? Does that sound like a good idea?'

'I'll make it,' volunteered Enid. 'You stay and talk

with Mum. She doesn't get a lot of visitors these days, do you, Mum?'

'Don't really want them either,' said Annie. 'It's better folk don't come bothering me.'

'Well, I shan't bother you,' said Maureen, 'but a cup of tea would be lovely.'

'Yes, a cup of tea would be nice,' said Annie. 'Are you making it, Enid?'

'I said so, Mum.'

Maureen saw the way things were, with Annie a little forgetful of what had been said, and hoping not to have to make an effort that she felt would be beyond her if she could avoid it. Yet she remembered Maureen from years ago very clearly. That was the route to getting Annie to relax and accept her as a visitor and then, gradually, see her as someone who could help make her life a little easier, Maureen decided.

She moved some of the clutter from the sofa and sat down. By the time Enid brought in the tea, Maureen and Annie were remembering thirty years ago and laughing about some incident involving one of Enid's older brothers.

'If you want to go, love, I don't mind,' said Annie. 'Maureen and me are just fine.'

'I'll stay and drink my tea first, Mum,' said Enid.

'I don't mind a visit from Maureen,' said Annie. 'She's no bother and it's good to remember the old days.'

*　*　*

Barbara continued to lie awake at night, her restless mind weighing up all her burdens. Perhaps it had got to the point at last when she should sell the car . . . No! The Manor and the Alvis were irrevocably tied to her memories of those few wonderful years of fun she and Marty had had together before his illness worsened and curtailed the good times: the parties spilling out into the garden on balmy evenings and the bedrooms all occupied with funny, noisy, gossipy, beautiful people. The so-called friends had all vanished when Marty died – had already found excuses to stay away when Marty got very ill. Barbara had been indignant about that at first, but they were never really her friends anyway, and fatal illness was a hard topic to discuss when you weren't close to people. There had been one or two unkind remarks she'd overheard, she now remembered, about her being 'an elderly chorus girl'. Marty's crowd knew she was not really one of them, for all he doted on her. There had even been a cruel suggestion that he had married her in order to have a devoted wife to nurse him through his last illness. Barbara refused to believe that then, and refused to believe it now. She had loved Marty with all her heart and he had felt the same about her.

But there was no going back to the old days. Barbara had to look to her future and Maureen Bancroft's fortune was key to her plans. After a few weeks of deliberation, Barbara decided that she would have to invite Maureen to The Manor. Then Maureen would see what a beautiful house Barbara lived in, and appreciate that it cost a lot to keep up, and Maureen, with her small ideas on life and her vast inheritance, which she hadn't much idea how to spend, would be only too happy to hand over a sum she would never miss to her glamorous friend, of whom she was so in awe.

Maureen let herself into 28 Mafeking Street, left her shopping in the hallway, kicked off her smart shoes and reached for the comfortable old ones she wore indoors.

'Eliza?'

'Hello, Mum. In here!'

Maureen followed Eliza's voice through to the kitchen where she was chopping salad.

'You look a bit tired, Mum, but in a good way. Did you have a lovely day with Stella?'

'I did. I've always had a soft spot for St Annes, and Stella knows it well. It was good of her to ask me to go with her on her day off. I love the seaside and St Annes has got so much more as well. We did a bit of shopping – I got a couple of books; I'll show you later – and had a delicious lunch. Then there was a concert in the bandstand on the Promenade, which was an unexpected bonus. Even Stella enjoyed that, for all she's one for more highbrow music.'

'It sounds perfect, Mum. I wish I'd been able to come too, but I can't leave Harry in the lurch just to join you and Stella gadding about.'

'Gadding about, indeed – cheeky madam.'

They both laughed. The inheritance was life-changing for Maureen, but it wouldn't provide for both her daughters for all their lives as well. They'd still have to make their own way, although Maureen hoped she'd be able to smooth away any financial difficulties they might encounter in their lives. Eliza was proud of the skills she was learning at the Short Cut and vowed she would never give up work, even if she could – if not there, then she would ply her trade somewhere else.

'There's some post for you.' Eliza pointed to an envelope on the kitchen table.

'About the house move, I expect. I'll look later. You sit down, love. You'll have been on your feet all day. I'll deal with the salad.'

'In that case I'll make us a pot of tea.'

Maureen had found a house in Clitheroe, just a few miles away, that she thought would suit her very nicely. It was quite large, so Eliza could have plenty of space of her own. They'd discussed it at length and decided neither of them wanted to live alone. There were gardens at the back and front, and Maureen was looking forward to being able to grow some flowers and maybe even some vegetables.

She'd already started to clear out her cupboards ahead of the move. It was amazing how much you hoarded without even realising.

This burst of energy for clearing out was partly inspired by the visits to Annie. Annie could be sentimental and liked to hang on to all kinds of useless old junk because of the memories it evoked, but she had slowly come round to the idea of Maureen helping her to keep her kitchen and living room clean and tidy, and was eventually willing to get rid of the old newspapers and magazines and other accumulated clutter that had covered so many surfaces. Annie had been more cheerful since she'd let Maureen help her, although she still tended to give short shrift to all her offspring when she spoke to Maureen about them. Maureen didn't take this too seriously because Annie wasn't particularly kind to Enid, and Maureen saw for herself how, despite being short of time and always at the beck and call of her family, Enid did what she could for her mother.

Enid was full of gratitude for Maureen's generosity with her time.

'If only Barbara had been prepared to give even a fraction of the time to her mother that you have, Maureen,' Enid had said. 'I know Mum's becoming forgetful, and that won't get any better, but she's so much happier now she isn't feeling overwhelmed by the mess she felt too tired to bother with. I think, when you've had enough, or you move house and it's too far for you to come here, we'll mebbe manage to keep ahead of the cleaning between us, Mum and me, now it's just a quick go-round, little and often, to bring the place back up to looking nice.'

This was good news, although Maureen was becoming fond of Annie. Yes, she could be short-tempered and dismissive, but Maureen had discovered a softer side to her that had been buried years ago under the exhausted mother with a houseful of rowdy and naughty children. She would keep in touch and visit her occasionally after she'd moved, she thought. Perhaps take her out to tea if she felt up to it. Everyone needed a little treat now and then.

'Theo's asked me to go round later,' Eliza said, as they were seated at the kitchen table, eating the salad. 'We've got a new song he wants to try out and he doesn't know if I'll manage it, he says.'

'I think he's being funny. Sounds like a trumped-up excuse to ask you round there,' said Maureen, without thinking.

They looked at each other.

'Do you think so, Mum?' asked Eliza, a little frown on her face. 'I don't think Theo's one for trumping up owt. We'll be practising the song without a doubt. I reckon if he wanted me just to go round, he'd just say, "Eliza, would you like to come round?" What would be awkward about that?'

'Nowt, love, of course. But you'd say . . .?'

'I'd say, "Why's that, Theo?"'

'Exactly. So what do you think Theo would say then?'

'I think he'd say it was for the pleasure of my company or summat. You know what he's like . . .'

'Mebbe. But I've seen the way he looks at you when you're singing together, Liza. Mebbe he's afraid that he might say summat that would create some awkwardness between you if he says what he really wants to, so he keeps it light.'

Eliza pursed her lips and looked down. She knew now what she felt about Theo – his easy smile, which could make her heart flip; the twinkle in his deep brown eyes; the attractive way his hair was greying at the temples – and sometimes she thought that he felt the same. But he was much older, and she remembered occasions when he'd been wise and clever and she'd been impetuous and daft. Perhaps his affection was mixed with a lot of indulgence for a silly young girl, the keen junior at the barber's where they both worked, and he liked her enthusiasm for her work, liked her singing, was generous enough to encourage her, but that was all.

Eliza had not dared to believe it was anything more than that. But Mum had noticed how Theo looked at her.

'Ah, love, why don't you just go and practise the songs?' said Maureen, clearly wishing she hadn't spoken. 'Mebbe I've got it all wrong. In fact, I'm sure I must have done. Singing those duets is a bit like acting and he always puts on a good performance. So do you.'

'Yes . . . yes, I expect you're right, Mum. Anyway, I shall go when we've washed up, if that's OK with you, and Theo will bring me home as usual.'

'No, love, I'll do the pots. I've got all evening. I'll put the wireless on and take my time. You get off.'

Eliza went to brush her hair and change into a print frock and then she set off with a kiss for her mother and a reassurance that Theo would bring her home.

Maureen had just waved her off when the telephone rang. It was Barbara Hayle, sounding very friendly and wondering whether Maureen would like to come to visit.

CHAPTER FIFTEEN

'I WISH YOU'D take me with you when you go to visit Barbara Hayle, Mum,' said Sylvia, sitting in Maureen's kitchen early on Tuesday evening, dunking a digestive biscuit in her tea. 'It's not fair that Liza's met her and I haven't. She sounds so unlike your usual sort of friends – Louisa, and Agnes, and that.'

'I've only seen her twice, Sylvie,' Eliza pointed out. 'And that's because she came here to collect Mum and then bring her back from her holiday. I haven't gone out of my way to meet her.'

'Mebbe not, but I'd like to. I've never met a film star—'

'She's not a film star, Sylvie,' Eliza reminded her, passing the biscuits to Maureen.

'—and I'd like to see all her lovely clothes and her car with the red seats, and I'd like to look round the house where she lives, and walk in the grounds. I've never been to a stately home. I expect it's full of mirrors with gold frames, and chandeliers and old paintings of

259

her relatives. And there'll be lots of souvenirs and stuff from the productions she's starred in.'

'I don't think The Manor is a stately home, Sylvia,' said Maureen. 'It'll certainly be a lot grander than here, but I think it's just a very big house, probably with large comfy sofas and other nice furniture, and roaring log fires in winter. Things that Barbara's mentioned over the years in her letters and when we were on holiday make me think it is beautiful, and I know she loves it. But I don't know about gold-framed mirrors and chandeliers. And I should be amazed if there are paintings of her family.'

She thought of Barbara's flouncy older sister and tough, fighting brothers from their childhood; her shouty parents, Annie always yelling at her misbehaving children in the chaos of their overcrowded little house . . . What a long way Barbara Wilmot had come from there to the fragrant, graceful Barbara Hayle of today. It was no wonder that Annie was so against Barbara now if Barbara had so wholeheartedly cast off her humble beginnings and reinvented herself, excluding her mother from her life. Quite how she'd done it was still a mystery and very astonishing, now Maureen came to think of it. Of course, Barbara had spoken about her career frequently during their holiday, although Maureen hadn't really been able to grasp what had happened when, exactly. Barbara had lots of colourful stories about her successes but, afterwards Maureen realised she hadn't volunteered much about how she'd got there in the first place. The thing about her was that she was now so much herself – the beautiful, gracious, successful actress – that it was easy to forget there had ever been an earlier version of Barbara, the one who was the bossy show-off daughter of Annie Wilmot. Barbara and Annie seemed now a world apart.

'Mum, are you listening? I said, I'd still like to go. Couldn't you telephone and ask her if I can come, too?'

'No, Sylvie. That would be rude. You can't just ask to be invited. You know better than that.'

'Why not? It wouldn't make any difference to Barbara, if she's got such a big house. It's not like I'd be under her feet or owt.'

'But that still wouldn't mean it was good manners to ask to be invited,' said Maureen. 'We may not live in grand houses, but that doesn't mean we don't know how to behave.'

'Yes, all right, Mum. But I hope Liza isn't going with you either, then.'

'No, Sylvie,' said Eliza with exaggerated patience, 'I am not going with Mum on Sunday. Mum's getting the train and Barbara's meeting her at Whalley station and driving her to Buckledale, as I think she told you five minutes ago.'

'All right, Liza. No need to get stroppy. Anyway, Mum, why are you going to Barbara's?'

'Because she's a friend and she's asked me to go, of course,' said Maureen, knowing full well she was evading the real point of the question. She still hadn't told the girls that she'd lent Barbara some money just to tide her over until her next role was secured. It made her feel slightly uncomfortable to think she was keeping it a secret from them, and she couldn't quite decide exactly why she was doing that. Perhaps she'd say something eventually, when it was all worked out, although by then there would be no need to mention it anyway. And it was, after all, her money to lend.

'It'll be nice for you to see this place, Buckledale,' said Eliza. 'I hope Barbara will show you round if it's a fine day for a walk.'

'I shall ask her, love. I'm interested to see it,' said Maureen. 'It will give me a taste of a more rural life for when I've bought my new house. I'm that excited. It's progressing very smoothly so far.'

Sylvia looked put out.

'What's up, love? I shan't be far away and nor will Liza.'

'I know, but it won't be like here, where you're just round the corner, will it? I shan't be able to just pop in like I am now. I'll have to make an appointment to visit, have an invitation.'

'Don't talk daft,' said Eliza.

Maureen said, 'We're not going miles away, just where it's a bit cleaner, a bit prettier. You and Des could visit anytime you like. You could come on the train or Des could bring you in the van.'

'Mebbe *we* could come and live with you in the new house on the edge of Clitheroe?' said Sylvia. 'I fancy a bit of fresh air and a garden.'

'Who's "we"?' asked Maureen, trying not to smile.

'Well, me and Des, of course.'

'And have you asked Des if he wants to live with his mother-in-law in her house in Clitheroe?'

Sylvia stuck out her lower lip but said nothing.

'Right, well, it's time for me to get the tea on,' said Maureen, turning to the fridge. 'Are you staying, Sylvia?'

'No, thanks. I've got to go and get ours ready. Des will be home soon.'

'Here, love, I saw some nice fish on the market earlier so I got plenty. Would you like to take this piece, if you can use it?'

'Oh, thank you, Mum. Better than the pie I've got, which can wait until tomorrow. Now you've got us a fridge as well, I don't have to worry about stuff going off in this heat.'

Maureen wrapped the fish and put it in a bag for Sylvia to take.

'In case we don't see you at the Waterloo tomorrow, I'll wish you a nice day on Sunday, Mum,' said Sylvia, 'and don't go doing owt silly with Barbara. Strikes me she's probably got quite a persuasive way with her, and I don't want you drawn into any of her fancy ideas, which you'd think better of, later.'

'That's the first sensible thing you've said since you got here,' said Eliza, smiling to imply it was a joke. Which it wasn't really.

* * *

'Now then, Annie, I notice you haven't a lot of food in your pantry. Would you like me to go to the shop for you or shall we go together?' asked Maureen.

'We'll go together,' said Annie. She paused and looked at Maureen. 'You know, love, you've been right good to me these last few weeks. Better than my own children.'

'But it was Enid who got us together, Annie,' Maureen said.

'Aye, Enid's all right, for all she's married to that fella . . . whatshisname. I reckon she's got her work cut out with him and his temper.'

Maureen was sorry to hear this. Enid had enough to do without having to put up with her husband being unpleasant to her.

'My own fella had a bit of a temper on him, too, so I reckon Enid was used to it before she married.'

Maureen vaguely remembered Barbara's father as someone to avoid although, having successfully avoided him, she couldn't recall any specific occasions when he'd been especially unpleasant. She just had an impression that he'd been a bad-tempered man.

'Yes,' said Annie, slowly putting on her outdoor shoes, 'he was quick to smack the children if they stepped out of line. Hit first, shout second.'

'Did he smack the girls, too?' asked Maureen, who had never smacked her children. 'Surely not.'

'Oh, aye, all of them. Even our Maggie was never too old for a good hiding.'

'I remember Maggie, a few years older than Barbara,' said Maureen, fetching the shopping bags, 'and the others, who were boys . . .'

'Geoff, Dave and Pete. I thought I'd finished when I had Pete, but then there was Enid.'

'And Brendan, your youngest? Isn't he much younger? Must have been a lot of years of child-rearing for you, Annie?'

Annie was concentrating on buttoning up her coat. Eventually she said, 'Brendan, yes. Over twenty years between Maggie and him. Ten between Enid and him. It was too much for me really.'

'I'm not surprised,' said Maureen. 'I don't think I'd have done so well.'

They left the house and made their way down the street at Annie's pace.

'Aye, my Joe used to whack 'em all to keep them in line, although Brendan came in for the worst of it. There was no pleasing Joe where Brendan was concerned. I reckon that's where he gets his own nasty temper.'

'Oh dear. Was he especially naughty?'

'No, not Brendan. That was Barbara,' said Annie, and pursed her lips to indicate the subject was closed, leaving Maureen wondering why Brendan had invoked his father's wrath so unfairly.

The shop was at the corner of the next street along. It was crowded with items, baskets of vegetables displayed on a table on the pavement outside. Inside, it had that familiar corner-shop smell of newspapers and cardboard boxes. Annie shuffled forward to the counter and Maureen wished Mary a good morning and handed her the list.

Mary went around the shop collecting the items, all the while chatting with Annie.

'Have you seen owt of your Brendan, Annie?' Mary asked, jotting down the prices on the bill.

'I don't remember him coming round lately. I'm not sorry about that. He's not good company. Have you seen Brendan, Maureen?'

'I don't know Brendan at all. He's not been to visit when I've been at yours,' said Maureen.

'Hmm, that figures,' said Annie. 'I don't expect owt of Brendan. He's too like Barbara for selfishness.'

'I don't think I've ever seen Barbara,' Mary said, leaning on the counter and starting to add up the bill.

Annie cackled at that. 'You'd remember if you had. Once seen, never forgotten,' she said. 'You'll not be seeing her either, Mary. Too grand for us, she is. A right madam, with her nose in the air, though I can't think why – she's got nowt to be stuck up about. She started a career on the stage but it never took off.'

What! Maureen thought her face must have given her away, but Annie and Mary seemed not to have noticed her astonishment.

'Mm, I'm sorry to hear that,' said Mary absent-mindedly, intent on her calculation. 'Right, that's two and fourpence, please, Annie.'

Maureen was all ears when the subject of Barbara came up but now the women had moved on to the finalities of the shopping trip and the exchange of coins was taking all their attention, while Maureen packed the tins and packages into Annie's shopping bag.

Then they began the slow walk back to Annie's house.

Maureen felt as if she was nearly exploding with curiosity about Barbara. Of course, she knew all too well by now that Annie and Barbara didn't get on. Barbara was very far from the attentive daughter, but whose fault was that really? Maureen knew nothing of the cause of the rift between them.

They reached number 52 and Annie put her key in the lock, which Maureen had oiled for Annie on a previous visit.

'Come in, love, and we'll have a cup of tea. You can make it,' said Annie.

'And we can put away the shopping together, if you like,' said Maureen, hoping for the chance to ask about Barbara while they did this, and in that way making lighter of the conversation than if they sat down and had a face-to-face discussion. That was unthinkable: Annie could be very blunt and would soon ask Maureen straight out why she wanted to know.

Maureen put the shopping bag on the kitchen table and Annie delved in and handed her the items one by one.

'So Barbara's stage career never took off?' Maureen asked casually, as an opener.

'No.'

'That's a shame. She was very keen, I seem to remember, when we were at school together.'

'She was.'

'Shall I keep this cheese wrapped, Annie? You don't want anything settling on it.'

'Better had. I do get flies in the larder sometimes, filthy things.'

'I remember going to see Barbara years ago when she was in the chorus at the Grand Theatre. She looked lovely in a spangly little costume – quite a short skirt – but then she had the legs for it.'

'Oh, aye? Yes, she's still got good legs, and knows it. I reckon it was how she looked as got her a place in the chorus, but she hadn't the talent to get further than that. She knew she looked all right, but could she act?'

Maureen waited for Annie to continue, then had to prompt her. 'Could she?'

'Could she what, Maureen?'

'Barbara – could she act?'

'No, that's what I'm saying. She could kick up her legs and look the part of a chorus girl, but she wasn't much good for owt beyond that.'

Maureen was aghast at this revelation. Could there be a mistake? Perhaps Annie had forgotten or was mistaking Barbara for someone else. It seemed unlikely, but she did get confused sometimes.

Not that confused. Not so much that she doesn't know the

truth about her own daughter's life. But how can this be true?
It's more than umbrage at Barbara's selfishness – and yet it
doesn't seem possible.

'So what happened?'

Annie's expression was shuttered now. 'She got by,'
she said. 'She married that fella in the end – oh, I can't
remember his name . . . Anyway, she never looked back
then. Lives in some splendour now, though I've never
been invited to see.'

'That's a shame,' said Maureen quietly.

She thought of Barbara's invitation to visit the
following Sunday. It was wrong that Barbara had invited
her, just a friend, to visit The Manor, but had never
asked her own mother.

Maureen went home that day with her head full of
unanswered questions. Barbara had failed in her
acting career? Surely not. Yet why would Annie make
up such a big lie? And why was she, Maureen, being
treated to a day at The Manor when Barbara's mother
had never been there in all these years? Was *that* even
true? Could Annie have been there and have simply
forgotten? Yet Annie's long-term memory was still
good. Perhaps the ill feelings between them had meant
Barbara didn't want her mother there . . . but might
that be because Annie knew the truth about Barbara
and her glittering career?

Well, there was only one way to find out.

* * *

As the week had progressed since Barbara's invitation for Maureen to visit, Eliza wondered if she should persuade her mother to let her go with her after all. Part of her thought that ridiculous: Maureen was a responsible adult who had brought up two daughters, mostly by herself, and who had had various jobs to support them all, and done every one of those jobs well. It was patronising and insulting for Eliza to treat her mother as if she were incapable of managing any situation, especially something as ordinary as a visit to an old friend. On the other hand, Eliza could not bury that niggling feeling she'd confided to Theo: that Barbara Hayle was playing a part, living an act, and what you saw was only what she wanted you to see. Which meant there was a possibility that there was another aspect to her that she didn't want you to see . . .

Eliza saw no point in repeating that conversation with Theo. She kept her misgivings to herself all week, but on the Friday she went round to see Anna-Marie after work to ask her opinion.

Anna-Marie shooed her young twin sisters, Bridget and Colleen, out of the sitting room, and moved a pile of newspapers, some books and a toy car off the sofa to make room for Eliza to sit down.

'Patrick's mending his bike in the yard – why don't you go and help him and keep out of Mum's way?' she called after the girls as compensation for taking over the room.

The twins rushed off delightedly to get in Patrick's way, and Anna-Marie set two mugs of terracotta-coloured tea down on the coffee table on top of a pile of news-papers and what looked like the twins' homework, and asked Eliza what was on her mind.

'Well,' said Anna-Marie when Eliza had explained, 'there's no reason why your mum shouldn't go and visit her friend, is there? What do you think this Barbara is going to do that should worry you, even if she is one for putting on an act? Why wouldn't your mum see through any act that's being put on, anyway? And she may not be as worldly as Barbara Hayle, but she's full of good sense. She and Barbara went on holiday together and, from what I hear, your mum had a great time.'

'It's true, she did.'

'So why wouldn't she have a nice time on Sunday, just the same?'

'You're right, of course, Anna-Marie, but I just don't want . . . her head turned by Barbara. Sylvia said summat much the same. I don't want Barbara to take advantage.'

'How do you mean?'

'I don't really know. I s'pose I'm just worried that Mum inherits that bit of money from her old employer,' said Eliza, using the phrase that she, Maureen and Sylvia had devised to make light of the legacy, implying that anything else Sylvia might have said before was an exaggeration, 'and suddenly Barbara Hayle is featuring in her life as she never did since they grew up.'

'But didn't you tell me your mum invited her to go on holiday with her because you and Sylvia were too busy at work to get away? She didn't say owt to Barbara Hayle about her legacy when she invited her, did she?'

'No, of course not. She's the last person to be showing off about what she has.'

'But why wouldn't they strike up a closer friendship now they've had a nice holiday together? Seems quite normal to me.'

Eliza thought about this. 'Yes, yes, you're right. Of course you are. I'm probably just being silly, worrying about whether Barbara is genuine. I reckon Theo thinks I am.'

'I'm sure he doesn't. Have you mentioned these thoughts to Sylvia?'

'No, I thought to have a word at the Waterloo on Wednesday, but she and Des weren't there. Anyway, Sylvia's been a bit odd recently. But, as I said, Sylvia did kind of warn Mum not to have her head turned. But then again, Sylvia wants to go with Mum but Mum said no.'

'Perhaps Sylvia is also wanting to keep an eye on your mother's friend, see her on home territory?'

'She didn't tell me if that was so. She talked a lot of rubbish about stately homes and chandeliers. If Mum's head were to be turned a bit, then Sylvia's is screwed right off.'

'Mm . . . or she might have just been making up a reason for wanting to go when really she wants to look out for your mum. I know she can be a bit . . . er, a bit selfish . . . sometimes, but she's not completely daft and she does love your mother, too.'

'Well, she's not going and neither am I so, whatever we think, it's Mum on her own.'

'I reckon you're being really good to look out for your mum. I hope I'd do the same for mine. But let her have a lovely day with her friend – what can happen in a day? – and if there's owt troubling you after that, you can do summat about it then. But don't underestimate your mum, Liza. It was all round town how she dealt with that horrible Herbert Nicholson – I think Stella Martin saw to that; she's one of us, for all she's a bit posh and works for Mr Felbridge himself – and I reckon some folk'd think twice about crossing your mother now, even though she's the nicest, kindest lady.'

Eliza laughed. 'Yes, you're right about that, Anna-Marie. I was getting all worried about Mum being so down and her job wearing her away, and then she rises up like a lioness and bites back harder! I should have remembered that. I reckon Mum is well up to dealing with anyone who crosses her.'

'It will all be fine, I'm sure. She'll have a nice time, and you'll be able to put your worries behind you.'

'I expect so. I wonder, though, had you ever heard of Barbara Hayle before she fetched up outside our house that day they went on holiday?' asked Eliza.

'Well, no, but she has to be about the age of our

mothers, so she was probably at the height of her career before we were born. It's not really surprising.'

'No, that's what I thought. But I did ask Theo, and he doesn't remember her either, though he said she might have been a big star when he was abroad or in the army.'

'Mm, Theo does know a lot more than we do about all the old musicals and theatre stuff, but what are you suggesting, Liza? The woman lives in a big house that your mum is going to see for herself, from what you tell me, and the car was real enough – Dad and Patrick are still talking about it. And I gather Barbara herself was quite impressive. You saw that. Your mum's looking lovely since she came back from her holiday, what with the smart new clothes and having her hair done, and I hope I'm not insulting anyone when I say that mebbe Barbara Hayle has had some influence there.'

'Right again, Anna-Marie. Oh, I'm just being daft . . .'

Anna-Marie leaned over and gave Eliza a hug. 'Daft is as daft does. Don't go doing or saying owt if you haven't real grounds to do so. It's good your mum has a friend to visit out of town and make a day of it. Everyone round here wants only the best for her. But if you decide there is owt to concern you, then I hope you'll come and tell Mum and Dad. And Theo and Harry would always do anything they could to help you and your mother, too.'

'Thanks, Anna-Marie. I'll remember that.'

Eliza went home with a quieter mind. She had been

fretting over nothing and it would be unkind of her to spoil Maureen's day out on Sunday with her own silly imaginings. She'd be wise from now on to keep them to herself.

CHAPTER SIXTEEN

MAUREEN TOOK THE train from Blackburn to Whalley quite early on Sunday. She would be at Barbara's before mid-morning and they'd have the whole day to enjoy together.

Since she'd seen Annie the previous Wednesday, Maureen had thought long and hard about what the old lady had told her. Of course, Annie could be intolerant and usually had little good to say about any of her numerous children. But surely this was more than just being unkind about Barbara because they had fallen out.

Maureen had decided not to tell Eliza, Sylvia or anyone else what Annie had said for the time being. If it all turned out to be nonsense, she herself would then be guilty of spreading lies about her friend. She really wanted to think the best of Barbara, despite knowing she had selfishly avoided helping her mother in her old age. What, after all, did Maureen know of their relationship?

On the other hand . . . oh dear, Barbara had confided

she was a little short of money since her latest role had fallen through, and she had accepted the loan. That hardly sounded like the position that someone with a sound financial footing from a successful career would find themselves in, but then the theatre world was probably a bit 'come and go', Maureen decided. After all, actors were a different kind of folk from, say, bank managers and others with 'steady' jobs.

Still, Barbara had been very friendly on the telephone, inviting Maureen to visit for the day, and Maureen was thrilled to have the chance to see The Manor, of which she'd heard so much in various letters over the years. Today would be a treat, a chance to see Barbara in her lovely home, and when she got back Maureen was looking forward to telling Eliza – and then, later, Sylvia – all about it . . .

Maureen had dressed smartly, in one of the summer dresses from Crosby's and a hat with a brim that shaded her face from the July sun. She was still grateful that Barbara had guided her on their shopping trip. What fun that had been in the end, after she'd overcome her nervousness at entering the plush quietness of the upmarket shop. How silly she felt she had been now. During these last few months, she had become so much braver. Miss Stevens's legacy had given her a confidence she had never had before, and she was feeling more and more at home with it. But that had all started with the holiday, and its success had been largely down to Barbara.

* * *

The train pulled up at Whalley and Maureen stepped off, slammed the door behind her and went out to the front of the station. There was the enormous car, all long and shiny, and attracting attention as usual.

'Hello, Barbara. It's kind of you to meet me here,' said Maureen, opening the car door and climbing in, putting a string bag with a cake tin in it on the back seat. As the day was fine and warm, Barbara had the roof down and sat there looking as elegant as her car.

'It's no trouble, Maureen, and as there's no bus from Whalley to Buckledale on Sundays you'd have had to walk otherwise.' Barbara trilled her pretty laugh. 'I'm so pleased to see you again.'

'I've brought a headscarf in case you had the roof down, love,' said Maureen, putting her hat on her knee and extracting her favourite old headscarf from her handbag.

'Your hair is nice, Maureen – did Eliza do it for you?'

'No, unfortunately Eliza only really cuts men's hair, and as there are now no men in our family – except Sylvia's Des, of course – we can't take much advantage of her skills.'

'I'd almost forgotten you had no brothers – or sisters, either.' Barbara put the car into gear and drove smoothly out onto Mitton Road and away towards Buckledale.

'Whereas you have . . . is it five?'

'Six,' corrected Barbara. 'More than enough . . . And you're looking so smart. Isn't that one of the dresses you bought in Somerton? I'm glad you decided not to give it away to either of your daughters.'

'Well, I listened to what you said and thought it made good sense.'

Barbara smiled. 'I do try to make sense,' she said almost shyly, 'even though people think I'm just a pretty face . . . a bit dim.'

'*Do* they?' said Maureen. 'You know, I wouldn't have thought it was wise to underestimate you, Babs. You've come such a long way in life; you didn't do that by your beauty alone.'

Barbara looked pleased at that. As she drove on, she asked how Maureen's plans for her future were progressing. 'Have you really decided to move house, Maureen? I would have thought you'd be quite happy staying where you are.'

'I'm in the process of buying a house as I'd dearly like a bit of garden. It's on the edge of Clitheroe and Eliza's going to live with me there, too, but I'd certainly be happy to stop where I am as far as my neighbours go, Barbara. I've got kind friends up and down the road, and round the corner. But we'll keep in touch and I'm not going far. You'll know yourself how important it is to have folk you can rely on around you when you're a widow, as we both are. And it's the give and take that strengthens friendships, of course.'

Barbara didn't answer and Maureen saw from the set of her face that she was concentrating on the road. She, too, turned her attention to the route, thinking it pretty now, past mid-summer, although she imagined it would look forbidding in January, with hilly open countryside, the trees bent with the prevailing wind. The villages they passed were mainly just tiny stretches of houses alongside the road, with farms behind. If the buses were infrequent, it would be difficult to live in the country without being able to drive. She'd chosen well with Clitheroe, she felt sure: fresher air and birdsong, but also transport and neighbours.

And here was Buckledale! Maureen sat up as the sign announcing the village appeared, half-hidden behind a flourishing hedge growing over the verge. It was certainly a pretty place, with stone cottages and a few more imposing houses along the road, a charming-looking church with a village hall and church fields next to it, a pub, which implied the camaraderie such as the regulars at the Waterloo shared, some small shops, and then, at the further end of the village, The Manor.

Maureen stared wide-eyed as Barbara turned in through the open gate and the Alvis crunched over the drive, skirting an extensive garden, with a lawn and flowerbeds, to the front of the house.

'Oh, Barbara, this is beautiful,' breathed Maureen.

Barbara turned off the engine and removed her rose-printed silk headscarf. 'Yes, well, Marty and I bought it together when we first married, and call me foolish, but I could never live anywhere else, remembering how happy we were here . . . remembering his dear face as we sat in the garden together or rehearsed at the piano.'

'I understand, love,' Maureen replied. 'I don't know that I will find it entirely easy to leave Mafeking Street when the time comes, despite having found somewhere new that will suit me nicely. The old house means so much to me. I lived there all my married life with Jack, as you might recall. I know life goes on and you can take the memories with you in your head, but the place itself helps you remember those good times, too. Still, there are always new memories to make, aren't there?'

Maureen reached out and gently patted Barbara's arm. She noticed Barbara was wearing a favourite blouse today, one she had worn a few times on their holiday, although there was a little black stain on the sleeve, now she came to look. Such a shame. She wondered that Barbara, always so smart, was content to wear it with what looked like an ink splash, but then perhaps she was very fond of it.

'Yes,' Barbara nodded, looking emotional. She sighed heavily and then clearly made an effort to gather herself. 'Come on in, Maureen, and have a cup of tea.'

She got out, came round, opened the car door for Maureen and offered a hand to help her out, then picked up the string bag for her from the back seat.

'How grand to live in a house with a name, not just a number,' said Maureen, seeing the house name engraved onto the brass letterbox as she took the bag from Barbara, then followed her.

Barbara unlocked the door and led the way in. Maureen looked all around, noticing the height of the ceiling, the stone-flagged floor, the wide staircase to one side, the attractive edging of stained glass round the tall narrow windows to either side of the front door. On a table in the middle of the floor was a cut-glass vase of beautiful red roses, lending a sweet scent, colour and elegance to the hall.

'So pretty. Did they come from your garden, Barbara?'

'Yes. It's such a nice day we can go and sit out there with our tea, if you like?'

'Oh, yes, *please.*'

'Come on through then, Maureen,' said Barbara, leading the way into the kitchen, where she put the kettle on to boil.

'What an enormous kitchen! I can see straight off that you take up but a fraction of the space,' said Maureen, glancing at the empty shelves. '*Spacious,* I think is the word.' She smiled widely. 'We're the opposite of spacious at home, but we'll have more room when we move.'

'Yes, I have plenty of room. In the end I gave most of the dinner service away to my sisters, who are able to make use of it. I don't need so much now Marty's gone and I'm away doing shows – or at least I was . . .'

'Ah, yes. No news of another part?'

Barbara shook her head forlornly. 'None, I'm afraid. Such a worry. But come and see the garden while I make the tea.'

Maureen put the string bag on the table and took out the cake tin. 'I've brought you a sponge,' she said. 'I made it last night.'

'Maureen, you angel. How did you know I wouldn't have any cake to go with the tea?'

'Just a guess,' said Maureen, kindly.

Barbara showed Maureen through the back door, and round into the garden, where two deckchairs were set up on the lawn with a little table, obviously moved from inside, between them.

'Oh, lovely!' gasped Maureen, taking in the sight of the abundant flowerbeds. 'I can smell the roses from here.'

'You look round and I'll be back directly with the tea,' said Barbara.

She went inside again, leaving Maureen to stroll across the lawn and on to the little herringbone paths between the flowerbeds, down to the bottom of the garden and back.

It was warm with the sun shining so brightly and no buildings crowding in to cast shadows; quiet but for the distant grind of a tractor engine, the sharp whistle of a blackbird perched on the rim of a little stone birdbath, the chatter of a few starlings stabbing at the further edge of the lawn with their sharp beaks. There were no voices of folk calling to each other from their doorsteps, or children kicking footballs or playing hopscotch. The air was clear and clean, rather like it had been in Somerton-on-Sea, but without the seaside saltiness. The setting was as peaceful and as beautiful as Barbara had told her it was.

Maureen looked up at the blue sky, dotted with high white clouds – not the smoke of thousands of chimneys – and then gazed over the colourful garden. She didn't know the names of any of the flowers except for roses, but the colours were so bright, the shapes so numerous and interesting, with ground-hugging plants flowing over low walls and tall spikey stems of flowers poking up amongst shorter, bushier ones, that she felt inspired to learn. Perhaps she, too, could achieve something like this, but on a smaller scale, of course. Start slowly with a few easy plants, even employ someone to show her and help with the heavy tasks . . .

Maureen turned back towards the house and the lawn with the deckchairs.

What an imposing place The Manor was. Probably Barbara gave a lot of parties for her theatre friends – odd, though, that she'd given away her dinner service – and all the rooms would be occupied most weekends. Not this weekend, though. Somehow it felt a little forlorn, Maureen thought, now she came to look at it. Why *was* that? She stared intently at the rear façade, trying to work it out.

The paintwork – that was it! The front was all smart with shiny paint, as if it had recently been renovated but, looking from here, Maureen could see that the window frames were peeling, even showing signs of rot, and much in need of attention and a coat of paint or two. Perhaps the painter was coming back to finish the job. Yes, that would be it.

And here was Barbara, returning with a tea tray – Maureen's cake on a plate – with cups and saucers and a matching teapot and milk jug, which she set down on the table.

'I'll pour and you can cut your delicious-looking sponge,' said Barbara.

'Lovely tea service,' said Maureen, bending down to serve the cake.

'Yes, I seem to remember Noël Coward gave it to me after I'd appeared in *Private Lives*,' said Barbara with a shrug. 'Such a dear man.' She poured a cup of tea for Maureen, added milk as she knew she liked it, and passed it to her.

'Thank you. Noël Coward – who'd have thought! How exciting. I love your garden, Barbara. I think I might try for summat similar, but smaller scale, of course, when I get my new house, though I expect it will be too late to achieve much this year by the time the move comes about. But, tell me, when is your painter coming to finish the house? Only I can't help but notice he's yet to do the back.'

'Oh, soon as he can,' said Barbara, 'but . . .' she took a deep breath, 'I'm afraid I might have to put him off.'

'Why's that, love?'

'Well, the front cost such a lot and I don't think I can afford to have the rear frames done just yet, what with the backer for the show pulling out . . . and other

things. So many bills to pay . . . Oh dear, I never
normally have this difficulty . . .' She gave Maureen a
helpless look, as if dealing with something beyond her
poor brain to fathom. Maureen was reminded of
another occasion . . . Yes, their journey to Somerton,
when Barbara, looking just this way, had got the factory
workers to put up the roof of her car. It had all been
an act then.

Maureen took a sip of her tea, thinking. 'When we've
had our tea, Barbara,' she said kindly, 'you'd better
show me any bills you can't quite manage this month,
and tell me all about it.'

She would listen and she would consider carefully,
she decided, just as she had with the choosing and now
the purchasing of her new house. She would not be
persuaded into doing anything against her better judge-
ment, and she would take one step at a time, not rush
in headlong. She was learning she could manage any
situation if she just thought it through. She had been
timid for much of her life, but now, at last, she was
learning how to be brave.

Barbara nodded silently.

The easiness between them had somehow evapor-
ated. Maureen felt her eyes drawn to the view of the
house, with the peeling window frames. At least the
roof looked sound, but there was a strangely empty
look to the place, almost as if it were unlived in, creating
an atmosphere of foreboding, a feeling that something
here was very wrong.

Maureen finished her cup of tea and declined another. 'Well, now, Barbara, shall we go in now and you can tell me what the problem is?' she said.

Barbara was gazing at the little flock of starlings, still pecking at the edge of the grass and chattering to each other. Her face showed unhappiness, even fear, and she appeared not to have heard Maureen.

'Barbara?'

'What? Oh, yes . . . yes, let's take the tea things and go in. It's getting quite chilly here.'

It wasn't. The sun was still shining and the breeze was gentle, but Maureen helped Barbara gather up the crockery and Barbara hastened inside, Maureen following with the cake.

'Let's go into the music room,' suggested Barbara. 'It's nice and light in there, with a view of the front garden.' She didn't wait for an answer but led the way to a room to the left of the hall.

The first thing Maureen saw in the large, high room was an enormous and very shiny grand piano. Heavens, it was so vast it looked as if you would be able to set sail in it. The top was down and on it was a silver-framed photograph. Maureen saw it was a picture of Barbara and a very tall and dashing-looking man in a broad-shouldered suit. She guessed this was Marty. Marty had one arm around Barbara and was holding a huge cigar in his other hand and grinning confidently at the photographer. Barbara had her hair longer than it was now, wound up in coils, and was wearing a fur coat over an evening dress. She, too, was smiling widely. The couple looked so happy, so assured, so glamorous.

'Darling Marty . . .' murmured Barbara. 'That was taken at a first night, not long after we were married.'

'You look lovely,' said Maureen.

This didn't tie in with what Annie had said about Barbara never making it further than the chorus. Annie must be mistaken, or else she was being deliberately unkind.

The huge room was cold now the sun had moved overhead. Maureen was pleased she'd kept her cardigan on. Barbara, she noticed, had two cardigans over the back of the chair at her table. On the table were a pot of pencils and an open book of music, which Maureen, having seen the busy scores Theo played, thought looked surprisingly simple, like the kind of thing a learner might play. It had sparse notes and the rhythm looked basic.

'So still no luck with another part in a show?' began Maureen, sitting down in one of a pair of neat, high-backed armchairs that Barbara indicated, while Barbara elegantly arranged herself in the other.

'None, I'm afraid. Such a nuisance, when I was relying on the one that's now cancelled. But the thing is—'

'But what does your agent say?'

'What?'

'Your agent, Barbara – isn't he looking for a part for you? If money's getting a bit tight, couldn't you take a role in the meantime that might not be as glamorous, as important as you're used to? You see, love, sometimes, if things aren't going so well, you have to make the best of it, compromise. Then, when you come through, you'll be able to pick and choose again.'

Maureen imagined a tall, dapper man with a luxuriant moustache and slicked-back hair speaking down a white telephone to Barbara from a well-furnished office, telling her the only role he had been able to get for her was as Juliet's mother, and Barbara, at the other end of the line, looking tearful and saying, 'But I'm not the motherly kind, am I?'

'Of course, you're right, Maureen, but at the moment I have no part and no show.'

'Well, I know you're used to being in demand, so it's no wonder you're upset. But surely you've been doing so well up until now? All those starring roles . . . How is it hard times at the first setback?'

'Because that's not the worst of it, Maureen. Oh, I can hardly bear to tell you what a silly and naïve woman I have been. It's just that I had no one to advise me and this man seemed so plausible, so trustworthy.'

Maureen felt her eyes growing round with horrible anticipation. 'What's happened, love?' she asked faintly.

'I invested some money in an unwise way,' whispered Barbara. 'Oh, I should have known it was all too good to be true. And I . . . I wrote this man a cheque because he told me I would have a really good return on my investment, but it's all gone terribly wrong.' She looked distraught and her voice trembled. 'I shan't ever see my savings again. He's taken my money and disappeared.'

'Oh, love . . . Did you contact the police?' asked Maureen, horrified.

'Of course, but he'd already got clean away. He's escaped the country and taken my money with him.'

'That's terrible. I am sorry. But who is this scoundrel?'

'A con man, a sham. I'm so sorry to burden you with this, Maureen. I should have known better than to believe him.'

'But his name, Barbara? Surely he told you his name, lured you in, like, to make you think he was genuine?'

'He said his name was . . . was Herbert Nicholson. But that is probably made up, of course. Goodness know what his real name is.'

Maureen swallowed and gave a little cough of surprise. She turned in the direction of the window, not wanting Barbara to see her face while she thought this through. What on earth was going on? Of course, it could be another Herbert Nicholson, not the one she had worked for, or maybe the con man had come across Herbert and had used his name.

Maureen took a deep breath and turned back to Barbara. 'I'm right sorry to hear that, Barbara. When did this happen, love?' She felt her heart beating quicker. She had to get to the bottom of this, but a part of her wished she didn't have to – wished she'd never come here. Whatever was going on, it involved lies from some quarter.

'Just after you sent me that cheque, Maureen. A few weeks ago.'

Maureen fanned her face. The room was cool but she suddenly felt very overheated. She wasn't used to lying and trickery. She breathed slowly, trying to be calm, to take her time.

'Awful, love. Your savings, you say?'

'Yes . . .'

'But why did you dig into your savings to write a cheque to this man? Especially when you told me you had bills to pay and I loaned you some money. Why not use your savings to pay the bills you needed to?'

Barbara looked exasperated. 'I don't know! Because I was duped by him. Because I was silly.'

'But where did you meet this man . . . this Herbert Nicholson?'

'In . . . Manchester. Yes, it was in Manchester. Where I went for an audition.'

'So you have had an audition?' asked Maureen. 'I know you've been worried that there were no parts for a woman your age, but I'm pleased you managed to get an audition. But not the part?'

'No, not the part. But never mind about the audition. The thing is, I gave this man a cheque and now I have hardly any money left at all. It's been stolen by this con artist.'

Suddenly a memory from her childhood sprang into Maureen's mind: Barbara coming round to play one day after school and some money that Maureen's mother had left on the sideboard disappearing. It had only been small change from the shop, but Maureen's parents had brought her up to be strictly honest, and the disappearance of the coppers had introduced a note of distrust in the friendship between the girls for a week or two. Maureen's mother had questioned Maureen and Barbara kindly but firmly, suggesting there had been a mistake and giving them each the chance to agree and produce the cash from a pocket, but Maureen hadn't got the money to return, of course, and Barbara – for it could only have been taken by her – was not going to confess and give it back.

Now, suddenly, Maureen thought she saw how things were with Barbara and it made her furious. Weren't they friends? How could Barbara treat her like this, as if she wasn't even worthy of the truth? It was so disrespectful, so downright rude. So underhand and sly and dishonest. Barbara hadn't even thought it necessary to get her story straight, as if any old made-up nonsense would suffice to trick the woman who was supposed to be her friend. She took a deep breath to tell Barbara this but just at that moment the telephone rang.

'Excuse me, I'd better answer that,' said Barbara, getting up and nearly running from the room.

Maureen leaned back in the chair and exhaled slowly. A part of her, the angry part, wanted to leave now, while Barbara was on the telephone, just pick up her things and go. Never mind if she had to walk all the way to Whalley, at least she'd be away from this web of lies.

But another part of her was intrigued. What on earth was Barbara's real story? Barbara had told her plenty of amusing little anecdotes of theatrical life while they'd been on holiday, but the timing of the events in these stories had never been clear to Maureen and, even now, it was something of a mystery just how Barbara had progressed from the chorus girl Maureen had seen at the Grand Theatre to the celebrated leading lady.

Well, Maureen decided, she didn't have to do anything she didn't want to. And she'd left her cheque book at home anyway. If Barbara wanted money today, all she'd get out of her would be the small change in her purse – just as Barbara had taken the small change that Maureen's mother had left on the sideboard all those years ago. How strange that that small incident had sprung into her mind just as Barbara's honesty was in question again, like a little warning sign.

Her courage strengthened, Maureen weighed her options. The idea of setting out for home on foot was absurd. She'd have to beg a lift to Whalley station, at least. So why not turn the situation round? Why not pretend to go along with Barbara and just see what she said? She'd know the worst of her so-called friend then; know how the land lay.

Maureen gathered herself to put on the first perform-ance she had ever attempted in her life, and waited for Barbara's return.

CHAPTER SEVENTEEN

O H, GOOD HEAVENS, Barbara thought as she went to answer the telephone, Maureen really was asking an awful lot of questions. What had got into her? Surely she could just accept that Barbara had been conned out of her savings? She didn't need all the details, did she? Why was she asking all that and not just accepting what Barbara told her? It was almost as if she didn't believe her, but how could that be? She'd lapped up all Barbara's theatrical tales before now. Maybe the story about the con man had been a rash element to introduce, but how else was she to account for having no money, despite her glittering career, just when her latest show had been cancelled?

Barbara needed to keep up the persona she had invented of the successful leading lady. That would allow her to 'borrow' from Maureen enough money to pay off her creditors, service the bank loan and perhaps live in a more civilised way – more in the style she and

295

Marty had enjoyed and less like she did at the moment – for a few months. The celebrated Barbara Hayle was someone an ordinary little person like Maureen would always want to be friends with, and she was a far safer bet for repaying a 'loan' than a poverty-stricken piano and elocution teacher would be.

In addition to this, Barbara could not now imagine living without the façade – the character of Miss Barbara Hayle, star of variety and light comedy – that she had invented and inhabited for so long. So long, in fact, that the real Barbara barely existed any more: the second-rate actress, the failed magician's assistant . . . and before that, the silly chorus girl who'd fallen hopelessly in love with a pianist in a theatre house band, and who'd thought he must really be in love with her when he'd offered to teach her to play for free . . .

All this passed through Barbara's mind as she went into her study, closed the door and picked up the telephone. The last few minutes had been a mite awkward, and she hoped it wasn't one of her creditors calling her, asking about some bill or other. That would really put the tin lid on the morning.

But no. Absurdly, it was the real Herbert Nicholson, the rather unpleasant man who came for elocution lessons. Barbara wondered if she'd conjured him up by borrowing his name for the con man when she'd got into a tight corner a few minutes ago. It was simply the first name that had come into her head.

Nicholson put on a ridiculous affected 'telephone voice' and spoke very loudly, as if the receiver was inadequate to convey the importance of his message or, indeed, the importance of himself. He wanted to book extra lessons because he was getting to know some 'very important people' and wanted to polish his 'refinement'.

Well, the truth about that would be better coming from someone who wasn't taking his money, Barbara thought. She booked him in for some extra lessons, writing his name in her diary against the additional days.

'Actually, I was going to phone you, Mr Nicholson,' she said then, thinking on her feet. 'I'm putting up my hourly rate by five shillings . . . Yes, it is a lot, but I have many overheads at The Manor and this is the first time I've raised my fee for a couple of years now . . . I always make sure you have a full hour of tuition, as you know . . . Yes, I can give you extra exercises to practise at home at no extra cost. That's not a problem at all. Would you still like to go ahead with the other lessons? . . . Excellent. I'm so glad. I shall see you on Tuesday at five thirty and then again on Saturday afternoon as usual. Good day to you, Mr Nicholson.'

She wrote down the new rate for Herbert Nicholson next to his name in the diary. Then she searched her desk for the pile of bills she had yet to pay. Satisfied she had everything she wanted to show Maureen, she went back to the music room.

Maureen was standing at the window, looking out to the front drive.

'Do you know, Barbara, I've just seen a man driving a van go round behind those trees over there. Is it summat you need to know about?'

Brendan! That's all I need today. Let's hope he stays over there and doesn't come here.

'Oh, I expect it's the pest controller, Maureen. A little vermin problem in the garage. Nothing to be concerned about.'

'Well, so long as you were expecting him. I thought I ought to say.'

'Thanks, Maureen. Now, please sit down. Oh dear, I'm afraid – and it really is quite a surprise to me – while I was seeing to the telephone, I noticed lying on my desk one or two bills – well, a few, actually – that I'd forgotten all about and, really, they should be paid quite soon. If not immediately.'

Maureen didn't look at all surprised. 'Better show me, then. As that con man took your savings. I think I ought to know the worst, don't you?'

'Oh, Maureen, you really are a dear.'

They sat side by side again in the armchairs as Maureen looked through the numerous bills very carefully, one by one, asking quite matter-of-factly about each. Barbara offered up each bill in turn, explaining only what Maureen asked.

At last they came to the very root of Barbara's ongoing difficulties: the bank loan and the reason for it.

'What was the loan taken out for, Barbara?' asked Maureen.

Barbara felt herself going a bit pink. 'Do you know, I can't quite remember exactly. I think to start with it was to cover some bills that Marty and I found it difficult to meet at the time.'

'"To start with"? What kind of things?' Maureen persisted with an encouraging little smile.

'Oh . . . just things we bought for the house . . . And the car. Yes, I do believe it was also to pay for the car. You see, we had to have a car. But not just the car. Other things like . . . the carpets and the furnishings. A house this size costs a lot to furnish well, but we did love to choose nice things for it. Good taste doesn't come cheap, you know.'

Maureen slightly raised an eyebrow but said nothing.

'There were some repairs we needed to do, as well.'

'Repairs?'

'Oh, the roof leaked a bit and then we found the whole thing needed replacing. But it was a sound investment because it stopped the rain coming in, which was getting to be a problem. And then we needed some rewiring done because the roof man told us it was a fire hazard. It was all terribly boring because that kind of thing costs a lot and is no fun at all, but we had to do it. Marty had bought some paintings and he said he didn't want to have them destroyed by fire.'

Barbara gave her charming laugh, remembering Marty's little joke. He had always found the fun in life, even when the boring old bills came in. The utilitarian nature of the new roof and then the rewiring had been offset by the more joyous purchase of more works of art and a fur coat for Barbara – the very one she was wearing in the photograph on the piano – since she had been complaining that life was starting to lack any luxury.

'I don't know if the piano was paid for by the loan as well . . . and of course we had to have holidays. We used to meet up with old friends of Marty's in Italy . . .' Barbara tailed off, remembering the sun on terracotta roofs, the long, long afternoons lazing in the shade, the red wine, the exotic local specialities that they loved to eat, so delicious after the drab food they'd had to endure in Britain for so long after the war.

'Holidays . . . yes . . .' said Maureen in a voice that made Barbara look at her. Her face was expressionless.

Barbara continued, 'At one time we had a couple of domestics living in, who cooked and cleaned, and we *had* to pay their wages otherwise they would just have left, and . . . and then there was Marty's treatment. He went to see a specialist in London, and then I brought in two very good nurses to look after him when he became so gravely ill . . . Their wages were always paid on time, of course. They were so good with Marty, so gentle . . .' Barbara's voice broke.

It was horrible even to think of that time, Marty dying by degrees and the medication getting gradually stronger so that in the end he was hardly conscious.

And so thin and pale . . . And the funeral – well, she couldn't have a shabby little send-off for him. She owed it to Marty to do things in the style in which he'd lived, a proper tribute: extravagant; bigger and shinier than anyone else's; his favourite food served generously to all his friends, and champagne to drink and toast his memory, of course.

Where were those friends now? Barbara had not seen any of them again since that day.

She put her hands to her mouth as if to hold back a sob and tears ran down her face. Oh, it was just all too much, remembering that awful time. After the funeral everyone just went away. The nurses had already left, of course, and Barbara found herself utterly alone in the house she and Marty had bought together at the beginning of their short marriage.

Maureen didn't say anything. She simply gave Barbara's arm a gentle comforting squeeze. After a minute or two in which she fought to master her grief, Barbara swallowed and, taking a lace-edged handkerchief from her sleeve, she carefully mopped her eyes.

'And you have to pay this much every month, Barbara?'

'Yes, I'm afraid so.'

'What would happen if you couldn't pay?' Maureen asked. She sounded very serious now but she still hadn't offered any opinion at all.

Barbara could hardly bear to say the words aloud. 'They would take the house,' she confessed.

'Could you ask for more time to pay, just until you find yourself some more work?'

'Not really, Maureen. I tried that once but then it was worse because the bank charges interest and so the interest grew while the loan didn't get smaller. I was running to keep up and had to . . . to sell a few things . . . to get back on course.'

'So you've been short of money for quite a while, I gather, and you've already tried to extend the loan?'

Barbara nodded.

Maureen got up and walked over to the window. She stood looking out for a few moments, evidently thinking, and Barbara felt her hopes rising. Maureen would be bound to bail her out now. The brief account of poor Marty's illness would melt the hardest heart, and Maureen's heart was very far from hard.

'But if you've been so very short of money, how did you come to have any savings for this con man, Herbert Nicholson, to steal? You could have paid off some of these bills or part of the loan, or more, or even both, instead of investing your money in some scheme with a confidence trickster. You see, Barbara, I don't understand.'

She looked directly at Barbara for a long moment, and it was Barbara who looked away first.

'All right, Barbara. Well, please answer me this instead. Your income from the theatre work you and Marty both had – didn't that meet your bills?'

'No.'

'Oh dear. I'm sorry to hear that. But why was that? I'm not sure what Marty did exactly, but I can see from that lovely photograph that he was the kind of man who was at the centre of things. And you – a star of variety, a celebrated comedy actress – didn't they pay you for all that work, love? Or did they just give you tea sets?'

Maureen was looking at her intently again. Barbara suddenly felt that Maureen's agreement to bail her out all rested on the answer to this. It was the moment of truth. The revelation that she was a liar would be hard to bear, but worse would be the exposing of the ugly truth about her failed theatrical career. At least she could keep that hidden. And this *was* only Maureen, no one important, and not anyone from around here. Maureen would go home to her little house in Blackburn with her bank account somewhat lighter and Barbara would continue to be the gracious retired theatre star, the lady of the manor in Buckledale.

'We didn't do any work.' There, it was said.

'What, none at all?'

'No.' Barbara took a deep breath. 'Neither of us worked in the theatre at all once we came to live at The Manor. We just sort of . . . retired from it . . . enjoyed life without working.'

'So that first-night photograph . . .?' Maureen nodded towards the piano.

'Someone Marty knew. We were invited to see the show and then to the party afterwards.'

303

'I see. In fact, I reckon I'm beginning to get the entire picture. And may I ask you summat else, please, Barbara?'

Barbara swallowed and nodded, reminding herself that Mousy Maureen had a kind heart and she was every bit as in awe of Barbara as she had been when they were schoolgirls together.

'Is the story about this Herbert Nicholson conning you out of your savings a complete invention?'

'What?'

'You see, Barbara, it just doesn't add up at all. Had you got savings, you wouldn't have needed a loan from me to pay your more pressing bills, would you? So I think you made up that story. In fact, the only true part of it is that there is someone called Herbert Nicholson, but so far as I know he's a brewery manager and a social climber, and lives in Blackburn. I doubt he's escaped abroad with your savings or anyone else's. Certainly he was still working at Felbridge Brewery last week.'

'Good heavens!'

'Quite. And given that you and Marty were living a life of idle luxury when you told me you were starring in variety all over the country, and given that your savings, far from been stolen, were spent by you and Marty, if indeed you ever had any savings – which I doubt because you took out a huge bank loan to support your way of life – then should I take it that your brilliant career is also a lie? Weren't you a chorus girl, never a star? You see, Barbara, I don't mind if that was the case one little bit, but what I do mind about is being lied to.'

Barbara was flabbergasted. How on earth had Maureen found that out? It must have been recently, too, because she had clearly believed everything Barbara had told her when they were on holiday. There was nothing for it but to admit the truth.

'You're right, Maureen. About all of it. There was no con man. Marty and I lived on what we could borrow, and yes, I never had any luck with the leading roles in the theatre.'

Maureen took a moment to digest this. She knew it was the truth at last, after lie after lie, for years and years. 'Oh, Barbara . . .'

'Yes, yes, I know, and I'm sorry I misled you—'

'I wasn't being misled, Barbara,' said Maureen severely. 'I was being lied to.'

Barbara looked taken aback. 'Oh, now that's a little unkind, Maureen. I only said—'

'You lied, Barbara, and you know it. You thought you needn't be honest with me, that either you couldn't trust me with the truth in case I thought less of you, or that it wasn't worth you bothering to be honest with me. If you can't even admit that, then I shall borrow your telephone and call Des and Sylvia to come and collect me. Don't worry, I shall leave you the money for the call, and then I'll go and wait at the gate. I can't think it'll take them all that long to get here and rescue me from your lies and deceit.'

'Maureen, no! Oh, how could you be so cruel? I admit I haven't always told the complete truth—'

'Always? It's been one lie after another! Oh, yes, Barbara, you're a good person to enjoy a holiday with – you've got style and beauty, and all kinds of loveliness that brightens up a day and adds a sense of fun to an occasion – but when it comes to basics, like honesty to a friend and even the kindness not to treat me like a fool when I'm offering to help you, well, I'm afraid you're a sad disappointment. I'm sorry to say this, Barbara, but it's clear to me that you've got yourself into a mess through your own stupidity and extravagance, and mebbe you should be getting yourself out of it rather than asking me, who you clearly have no regard for, to help you.'

'But you offered to help me,' whined Barbara. 'You said you wouldn't let me sink or swim alone.'

'That was before I discovered that it was just lies and more lies with you.'

Barbara rose from her chair and started to pace about the room, clutching her little handkerchief.

'But I had to, Maureen,' she pleaded. 'You see, I've been the theatre star for years. I live and breathe that role. I can't just drop it now. Everything – the house, the car, the clothes – is about me being that glamorous woman. All this . . .' she indicated the house with a flap of her arm, '. . . it's who I am.'

'What, the crumbling old pile with a dodgy roof you bought? Summat that looks splendid on the surface, until you look closer and then you see just how shabby it really is?'

'Heartless!'

'True! Trying to make out what a shining star of the theatre you are when the truth is clearly that you weren't the talent you pretend to be, and I reckon you weren't even prepared to try very hard. You'd rather scrounge off other folk.'

'No! No, I was up for any role, I was willing to try anything to get my big break, but it never seemed to come. I kept going, taking what roles I could get – I even worked as a magician's assistant for a while, though it was awful being contorted into boxes on stage, and the rabbits' fur made me sneeze – and my big break was really when I met Marty and we got married. I had a wonderful husband and the life I'd always wanted . . . that I'd dreamed of . . . and we didn't even have to work for it. It didn't matter at the time that we might have lived a little optimistically, a tiny bit beyond our means, when we had such style and Marty knew so many rich and famous people. But then Marty became ill – he was ill already but I didn't know for a while.'

'There was no excuse, the pair of you buying a manor house and a posh car and a grand piano you couldn't pay for. Living high on the hog, running up bills for a way of life you couldn't possibly afford wasn't going to stop him dying, was it? Or mebbe you thought it was.'

Barbara sank onto her armchair then and gave herself up to sobbing until Maureen thought she had been too cruel; she even felt a little bit sorry for her friend. She'd no doubt that behind the lies and the falseness was a woman still grieving for the husband she had lost. Maureen knew what bereavement felt like.

'Ah, lass . . .'

Barbara continued crying and Maureen turned away and went to the window again to give her time to gather herself. She looked out over the drive and the large front garden. It certainly made a suitable setting for the grand house, the neat gravelled carriage drive, flowerbeds and shrubs to the side of the lawn, a variety of trees along the roadside to provide privacy. But as she moved closer to the window, her attention was caught by the once-glossy cord, now fraying and discoloured, tying back the long, thick curtains. The curtain lining, too, now she looked, was worn into tatters along the pleats. She'd never let her own curtains get so ragged without mending or replacing them. But then her curtains were made from remnants from the market.

She sighed and went to sit beside Barbara, who was still crying. 'Barbara, please pull yourself together or we'll never make any progress. I know it's upsetting, but you brought this about yourself – it wasn't summat that just happened to you – and now you must make an effort to face up to it and devise a plan to get out of it.'

'Oh, but, Maureen, please don't leave me to do it all on my own.'

'I'll help you, but in return you have to be straight with me. We'll work out what's best to do. I don't know a lot – far from it – but I reckon if we work out the basics, face what needs doing, we can then get some advice from wiser heads. It's surely only like house-keeping, but bigger, and we all know how to stick to a household budget . . .' Maureen tailed off as she realised where this was heading. 'Well, most folk do,' she finished.

'Yes, all right,' said Barbara in a small voice.

'Now,' said Maureen, 'tell me – honestly – how much money is coming in, if any. Do you have any income . . . at all, Barbara?'

'I teach the piano and elocution every day except Sundays,' said Barbara stiffly.

'Good heavens, I'd no idea, but then why would I when you told me you worked in the theatre? But this is good news.'

'Is it?' asked Barbara, looking glum. 'I earn several pounds a week from that, but no more. It feels like the most awful come-down.'

'From what? It sounds to me like it's summat you are good at if you have enough pupils to teach on six days a week, even if it isn't a big earner. Do they come here to have their lessons?'

'Yes, of course. The Manor is part of the appeal of the lessons. Most of the pupils like to come for private lessons to a house called The Manor and be taught to play on a grand piano or taught to speak by me, a former star of the theatre. I can charge more than most teachers would. It makes it all a lot more special, somehow, than if they just went to any old house and were taught on some shabby upright by a warty old person with a cough and bad feet.'

'Good heavens, Barbara, you are quite the most snobbish person I have ever met,' gasped Maureen.

'Perhaps, but I can also recognise and use it in other people. That's part of why I've kept the car. Of course, the other reason is that it was Marty's and he bought it for both of us to enjoy—'

'With the bank loan you still have to repay.' Maureen felt she had to bring the conversation back to the point.

'Yes, yes,' said Barbara impatiently. 'But you must remember when we were on holiday – in fact, only this morning when I came to collect you from the station – how everyone's eye is always drawn by the car; how at the places where we stopped, the staff were very attentive towards us – much more so than to other customers. It was the car, announcing to everyone that we are people not to be overlooked, we are *somebody*. The car has proved very useful in the past and I do believe it will again.'

'I understand what you're on about, love, but it's plain to me that this house and that car are not the sort of thing a person whose income is just a few pounds a week from teaching music and posh speaking can afford. I'm surprised you've kept going for so long. If you keep on like this, soon you'll not be able to pay either the bills or the loan, and then what? In fact, that moment has already come, hasn't it? It's the reason you asked me to come here, I reckon.'

Barbara huffed and slumped down in the armchair. 'So what am I supposed to do? Oh, Maureen, you did say you'd help me out. I'm sure if you were to write me a cheque I'd then be able to pay who I needed to and I'd manage for a bit longer.'

'Only to sink without trace later, my loan not repaid. No, don't start arguing, Barbara. I'm sorry to have to be blunt, but it seems to me that it's time someone made you face the truth. You're just putting off the evil day. I said I'd help and I will, but only to try to advise you what to do. I can't take you on like a life sentence.'

'A *life sentence?* What on earth do you mean?' Barbara looked affronted.

'Well, if you don't mend your ways and face up to what is possible on your earnings, you'll soon need another cheque from me, and then another. That's no use, is it? I'd run out of money, too, and then we'd both be in the drink without lifebelts. And besides, I have my girls to think of, and – have you thought of this – I might want to spend my money on summat for me, rather than bailing you out over and over?'

Barbara sighed. 'But I thought you were proud to be my friend. I'm a famous star, and when we were away you loved it that I attracted all the best attention and added glamour and a sense of luxury to what –

quite frankly, Maureen – wouldn't have been half the holiday it was without me. I was in the limelight, and you *did* like it that a little of that shone on you, too. I bet you've spoken to everyone you know about your friendship with the celebrated actress Barbara Hayle. You have your inherited fortune, but you haven't much idea how to live well on it without me to show you, have you? You're only moving from Mafeking Street because I've shown you a better way to live beyond your little terrace, and in return I just thought you'd be pleased to help me.'

Maureen was suddenly furious, reading into Barbara's words what her so-called friend really thought: that Maureen's legacy was wasted on her, and with a little flattery and a shopping trip she'd be buttered up to part with as much money as that 'friend' could relieve her of. She had been lied to and she was being used in a cruel and calculated way.

'Enough of your nonsense, Barbara. Is there no end to your selfishness and your self-regard? You're worse than you were when you were twelve.'

'What was wrong with me when I was twelve?'

'I reckon you might have to work that out for yourself, but you're forty-five now and it's time you grew up.'

'Don't ever say my age aloud again,' hissed Barbara. 'It is not to be broadcast, do I make myself clear?'

'But it is your age, isn't it? Same as mine. Oh, you are a monster of vanity. As if I'd boast about my friendship with you. For goodness' sake, no one's ever heard of you! I cannot help you if you're so bound up in your pretending that you can't cope with the truth . . . about anything!'

Maureen gathered her handbag up off the floor and her hat from where she had left it on the table and stood up. 'Right, I think it's time I made that call to Sylvia and Des and then I'll let myself out.'

She went out into the hall and then along to where she thought she'd heard Barbara's telephone ringing earlier.

The study was an untidy little room dominated by a desk and chair, and with piles of music and sheets of printed speech exercises – tongue-twisters and poems, Maureen saw at a glance – on the shelves, the desk, the chair. Also on the desk was a long calculation scribbled on a piece of paper, some of the figures crossed out, others added to the total to make a further calculation. They were obviously sums of money, and the untidy scrawl and deep impression of the pen on the paper reflected Barbara's mood about that exercise. Beside it was a diary open to display the following week over a double-page spread. The name – good heavens! – 'Herbert Nicholson' was written against the space headed Tuesday, with '+ 5s' next to it. Now the little mystery of how Barbara had pulled out that name to give to her fictitious confidence trickster was solved. Maureen realised at once that Herbert was taking elocution lessons – he'd betrayed his lack of interest in music when she worked for him, much to Stella's disgust, she remembered – and that Barbara was making him pay through the nose. Served him right!

Maureen dialled Sylvia and Desmond's telephone number and luckily it was Des who answered. Being a man of little imagination or curiosity, he asked no questions but said he'd be at the gate of The Manor, Buckledale, to collect his mother-in-law as soon as he could. Maureen then put a shilling beside the telephone, which would more than cover the cost of the brief call, and came back out into the hall.

Barbara must still be in the music room. Maureen went to the doorway to say goodbye. Barbara's golden curls were just visible behind the high back of the armchair.

'Thank you for the tea, Barbara. Please keep the cake and the tin. I shall go and wait out of your way.'

Barbara sprang up from the chair, her face contorted in anguish. 'That's right, you go! Leave me! You said you wouldn't leave me to sink or swim alone and you lied! Just go, get out and leave me to my fate. Cruel! So cruel . . .' She sank down again, sobbing loudly.

Maureen had seen enough for one day and could cope with no more. She went quickly to the front door and let herself out.

CHAPTER EIGHTEEN

MAUREEN CRUNCHED DOWN the gravelled drive to the gate, which was open, and went out to the lane, being careful not to glance back. It was possible that Barbara would be watching her leave and she really didn't want to see the expression on Barbara's face. She looked at her watch: half past eleven. Desmond would be at least forty minutes, even if he left home straight away. There was time to have a walk into the village and see what it was like. She had hoped Barbara would show her round while they exchanged news, and Maureen would meet Barbara's friends and neighbours, but this was not to be.

There was no pavement, just a grassy verge, but the road was deserted and the sky continued blue with just the haziest of high fair-weather cloud in the distance. As Maureen walked she felt her fury start to drain away. Oh, she was still angry with Barbara – it was clear now that Barbara regarded her with no affection, just as someone to use, to sponge off, and to show off in front of – but Maureen decided to make an effort to put that behind her. After all, what did it matter? She had her darling daughters and other, real friends, people she could trust and whom she loved – what need had she of Barbara's false friendship? It was disappointing, but it was better that she knew the truth . . .

The green of the hedges was intense, the smell of grass the freshest Maureen had ever experienced. The air was just so *clean*, so clear, that it was a treat to breathe it.

At a field gate she stopped to look over at some cows grazing. They in turn looked up to stare at her and, after a while, a couple of them sauntered heavily over, breathing hot cow-breath and bringing with them flies and the sweet mucky smell of cowpats. They were bigger and broader than any cows Maureen had ever seen before – her experience of farm animals not being extensive – just as the green of the leaves was greener and the blue sky was higher and bluer than any sky before now. Oh, but this was heaven . . .

She walked on and soon came to the first of the village houses, a stone cottage with a small front garden, a low wall enclosing it. There were flower-filled tubs and window boxes, roses and other flowering plants packed into the little space, and a row of tall plants with pink flowers bordering inside one wall. An old man was sweeping the path to the blue-painted front door. He looked up, hearing Maureen's approach.

'Good morning.' He touched his hand to the peak of his flat cap.

Maureen stopped outside the gate. 'Morning. I'm just admiring your flowers. What are they called, these tall ones?'

'They're hollyhocks,' the man said. 'These are self-seeded. I just let them come up and see to themselves, really.'

'I wonder if I could manage that,' smiled Maureen. 'I've never grown flowers and I haven't a garden of my own yet, although I hope to have one very soon.'

'Where do you come from then, without a garden?' asked the man.

'Blackburn. At the moment I live in a terrace with just a backyard for the coal house and that.'

'You're a way from home, missus, on a Sunday morning.'

'I just came to visit. I'm off back when my lift turns up.'

'Not much to see in Buckledale.'

'I think it's a nice place, what I've seen of it,' said Maureen. 'Pretty and peaceful.'

The old man chuckled. 'Prettier than Blackburn, anyway. Have you been right round the village?'

'No, I've just walked from The Manor.'

'Oh, yes? Know her, do you?'

'Who's that?'

'Barbara Hayle.'

Maureen shook her head, not wanting to speak a lie but not willing to give up the chance to learn

317

something from this man, if only how Barbara was regarded in the village. He might well be unhelpfully discreet if he thought Maureen knew Barbara.

'I saw the house – what's *she* like?'

'All right.'

'Not a friend of yours?'

'No. I reckon as she hasn't any friends. I go there to do her garden, but never see no one up at The Manor but them as pay for her to teach them to play the piano and to talk posh, and some fella in a van what's up to summat in those outbuildings.'

'No friends at all? That's a bit sad,' said Maureen.

'Yes. I feel sorry for her, really. Reckon she's down about her husband dying. There was always a crowd there when he was alive, before he got ill, but since then she's been very much on her own.'

'I'm sorry to hear that. It can be hard to manage alone.'

'Aye.' He lowered his voice. 'Struggling, she is. Keeps up a good face, always looks the part, but I reckon there's not much behind it all these days. Most of the rooms are empty of furniture.'

This was news. Maureen had seen the kitchen, which did indeed have an empty look, but the music room was furnished and the study was certainly functioning. The entrance hall was a picture of elegance, possibly a calculated first impression. There were, however, many other rooms than these, and Maureen had not been invited into any of them. Had this been because

Barbara had not wanted her to see they were empty? Certainly unfurnished rooms would account for the oddly desolate look of The Manor from the back.

'What's happened?' Maureen felt deceitful but she was getting information more readily out of this old fella than she had out of Barbara herself.

'Sold almost everything, piece by piece,' he confided. 'Only a matter of time before the bailiffs come and take away the rest, I reckon.'

'Oh dear! I wonder, as you say she gives lessons, that her pupils don't pay.'

'Oh, I'm sure they do, the kind of folk what goes there: respectable, well-heeled, judging by their appearance, and many arrive by car. But I reckon she must be too far in debt to get out now. The husband was a flash kind – charming, but champagne taste, if you know what I mean, and that costs, whether or not you've got owt to support it. But when he went and died, well . . . things soon started going downhill after that. She used to be a big name in the theatre, apparently – I've never heard of her, but then I know nowt of theatres – but I never see theatrical kind of folk round there these days, looking out for her. No family nor owt, either.'

'Goodness, poor lady,' said Maureen, wondering where Barbara's numerous siblings fitted in with this piece of information. Hadn't she said she'd given her dinner service to her sisters? But Enid had told her that she and a brother were the only ones living locally. 'Everyone needs family and friends.'

'Aye, it's a bad job for them as hasn't got none, especially when they're in trouble.'

'Mm . . . well, I might continue my walk, see what there is to see before I go home. Goodbye, Mr . . .?'

'Gathercole. Good day to you, missus.'

Well, that had been an interesting conversation. Barbara hadn't said anything about having to sell her furniture. Strange that she should live in a largely unfurnished house – if Mr Gathercole was correct in what he said – yet still drive around in the huge car. But then the car was all part of the show, whereas few but Barbara would know the house was unfurnished, especially if she never had any friends visiting. Just as the front windows of The Manor were painted and maintained but the back ones were shabby and decaying. With Barbara, all was for show and vanity. It was very sad.

Maureen checked the time and walked on until the houses petered out. She turned at the edge of the village and strolled back towards The Manor, looking behind her when she heard a vehicle approaching, but it was just a passing car. She went to stand at the side of the road near Barbara's gate, but out of sight of the house, to wait for Desmond.

She'd been waiting for a few minutes when the van she'd seen arriving at The Manor earlier came out of the drive end. The driver paused to see that the way was clear and then pulled out and passed directly by Maureen. The man, probably in his late twenties, was quite good-looking and looked vaguely familiar, although Maureen couldn't place him. No, she must be mistaken. There was no reason she would have seen this pest controller before.

He drove away without glancing at Maureen, and within seconds had passed Desmond, who was slowing to read the house name on the wall beside the gate.

Sylvia was with him, craning her neck as he turned the van in the gateway. She opened the van door.

'Mum, what's going on? Why did you call for a lift home? Are you all right?'

Maureen climbed in the front and Sylvia shuffled along to make room. 'Hello, Sylvie. Thanks for coming to collect me, Des. I'm fine, love. There's no need to worry.'

'But what happened? I thought you'd be staying all day and Barbara Hayle would take you to the station.'

'We had a change of plan, love, that's all. Nowt to worry about.'

'Can you wait, Des, while I have a proper look at the house? Ooh, it does look grand. Do you think Barbara would mind if I just went in to look?'

'I think she might,' said Desmond, surprisingly. ''Specially as there's been a change of plan.'

'Oh, but I do want to see what it's like—'

'I think I'd like to go home, Sylvie, if you don't mind. I'll tell you all about it later, but it's been a very tiring morning and I might need to have a little nap on the way home,' said Maureen, leaning her head against the window and closing her eyes.

The visit to Barbara had given Maureen a lot to think about. The easiest course of action would be to cut Barbara out of her life and let her manage by herself. She really had behaved in the most outrageous way, and who wanted to be friends with someone quite so deceitful, so disdainful of her friend, so manipulative and vain? Thank goodness Maureen had got to the bottom of at least some of Barbara's situation before she'd agreed to go home and write the ridiculous woman a huge cheque to allow her to keep up her pretensions. There was no doubt that if she had, she would never see her money again. Barbara would spend it on what bills she simply had to pay and then would keep herself in the style to which she was accustomed – the style she thought was her due.

Oh, but there had been *some* worthwhile outgoings: having the piano tuned; the sheet music. Barbara obviously took her job as piano and elocution teacher seriously, and she'd devised this role to shore up her failing finances as best she could, but trading on her invented past as a successful actress. It seemed that everything Barbara did was tied up with this fiction. She was a hollow person, a woman who hardly existed in reality. Yet ironically, the tiny part of her that was genuine – the piano and elocution teacher – was of far more worth than the rest.

There had been nothing offered to eat but the cake Maureen herself had provided; no sign that there would be any food had she stayed until lunchtime. That would have been interesting. Maureen imagined Barbara suddenly saying they must go out for lunch, driving them somewhere expensive in the car, where everyone would see their arrival and would be fussing around them, and then, somehow, Maureen herself would be the one paying, just as she had on their holiday. Of course, she wouldn't mind that; it was the lie behind it that she would object to.

Barbara hadn't eaten much while they'd been away. Perhaps she was used to eating only a little because she couldn't afford to do otherwise, or she had to be so slim to fit into the beautiful clothes she wore, mostly discounted samples, the bills for which remained unpaid.

Oh, it was all very sad and such a mess . . .

Not your mess.

'Mum? Are you OK? There wasn't some upset, was there?' asked Sylvia kindly.

'I'm all right, love, don't you worry. Just got a few things to think about.'

'It'll be gone lunchtime when we get home. Come and have summat at ours and then Des will take you home – Liza won't be expecting you until later. And I promise not to ask you owt. But you know that me and Liza – and Des, too – we'd do what we could to help if you needed us.'

'Thanks, Sylvie. You're a good girl. I'm lucky to have you – all of you.'

Poor Barbara – she might have the looks and the style

but she had no support from her family, for whatever reason, no friends and no money. Worse, she was well and truly stuck with the life of lies she had invented, bound up with The Manor, from which she seemed unable to part, even though it was like a stone around her neck, sinking her ever deeper into financial trouble.

She's pathetic. She's not your problem, Maureen. Forget her.

Eliza had spent Sunday morning round at the Mulligans' house, chatting and laughing with Anna-Marie, and then Agnes and the twins when they returned from Mass. Bridget and Colleen were funny and noisy, and they liked Eliza to teach them the words of the songs she sang in the Waterloo.

Eliza declined an invitation to stay for lunch. Maureen had left her something to eat, and besides, Eliza wanted to continue sorting through her clothes and boxes of old things she'd kept from her childhood. The house Maureen was buying was much bigger than 28 Mafeking Street and there would be plenty of space for everything in the rooms Maureen had offered Eliza to have as her own part of the house. But it would be silly not to have a throw-out now.

She was sitting on the floor in the front room, surrounded by old books and toys and some unfinished knitting she'd forgotten about, when the doorbell rang. She glanced through the window and saw Theo on the step, so she rushed to open the door.

'Theo, what a nice surprise. Or have I forgotten you were coming round? Come in.'

Theo stepped inside. He was carrying a bunch of flowers – white roses, no less. 'No, we didn't make an arrangement. But you did say your mum was going to see Barbara Hayle today so I thought you might be alone . . . lonely.'

'I was at Anna-Marie's this morning. The twins are so funny. They reckon Anna-Marie and Michael are going to marry because they saw them kissing.'

'Do they indeed,' smiled Theo. He held out the flowers to Eliza.

'For me? Oh, they're beautiful. Thank you, Theo. You're very generous. Come through and I'll put them in water. Would you like a cup of tea?'

'No, thank you.'

'Have you had owt to eat? I can quickly make you summat if you like?'

'No, thank you.'

'Shall I—'

'Liza, would you please stop talking for a moment so that I can say something?'

Eliza's mouth made a silent 'Oh' but she said no more. She turned from the sink with a vase of water for the roses in her hand and put it down gently on the kitchen table. Then she stood quite still. Suddenly her heart was pounding.

'You see, I've been thinking about this, and worrying, and wondering if it's a mad idea and if I'm making a complete fool of myself, what with me being so much older and having been married before – I think I once told you my wife died very young – and you being so young and lovely, and with your whole life ahead of you. And maybe you wouldn't want to be shackled to an older man, and I'm just being selfish, but I just thought if I didn't ask, I'd never know for certain. And I wouldn't want to go through the rest of my life wondering if I *should* have asked you and maybe, just maybe, if I had, you'd have said yes and made me the happiest man on earth.'

'Theo?' Eliza hoped she wasn't thinking the wrong thing. He had never shown such uncertainty before. He always seemed to know exactly what was the best thing to do. She was filled with a rush of hope, combined with fear that she was wrong – that she just couldn't be this fortunate. 'What is it you're saying?' she whispered.

'I'm saying, Eliza, that I love you more than anything.'

He started to bend his knee and Eliza knew she had to spare him that. She wanted to laugh, at his absurdly comic move, but also with the joy of her hopes realised.

'Oh, please, please, Theo, don't get down on one knee.'

'No, quite right. A ludicrous idea. Such a cliché.' He reached for her left hand and kissed the back of it. 'Please will you marry me?'

It was what she had dreamed off – increasingly often of late – and had never dared to speak of aloud, even to Maureen. It seemed too much to hope that this dear man, so attractive, clever and funny, would want her –

Eliza Bancroft, a barber's assistant, aged twenty, who had never been anywhere or done anything – to be his wife.

'Yes, Theo. I love you, too. Yes . . . of course I will.'

'Oh, thank you. Oh, thank goodness,' he said, his voice betraying genuine relief and gratitude. 'I can't imagine my life without you in it and I promise to take care of you always.'

'Darling Theo . . .'

Eliza stepped forward and Theo enveloped her in his arms and held her very close. 'My darling girl,' he muttered into her hair, and then he kissed her and she kissed him in return, so that soon each was kissing the other at the same time, and this delightful muddle of exchanged kisses went on for a while.

'I was so worried you'd think I was being a stupid old man,' Theo confessed eventually, 'that I was deluded and cutting a ridiculous figure.'

'Of course not,' Eliza said emphatically. 'And, please, do stop referring to yourself as old. Are you trying to put me off already? You're lovely, and so young at heart that you will never be old to me.'

'Darling girl . . .'

'Our marrying makes the most perfect sense. We can sing together whenever we want to, and our home will be full of song and laughter.'

'Song and Laughter – it can be the name of our double act.'

'And you're such a good cook that I will eat like a queen, which is a good thing because you know I haven't much talent for cooking and one of us has to be able to do it well.'

'Do I detect an ulterior motive already?'

'But the most perfect sense of all is that we love each other and so we *should* be together.'

He held her closely to him and kissed her again, then pulled away to look into her eyes. 'You always did speak wisely, Liza.'

'Ha, love has made you blind, or rather, deaf, as you know I'm often wrong about many things. But about this we're in agreement, and we can't both be wrong, can we? So, as I say, it must make perfect sense.'

'Do you think I should have asked Maureen's permission to marry you? She is your only parent, after all, and you two are so very close.'

'Well, we might want to tell her our intentions together, as a . . . a formality, Theo, out of politeness, like, but I reckon Mum won't stand in the way of our happiness, do you?'

'What time is she back from Barbara Hayle's?'

'I don't know. Sometime later, I think. Not yet, anyway.'

The telephone rang then, and Eliza ducked under Theo's encircling arm and went to answer it.

'Bancroft, hello?'

'Liza, it's Sylvia. I just wanted to make sure you were in. Mum's at ours and Des is just about to bring her home. There was some kind of upset at Barbara's and Mum asked us to collect her.'

'Upset? Is Mum all right?'

'She's fine. She's not said much but she's quite cross.'

'Goodness . . . well, I'm here so I'll see her in a few minutes. When I find out what's happened, I'll tell you.'

'Of course. I'm bursting to know.'

They said goodbye and Eliza went to tell Theo that Maureen was coming home early.

'Some kind of falling-out with Barbara Hayle, it seems.'

'I had better get out of the way, then, Liza. It's none of my business and I doubt I can help, although you know where I am if I can. I'll see you tomorrow at the Short Cut.'

'I won't say owt to Mum today about us. Mebbe you can come back here with me one day this week after work, when this has blown over, or died down, and we can tell her together then.'

'Yes, my love. We'll make sure Maureen's OK before we tell her our news.'

They parted with another series of kisses, and then Eliza waved Theo off and went to arrange her roses in the vase before she got distracted by Maureen's arrival back.

CHAPTER NINETEEN

T HE NEXT DAY Eliza told Theo all that Maureen had found out about Barbara and what a false friend she was. Maureen was quite down about all the lies she'd been told by Barbara, and Eliza and Theo agreed they wouldn't spring their news on her when she had enough to think about already. 'I'm that confused,' Maureen said to Eliza that evening, unable to put Barbara's deceit behind her. 'I honestly thought we were friends. To think that all these years she's been lying to me! I had no idea until Annie told me about the real Barbara and, even then, I didn't believe her. I feel bad about that, too: almost dismissing Annie as a vindictive and batty old woman, when she was telling the truth.' 'Are you going to tell Annie that you've discovered the truth for yourself, Mum?'

'No. It would only raise bad feelings and upset her. I think Annie's happiest if she's not thinking too much about Barbara. Of all her children, she seems to like her the least.'

'I wonder why,' Eliza said, deadpan.

In the meantime, Maureen had something else to think about. When she'd got home the previous day she'd eventually seen, on the kitchen table, the most beautiful vase of gigantic white roses.

They didn't look like the kind of thing Eliza would buy for herself. Maureen took them through to the sitting room.

'I found these on the table, love. I thought you'd want them in here. Did someone give them to you?'

'Oh, thanks, Mum. I forgot and left them there when you came home. Yes, Theo brought them. Aren't they lovely?' 'Very generous of him,' said Maureen, carefully. 'Did he give you them for any particular reason?'

'He just thought I'd like them.'

'I see . . .'

Oh my goodness, thought Maureen, these roses weren't just a casual present. The man who gave a woman roses like these was, without a doubt, very serious about that woman.

She had hoped to put off wondering quite what she thought about the very clear and deep affection between Eliza and dear, kind, funny Theo, the man who she spent so much time with and talked about endlessly, but who was more than twice her age. Was Eliza setting herself up for future unhappiness, even loneliness? She wouldn't wish it on her darling girl.

* * *

On the Wednesday, at the Short Cut, Theo suggested to Eliza that he come round to collect her and Maureen and take them to the Waterloo. It would do Maureen good to have an evening with her friends and some cheering music, and of course, there would be something to celebrate, too. It was time to tell her of their plans. Eliza agreed and made a special effort to do her makeup and her hair carefully. This was an important evening. Somehow Maureen had caught her mood and came downstairs wearing a very pretty dress – one of the ones she'd bought in Somerton-on-Sea but thought a little dressy to wear too often. She'd bought Eliza a soft cream-coloured cardigan with tiny bugle beads set around the neck and in a rose pattern down the front, which looked perfect with her beloved performance frock, and she was pleased to see Eliza wearing it now.

'Don't we look smart?' Eliza smiled. She glanced through the front window. 'And here's Theo. Now there's a man who knows how to dress.' She went to the door.

'Is your mum OK? Shall we tell her now?' whispered Theo.

Eliza nodded and squeezed his hand.

Theo went into the front room.

'Hello, Maureen. You look amazing,' he said.

'Thank you, Theo, but I think "amazing" is more suited to you this evening. Is that a waistcoat you're wearing under your jacket?'

'It certainly is. Embroidered by nuns, no less.'

Eliza giggled. 'You're having us on.'

'No, it's true, I promise. You see, I'm hoping to catch the benevolent eye of the Divine and then all will be well. The thing is, Maureen . . . well, I hope you don't mind me rushing in but I simply have to say: I am madly in love with Eliza and I've asked her to marry me. Eliza's said yes, but, well . . . we're both hoping that we can marry with your blessing.'

Theo and Eliza looked at Maureen and Eliza held her breath. Maureen said nothing, but her face reflected a series of thoughts passing through her mind: happiness but also some anxiety. She pursed her lips, and then put her hands to her mouth as if she was wondering what to say and how to say it, and then she took a deep breath . . . and by this time Eliza felt she was ready to elope, she was so full of misgivings about Maureen's reaction. She felt Theo taking her hand and giving it a supportive squeeze.

'Mum . . .?'

Just then the doorbell rang and, through the window, Sylvia and Desmond could be seen outside. Eliza and Theo looked at each other.

'I'll let them in. Can't keep them on the step,' said Eliza crossly, thinking that the timing was typical of Sylvia, but also that at least Sylvia and Desmond's presence would put off herself and Theo having to hear Maureen's reservations about their marrying.

'Hello, Liza,' said Sylvia, beaming joyfully, bursting into the house in a cloud of rosy perfume. 'We've got some great news and I've been dying to tell you and Mum, and we've decided that now's the time,' she announced loudly as she tottered into the front room on her high heels, Eliza and Des following. She flung her arms around Maureen. 'I'm going to have a baby. Des is going to be a dad and you'll be a grandma, Mum! Isn't that exciting?'

Maureen didn't look at all surprised. Eliza thought she might already have guessed, as Sylvia had been moody – moodier than usual – of late. Maureen did look extremely happy, though, and hugged Sylvia to her.

'Such good news, my darling . . .'

'It is,' agreed Eliza. She gave Sylvia a hug. Now she understood why Sylvia didn't want Maureen to go to live very far away. Any woman would want her mother nearby to advise her about a first baby.

'Oh, hello, Theo,' said Desmond, grinning.

'Desmond, congratulations.' Theo, displaying manners that were never less than perfect, set aside any thoughts about Maureen's reaction to his and Eliza's own announce-ment and shook Desmond's hand. 'Congratulations to both of you.' He went over and kissed Sylvia's cheek.

'Hello, Theo. Sorry for barging in like that,' said Sylvia. 'I didn't know you'd be here.'

'Well, the thing is,' said Maureen, smiling, but as if she'd decided to pull herself together, 'you're not the only one with news. Eliza and Theo are going to be married.'

'Well, I never,' said Sylvia, looking nonplussed, as if it was she who had had her thunder stolen. 'There's a surprise.'

'Really, love?' asked Desmond. 'Makes perfect sense to me. Congratulations in return, the both of you. Anyone can see you're made for each other.'

He and Theo shook hands again, and then Desmond kissed Eliza's cheek and remarked how pretty she looked this evening.

Eliza caught her mother's eye then. Maureen's face had so much showing in it. Somehow she managed to look happy and sad at the same time.

'Shall we go and celebrate at the Waterloo, then?' said Desmond. 'Come on, Sylvia, love. I'll find you a chair with the other mothers.'

He and Sylvia led the way out, Sylvia taking her mother's arm outside and preparing to talk about her pregnancy all the way to the pub.

'I'll lock up,' Eliza called after them, and waited with Theo to let them get ahead.

'Oh dear, do you think she's upset?' said Theo.

'I had hoped she'd be delighted for us. I know how much she likes you, Theo, and, well, what has she to mind about? Anyway, with Sylvia and Desmond trumping our news, at least she has summat to celebrate this evening.'

'Oh, sweetheart, don't be down. We're going to be married and we'll be the happiest people on earth. Your mum will come round. She only wants the best for you.'

'And the best for me is you, Theo. Why wouldn't she see that?'

'I intend that she should, but we'll just have to give

her a bit of time to get used to the idea. At least Desmond got to the heart of the matter with remarkable speed: that we're made for each other.'

'Which for Des is a pretty sharp observation.'

Theo smiled. 'Be nice, Eliza.'

The announcements at the Waterloo that evening made what would have been a normal Wednesday evening into a party, and everyone lost count of the rounds of drinks that were bought to toast the happy couples.

'A grandma,' said Agnes, beaming and patting Maureen's hand. 'Who'd have thought you'd beat me to it, and me the mother of five, and my Kathleen older than Sylvia and still not hitched? Ah well, I'd better get knitting, hadn't I? It'll be good to have *someone* to knit a little matinée jacket for.'

'Ah, Agnes, love, it's only a matter of moments before your Anna-Marie and young Michael McBride announce their engagement,' said Maureen.

'Aye, I suspect you might be right. The twins think so anyway. Perhaps our girls could have a double wedding.'

'Well, that would be up to the brides. Eliza will do as she wants anyway.'

Agnes looked sharply at her friend. 'What's the matter, Maureen? It's not like you to be critical of Liza.'

'Oh, just ignore me.'

'No, love, tell me what's wrong.'

'Well, part of me's really pleased that Liza and Theo are getting married. Des said earlier that they're made for each other, and he's right. But it's just that Theo's so much older. I don't want my girl to be left a young widow like I was. She could go half her life without him.'

'Theo's not old yet, though, Maureen. He's what, mid-forties? Your Jack was ill, and that was a tragedy, but there's no reason to think Theo won't live to a good age, is there?'

'Not as far as I know. But it's so hard to be a widow and know you'll be alone for the rest of your life.'

'Do you know what I think, Maureen?' said Agnes stoutly. 'I think you're talking nonsense. You should be pleased that Eliza has found such a good man. There's many a young fella out there who's not worthy to clean her shoes, and she's got herself a good 'un. Just be glad, see the good in this – of which there's a great deal – and stop being such a misery. Your Eliza's marrying the love of her life and your Sylvia's going to have a bairn, and if there's owt to grumble about in that then you're not the woman I thought you were.'

Maureen was startled to be told off so roundly, but one of the things she liked about Agnes was that she was genuine and plain-speaking: a good, reliable friend. What a welcome contrast to Barbara Hayle, who was false and deceiving through and through.

'Well, that's me told! But you know, Agnes, I expect you're quite right. I'm being daft.'

'None of us knows what's going to happen in life, Maureen. Don't you think we have to grasp our happiness when we can? Some are never happy; those of us who have the chance to be are the lucky ones, aren't we?'

'You're right again, of course. I am happy for them really, but I just can't help worrying.'

'And how is that going to help anything? You can worry yourself to an early grave, and all for nothing. Come on, Maureen, love. Accept and embrace the good, otherwise you'll tarnish it. Don't let them remember that the night they celebrated their engagement, you had a long face.'

'No, that would be awful. I shall go and hug them both and give them my blessing. I shall do it now.' She rose to go to Eliza and Theo, who were chatting with Harry at the bar, but Sylvia came over and sat herself down beside her mother.

'Don't go, Mum.'

'I just want to say something to Eliza . . .'

'I've said I'll knit a little jacket for your baby, Sylvia, love,' said Agnes. 'Shall I go for white?'

'Thanks, Agnes. That's so kind of you. Yes, that might be best, and then when the baby's born you can sew some buttons on in pink or blue.'

'Ah, there's nothing beats tradition,' smiled Agnes. 'And your baby won't be the only one in white. It's very exciting.' She nodded across to Eliza.

'I only hope Eliza will hold off setting the date until after I've had the baby,' said Sylvia. 'I don't want to be fat and pregnant in the photos. If she waits until I've got my figure back, then I could be her matron of honour. I fancy a mauve dress, or mebbe pink with puffy sleeves . . .'

Maureen rolled her eyes. 'Sylvia, the decision about the date is Eliza and Theo's, not yours. The decisions about bridesmaids and dresses are Eliza's.'

'Yes, all right, Mum. But I hope Eliza will consult me.'

Sylvia moved off to find Desmond, and Maureen leaned in to Agnes. 'Honestly, I wonder about Sylvia sometimes. Only she could make Eliza's wedding about herself.'

'Well, she'll be like a lioness with her cub when the baby's born, which has to be a good thing,' laughed Agnes.

'And now you've given me a boot up the backside I think without any more delay I should go and tell my darling girl and that fine man how pleased I am at their wonderful news.'

She moved off to the bar to do so.

'Eliza, Theo,' she said, joining their group, 'I couldn't be happier you're to be married.' She put an arm around each of them and they put their drinks down on the bar and hugged her back. 'I know you are made for each other. Many go their whole lives and don't find true love, and I know how fortunate you both are. You are meant to be together – anyone can see that.'

'Thank you, Maureen,' said Theo. 'I shall never do anything to make Eliza regret her decision. She's a woman in a million. As are you, Maureen.'

'I'm not sure I can do the maths to work out how

special we are, Mum,' laughed Eliza, 'but I can tell you are properly pleased for us . . . and – heavens – you'll be Theo's mother-in-law!'

'Now that,' said Maureen, beaming at Theo, 'is a real privilege.'

Eliza pressed a glass of delicious fizzy wine into her mother's hand and the whole company raised their glasses: 'To each of you and all of us.'

Eliza's engagement and Sylvia's pregnancy were two milestones in Maureen's life to lift her spirits. The other good news was that the house she was buying looked set to be hers in just a few short weeks and she was filled with the energy of new beginnings and fresh plans. But she could not quite let go of her worries about Barbara. Barbara was in deep trouble. It was trouble of her own making, sure enough, but Maureen felt, despite everything, that she had abandoned Barbara too quickly.

The gate to The Manor was closed. Brendan got out of his van into the pouring rain to open it, then climbed back inside again, dripping and cursing, to drive round to the outbuildings. The light was strangely gloomy and autumnal for August, and the chilly rain was set in for the day.

There was no one around, as the closed gate had implied. Often on weekdays there was a car parked in front of the house, belonging to one of Barbara's pupils or the parent of one, but today there was no sign of life at The Manor at all. Not even that old fella who did the garden . . . Brendan couldn't remember his name. Well, it certainly wasn't a day for gardening, especially for the elderly.

The fact that the place looked deserted was fortunate. Brendan wasn't keen on having to keep a lookout for nosy parkers, but he could hardly ask Barbara when she was unlikely to have anyone here. She'd be wanting to know why. It was bad enough that Con had begun asking questions – in an oh-so-casual way – about the reason for keeping surplus stock so far out of town until there was room for it at the shop. Brendan had brought his colleague here a couple of times to help lift the heavier pieces of second-hand furniture, but had not encouraged Con to touch anything that he himself was not directing to be moved.

Now he opened the middle one of the buildings and went in. He'd got a couple of little cabinets in here that he'd searched thoroughly for forgotten heirlooms and he now thought he might take back with him. The place smelled of damp, even in high summer. He noticed the rain was coming in at the top of the door, although the door had been firmly closed, and it was also running down the side wall. There must be a hole in the roof. That was a nuisance. Trust Barbara to rent him some sound- and substantial-looking outbuildings, which then turned out to be decrepit and decaying. That was pretty much the story of The Manor, from what he could gather. Hadn't Barbara and Marty been nearly bankrupted over the roof at one time? Evidently they had spent money only on renovating the house, not the other buildings.

Brendan looked around and saw wet rot at the foot of the doors and then, to his horror, that the roof was sagging. The heavy rain of these last couple of days had shown up these structural weaknesses where none had been apparent before. It must have been the precise direction the wind was blowing, funnelling the rain right inside and also onto the most vulnerable part of the structure above.

He went out and unlocked the doors to the building nearest the garage. This was nothing like as wet inside, although it was far from watertight. It was also completely full of furniture and there was no room to move anything over to here.

What must the garage be like, where Barbara kept that fancy car? She wouldn't want the roof falling in on that. Brendan decided he'd better mention the decay to her, if only because he wouldn't be able to sell the car if it got crushed by a collapsed roof. She said she'd never part with that car, but Brendan was hopeful and prepared to wait. She'd sold most of the furniture in the house; it was only a matter of time before the motor had to go, too. She'd be wise to ask him to sell it for her sooner rather than later, with the state of these buildings.

Finally, he went to the furthest along and unlocked that. Oh Lord, this was the worst of them. The underside of the roof was stained with a huge watermark. The rain had formed a large wet patch on the floor by the outer wall, and the water had dripped onto some of the old furniture, causing a stain down the side of a pine dresser and on the wide lower shelves of a bookcase.

Well, at least Con would be able to put right the damage. The old stuff never made much in the shop anyway, unless it was given a new lease of life, old varnish stripped off and then the wood polished or given a coat of paint. Still, Brendan thought, he'd have to take some of this away with him soon. Like Barbara's car, it would be no use to anyone if it was crushed, or ruined by water beyond renovation.

What did have to be removed – and now – was a box of items Brendan kept hidden in one of the locked drawers of an old bureau. Should the bureau be reduced to matchwood beneath the fallen roof, these items might come to light before he could get to them, which would be very bad news indeed.

Brendan checked outside – no one in sight – then eased himself through the narrow space he'd left between two close-standing wardrobes, then edged across the front of a linen press, round a chest of drawers and through to a clearer area, behind where he was able to access the bureau quite easily. The key to the drawer was on his keyring. The box was nothing more than a cardboard shoebox.

Brendan picked it up, thinking. He could take it home, but he lived above the shop and that made his flat vulnerable. Any suspicions about his stock at The

Remove – which had happened in the past – and the flat could come under police scrutiny, too. No, better the contents of this box were nowhere near him, nowhere anyone would think of looking, until he'd got a suitable buyer lined up. He'd been trying to do this for a couple of weeks now but without success.

He took off his jacket, wrapped the box in it, then shut and locked the bureau and edged his way out. He ran to his van to put the box inside, then back to close and lock each pair of doors. Then he retrieved the wrapped box and hurried round to the front of The Manor.

Brendan was pleased to make the shelter of Barbara's imposing porch. He let himself in quietly at the front door with the spare key he had never returned to Barbara. The house was completely silent. He put the box down very gently, took off his shoes, padded to the kitchen and peeped round the door, which was open a few inches. Deserted.

He tiptoed back into the hall and listened. The house was totally silent but for the distant faint ticking of a clock in one of the rooms. Perhaps Barbara was out. Quickly and silently, Brendan checked she wasn't asleep on the sofa in the drawing room, or sitting at her desk in the untidy study, where he sometimes found her, often in a bad mood, papers strewn before her. She might, of course, be upstairs. He needed to be quick and quiet.

He picked up the box, still wrapped in his jacket,

and ran as quietly as he could up the carpeted stairs. At the top there was one long corridor with rooms off to either side, the doors all closed. Brendan knew, because he had been all over the house when Barbara had been away, that her bedroom was the first on the left, overlooking the front, and that there was just one other of the many bedrooms still furnished, which was at the other end on the right. He ran silently down to this room and turned the door handle slowly, opened the door and went in, pushing the door almost to behind him.

The room looked over the back garden, where the rain was hammering down, causing the roses to sag, and splashing in deep puddles on the uneven brick paths. A couple of birds sat on the wall to the side, miserable like sentries enduring their watch, the rain beading on their dark feathers. The room felt cold, the house gloomy and sad. Why did Barbara like it here so much? It must be awful, all alone, on a long, dark, freezing January night . . .

Brendan brought himself back to the task in hand, realising he'd wasted valuable moments being distracted.

He turned away, shrugging on his jacket, but immediately something flew at the window and there was a thud as the black creature collided with the glass, leaving a faint impression of feathers, like the ghost of a bird, on the pane. Brendan gasped in shocked surprise, his heart pounding, his stomach flipping right over. After a minute or two in which he didn't move at all, his racing heart slowed and he swallowed down his nervousness.

Daft bird. That's all it was. Just some stupid creature . . .

Mindful now of wasting time, he quickly pulled open the third drawer down in a mahogany chest of drawers set between the room's two windows. To hide anything in a top drawer was too obvious. The last but one down was safer. He had just put the shoebox at the back of this drawer when he heard a door opening and then the faint sound of someone approaching. He stayed absolutely still. It must be Barbara. There was no need to worry; why would she come in here now if he stayed silent?

Then there was the sound of a door opening close by and he realised she had gone into the bathroom. He pushed the drawer to as silently as he could, though the last little bit stuck and would need to be opened again and straightened to close properly. There was no time to do that and risk making a sound; it was all but closed anyway.

Brendan put his head carefully round the door. The corridor was clear, but he had to move quickly. He pulled the door almost to – the click of the latch might be heard – and belted along on tiptoe to the stairs, then down and into the hall. Stopping only to pick up his shoes, he went out in his stocking feet, hearing the bathroom door open as he did, and closed the front door as gently as he could, standing on the wet door-step outside to put on his shoes.

Crikey, that had been close. Barbara had given up

asking for her key back recently, but she certainly would have been asking now if she'd found him upstairs in her house, in the spare room, where he could not possibly have any business.

She must have been asleep earlier, but what if she heard him leaving now from her bedroom, his footsteps crunching on the wet gravel, and wondered what he was doing lurking outside her front door but not making himself known?

Then he had a brilliant idea. He rang the doorbell vigorously a couple of times and waited in the cold and wet for Barbara to come downstairs and answer it. Eventually she did.

She was wearing a red silk dressing gown with a quilted collar, which would have looked very striking with her blonde hair and beautiful face, except that today her hair was lank and her face was pale and drawn. Brendan couldn't remember ever seeing her without her makeup before.

'Brendan, what do you want?' she asked, frowning and looking at him through narrowed eyes.

'Well, that's charming, Babs, I must say,' he said chirpily. 'Just thought I'd drop by and see about some stuff I'm keeping in your buildings, and what do I find but the water's getting in. The structures don't look too safe to me.'

Barbara heaved a huge sigh and patted her forehead with her hand. 'Please, Brendan, do you have to bother me with this now? Can't you just fix it?'

'Not really, Barbara. Not my buildings, see?'

'Oh, for goodness' sake, can't you see I'm feeling beastly? Don't stand there on the doorstep letting the cold and rain in. Come in, if you don't mind risking the lurgy.'

'You do look a bit off colour. I just thought you might always look like this without your face on.'

'Don't be ridiculous,' snapped Barbara, on the verge of tears.

'What's matter with you?' Brendan asked nervously. 'It's not catching, is it?'

'I don't know – I don't suppose so – but I do feel dreadful. My head is absolutely pounding. I've had to cancel the lessons – what there are of them at this time of year. And that's not helping, either.'

'What?'

'The pupils – they're nearly all on holiday. I've had to cancel what few there are because of my headache. Don't be dense, Brendan. I can hardly bear to speak.' She sank onto one of the hall chairs, looking thin and ill.

'Well, I'm sorry to bring you bad news about the outbuildings. Do you want me to find a fella to fix them? I know a builder who might be free to do it cheapish, but you'll have to pay him in cash up front.'

'And how am I to do that? Oh, Brendan, please either make me a cup of tea or go away. You're not helping.'

'Come on, Babs. Go and sit on that lonely sofa of yours and wrap yourself up in that blanket you keep

349

to hand. I'll light the fire and then make you a cuppa. How does that sound?'

'All right . . . But please don't talk about builders. If you do, I think I might just collapse under the strain.'

Brendan, satisfied that whatever was wrong with Barbara was not catching, went to light the fire in the drawing room while she followed him, dragging her feet and pressing her hand to her head. It was probably just her nerves buckling under the burden of keeping the whole show on the road, he decided.

He went to make her a cup of tea. The fridge was nearly empty. Still, at least there was some milk. He wondered vaguely what she would have to eat tonight. Probably she was too poorly to want anything, which was just as well in the circumstances.

'Here you are,' he said cheerfully, with the air of a man making a grand gesture, bringing in the tea and putting the cup and saucer down on the floor next to where she lay on the sofa.

'Thank you, Brendan,' Barbara said faintly.

Just then the telephone rang.

Barbara groaned. 'I can't face answering that. Just let it ring.' She reached for her tea but they were both listening to the ringing telephone, which made thinking of anything else impossible. Brendan started to bite his nails.

'Just leave it, Brendan. It will stop in a minute.'

'I think I should get it, Babs. It might be important.'

'It might not be.'

'Then why ring at all?'

She lay back on the sofa and pulled the blanket over her head. 'Oh, for goodness' sake, go and answer it if you must. Tell whoever it is that I'm ill.'

Brendan ran off to get the phone. What a relief when he picked up the heavy receiver and the ringing stopped. He immediately felt calmer.

'Good afternoon. The Manor,' he said, thinking he sounded like a butler and suppressing a grin.

'Hello? Oh dear, sorry to bother you. I'd like to speak to Barbara Hayle, if she's there, please.' It was a woman's voice, an ordinary-sounding woman.

'I'm afraid Miss Hayle is not available.'

'Oh. Is she all right? It's just I've been worried about her. I've tried to ring her a couple of times before now. Who am I speaking to, please?'

'I'm Barbara's brother Brendan,' said Brendan. 'Barbara's ill.'

'I'm sorry to hear that. I hope she's not very poorly.'

'She can't speak right now but I'll give her a message if you want?'

'Yes, please. But is she very ill?'

'She says she's got a bad headache. I reckon it's her nerves. She's cancelled all her lessons. Are you one of her pupils?'

'No . . . oh dear, poor Barbara. Well, I hope she's better soon. How long has she been ill?'

'I don't know. She's been in bed and she looks a bit rough.'

'Oh dear. Well . . . I hope she's better soon. Please tell her Maureen Bancroft called and when she's better we should meet up and I'll see what I can do.'

Maureen Bancroft. Well, who knew? The mother of that stuck-up Eliza who fancies herself as a singer. And offering to 'see what she can do'. Sounds promising.

'I'll tell her that, Mrs Bancroft. Goodbye.'

When he went back to the drawing room, the fire had gained a little heat, but Barbara was still huddled under her blanket.

'That was Maureen Bancroft.'

'Hmm . . . what did she say?'

'She said "Oh dear" a lot, but she also said when you're feeling better you should both meet up and she'll "see what she can do".'

'What did she mean by that?'

'How should I know? I don't know the woman. I could hardly ask her to explain herself, could I?'

'Don't snap at me, please, Brendan. My nerves won't stand it. It was Maureen Bancroft that made me ill in the first place.'

'What do you mean?'

'Offering to help me out and then leaving me high and dry.'

'Well, she's offering again now.'

'I think, Brendan, that what she's probably offering is to list my unpaid bills in alphabetical order. She certainly isn't offering to pay them, even though she could. She said she couldn't take me on "like a life sentence". So insulting.' Barbara fought back a sob and patted her forehead gently, then closed her eyes.

'Couldn't you ask her over, make a fuss of her, butter her up, like?' Brendan asked. 'She's bound to be impressed with your gaff. Doesn't she live in some ordinary little house in Blackburn?'

Brendan's words suddenly seemed to remind Barbara of something. She raised herself on the sofa cushions. 'Sit down, Brendan, you're making my neck ache.'

Brendan sat on the floor beside the sofa. 'What's up now?'

'I've just remembered something Mum said.'

'You went to see Mum?' He smiled incredulously: he wished he'd been there to see that conversation!

'It was awful. I shan't go again. That woman's going clean off her head, and she lives in complete squalor. Anyway, she asked me to go although I wish I hadn't wasted my time. She said she'd heard that you were up to no good and would I warn you to behave yourself.'

Brendan's smile disappeared as if it had been snuffed out. 'And how did Mum say she'd heard this?'

'Oh, it was some ridiculous story about some woman who's her friend at the corner shop telling her. That's why I didn't think anything of it until you mentioned

Blackburn. I thought it was nonsense, and I'm only telling you now because you reminded me. If you want to know all about it, you'll have to ask Mum.'

Brendan frowned. 'When was this?'

'Oh, ages ago.'

'What, last year? Since Christmas?'

'No. Calm down, will you? It was a few weeks ago, perhaps last month.'

'Right . . . Well, thanks for telling me at last.'

'No need to get in a bate. It was only Mum, and she's not exactly reliable, is she?'

'And who is this friend at the shop?'

'Oh, Brendan, don't get all worked up. How should I know? I can't even remember the woman's name. I expect Mum's got the wrong end of some tale she's overheard or dreamed up and it's all a lot of nonsense. If you're not heading for any kind of trouble, it needn't bother you what Mum said, and if you are, well, you've been warned to behave yourself, haven't you?'

'Right. Well, now I know. Thank you, Babs. I'll leave you with your tea, and if you do want to use that builder fella for the outbuildings, then you'll have to let me know. But I reckon you should think about it seriously. I'm not sure I want to be renting owt that's falling down. What say I have a reduction on next month's rent, say fifty per cent, and then we'll see how you get on with the maintenance?'

Barbara's eyes flashed fury. 'You heartless beast! Kick a girl when she's down, why don't you?'

'Look, Babs, it's not as if—'

'Just go. Get out of my sight! And don't bother to come back!'

Brendan retreated, leaving Barbara spitting venom behind him: 'Get out . . . get out . . . get out . . .'

CHAPTER TWENTY

'THE QUESTION IS whether Theo will want to live with his mother-in-law, isn't it, Liza? He may want to stay in the house where he lives now—'

It was a Thursday evening and Maureen and Eliza were sitting down to eat. 'It's only rented, Mum, not his own house.' Eliza helped herself to runner beans. 'Mm, these look good. I reckon you could grow these when you get gardening.'

'Or he may want to find somewhere new: a new beginning for the two of you together,' said Maureen. 'Of course, I'll buy you somewhere, if that's what you both want, love. It can be my wedding present to you. It's about what you want. Nothing else matters.'

'Oh, Mum, that is so generous of you, thank you. But, it's also about what *you* want. You see, we – you and I – were going to live in the new house together, and we'd got all sorts of plans for it, the two of us. But now Theo and I are getting married, and if we decided to live elsewhere you'd be all alone.'

'That's all right, love. I never thought you'd live with me for ever. I needn't be alone – I could always get a dog,' Maureen said.

'Ha, replace me with a dog? But seriously, you chose that house with us in mind, loads of room for us to live together, and also each with our own space, and now it might be just you. Won't it be too big?'

'Well, why don't you take Theo to see the house? Then if he hates it, or hates the thought of living with your mother, then we'll know and can plan accordingly. How does that sound?'

'It sounds to me, Mum, as kind and thoughtful as you always are. But you've changed these last few months, and it's nice to see how you're doing what you want and not just giving of yourself to everyone else. Do you remember in spring, working for Herbert, how downtrodden and fed up you were? Now you'd have told him which way was up long before it came to that. In fact, I think you should go back to work at the brewery just so you can do that.'

Maureen laughed. 'Ah, the fearsome Miss Ramsbottom is keeping Herbert in line, I gather from Stella, and – I never thought I'd say this – the call of paid work is not what it was. There's no going back to the brewery or anywhere else for me. Of course, when I'm settled where I am to be, I might think of summat I'd like to do just because I want to and not because I have to. Mebbe I'll start a little business of my own. We'll see.' Maureen passed the mint sauce to Eliza, then started on her mutton chop. 'Being able to be independent has changed my life, Liza. I was always worrying about keeping us going before, and being hard up does crowd your thoughts with worry: the fear of what might happen if the job goes or you're ill. Now, well, I have security – for myself and for you and Sylvia, too – and, best of all, I've learned that I don't have to take any nonsense from anyone. I bless Miss Stevens every day for that.'

'I feel certain that's what she wanted when she decided to leave her savings to you.'

'Now, let me know if Theo would like to see the house and I'll call the agent.'

'Thank you, Mum.'

'And, speaking of calling folk, there's someone I've been trying to speak to for days, and that's Barbara Hayle.'

'What? I thought you'd washed your hands of her. She's not to be trusted, you know that.'

'I spoke to her brother earlier in the week. He just happened to be there, I think, and he said she was ill, which explains why she wasn't answering the phone before.'

'How ill? Dying?'

'Liza, don't be heartless. He said she wasn't well, had a headache and had been in bed. I've rung again since, but no one answers. What if she's all alone and needs help?'

'Then she can telephone for it.'

'But who will she phone? Oh, Liza, I don't want to fuss, but she has no friends visiting and she seems to have fallen out with all her family.'

'Except the brother was there.'

'Mm, Brendan, I think he's called. I've never met him. He's a lot younger than the others I knew when Barbara and I were at school.'

'Brendan? That's odd, Mum.' Eliza put down her cutlery, thinking, puzzling. 'I met someone called Brendan a few weeks ago. He's not very nice. He deals in second-hand furniture. He came to the Short Cut but I doubt he'll be back. Not Hayle, though. Wilmot.'

Maureen, too, stopped eating. 'But that's what this fella must be called. Barbara Hayle is a name Barbara invented for herself many years ago, and I can't think of her by any other now, but Annie is Mrs Wilmot.'

Eliza looked serious. 'I didn't know that. It's surely the same man. That is so strange.'

'So what happened with this Brendan Wilmot?'

'It was odd and not nice at the time, but in the end it was nothing. He was a nuisance, but Theo turned up and saw him off. I've not set eyes on Wilmot since. He offered to walk me home from the Waterloo one evening when you were staying on to chat with Agnes. Anyway, it seemed like he knew just where to go, where I lived, and I wondered if he'd followed me home one time.'

'What a horrible thought.'

'Yes, some awful fella creeping about behind me in the street. Also, he was asking rather intrusive questions about my circumstances, not the kind of thing you'd ask someone you'd only just met: whether I was paid for the singing, whether I was going to continue working at the Short Cut. I thought he somehow might have heard about your legacy.'

'If he's Barbara's brother and she's told him about my inheritance, then that would explain that, but what's it got to do with him, and why would he find out where you live, but in a secretive way?'

'Have your dinner while it's hot, Mum . . . It could just be coincidence – that he came to have his hair cut at the Short Cut and took an interest in me, but it was quite an unsettling sort of interest.'

'I'm sorry, love. I wish I could explain but I don't understand . . . Anyway, he answered Barbara's telephone the other day and I asked him to tell Barbara, who he said was too ill to come to the phone, that I could go and see what I could do for her.'

'Mum! You've been and done that already. You can't keep her going *and* buy your lovely new house and live a life doing exactly what you want, as you deserve to after all these years. She'd be a major expense for the rest of your life – or until you ran out of money. The woman seems to think she's entitled to live in a style far beyond her income and, as she can't afford it, someone else – *you* – will pay for it for her.'

'I know that, love, and I told her as much. But she's floundering. It may be the worry that's making her ill. She needs a sensible head to help her decide what to do, what course of action is best. I shan't give her any more money. I decided that when I visited. She needs a different sort of help. She has to start being realistic about her life: about who she really is and how she can afford to live, not these silly fantasies she puts about to feed her vanity.'

'Oh, Mum, I don't know . . . You're such a good person, so kind. I don't want that awful woman taking advantage, and she will! I don't trust her at all. She's nowt but a complete liar.'

'Well, I did have a thought, Liza. I wondered if you would mind going with me – we could go on Sunday, if you're not busy – and then – oh dear, this sounds awful – it would be two against one. We'll have strength in numbers, and if Barbara isn't prepared to listen then we'll simply leave.'

'Yes, of course. In fact, I insist that I do. I think I might ask Theo if he can take us. Not only would the car be helpful but so would Theo. He's always so level-headed and he'd boost our numbers, too. I reckon the three of us will be more than enough for Barbara Hayle.'

'Liza, that's a very good idea. Theo's presence alone would give me courage and bolster my resolve. I thought I could help Barbara decide what to do about her debts. I could give her Mr Lambert's telephone number at Lambert and Goldsworthy. I'm sure he will know what Barbara should do to get herself out of this pickle. I'll call Mr Lambert myself first and ask if that's all right, and say that he's to send his bill for advising Barbara to me.'

'You're a good friend to her, Mum, far better than she deserves. But I expect Mr Lambert will simply tell her she'd better sell the big house and the car and then pay her bills. I just hope Barbara realises that people are trying to help her, and that she starts listening instead of putting on her act.'

'Yes, well, let's see how things are when we get there – whether she feels up to listening. With you and Theo there to support me, love, I reckon I can manage her. I'm not proud of the way I walked out on her last time, and I think if I make one last effort with her but keep my temper this time, then I shall have done everything I can.'

Brendan stood biting his nails in the doorway of The Remove, making up his mind to go out into the murky evening. It was a drizzly Saturday and he was reluctant to leave the shabby comforts of his own flat, with its curious mixture of second-hand furniture and the shiny new radiograms he'd bought recently in two of the rooms. More than that, he really didn't want to go to see his mother, but since Barbara had told him that muddled half-story about what Annie had said to her, he needed to find out what was behind it, especially *who* was behind it, and whether there was anything to worry about. Or anyone he needed to deal with. He didn't want to have to lie low and hang on to the contents of the shoebox once he had a buyer lined up – or retain for longer than necessary a few of the bigger items still stored in the leaking outbuildings at The Manor, which might need a bit of organising to shift unnoticed by anyone. He needed to be shot of them all, quickly, and have the money in his pocket.

He set out for his childhood home wearing a flat cap against the light rain, huddled into his creased and worn mackintosh and nervously smoking a Capstan Full Strength. The walk to Annie's house in Avery Street took only a few minutes, but it wasn't one that he took very often.

The pavement outside number 52 was greasy and dark in the premature gloom of twilight. Brendan didn't have a key so he knocked on the door.

'C'mon, Mum, c'mon . . .' He ground out his cigarette on the doorstep.

He thought he saw the curtain twitching at the front window of the house next door but he wasn't sure. He began to feel foolish, standing out on the pavement like someone who wasn't welcome or had nothing more important to do, while his mother made up her mind to come to open the door.

Eventually Brendan heard the lock click and there was Annie. She looked at him hard for a moment, as if trying to remember who he was.

'Hello, Mum.'

'Brendan. What are you doing here?'

'Come to see you, haven't I.'

Annie looked as if she thought this was bad news. 'Well, I suppose you'd better come in.' She stood back to let him over the threshold and then closed the door.

'Shall we go and sit down?' asked Brendan. He didn't want to be standing in the narrow hall where, towering over Annie, he felt too big for the house.

Grumbling under her breath, Annie led the way to the sitting room at the back. Even Brendan could see that it looked a lot cleaner and tidier than it had the last time he'd been here, earlier in the year.

'What's happened here?' he grinned. 'Discovered where the dustbin is, have you?'

'Make us a cup of tea, Brendan, will you?'

'No, I'm not stopping, Mum. I just came to ask you summat.'

'Oh, go on, Brendan, make me a cup of tea.'

'No, I told you, Mum, I'm off in a minute, when you've told me what I came to find out. It was summat Barbara said, summat she said you know about. I think it's important.'

Annie sat down, looking sullen. 'You always were an awkward so-and-so, Brendan. Well, I doubt there's much I can tell you that you'll want to hear. If you want to know all about it, you'd be better asking Barbara. It's for her to tell, really.'

'What are you talking about, Mum? It was Barbara said I should ask you.'

'Typical Barbara, never taking responsibility. Well, she can't pretend she doesn't know all about it – how could she not? If she's ready to tell you she should, not expect me to.'

Oh Lord, thought Brendan, *no wonder we've all given up on her – all except Enid, that is. She's as mad as a fish.*

He paced around, beginning to wish he hadn't come here. He was wasting his time. Perhaps he should go back to The Manor and interrogate Barbara. The trouble was, she was so full of lies, there was no knowing the truth with her any longer. And she'd said she was ill. He'd give it one last go with Annie.

'Look, Mum, will you try to talk sense for once?' he snapped at her. 'Just tell me this thing that you say Barbara knows, then I'll leave and be out of your way. Otherwise I'll just be going round in circles, you and Barbara batting me between you.'

'Aye, well, we never managed that before,' said Annie. 'It was me that ended up holding the baby.'

'Now what are you on about?'

'Barbara. She left her baby with me while she went gallivanting off back to the bright lights.'

Brendan suddenly had a very nasty feeling that he'd rather not know any more, but his mouth seemed to have a mind of its own. 'But Barbara hasn't had a baby,' he said slowly.

Annie cackled. 'But that's the secret, don't you see? You're Barbara's baby.'

'What! No, no, that's ridiculous, Mum. You're getting

366

confused. Barbara's my sister, not my mum. You're my mum, God help me.'

'Told you there was nowt I could tell you that you'd want to hear,' said Annie triumphantly. 'I sometimes forget and think I'm your mum, but in fact I'm your grandma.'

Brendan sank down on the sofa. Annie could be spiteful, but she'd never make up such an elaborate lie just to be unkind. Nor was she so feeble-minded that she'd imagine this was the truth if it wasn't. 'How can this be? How did Barbara manage to keep this quiet?'

'Well, Barbara's an expert at secrets. I'm surprised you don't know that. It was easy really. She gave birth to you when she lived out of town. Somehow she must have hidden herself from her theatre friends, 'cos so far as I know nobody ever suspected. Or if they did know, she never said owt to me about it. Then she turned up with you and it was: "Here's my baby. You can take care of him. You know all about babies and I've got my career to think of." Then she was off, leaving you here. Course, you were a helpless and sickly little thing and – I'll not tell a lie, Brendan – I thought I'd never rear you, that I wouldn't be burdened with you for long. I'd had enough of babies with six others. Bloomin' babies all my life, but I couldn't just put you out, could I?'

Brendan's light blue eyes were wide with shock. 'She just left me? You were "burdened" with me?'

'Well, you know Barbara.'

He swallowed. He felt breathless and his throat was tight. 'It seems not. I thought she was my sister. I knew she was selfish but I'd no idea how much. Oh, I can't believe it.'

'Don't take on, lad. It's old news now.'

'Not to me it isn't. She has a heart of stone – no, she has no heart at all. She's heartless! She's like a picture or a doll: all on the surface for effect but no feelings underneath at all. Except about herself.'

Annie delved into her pinny pocket and mopped her eyes with the crumpled handkerchief she'd drawn out. 'She's that, sure enough, lad. I can't think how I came to have such a child. The others, 'cept for Enid, are all selfish in their own ways, and I'm including you in that – but Barbara knows of nowt in the world except what matters to her and what she wants.'

Brendan put his head in his hands, feeling lost now; his whole life undermined, his whole sense of self cast adrift. He felt in his jacket pocket for his cigarettes and matches, then lit one and blew a thick cloud of noxious smoke above Annie's head.

'So who is my dad? Do you know, Mum?'

'Don't take on, lad, though you're right to call me "Mum" still. I'm more of a mother to you than her ladyship ever was or ever will be. What was it you said?'

'My dad – do you know who he is?'

'Some musician fella, she might have said, but I forget now. We never saw him. Can't even remember his name, if I ever knew it. I wonder if she can either.'

Brendan sat back on the sagging sofa, smoking hard. 'Well, this is all a surprise, Mum. I thought you were going to tell me summat about getting into trouble.'

Annie laughed loudly at this. 'Ha, ha, it was Barbara that got into trouble! And now look how stuck-up her ladyship is. She thinks herself too good for the rest of us.'

Brendan stood up and stabbed out his cigarette in a saucer. Then he stomped around the little room, muttering to himself, trying to think straight.

Annie mopped her eyes again and blew her nose. 'What?' she said, raising her voice. 'I can't hear you, Brendan. Sit down, son. Don't take on so.'

'That a mother should just leave her baby like that! I can't believe it. Yet I can, with Barbara. To give me up – to hand me on like an unwanted parcel – just for her so-called career. And look where that's got her! She gave me up for that – for nowt but her own vanity?'

'Ah, c'mon, Brendan, love. It can't be helped. I told you you wouldn't like to hear it, but you would ask. Now make me a cup of tea and then sit down. I don't get many visitors . . .'

'Visitors?' Brendan looked at Annie as if he couldn't understand what she was saying. 'No . . . no, Mum, I've got to go. I've got to go and see Barbara and . . . and . . .' He rubbed his eyes. 'I've got to go. Now. I'm going . . .'

He strode out of the hot little room and down the

hallway. He could hear Annie calling after him, her querulous voice increasingly frantic.

'You can't go to Barbara's now, Brendan. You'll see it all different in the morning. I told you you wouldn't want to hear – I warned you, and now look. All angry and hot-headed. Wait till you've calmed down. Oh dear . . . oh dear, it's all such a mess . . . Brendan, wait!'

Brendan ignored her, let himself out of the house and slammed the door. It was raining heavily now and he turned up the collar of his mac and shoved his hands in his pockets, hunching his shoulders with the weight of his cares as he strode off home.

By the time Brendan opened the little front door to the side of The Remove, mooched wearily up the stairs to the flat over the shop and took off his soaking coat and cap, he was still feeling angry, but his anger was colder, harder, set into his soul rather than a flare of temper.

Mum . . . Grandma . . . no, *Mum* was right, he thought. He'd go to see Barbara when he was calmer. He'd work out exactly what he'd say and do, and then . . . and then, he wouldn't be distracted by her excuses, or her pleading with him.

CHAPTER TWENTY-ONE

Theo's car drew up in front of The Manor. It was a dismal morning, the weather autumnal, despite this being only August. The air felt damp and already there were green berries, hard as marbles, forming on the hawthorns on the roadsides. There was a feeling of decline, of valediction to the day.

Theo came round to hand Maureen out of the front seat, and Eliza got out of the back, stretched her legs and smoothed down her skirt.

'Heavens, Mum, this is very grand,' she said, looking up at the façade of the house.

'I think I said summat much the same to Barbara when I came here that time.' Maureen gazed around. 'It's changed a bit even since then, though: less smart, somehow, not so well cared for. The grass has grown, and I see those rose shrubs haven't had the old flowers removed.' She looked down and saw tiny weeds starting to sprout up through the gravel of the drive.

She thought of Mr Gathercole, the gardener, whom she'd met by chance. Possibly Barbara had asked him not to come here any more, if she couldn't afford to pay him. Already that had made a difference to the garden. Maureen hoped it hadn't made a vital difference to Mr Gathercole.

'I just hope we haven't had a wasted journey,' said Eliza. 'You only have Brendan Wilmot's word for it that Barbara's ill in bed, although you did say you've tried to telephone her several times and got no answer.'

'Well, if she's still feeling ill, she probably won't want to get up to answer the phone,' said Theo, 'although I suspect Brendan Wilmot is not a man whose word can be relied upon.'

'No, I meant what if she's left, gone away?'

'One way to find out, Liza. Do you want to ring the doorbell, Maureen?'

Maureen stepped forward and did so. Then the three of them waited in silence. Maureen realised she was holding her breath. It was as if something important, or possibly awful, was about to happen.

'Mebbe she really is ill and asleep in bed,' said Eliza after a couple of minutes.

'Or she has gone away, as you said,' Theo added.

Maureen rang the bell again, they waited and still nothing happened. Then she tried a third time.

'Oh heck, you don't think she's lying there dead, do you?' said Maureen, looking worried.

'No,' said Eliza. 'I don't reckon she's dead of a head-ache. But she might still be feeling ill with it. Or she's no longer here. How can we find out?'

'Let's go round the house and see if we can see any clue that she's inside,' suggested Theo. He went to the front window to the right of the door and looked through.

The room was dominated by a gigantic piano. He gazed at it with admiration, then turned his attention to the rest of the room. It was unoccupied but looked as if someone might have just left it, with a couple of cardigans draped over a chair and papers lying untidily on a small table.

'Shall I go round this way and you and Maureen can take the other direction? We'll meet at the back.'

'Good idea,' said Eliza. 'C'mon, Mum.'

The women set off via the other front windows. The room there had very little in it that they could see; certainly no Barbara. So it proved with the many other rooms, although the women looked carefully, deter-mined not to miss Barbara if, heaven forbid, she was lying unconscious on the floor.

The kitchen was on Maureen and Eliza's route, and Eliza tried the back door in the unlikely event that it might be unlocked. It wasn't. When she looked through the window, the kitchen was empty, too: just a milk bottle carelessly left out on the table and a little one-cup-size teapot. It looked sad, neglected.

'Nothing,' said Theo, meeting up with them at the

edge of the lawn at the back of the house. 'Mm, I can see what you mean about these window frames, Maureen. The whole place shows a very different face at the back.'

'Somehow you know there's not much furniture in the rooms, even from the outside,' said Eliza. 'It looks . . . abandoned, really.'

She turned round to survey the huge garden with its stretch of lawn and the interweaving paths and flowerbeds beyond. The flowerbeds looked in need of tidying and the lawn was dotted with weeds, raising their bold heads above the level of the grass. A few starlings pecked at the edge of the lawn.

'I remember those birds were here last time,' said Maureen. 'I wonder what attracts them . . . Right,' she went on, determined to see this through, although the whole enterprise was already beginning to look like a waste of a day, 'I've had you bring me all this way, Theo, and I'm determined that it won't be for nowt. We're not ready to go home yet. Eliza, shall we try that back door again?'

They all went round the side to the kitchen door. Maureen remembered Barbara showing her out through this door to the garden when she visited. At that time she didn't know how bad Barbara's difficulties had become. Now she fought down a growing fear that they might have proved overwhelming.

The door was undoubtedly locked.

They stood there looking at each other.

'I wonder if I should go to the village call box and telephone the police,' said Maureen.

'But we don't know if Barbara's here or not. She might just have gone away. She has every right to do as she likes,' Eliza said.

Maureen looked up and down this side of the house to see if there was a ladder, an upstairs window open . . . anything that might aid access. Suddenly her eyes alighted on a little potted geranium by the back corner of the house. Where did everyone keep their spare key? Under a plant pot near the door, of course. It was such a well-known hiding place – everybody used it – and no matter that she now lived in a manor house, Barbara would surely remember this rather insecure idea from her earlier life.

'I'll just look under that plant pot,' said Maureen. 'You never know.'

Sure enough, there was a single long, slim key.

Theo laughed. 'It's so obvious.'

'I wonder if the Queen keeps her spare key under a pot near the back door of the palace,' Eliza laughed.

'Under a sentry box, perhaps,' said Theo.

'Right, let's see if it fits. I feel like Alice in Wonderland,' said Eliza, taking the key from Maureen and inserting it into the back-door lock. It fitted and turned smoothly.

Maureen, Eliza and Theo looked at each other.

'It feels wrong, like we're trespassing,' said Maureen.

'Well, now we've got the door open, I think we're going to have to go in,' said Theo. 'We should make sure Barbara's all right if she's here, and if she isn't here we'll just leave, lock up and return the key to where we found it. Come on. But we must be careful not to frighten her by bursting in on her if she's here.'

The huge kitchen, with its vast empty shelves, didn't look as if it had been entered for days. The tiny teapot was stone cold, with the dregs of tea leaves in the bottom, Maureen saw, lifting the lid.

'I think we should try upstairs,' said Theo.

'Shall I go first, as she knows me?' suggested Maureen bravely.

They went out into the entrance hall. On the table in the centre was a vase of flowers, the blooms all brown and dead now, the water yellowed and scummy. Maureen remembered the roses in the vase last time she was here, and she was filled with fear for what might have become of Barbara. This search for her old friend had grown in importance and was now vital. She had to know that Barbara was all right.

'Right . . .' she took a deep breath. 'Barbara?' she called, and her voice sounded like a terrible intrusion in the silence. 'Barbara, it's Maureen. Are you there, love?'

There was no reply.

'Right, Barbara, I'm coming to see if you're upstairs and you need help,' said Maureen boldly – far more confidently than she was feeling – and led the way up, Theo and Eliza close behind.

At the top of the stairs was a long, wide corridor, a small, high window at the end, with doors closed on either side, except for the last one on the right. This was open slightly, the light from inside throwing a shaft of brightness onto the green carpet.

'Might be her bedroom,' said Eliza softly, pointing.

'Let me,' said Theo. He went down to the door and pushed it slowly open. What he saw was clearly a spare bedroom, with a chest of drawers between the windows and a bed not made up, the pillows and eiderdown piled up in the middle of the bare mattress. There was a curious faint pattern, like feathers, on the window, as if a bird had flown into it.

Maureen was right behind him, looking all round. 'Not in here, and this doesn't look as if it's her room. Right, let's try them one by one.' She raised her voice again, although it sounded trembly now. 'Barbara? Barbara, can you hear me? It's Maureen,' she called over and over as she opened the doors to the rooms, working her way back down the first side while Theo and Eliza tried the rooms on the other side, which looked on to the front garden. On Maureen's side there was a bathroom, then another three bedrooms – completely empty, as if Barbara had moved out and taken all her furniture. Although Maureen had learned the truth behind this situation from Mr Gathercole, it was still a surprise to see so many bare rooms in the house.

At last Eliza opened the door at the end next to the stairs and there was a figure huddled in the rumpled bed. The air smelled stale, as if it had been breathed for days and not refreshed, but also of sweat and, behind that, a lingering floral scent, like old perfume.

'Barbara? Mum, Theo, she's here!' Eliza rushed over to the woman in the bed. But she didn't look much like the lovely Miss Barbara Hayle. For a moment Eliza was just thankful to see that she was breathing, but her gratitude immediately gave way to astonishment. Was this really Barbara, with her matted hair, her colourless face with sunken cheeks and etched with lines from her pillow, her figure, from what Eliza could see, now more skeletal than merely slim?

Maureen burst in, Theo following closely.

'Barbara? Is it you?' Maureen rushed over and raised her on her pillows. 'Oh, Barbara, I've been so worried. I've been trying to call you.'

'Never mind about that, Mum. I'll go and get her some water and, Theo, p'raps you could raise that sash and let some air in.'

Eliza ran off down to the kitchen and Maureen asked Theo to fetch a wet flannel from the bathroom so that she could bathe Barbara's face.

'There, love, I'm here now. We'll soon have you feeling better. I can see that you've been ill and all by yourself . . .' Maureen crooned while she gently washed Barbara's face.

Eliza returned with a glass of water, which Barbara gulped down. Immediately she looked better.

'What are you doing here? So many people . . .'

'Just me and Eliza and her fiancé, Theo,' said

Maureen. 'What's been wrong, Barbara? You don't look very well.'

Barbara looked weepy. Her eyes were shadowed, and without her makeup she appeared a lot older than when Maureen had last seen her. Her hair was greasy, the curls darker and lank, with a hint of dullness at the roots.

'I think I had a horrible bug or something, Maureen. Such a headache, and so exhausted.'

'Have you taken any medicine?'

'Not lately.'

'Do you have any aspirins?'

'In the drawer in the music-room table,' said Barbara. 'The pupils give me such terrible headaches . . .'

Eliza ran off to find them without being asked, then returned with the aspirins and another glass of water.

'Take two, Barbara. And I think you'll feel better if you have a proper wash. Shall I run you a bath, not too hot?'

'Yes, please, Maureen.'

'And then clean clothes, if you feel up to dressing. That will help you feel more normal. Then mebbe you could come down and have summat to eat. See how you feel after the bath.'

Barbara looked tearful again. 'It's hopeless. There's nothing here.' She began to cry in earnest. 'I haven't even got any food. I can't manage any longer with nothing.' She flung herself down in the bed and pulled the covers over her head, sobbing loudly and extravagantly.

Maureen, Eliza and Theo looked at each other. Eliza's eyes were round with fear.

'Shall I go down and call a doctor?' she whispered.

'Let's see how she is when she's up. She doesn't feel feverish,' said Maureen, taking control in her motherly way. 'Why don't you go and run Barbara her bath and, Theo, please would you bring in the picnic and mebbe set it out on the kitchen table?'

They went to do as she instructed.

'Please don't cry, Barbara,' said Maureen after a minute or two. 'I'm here to help. I heard you were feeling poorly, but you've had your aspirins and Liza's running you a nice warm bath, and Theo, who's a very good cook, has brought a picnic. We can eat it in the kitchen. I guessed you might not have much in.'

Barbara's crying subsided surprisingly quickly then, and she raised her head and wiped her eyes on the sleeve of her grubby nightdress. She didn't look too upset for someone who had been crying in earnest, and it passed through Maureen's thoughts that, although Barbara clearly had been ill, she might now be putting on a bit of an act.

Barbara nodded. 'Thank you, Maureen. You're a good friend.'

While Barbara was in the bath, Maureen and Eliza changed the sheets and, having found the cleaning things in the kitchen, quickly dusted round Barbara's bedroom and went over the carpet with a sweeper.

It was while she was dusting the dressing table that

Maureen noticed, on an oval porcelain tray next to Barbara's beautiful little watch, a ring like a tiny flower made of diamond chips. Her sharp intake of breath had Eliza hurrying over to see.

'What, Mum?'

Maureen held up the ring wordlessly.

'Your ring! What on earth is *that* doing here? It *is* your ring, isn't it? It was stolen in the burglary, but what's that got to do with Barbara?'

Maureen swallowed and tried to think clearly. 'I don't know, love. I don't understand at all.' She looked worried; the day was proving full of nasty surprises. 'It's impossible that Barbara stole it herself – we were on holiday together when the burglar broke in – but there's no doubt about it, it is my ring. I recognised it straight away – so did you – and I've never seen another one quite like it.'

Eliza spoke quietly, as if Barbara, who was soaking in a deep bubble bath, might overhear and appear at the door at any moment, like the Fairy Carabosse in a pantomime, waving her wand and casting a bad spell on them. 'Well, you're not leaving here without it. It's yours without a doubt. Mebbe Barbara bought it somewhere, or it was given to her, or . . . I don't know. But you're going to have to ask her, Mum. You can't just take it without saying owt. She might not know it's stolen, and then she'll think you've stolen it from her!'

'Oh, what a muddle,' sighed Maureen. 'I'll see how she is when she reappears.'

'I don't care how she is,' hissed Eliza. 'It's your ring – Dad gave it to you – and if you don't take it back today you'll never get it back at all. You're going to have to ask her where she got it. And then we'll see if we can make head or tail of whatever lies she dreams up this time.'

'Liza!'

'No, Mum. I think it'll take all three of us to face her down, given that she's got more face than most normal people. I'm remembering now what she's like, how she puts on an act, and I reckon it's dangerous to feel too sorry for her. She'll take advantage.'

'Liza, be quiet. I will ask her. But, please, try to be kind. Barbara's had a migraine or some such, and I'm certain the worries about her financial difficulties have brought her very low. That's what I'm here to help her sort out, but,' she sighed heavily, 'this is getting ever more complicated.'

'Well, just remember, Mum, she's been lying to you for years. I'd be very careful what I believe of her tales, if I were you.'

In less than an hour, Barbara was almost miraculously restored to something resembling her usual self. She was clean and fragrant, Eliza had helped her with her hair, and she had even made up her face, although the effect wasn't quite as glowing as usual, what with the bags under her eyes and her pallor. She looked too thin in her plain jumper and well-cut skirt, in need of some good food.

'Not too bad for a youngster,' was her verdict on the way Eliza had done her hair, with few tools available to her. 'I usually have my hair done by a little man in Preston and he's worth the journey.'

Maureen imagined Barbara, all tall and slender, arriving at a hair salon run by gnomes, and they running around after her like the dwarves in the film of *Snow White*. She guessed from Barbara's restored superior attitude that she was feeling much better already.

Theo's picnic was a delicious success and they all four felt better for it. He'd even remembered to bring some milk so they could have cups of tea, without which no situation, good or bad, could be faced.

'So,' said Maureen at last, when she and Barbara were seated in the armchairs in the music room, and Eliza and Theo were sitting to one side on the piano stool, 'I said I am here to help you and this is the help I'm giving. I've got someone else, who knows a lot more than I do, to offer proper advice and guide you towards professional help.'

'I can't afford professional anything,' said Barbara disconsolately. 'I've got to face it, this is the end of the road for me.'

'No, Barbara, really, I've sorted it all out for you. The gentleman is called Mr Lambert at Lambert and Goldsworthy. He's a solicitor and he thinks he'll be able to point you in the direction of all manner of experts on difficulties such as yours, the kind of folk I don't know owt about. If you call him, he knows I will see about the subsequent bills for the advice, never fear. But you have to do this yourself, Barbara. And you have to take notice of what folk tell you.'

'But, Maureen—'

'No, Barbara, you *must*. No matter how things have been, no matter how bad they are now, they can be better, but only if you face up to it, keep both your feet on the ground and live in the here and now, not some daft fantasy world, which would be very nice if this were a film or a play, but sets you on a hiding to nothing in the real world.'

'Be an ordinary, dull, boring little person, you mean.'

Eliza opened her mouth to speak but Theo dug her gently in the ribs with his elbow. She remembered she'd promised to let Maureen handle this. She was only there to back Maureen up if necessary.

Maureen reached over and took Barbara's hand. 'Dear Barbara, you could never be ordinary or dull and boring, but you have to realise, love, that gadding about pretending you're summat you're not doesn't make you special. But rather it takes away from the specialness you do have by coating it in lies and deceit. You see, you have found a role teaching piano and elocution, and you have quite a few pupils, from what you told me. You said you were teaching six days a week—'

'But I hate it! I hate most of the pupils and I hate their stupid parents even more. The piano pupils are the worst. Most have no talent and no interest either. Teaching them here, at The Manor, on that wonderful piano, is the only thing that makes the lessons bearable for me.'

Maureen sighed. 'Well, mebbe you can find summat you'd rather do, Barbara, if you dislike teaching so much, but you can't go on as you have been and continue to live here. You have to pay your bills and you have to pay off the loan if you are to keep the house that means so much to you. Couldn't you bear to do the teaching with more enthusiasm, knowing it helps you to keep The Manor? You will have to think of other ways to improve your income, too, mebbe working at two or three jobs, same as a lot of folk have to do to make ends meet when times are hard.'

'Like what?' Barbara asked, looking sulky. 'This is sounding worse and worse. You'll have me scrubbing floors, next thing I know.'

Maureen was furious for a moment. Trust Barbara to get on her high horse and start sneering at the friend who was trying to help.

'You could sell the car. You could take in lodgers,' snapped Eliza, clearly conscious her mother was being insulted.

'Open the garden to the public, serve teas on the lawn,' added Theo, pleasantly. 'You could sell The Manor to be developed as a hotel with the condition that you continue to live here. You could play this gorgeous piano to entertain the guests in style.'

'You could hire out the car for weddings or to take people on excursions,' said Eliza.

'Become a chauffeuse?' Barbara asked, affronted.

'Why not, if it made you a living? And you'd be able to keep the car as a business expense.'

'Eliza's right. You could be the most stylish female driver in the county – in the country,' said Theo.

'Honestly, Barbara, you have so much going for you, a beautiful woman with such style and talent,' said Maureen. 'Why would you throw it all away just because you can't move forward, can't admit that the kind of life you led with Marty is over now? It's time for you to leave that and its trappings behind – long past time – and move on by yourself to the next stage in your life. That's what you have to do. Have a think, love, about all the things you could do, and then see if Mr Lambert can put you in touch with someone who can help you while you also sort out the other problems.'

'Perhaps I could think about it,' said Barbara sullenly. 'Please give me this Mr Lambert's telephone number, Maureen. I'll call him tomorrow.'

Maureen got up and put the number, which she'd already written out on a sheet of her writing pad, in the middle of Barbara's table.

'Good, Barbara. I hope you will find him helpful.'

Barbara was gently patting her forehead and frowning. 'I think I might have to have a little lie-down,' she said. 'I'm finding it so difficult to sleep at night, what with the worry and the birds tapping at the window.'

'Birds? Surely not,' said Maureen. 'What birds would

be flying about at night, 'cept for owls, and I'm sure they wouldn't be at your window?'

'Birds. They tap away. Tap, tap, tap. So menacing. I have to keep the window closed. In fact, Theo, would you please go up now and close the window in my room, and in the bathroom? I can't risk them flying in. Please make sure they're properly closed.'

Eliza and Maureen exchanged glances.

'Of course.' Theo went at once, and with surprising grace considering the request had been more of an order.

'Well,' said Maureen bracingly, 'I'm sure if the windows are closed you have nowt to fear.'

Barbara gave her a sidelong look but said nothing.

'Now, Barbara, I have summat to ask you and – please don't take this the wrong way – but where did you get this ring?' She held up her ring, which she'd taken from the dressing-table tray while Barbara was in the bath. 'You see, love, this is without a doubt my engagement ring, which I lost earlier this year.'

'It is,' said Eliza, before Barbara could start to spout some made-up story. 'We both recognised it straight away.'

Barbara's face betrayed a whole series of thoughts – she evidently wasn't feeling well enough to employ her full acting talents today – and then she said, 'I found it.'

'When was this, Barbara?'

'Earlier in the summer.'

'And where did you find it?'

'Here. In the gravel. It was just lying there.'

'What, outside the house?'

'Outside my outbuildings, round the side, where I keep the car.'

'Well, I never. How could it possibly have got there, do you think?' said Maureen, while Eliza began running her hands through her hair and fidgeting on the piano stool. Theo came back, sat down again beside her and took her hand, cradling it between both of his.

'I don't know. Does it matter? You say it's your ring and I believe you. I only kept it to wear because it's a pretty little thing. You can have it back, of course.'

'Thank you, Barbara,' said Maureen ironically, putting the ring on her finger where it belonged. 'But I think it does matter. You see, Barbara, the ring was stolen from my house in a burglary while you and I were in Somerton, and I can't understand how it got from the burglar to outside your outbuildings.'

There was a long, long silence. Eliza looked as if she might burst, but she pursed her lips and let everyone's thoughts trundle round to the only possible conclusion.

'I don't know,' said Barbara eventually. 'Apart from the garage, what happens in those buildings is nothing to do with me.'

'Then who is it to do with, Barbara?' asked Theo gently. 'I'm sure you must know who is around there, coming and going at your beautiful property.'

Maureen suddenly remembered the man in the van

she had seen driving round. Barbara had said he was the pest controller, but when Maureen had caught sight of his face later, by the gate, he had looked strangely familiar. There was only one person it could be, and she realised now that she had recognised him from the Waterloo one evening, standing talking to Eliza. He was without a doubt the man who had been a nuisance to Eliza, knew where she lived and had asked her intrusive questions regarding her income. Hadn't Eliza said he dealt in second-hand furniture? He was also the man who had answered the telephone the other day and told Maureen that Barbara was ill.

'I do,' said Barbara. 'It's my brother Brendan. He keeps some things locked up there.'

'What kind of things?'

'How should I know? They're to do with his business, nothing to do with me.'

Theo's face didn't change from an expression of mild interest. 'And this brother, Brendan – Brendan Wilmot? – would you say it was possible that Maureen's engagement ring got onto the drive outside your garages via him?'

'I really have no idea,' said Barbara with an indifferent shrug.

'But it looks likely, doesn't it, Barbara?' said Maureen. 'You see, love, this is a very serious thing – having my house burgled and my ring taken. It's upsetting to think someone's been in your home and gone through your things, looking for owt they might take. And what if

Eliza had encountered the burglar in the house? She would have been very frightened and she might have been hurt. She only just missed him, as it was.'

'Brendan would never be violent,' said Barbara. 'Even if it was him, which I doubt.'

Eliza and Theo looked at each other, remembering the incident on the doorstep after Brendan had insisted on escorting Eliza home.

'So you admit it's possible that Brendan that took my ring?' said Maureen.

'No! I don't know, Maureen. He might have bought it from someone else. He does deal in second-hand goods.'

'Bought it and then dropped it? Oh, Barbara, I think you're just covering up for him. I was very upset to have it stolen, my engagement ring, and I went to the police. Now I should go and tell them it's been found, and of course they will then be asking where.'

'No, please don't do that, Maureen. Whatever the truth of this situation – and Brendan isn't here to speak for himself – I shall make sure nothing like this happens again.'

'What do you mean?' asked Eliza fiercely. 'Those are just empty words, especially as you're trying to deny it is him that broke into our home. It's a police matter and Mum is going to report what she knows. I reckon Brendan Wilmot is a thief and he should be arrested.'

'No. *Please* don't do that,' Barbara said insistently. 'If he did take your little ring – and we don't know that he did – it will have been just the silliness of a young man who really should know better. I'll have a very strict word with him to be absolutely certain that nothing like this ever happens again.'

'But, Barbara—'

'Please, Maureen. Let me sort this out. You have, after all, got your ring back, which is the most important thing. No harm has been done, has it? The police are much too busy to be worrying about arresting anyone when the supposed stolen item is found again. They might even think you lost and found it yourself and are making up the whole story to cover your own carelessness, which would be very embarrassing for you. I believe they keep a record of these things, and they might not believe you if you ever went to them complaining again. Best all round if you let me deal with it, wouldn't you agree?'

Eliza looked ready to explode but Theo was squeezing her hand, silently urging her to be quiet, while his eyes pleaded with Maureen to agree.

Maureen read the situation on the piano stool and breathed deeply to dispel her anger at Barbara. She would go along with what Theo was signalling.

'Yes, all right, Barbara,' she said coldly. 'But just make sure that you do. P'raps you'd be good enough to telephone me when you've had a word with Brendan Wilmot so I can be sure you've done as you say.'

'Of course, Maureen. Whatever you wish. And now my head is spinning and I'm finding this inquisition far too much to deal with while I'm feeling so delicate. Thank you for your help and concern today. Would you mind letting yourselves out – you may use the front door, of course – and I shall go up and rest.'

'I can see that you're flagging,' said Theo kindly. 'Would you like another cup of tea bringing up? I'm sure Maureen will be happy to make you one while Eliza and I tidy away the food left over from lunch into your fridge, if you'd like it, and then load up the car. Then we'll be on our way.'

'Thank you. That would be very kind,' said Barbara graciously, with a faint smile.

She rose majestically and went slowly from the room, leaving Maureen and Eliza exchanging astonished glances.

'Right, let's get on,' Theo said cheerfully, leading the way back to the kitchen.

As soon as Maureen, Eliza and Theo were in the kitchen, he closed the door and ushered the women away across the room so there was no danger of being overheard.

'I think I might just grab one of those kitchen knives and go up and kill her,' said Eliza. 'The woman's a monster.'

'"No harm done" indeed,' snapped Maureen, 'when you both had to deal with nearly encountering the burglar, and the broken window, and I was distraught about having my engagement ring stolen. Not lost but actually *stolen* by that woman's brother.'

'Well, don't worry, Maureen. You may keep your word to Barbara Hayle but neither Liza nor I said anything about not going to the police. In fact, I think we'll go together, make sure we haven't forgotten to mention any details. Now, Maureen, would you like to make Lady Barbara her tea – no added strychnine, please, though the temptation may prove almost overwhelming – while Liza puts the leftover food in the fridge and I, meantime, will nip round to these outbuildings and have a quick look at what's there.'

'Oh, do be careful, Theo,' said Maureen.

'I intend to. I'll just go and unlock the car for you, Liza, and then you can put the picnic baskets in when you're ready.' He left through the back door and Maureen and Eliza heard his footsteps crunching on the gravel as he went round to the car.

Maureen took Barbara her tea up in a pretty cup and saucer, which she remembered from the day she had been at The Manor and they'd had tea together in the garden. Their relationship had changed that day, and this afternoon, Maureen felt, it had tipped irrevocably into dislike on her part. Possibly Barbara had always felt dislike for her; she didn't know. She felt sorry for what had been lost, but their friendship had run its course and it was over. She knew it was unlikely that she would see Barbara again.

'Here you are, Barbara,' she said, and put the cup and saucer down on Barbara's bedside table.

'Thank you, Maureen. That's very kind of you,' said Barbara, lying on top of her clean bed, fully dressed. She closed her eyes and put her hand gently to her forehead, as if her head was hurting.

'Don't forget to call Mr Lambert. As I say, you won't have to worry about the cost of any help. And there's plenty of the picnic lunch left for you in the fridge.'

'Thank you, Maureen. And please thank . . . your relations for me. So kind . . . But remember what I said. I shall have a word with Brendan and see he keeps to the straight and narrow.'

Maureen ignored this as there was no answer she could truthfully give that Barbara would want to hear. Instead she said, 'I think, Barbara, you might want to resume giving your lessons next week, if you feel better. Just so you have some money coming in.'

Barbara sighed in a long-suffering way.

'And I'll leave you this.' Maureen silently put down an envelope containing some money beside Barbara's tea. She'd been to the bank and withdrawn the notes on Friday. She hadn't mentioned this to Eliza or anyone else.

Barbara didn't move or open her eyes. 'I must say, Maureen,' she said quietly, 'I can't help but be a little disappointed in you. I thought you'd have had a little more vision, a little more style. I hoped that you could have been more like me, seen the import-ance of being larger than life, out of the ordinary, but in the end you're just an ordinary, dull little woman worrying about her cheap little ring. And such a waste of a legacy . . . What I could have done with that money . . .'

Maureen resisted the temptation to pour the tea over Barbara, took a deep breath to calm herself and went to the door.

'Goodbye, Barbara,' she said. 'Look after yourself.'

She turned and walked out, closing the door behind her.

CHAPTER TWENTY-TWO

MAUREEN GOT IN the car and sat for a few moments, looking tearful.

'You all right, Mum?' Eliza asked from the back.

Maureen nodded. 'Well, at least I know Barbara's not gravely ill, and I've done all I can for her, I reckon.'

'You've done a great deal more than most would, Maureen,' said Theo.

'Do you think she will call Mr Lambert?' asked Eliza.

'I don't know, love. It's up to her.'

Eliza reached forward and patted her mother's shoulder. 'You were brilliant, Mum. That woman's a piece of work but she won't ever underestimate you again.'

Maureen shrugged, then mopped her eyes with her handkerchief. 'She won't get the chance. I reckon I need to put Barbara Hayle behind me now. We're done. At least I got my ring back. That was a bonus I didn't expect from today.'

'Did you see anything in the outbuildings, Theo?' Eliza asked.

'No, they were securely locked, which in itself might be significant. Now, are you ready to go home, Maureen?' he asked kindly.

'Yes, please, Theo. Let's enjoy the beautiful country-side along the way and put Barbara Hayle out of our minds for the rest of the day.'

Theo drove off down the drive to the road, then stopped so that Eliza could jump out and close the big gate behind them.

She had just fastened the gate when she heard the engine of an approaching vehicle and a shabby-looking van pulled off the road and came to a stop right beside the car. Eliza saw straight away that the driver was Brendan Wilmot, and he looked extremely unhappy – angry but also upset. This much emotion couldn't possibly have been conjured up instantly by the sight of herself, her mother and Theo, could it? Surely not.

Wilmot got out of the van, a noxious cloud of cigar-ette smoke escaping with him into the clean country air, just as Theo got out of his car.

'Maureen, stay here,' he said. 'Eliza, darling, please get in.'

'No, Theo. I need to hear what Brendan Wilmot has to say for himself.'

'What are you doing here?' snarled Brendan. He really did look quite terrible, Eliza noticed: red-eyed, unshaven, crumpled, as if he'd been up all night or slept in his clothes.

'We've been to see Barbara,' said Theo. 'We came to help her, but it turns out she was quite helpful to us.'

'Helpful? I gather the kind of help you offer isn't the kind she wants. Too little, too late now,' said Brendan. 'Now, can't you just shift your car out of my way?'

'Thing is, Wilmot,' said Theo, ignoring him, 'Barbara was able to restore to Mrs Bancroft a ring that means a very great deal to her, and which we think was brought here by you after you'd burgled her house. You might remember the evening: Eliza and I saw you shinning up the back wall.'

Eliza thought Brendan would try to deny it or else, worryingly, he would become confrontational. His reaction, however, was quite unexpected.

'What? What do I care about you and your stupid stuff and your stupid little lives? Don't you think I haven't got more important things to think about, eh? Just clear off and let me drive in.'

'So are you denying it?' asked Theo.

'Shush, Theo. Mebbe we'll just go,' Eliza murmured, taking his arm. Something was happening here that had nothing to do with the stolen ring.

'Didn't you hear me? I said get out of the way,' snarled Wilmot.

'Not till you explain how Maureen's ring came into your possession,' said Theo. 'You see, Wilmot, you can't just shrug it off, pretend it's nothing to do with you.'

Maureen got out of Theo's car then and came round the front of it so that she was standing on the other side of Wilmot.

'It's all right, Theo,' she said calmly. 'Now, Brendan, I'm Maureen Bancroft and we spoke on the telephone the other day. You told me Barbara was ill and I reckon you're worried about her. But we've just been to see her and she's feeling a lot better. I can understand your worries, but she really is quite all right.'

'Worries?' said Wilmot, looking astonished. '*Worries!* You know nowt. *Nowt at all!* Just go, go away and don't come back. Interfering in other folk's business, do-gooding, like you even care.'

Maureen opened her mouth in surprise, but no sound came out.

'Come away, Mum,' said Eliza. 'Theo, let's go . . . please.'

'Yes, Eliza. You're quite right. But you haven't heard the last of this, Wilmot.' He climbed back into the car, while Eliza got in the back and Maureen, still looking dumbfounded, sat back next to Theo.

Brendan Wilmot resumed his seat in his van, slamming the door unnecessarily hard, and sat scowling, waiting for Theo to pull out of the drive and give him room to open the gate.

'I reckon that lad is very troubled about summat,' said Maureen.

'So he ought to be,' Eliza replied, as Theo pulled out to the left, towards Blackburn, home and sanity, which it seemed to her they had left behind days ago, so trying had the time here been. ''Cos very shortly he's going to get his just deserts.'

Barbara heard the front door close behind her visitors.
  Silence.
  Thank goodness they'd gone. Maureen really did fuss. At least the bed was clean and sweet-smelling . . . Barbara turned then and saw the envelope on her bedside table. She picked it up, opened the unsealed flap and took out a wad of green banknotes. She counted it quickly. There were twenty-five pounds. Well, that was thoughtful of Mousy Maureen, though it was a shame she hadn't made it thirty . . . or forty. Barbara took the little clutch bag she'd stolen from Crosby's out of her wardrobe and put the money inside.
  Then she quickly drank the cup of cooling tea and went to take the cup downstairs. The upstairs corridor was more brightly lit than normal. Typical: those rude, careless people had rampaged through the house and left all the doors open. They'd evidently been every-where, uninvited, looking in the rooms, seeing how she was reduced to living. It was intrusive and humiliating. These rooms were private, for her eyes only. She put her cup and saucer on the floor, then went down the corridor, checking the rooms to make sure they were as she'd left them: that all the windows were closed.
  At the end on the right was the spare room, which she kept furnished because, you never knew, there

might just be, one day, someone who wanted to visit and stay overnight, an old friend from those lovely days when Marty was alive. You couldn't not have a bed for a visitor, just in case there ever was one . . . one day.

Barbara opened the door wider and went in. There, right in front of her, on the window, was the faint imprint of a bird. She gave a little squeak of distress before realising what it was and how it must have come about.

Not just tapping to get in but flying at the windows, hurling themselves against the glass!

They were getting bolder, more determined. But they would not get in. They would not! She stood back from the window and craned her neck to see down into the garden. There, on the wall, were five starlings, waiting.

Barbara stepped away, trying to calm her panic. They hadn't seen her. Good. All was well.

It was then that she noticed one of the drawers in the chest between the windows was askew. Those rude people had not only been in every room but had looked inside her furniture, too. It really was an affront to decency. She pulled the drawer right out to straighten it where it was jammed on the wooden runners and there, inside, towards the back, was a shoebox.

She took it out. It was quite heavy. Could it be hers and she had forgotten about it? No, she was certain she had never seen it before. It was not especially clean, and when she turned it round one side said 'Size 10', which was her dress size but certainly not her shoe size.

She glanced up and her eyes met the ghostly bird pattern on the window. She closed the drawer with a little effort, picked up the box and retreated to her bedroom where she sat on her bed and removed the lid from the box.

The inside was lined with crumpled newspaper, and nestling within that were some pieces of jewellery. Barbara's eyes widened as she tipped them out onto her eiderdown, and she felt her smile growing wider and wider as she lifted them up one by one to examine them.

There was a gold pocket watch, substantial and weighty; a necklace of little diamonds embedded along a chain; a pair of pearl drop earrings; a brooch shaped like a long, slim bar made of alternating diamonds and rubies; a massive opal ring; a three-strand pearl choker; a lady's dress watch, its tiny face surrounded by diamonds. Inside a layer of newspaper, which must have been below this first cache, were more earrings, made of garnets set in gold, and two diamond rings, though not quite as big as the opal. This was expensive jewellery, a hoard of treasure, no less.

Barbara looked through the pieces and then put them down carefully so that there was a line of precious items along the middle of her bed. She felt her stomach doing a little flip of excitement. Then she smoothed out the crumpled newspaper and looked for a date, some clue as to when these wonderful things might have been put in the box. The newspaper was the *Daily Sketch* and it was dated 12 July 1956: just last month.

Brendan!

But of course. Who else could be responsible? Barbara had to smile: the use of the *Daily Sketch* was a giveaway in itself. If she had wanted to ignore the warning her mother had been trying to give her, shrugging it off as the muddled wanderings of a frail mind, then here was evidence that Annie, far from getting worked up over nothing, was for once in her life the mistress of understatement.

And now this jewellery was in Barbara's hands. How very fortunate. The universe had heard her silent pleas for help and it had provided. The timing was perfect.

Oh, but when would Brendan be back to collect the hoard? He must have hidden it here recently, judging by the date on the newspaper. No one would want to have to hide these precious things for long. He would find a buyer as quickly as possible, and then get rid of them before they came to the attention of anyone else.

Ha! Should have moved a bit quicker, Brendan.

Barbara opened her wardrobe and reached to a shelf at the side, which held handkerchiefs and stockings. She removed a few handkerchiefs and wrapped the jewellery quickly and carefully so that soon there was a heap of little white cotton parcels. Then she took a substantial leather handbag from a lower shelf in the wardrobe and put the parcels in the bottom, the roomy side pockets, the inside zip pocket. She added the little clutch bag containing Maureen's gift of cash, which fitted neatly in the main compartment, and put the handbag back where it had been in the wardrobe. She put the shoebox out of sight under the bed.

She'd have to work out what to do now: how to sell these things as soon as she could, and how to deal with Brendan. That was going to be tricky, but with luck he wouldn't be checking on his hoard for a few days at least. She hoped not. If he came back for it now, she'd be sunk.

Just as that thought passed through her mind, Barbara heard a distinct and loud staccato sound at the front door. The tapping of sharp and cruel beaks. Instantly she was filled with fear, but it wasn't an invasion of birds, it was the sound of a key being inserted into the lock! She went to the top of the stairs to look and gasped in horror as the door swung open, bringing a gust of cool air.

Brendan stood on the doorstep. He looked angry, almost as if he knew she'd taken the jewellery, but how was that possible?

'Oh, Brendan. What a surprise! Please, close the door.' Even to Barbara's own ears her voice sounded high-pitched and nervous. 'I was just going to lie down. You know I haven't been well.'

Brendan did as he was asked but he still hadn't said anything. He stood on the doormat, looking up at her as if he couldn't believe what he was seeing.

Barbara saw that he wasn't going to take the hint to leave. She decided to adopt a different tactic.

'What's the matter?' she asked, coming down, smiling as if she was pleased to see him, putting on her act.

'You know,' he snarled.

'What do you mean? I really have no idea what you're talking about.'

'Which just shows what a liar you are, Barbara. Or should I say "Mum"?'

Barbara's stomach did a full somersault and for a moment she thought she might faint, but she fought to maintain her composure, clutching the banister and swallowing down her panic. She hadn't seen this coming now, but perhaps she could yet brave it out. 'D-Don't be silly, Brendan.' She tried to smile, to sound light and indulgent, but she felt her smile slipping.

'Silly? *Silly!* You ridiculous woman, still pretending, when even you must realise the game is up. Are you so stupid? Or mebbe you've swept the truth under the carpet for so long that you really have forgotten what it is. I went to see Mum . . . Grandma . . . Annie, and learned that you're not my sister after all. You are my mother!' he shouted, his voice trembling with emotion, his face contorted with anguish.

Barbara swallowed but said nothing. All this was so completely unexpected that she had no idea what to say.

'Do you think that doesn't matter – that I wouldn't mind that you have never told me the truth, never claimed me? Do you reckon that it makes no difference, just because it's more convenient for you to carry on living the lie? When do you ever think of anybody but yourself?'

406

By now Barbara was in the hall and he came towards her and made a grab for her wrist, pulling her roughly towards him.

'Ow, Brendan, get off. You're hurting me.' She tried to pull away but he held on tighter.

Brendan took her jaw in his large hand and twisted her face towards him, holding her too tight. 'Look at me, Barbara, and tell me that I am your son. Go on! Tell the truth for once in your life. Admit you abandoned me with Annie while you swanned off back to the chorus line.'

Barbara couldn't say anything as he was squeezing her face too tightly. She struggled to prise his hand off and eventually he released her.

'Well? Was it worth it, giving up your baby for a place in the second row of the chorus?' he snarled in disgust.

'I thought it was for the best,' whispered Barbara, rubbing her jaw where he'd squeezed it painfully. 'I had paid work and . . . and I thought it would lead somewhere. I was going to be a star.'

'A star? That's rubbish and you know it. You chose that daft fantasy, that pipe dream, over your own child? You are selfish through and through.' He stepped towards her and pushed her with all the force he could so that she fell backwards onto the hall floor.

'Aaahh!' Barbara's arm made contact with the stone flags first, at least saving her head, and she lay there winded and bruised while Brendan stood aggressively over her.

'Annie said you just left me with her, like an unwanted parcel. You probably thought I would die – Annie did – and then you could forget I'd ever existed in the first place. I bet that's what you hoped. That's the truth, isn't it? And you'd continue on your merry way and never look back.'

Barbara struggled to sit up. 'No, that's not true. You know nothing about it. It was hard for me to make enough to keep myself, never mind a baby. And what would I have done with you when I was working? I couldn't have just left you.'

'So you *just left me* with Annie. Didn't even ask her. Just dumped me and scarpered. Who is my father, Barbara? Do you even know?'

'Too cruel, Brendan. Of course I do.'

'Well, I don't. I thought my dad was that angry bastard who showed us all – but especially me – the back of his hand all the time. So who, then?'

'He . . . he was a pianist in a light orchestra. Lionel Layton, he was called. He said he'd teach me to play and there would be no charge for the lessons but, of course, there's always a price.'

Barbara got to her knees, rubbing her elbow.

'Well? Go on,' snarled Brendan.

Barbara took hold of the banisters and pulled herself up, holding tight to the newel post.

'I thought he was a nice man, I thought he was in love with me. The lessons were fun and I learned very quickly. It was all just perfect for a while. And then I told him I was pregnant and that's the last time I saw him. He left the orchestra, just like that. I tried to find him but he'd gone for good and the other musicians, well, if they knew, they weren't letting on. They told me to forget him, that he was engaged to marry someone else.' She would never forget the look of pity in their eyes.

'And that was a reason to keep him a secret all these years, was it? To have me believe M— Annie and *him* were my parents?'

'But they were, in a way. They gave you a home. I told you, Brendan, I couldn't afford to keep you. I wasn't able to. I'd have had to give up everything I was working towards, all my dreams—'

'Your dreams! So you're back to the pretending and the fantasy world you live in. Why isn't the real world good enough for you, Barbara? There must have been years when you could have told me the truth. Instead, I had to put up with Annie treating me like some inconvenient little afterthought, and Dad, snarling and lashing out at everything and every-body because he couldn't cope with his life of disappointment, married to Annie, six children of his own, plus his daughter's little bastard, and life one long, relentless struggle. I bet you never were going to tell me, were you? I bet you'd almost forgotten that you have a son.'

'That's not true, Brendan. I never forgot that.' Barbara rubbed her arm. It hurt a lot and she wondered if the bruises were showing already. 'But the time went on and it never seemed like the right moment.'

'Oh dear, poor you. How difficult that must have been for poor Barbara. So why was it never the right moment? Right for who? What you mean is that you just didn't want to tell me. It was just better for you to keep quiet. Because in your pretend world you were still going to be the star, and a bastard child would have got in the way, tarnished your reputation, is that right? You couldn't have your grubby little secret coming to light, could you?'

'I don't have to explain myself,' Barbara said, beginning to retreat upstairs. 'Please just go away, Brendan. You know I've been feeling ill. You've no idea what a struggle my life's become—'

'Struggle? Don't be so pathetic. Am I supposed to feel sorry for you? You could have told me that you were my mother when Marty died. You could have pretended that I was Marty's son: just a widow with a grown-up son, nothing unusual in that. We didn't have to make a life together, but at least I would have known who my real mother was; known that you cared even a little bit, that you tried to make it right in the end. Instead, you preferred to keep living the lie, pretending I'd never been born to you. It was all so much easier for you.'

'No, you don't know what it's like for me, how awful it's been since Marty died . . .'

'Oh, don't start that again. What's that got to do with

anything? You're hopeless, Barbara. You're worse than Annie. At least she told me the truth in the end, but your whole life is just one great big fat lie.'

'Worse than Annie? No!' Barbara thought of her mother: her dirty, untidy little house, her shapeless old clothes and swollen feet, her frizzy hair, which she mostly cut herself, and her plain, jowly face; her forget-fulness and her complaining. Barbara could not think of a worse insult than to be compared unfavourably to Annie. 'Go, Brendan. Just get out and don't come back. I don't want ever to see you again. Worse than Annie! How could you say such a thing?'

'Because it's true. Annie's getting muddled in her old age, but you are years younger and completely mad. Your selfishness and vanity are like an illness—'

'No!' Barbara screamed. She ran up the stairs to get away from Brendan and his accusations. A pair of outdoor shoes were just inside her bedroom door, and she picked them up and hurled them with all the force she could at Brendan's head.

The first missed by inches, but as he dodged that successfully the second followed swiftly after it and hit him directly in the face. He staggered back with a cry of rage, his hand over his nose, blood gushing through his fingers.

Barbara, immediately horrified at what she'd done, came halfway down, fixated by the gory scene.

'Brendan, I'm sorry. I didn't mean to. I'm sorry, but when you said I was worse than Annie—'

Brendan was quick, despite his injury, and he bounded up the stairs towards her with a roar of intent. The look on his face and the blood dripping from his nose made a terrifying spectacle.

'No, Brendan, no!' Barbara shrieked, trying to get into her room where she could lock the door, but he grabbed her and tried to spin her round to a lower step so that he was above her and could push her down the stairs.

She hung on to the banister rail for dear life, trying to move upwards and get to the relative safety of her room. She willed herself not to let go as he struggled to pull her off and send her down with one strong push. They grappled together, and all the time he was yelling, 'I hate you I hate you I hate you . . .' When she could no longer hold onto the banister with both hands, she tried to snatch hold of a fistful of his hair, but it was too short to allow her any purchase and he was stronger and managed to bat her arm away. She knew she was seconds away from being flung down into the hallway. She must not let go of the banister, she must not! She hung on as he struggled with her, the blood from his nose running over his chin and down his front.

Then, as she was forced at last to let go and he was bearing her weight, he lost his footing, and with a discord of screams they fell together down the stairs.

* * *

Barbara lay quite still. She did not open her eyes. After several minutes she decided she would have to attempt to move, so she opened one eye and saw she was at the bottom of the stairs, lying mostly on top of Brendan. He was lying quite still but she was too close to see if he was badly injured. She put out a hand to the floor to lift herself. Her arm hurt; every bit of her hurt. She wanted to wait for a while, just lie here and see if she felt better after a bit, but it was growing dark and soon she would be lying here in total darkness. It would be better not to do that.

With a groan she made an effort to get up, managing it at the third attempt. Her knees were very sore where they had made contact with the floor, but it became apparent that she had been saved from far worse injury by Brendan, who had broken her fall.

In the grey twilight, Barbara limped very slowly over to the light switch and pressed it down. She had to steel herself to look. She didn't want to see what had happened to Brendan, but she had to.

Brendan was lying on his back. A pool of dark blood had formed on the stone flags around his head and it was clear that he was dead.

Barbara sank down on the bottom step of the stairs, not looking at Brendan's body and breathing through her mouth in little gasps. She did not love him – she never had – she was not the motherly kind at all, and he'd been nothing but a trouble to her. She should be relieved he was gone, but all this was a terrible mess and she'd have to see it through.

Think, Barbara, think!

The temptation to leave, to take the stash of jewellery and run, was almost overwhelming, but she knew she wouldn't get far. As soon as Brendan's body was discovered, the police would be out looking for her. They'd think she'd murdered him and tried to do a runner. That's what it would look like, and if they arrested her, she'd have a hard time proving that she was the victim.

No, far better to instigate the police presence, to get her own story in first so that no one would even think there was any other aspect to this tragedy.

Very slowly, groaning with the pain in her knees, Barbara went upstairs. She wanted to sit down and examine her bruises but there was a more important task to be done.

She collected the big handbag containing the jewellery from her wardrobe, painfully knelt down to reach the box from under the bed, and carried the bag and the box slowly downstairs, where she hung the handbag on a peg just inside the front door, next to her coat, right where anyone entering the house would pass by it. Then she collected the shoes she'd thrown at Brendan from the hall, averting her eyes from the horrible sight of the blood and his stiffening face, his mouth partially open, and put them neatly under the peg.

Next she went to the drawing room, bending down with some difficulty to the fireplace, where she put the box and its lid upside down among the cold ashes,

414

then struck a match and watched as the flames began to lick vigorously around the cardboard.

Finally Barbara went to her little study, picked up the telephone to call the police, and prepared to put on the performance of her life.

CHAPTER TWENTY-THREE

MAUREEN TURNED OVER the soil in her back garden, breaking it up, working in a spadeful of compost, and then straightened to ease her back. Jasper, her little dachshund, sat in a sunny spot nearby, making the most of the bright day, enjoying the company of his mistress. The sun was beginning to have some warmth in it: spring was here at last.

Already the daffodils Maureen had planted in autumn were beginning to flower. She had dreamed all her life of a garden bright with daffodils in spring. Now she was out here every day she could be, delighting in the changes that took place with the seasons. There was so much to learn, she thought, that if she read her growing collection of gardening books every evening, and worked all day every day at the practical tasks, she would still never know it all. She'd joined a local gardening club, and the folk there could not be more welcoming, or more generous with their time, helping a beginner. There was plant-swapping, good company, new friendships.

Maureen had in mind that she might one day have learned enough to start up a little market-garden business, employ an assistant, and they'd potter around gardening together, but she was keeping this a secret for the moment. It might yet turn out to be just a dream. The time to announce her intentions was when she knew what she was doing! It felt good to have something to aim for, though, to have dreams that weren't just fantasies but might, with some effort and enthusiasm, be attainable. She had Miss Stevens's legacy to thank for that. It had given her independence and time for herself. She was a woman of property, a woman who was learning to be fearless, who was daring to find her own way and whose life was full of plans for herself and her growing family.

She'd bought a very large greenhouse and had had it put up to one side of the garden. When the weather was wet or cold, as so often in early spring, she was in there sowing seeds and potting on her early vegetable crops. Theo took a close interest in the vegetables she was growing, suggesting the kinds of things he'd like to cook for them all, and Maureen thanked God every day that Eliza had married this kind, sweet-natured, gentle and talented man, and that he and Eliza had taken up the offer to share Maureen's house with her. Maureen knew she had been wrong to have even the slightest reservations about Eliza's marrying Theo.

Agnes had been right: who would not want to grab happiness with both hands, wherever it was to be found?

'Mum! Come on in. Sylvia and Des are here with baby Sarah,' called Eliza from the back door, and Maureen stuck her spade in the ground, pulled her leather gloves off her hot hands and went back towards the house, Jasper following on her heels. On the doorstep she sat down and untied her muddy boots, then padded inside in her warm stripy socks.

'Ah, love,' she gave Sylvia a hug, 'thank you for bringing the little 'un to show us.'

'I thought it would be nice for Sarah to have a little trip out, see her relations and breathe the cleaner air,' said Sylvia, smiling adoringly at her baby.

'Isn't she beautiful? And you look like the perfect mother – obviously a natural. And it's lovely to see you too, Des, looking every bit the proud father.'

Des was holding the carrycot that Maureen had bought for her granddaughter and gazing transfixed at his tiny child. 'And why wouldn't I be? She's a cracker, isn't she?'

'Des, do put her down,' said Sylvia. 'No, not there. She might tip over. Put the cot on the table out of the way of the dog.'

The inquisitive dachshund was keen to see the new baby, too. 'Liza, take Jasper into the drawing room, will you?' said Maureen with a little wink at her younger daughter. 'There now, all safe. Now let me look properly . . .'

The baby was suitably admired and cooed over, and Sylvia kept saying how like herself she thought her daughter was. Of course, Maureen and Eliza agreed, although Sarah just looked like a very small new person, with perfect, rather pink skin and a sleepy little face with a button nose. She really was very cute.

Theo came in to say hello and admire the baby, and then announced he'd laid out a little tea party in Sarah's honour in the dining room.

After everyone had eaten the savouries, which were delicious dainty bits and pieces on triangles of toast – 'baby-size food, though it's a shame she won't be able to join in until she's acquired some teeth' – Theo went away and came back carrying a plate stacked with, of all things, home-made jam doughnuts.

'I didn't know it was even possible for folk to make these,' said Des, tucking in with enthusiasm. 'I thought they only came from bakeries or were made in factories, like.'

Sylvia refused one at first, muttering about regaining her figure, but within two minutes she had succumbed to temptation.

'I'd be mad not to,' she said, licking sugar off her fingers and showing something of a new tendency not to take herself too seriously. 'Theo, please, would you make Sarah's christening cake for us? I can't imagine anyone would make a better one.'

'It would be an honour,' said Theo. 'Just tell me what

you'd like and about how many guests you'll be having, and I'll do the rest.'

'Where did you learn all this fancy cooking anyway?' asked Desmond.

'I used to be a cook in a restaurant,' said Theo, 'a long time ago.'

He did not add that he'd owned the restaurant with his first wife, Marguerite. He'd told Eliza all about her – all about his life in France, learning to cook – but he felt it insensitive to refer to Marguerite often in front of Eliza. After Marguerite died, he'd told Eliza, he'd sold the restaurant, unable to face continuing there alone, and come back to England, just as war broke out. He'd joined the army, and when peace was declared he had decided to learn to cut hair and gone to work with Harry Mulligan. Now he was married to Eliza and, he'd said, his life was complete, and he would probably not be trying another new career for the time being because this marriage was enough for him and he couldn't be happier.

'Oh, but, Theo,' she'd replied in mock dismay, 'I had hoped we'd discover all kinds of new things together, even while we work for Harry. You know all sorts and I've only just got going.'

'I didn't say never,' Theo had answered. 'Can we just be married and settled in our lovely home for a bit before we go out on a limb with something new?'

'Only if you teach me to play that grand piano,' she said. 'I fancy spending our evenings playing duets –

Song and Laughter, remember? – but I've a lot to learn if I'm ever to play half as well as you can.'

Barbara had written to Maureen out of the blue in the autumn, telling her she was selling the piano, had remembered that Theo played, and naming a very high price if Maureen would like to buy it. Maureen didn't mind paying, although she knew the piano was over-priced. She'd had it moved to her house in Clitheroe at enormous expense. She pretended it was an invest-ment, but really it was a present for Theo.

Barbara's letter said she was selling The Manor. She didn't mention the cash that Maureen had given her when she'd visited The Manor for the last time, but Maureen was not surprised by this. She was pleased to hear that Barbara was doing the sensible thing at last, although she didn't believe wholeheartedly in that. Barbara had never shown much of a tendency to be sensible before now, but then everybody could change, and perhaps the horrible accident that had killed Brendan Wilmot, and which had been reported in the newspapers, had brought her down to earth at last.

Maureen didn't expect to hear from Barbara again. Maureen was no longer the shy, admiring friend that Barbara had known, and their friendship could never be resurrected on the old footing, which Maureen thought was a very good thing. She had moved on in life and she only hoped that Barbara had been able to, too.

* * *

Barbara went round all the rooms of The Manor for the last time, checking the doors and windows were closed. It was a bright spring day, a good day to start a new life, she thought, albeit one that had been forced upon her by circumstances. What had remained of her furniture was sold. Con at The Remove, who turned out to be a hefty young woman called Connie – the granddaughter of Annie's friend Mary, and it tran- spired, Brendan's business partner – had taken away the last of Barbara's belongings in her van early this morning. Before that, she'd removed Brendan's house-clearance items from the outbuildings.

The police had been through Brendan's store after Barbara had tipped them off about finding a ring on her drive, which had turned out to belong to an old friend whose house had been burgled. She hadn't known if there would be anything to find, but it turned out there were several silver teapots and some vases, plus a few porcelain figures wrapped in old newspapers in the bottom of a wardrobe. None of this was as exciting as the jewellery that Brendan had hidden in her spare room, but it had some worth, and the tip-off was enough to satisfy the police as to Barbara's honesty and willing- ness to help them, diverting their attention from any thought of searching her house for stolen items.

There was literally nothing left of Barbara's that couldn't go in her case in her car, except for her fur coat, which was on the peg by the door, and her big leather handbag.

The handbag was far lighter than it had been on that fateful evening when the police had arrived, with an ambulance crew, and taken away Brendan. Barbara had answered the police officers' questions as best she could, although she'd been understandably distraught that Brendan had turned violent when she had tried to tackle him about his thieving and, in the ensuing struggle, he had fallen to his death. While she wept inconsolably, Barbara considered with secret amusement the irony of the police passing in and out of the house right next to a handbag containing a fortune in stolen jewellery. The stolen goods, fortuitously shut away behind those heavy padlocks in her outhouses, had been little enough to give up when the jewellery was still safely in her possession, and Maureen Bancroft and her daughter, Connie from the junk shop, and Barbara's own mother had been interviewed and added what they knew, which nicely supported Barbara's story.

Later, a tentative telephone call to an old acquaintance of Marty's led to a chain of calls to people who knew people, and Barbara had been able to sell the jewellery. She half understood that eventually the most precious pieces had reached some very clever and talented jewellers who could refashion them into new items, but she knew nothing of who these people were. She realised the long chain of contacts had probably cost her a lot more than taking a more direct route with these sales, but it was nearly impossible that the stolen items would ever be traced back to her, so it was worth it.

And now here she was, ready to start her new life. She had petrol in her beautiful car, she had the last of her furs – the one Marty had bought her to offset the sheer dullness of the expense of the new roof and rewiring – and she had, sewn into the linings of various garments and in the inner pockets of her handbag and her case, a very large amount of cash from the sale of the jewellery. Her hair was now short and brunette, something like the style of Maureen's daughter Eliza, and her complexion was like porcelain. She looked many years younger than her age and she knew it.

She had come to terms with having to sell The Manor in the end. She'd been mistaken to think holding on to it could help retain the heady days of her marriage to Marty. Those days were forever in her memory, and that was all she needed. It had taken her a long time to realise that but, now that she had, she could move forward with her life. The Manor, of late, had become associated in her mind with the struggle to pay her bills and the loan, the cold in winter, the selling off of the furniture, the drudgery of teaching the piano and elocution, the frightening birds invading her dreams and then the death of Brendan. The eradication of the bloodstain on the hall floor could now be someone else's problem . . .

Barbara had already left her keys with the estate agent. She locked up and posted the spare key through the letterbox, then, carrying her coat and bags, went round to the garage.

The doors had dropped on their hinges and they scraped on the gravel as she struggled to push them open. Yes, she was pleased to be going, leaving all this behind. She'd done her best but, in the end, it had proved to be more than she could manage. She backed out the car, got out to put her coat and bags inside, then drove down to the gate.

As she turned to close the front gate for the final time, she paused to give The Manor one long last look. The sun glinted on the windows. It looked a fine house still, although the front garden was neglected. A few birds flew over the roof, calling and chattering. They circled, and more joined them, until they formed a flock, wheeling and swooping. Their voices were chirpy and bright in the sunny air, clamorous, almost as if they were laughing, seeing her off.

Barbara wiped away a tear, breathed a long sigh, then straightened her shoulders and got back into her car. She pulled out into the lane, turning right, away from the village, and drove west, towards Liverpool, towards a ship for America. Her new life would be in films, she had decided. She was Miss Barbara Hayle, a star of variety in England, beautiful, poised and with just the smart clipped accent that she'd heard Americans admired. She didn't doubt for a single moment that she would make it in Hollywood.

Above The Manor the starlings circled overhead once more, calling mockingly.